Absolutely FR

E

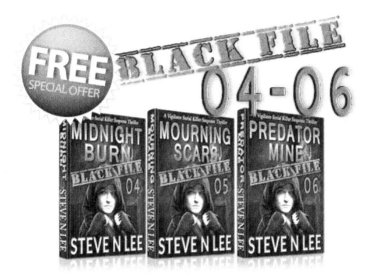

You get three free books with this edition:
Black File 04
Black File 05
Black File 06
See the Table of Contents in each book for details.

Angel of Darkness

Books 04-06

Steve N. Lee

Copyright

Published by Blue Zoo, Yorkshire, England.

Angel of Darkness Books 04-06

Midnight Burn

Mourning Scars

Predator Mine

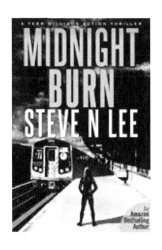

Midnight Burn

Angel of Darkness Book 04

Chapter 01

IN THE SHADOWS of her apartment building's doorway, a dark figure lurked.

"Oh, hell." That was all she needed. Slouched in the back of the yellow cab, Amelia buried her face in her hands and heaved a great breath. She didn't need to see the figure clearly – she knew who it was. And she knew if he hit her once more – just once – she was out of here. And this time, she meant it.

Raking her fingers back through her long brown hair, she groaned. Arriving home nearly two hours later than she'd agreed, she'd hoped to be able to creep in unnoticed while Ethan was asleep. Not because she didn't want to disturb him, but because she didn't want a fight. Well, that idea was shot.

As the cab swung in to park behind Ethan's rusting pickup truck, she dabbed her crotch with a crumbled tissue to remove any lingering traces of the guy from the bar, and with it, any lingering traces of the escape plan he provided. She smiled. Those ten minutes in the toilet stall were the highlight of her week. She couldn't remember the last time she'd felt so good. Felt so wanted. Felt worth something.

She noticed the dark eyes of the taxi driver staring through his rearview mirror. She knew he didn't have an angle to see her hand inside her panties, but he could see enough. The last thing she needed was him thinking she was coming on to him. Ewww. That beard scraping her face raw? And that gigantic belly pounding into her? Oh, God, she'd puke.

She arched an eyebrow at him. "A little privacy, huh?"

The driver looked away.

Seconds later, the cab stopped and the driver turned to her. "Fourteen fifty."

His accent was thick. Foreign. She didn't know where he was from and she didn't care.

As she yanked the door open, she pushed two scrunched bills at him. "I got ten bucks."

His dark-skinned hand caught her bony wrist. He was so big compared to her, it was like an adult holding a child by the arm.

He glowered. "Fourteen fifty!"

She snatched her hand away. "Hey, you got a free floor show."

She clambered out and into the shadows of her building, its six-story patchwork of darkened windows, broken only occasionally by a lit one, suggesting that the city that never sleeps actually did.

The taxi driver clambered out too. "Another four dollars fifty."

A cool wind biting at the summer's night, the chilly air coaxed goose bumps from her bare thighs. Her yellow skirt might look fabulous but it offered as much warmth as a silk scarf tied around her waist. She hugged herself, bouncing gently from side to side.

She said, "Look, that's all I got."

"Then maybe I call the police."

"Call. You think they'll give a crap?" She turned to leave.

From out of the shadows, a guy with muscles oozing out of his white undershirt marched towards her.

Under her breath, she said, "Oh, shit."

Ethan scowled at her. "You know what time it is?"

Meanwhile, the taxi driver had appeared beside her. "Another four fifty. Or there'll be trouble."

Ethan turned to him, arms folded over a proud chest. His stare drilled into the driver for a moment before he said anything. "Trouble? Over five bucks? Is it worth five bucks to get your face all messed up?"

The driver backed away, hands up, shoulders hunched. "Okay, okay. No police. No trouble."

"Damn right." Ethan's scowl swung back to Amelia. "Well?"

"Well what?"

With his cab between them, the driver obviously felt more courageous. He pointed at each of them. "You I won't forget."

"Is that so?" Ethan stabbed a finger at the driver, his bicep bulging. "You want a keepsake, just in case?"

He slammed a kick into the taxi's rear door, denting it.

The driver shouted, "The police, they give a crap now!"

Ethan lunged, as if he were about to race around the car at the driver.

Frantic, the driver fumbled opening his door, then jumped in his cab and shot away.

Ethan turned back to her. "So this is what I get for letting you go out with your friends?"

"*Letting me?* You *let* me go out?" She snickered.

"Think this is funny, huh?" He had that wild glare in his eyes – the one that always led to bruises appearing on her body which she had to lie to her friends about.

She flinched. "No, no. I'm sorry. Honest." She shrank back from him. Tried to be even smaller than she already was.

An old man with a cane limped towards them – the neighborhood weirdo all the local kids called Hop-along.

Though she always slapped on cosmetics to hide the evidence, the whole block knew Ethan was violent. Being in charge of the Neighborhood Watch, surely Hop-along would see how menacing Ethan was being and help her.

She caught Hop-along's eye. Silently pleaded for help.

The old guy immediately looked away. Stepped off the curb to cross the road. Never said a word.

She was on her own. As usual.

Further down the street, red brake lights caught her eye as her taxi slowed and hung a left. She ached to be sitting in it.

Ethan grabbed her by the arm. Shook her. "Hey, I'm talking here. Pull that silent shit and don't blame me for what happens."

She looked up into his eyes. "Ethan, really, I'm sorry. I just lost track of time. Okay?"

"Lose track of your cell phone as well?"

"I turned it off. I was having a good time."

"Oh, yeah? Who with?"

She wriggled free of his grip. "You know who. I told you. The girls – Becks and Trish and the others."

"And…?"

"And what? That's it."

Ethan glowered at her, arms folded, his biceps gleaming under the streetlights. "So, no one else?"

"No. Just them. So can we go in now? It's goddamn freezing." She reached out to touch Ethan's arm, but he shrugged her off.

He said, "So how come Blaine saw you with a guy in Shades?"

Oh, hell. "Blaine? Blaine! You believe a screwed-up dopehead like Blaine over me? Jesus, most days that guy wouldn't recognize his own mother if he was banging her."

"So what's this?" Ethan thrust his phone at her. It displayed a photo of her cozily chatting with a man at a bar, her hand on his arm. It was dark and her face was mostly obscured, but it was clearly her.

"That's not me." She pushed the phone away.

"No? Same hair. Same skirt."

"Like I'm the only girl with brown hair and a yellow skirt? Jesus, Ethan, get a grip."

His eyes widening into that glare again, she knew she'd pushed him too far.

She smiled. "Look, let me fetch some beers and smokes from the store" – she stroked her hand along his forearm and gazed into his eyes – "we'll put on some music and I'll show you how much I missed you tonight."

He pulled back again. "Don't go trying that sweet talk shit. This time I got proof."

"So what do you want, Ethan? To smack me around a bit? Then say you're sorry so I'll blow you?"

He leaned right down in her face. "Don't push it. I'm warning you."

"Warn who you like." She turned away, praying he wouldn't lash out at her. "I'm buying beer. Drink it or don't drink it. See if I care."

She flounced down the street, hoping a trip to the store would give her time to concoct a decent story. She'd call Becks for backup too.

He shouted after her. "Don't think this is over, because it ain't!"

Christ, was she sick of men walking all over her. Well, that was going to change. She deserved better so she was going to have better and to hell with anyone who got in her way.

She marched toward the end of the block. Now, how was she going to twist her story so Ethan would buy it long enough for her to figure out what to do next?

At the corner, she turned left onto Chiltern. The wind gusted through the concrete canyon. She shivered and tightly hugged her arms around her chest.

Ducking into the setback doorway of A Taste of Napoli, she hunched over her cupped hands to light a cigarette. The wind extinguished her lighter. She tried again. But failed again. "Goddamn it."

She thought she heard a voice, so she glanced towards the street, but she saw no one.

She tried her cigarette for a third time.

Something touched her right upper arm. She jumped. Pulled away. As far into the corner of the darkened doorway as she could.

Chapter 02

SILHOUETTED BY A streetlight stood a tiny, lopsided figure. "Is everything alright?"

"I've got a knife!" Amelia hadn't, but the figure didn't know that.

The figure moved nearer, a hand out toward her. "It's okay. It's me: Mr. Ridley. I just wanted to check you're okay."

It was Hop-along, the old man with the limp who could've helped her but didn't.

Batting his hand away, she said, "What's your fucking game? Keep your hands to yourself, you old pervert." She bustled passed him back onto the street.

"Jesus, you're old enough to be my grandpa." She scowled at him. Men, what the hell was wrong with them?

He said, "I'm sorry. I was only—"

"Only trying to cop a feel. Hell, I'm not surprised all the kids think you're a creep. Do you try to feel them up, too, you fucking pedophile?"

His wizened face hung in shock. He looked as pathetic as a dog that had taken a dump on the carpet and knew it was in for it.

He hobbled closer. "Please, Amelia, that's a horrible thing to say. I'm only trying to help."

"Trying to take advantage, more like." She snatched her phone from her purse and pointed it at him. "Well, not of me, you're not. I'm gonna put your photo online. Tell everyone what a pervert you are. See you chased out of the neighborhood. Have Child Services at your door. Fucking pedophile!"

"Please, Amelia. Don't." Cowering, he crossed his arms in front of his face to hide from the camera in her phone. "I'm sorry. I didn't mean to upset you." He backed away.

He looked like he was about to cry. Christ, talk about sad. A grown man crying over names he'd been called. But it served him right. He should've helped her. Neighborhood Watch her ass.

It was usually men making her feel weak and useless – it was good to finally know what it was like to be on the other side. Watching him squirm, she felt strong, dominant, unstoppable.

As she walked backwards, she kept her phone aimed at him. She chanted, "Pedophile. Pedophile. Pedophile."

He stood gawking at her. Frozen with shock.

"See you on Facebook, pedo." Continuing down the sidewalk, she laughed. The night no longer felt so chill. Her luck no longer felt so bad. She strolled toward the store, head high.

As she neared it, she realized the car parked across the street from Patel's Convenience Store was a taxi cab. She thought nothing of it, until she was almost even with it and spotted a large dent in the rear door – a dent that looked as if someone had kicked the metal panel.

The interior was too dark to see if anyone was inside, but she wasn't going to let that sleazy driver have the satisfaction of hassling her again when he saw she was lying about having no money.

Crossing the road behind the cab, and empowered by abusing the old man, she paused in the middle of the street just long enough to flip the darkened cab the finger. Laughing, she headed into the store.

Back on the street moments later, she bounced down the sidewalk for home, with four cans of beer in a white plastic bag.

The darkened taxi was still parked, but there was no sign of the old man. She'd felt powerful after her fight with Hop-along, but now, her adrenaline drained, the street felt so much darker, so much more threatening.

She glanced back at the taxi shrouded in gloom. The driver was a big guy, a giant compared to her. Still, with his blubbery belly she'd easily outrun him if he tried anything.

She crossed the street and rounded the corner. No matter what trouble you were in, once you were within spitting distance of your home, you knew everything was going to be just fine. Usually. Walking along the deserted street, Amelia shivered again. But not from the cold. This time, she shivered because she was sure she wasn't alone.

She spun around.

Scoured the shadows.

Gloom hung in doorways. Blackness bled out of alleys.

She scanned the darkness.

Nothing moved.

In a city of eight million people, the silence was unearthly.

Amelia backed away, peering into the shadows. She couldn't help but feel someone was watching. Someone was waiting. But who? And waiting for what?

The street she knew so well suddenly felt so much darker, so much lonelier.

Turning for home, she quickened her pace.

It was just her imagination. There was nothing there. What was she? A goddamn child?

But she shuddered. And again glanced over her shoulder.

There was someone there. Somewhere. She goddamn knew it.

Again, she quickened her pace.

Marching toward her building, she looked at the windows of Hop-along's apartment. Because of her fight with Ethan, Hop-along had born the savage brunt of her frustration. He hadn't deserved that. He was weird, yes, but he meant well. And like he could've helped. An old cripple taking on Ethan? Hell, Ethan would've busted up his other leg just for the hell of it. No, it wasn't Hop-along's fault. And calling him a pedophile was a horrible thing to have done. She'd apologize to him the next time she saw him.

A shudder ran down her spine. She looked behind her again. It was weird how people could tell when someone was watching them. Weird. And scary. She squinted, straining to pick out any figure hiding in the blackness.

Still nothing. Nothing but looming shadows.

Hell, she wished the little old man would pop up now with a cheery word and that crooked smile of his. She was sure someone was stalking her. Lurking in the darkness, just out of sight.

If she hadn't fought with Ethan, she'd call him and make him come down to meet her, even though she could now see her apartment building. It wouldn't be the first time he'd busted up some whack-job for hassling her.

"Oh, hell." *Ethan.* What was she going to tell him? In fact, would she be able to tell him anything if he'd flown into one of his rages because she'd dared to walk away while he was still talking?

Her pace slowed to a crawl. She needed a good story. A convincing story. She couldn't go rushing home until she had one he couldn't rip apart.

Okay, she'd tell him the guy in the bar was an old work colleague. No – a gay work colleague. Oh, yeah, that was it. Say she'd shown him Ethan's photo and he'd said what great muscles Ethan had.

Oh, damn it. Ethan wasn't the smartest guy she'd ever dated, but he wasn't that dumb. What the hell was she going to tell him?

Dawdling to stall for time, her door just yards away, she again took out her phone. Becks would know what to do – she had a sixth sense when it came to lying to guys. But Amelia didn't just need advice, she needed to hear a friendly voice – whoever was following her was creeping her out.

Amelia flicked through her address book and hit Becks's number.

The phone to her ear, Amelia thought she heard a noise behind her.

The hair on the back of her neck prickled.

She whipped around and—

Chapter 03

SITTING ON THE ground beneath her favorite willow tree, Tess slowly exhaled.

Amid a gentle mist clinging to the water's tranquil surface, ducks quacked on the small lake. The sun hovered above the tree line but the world was yet sleepy, chilled, still.

At the foot of her tree, Tess sat deep in meditation – completely enveloped in a world of her own making. But then, didn't everyone live in their own tiny world? While global affairs were beyond an individual's grasp, the everyday world a person created for themselves was under their complete control: their choices shaped their life. Unfortunately, like every other person on the planet, Tess often made the wrong choices, so her world was far from the utopia her philosophy decreed it had the potential to be.

Her breathing steady, eyes closed, Tess slowly emerged from her meditation. A sound had disturbed her. A sound unbefitting her favorite place. A sound of distress. Something was wrong.

With blue eyes as sparkling as the dew-laden grass, she scanned the park for the cause of the problem. Nothing.

Unfurling from her lotus position, she drew a deep breath and then stood. For a few seconds, she shook her muscles loose and worked her joints.

Snagging her black backpack from the grass, she turned toward the small bay in which rowboats could be rented during the park's official opening hours. She glided along the dry dirt trail with the grace of a dancer who'd graduated top of her year at Juilliard.

Again, a noise shattered the stillness – an eruption of honking. But it wasn't the usual traffic in the background. No, this was something living.

Rounding a clump of conifers, Tess saw three men on a narrow wooden jetty which crawled out over the lake on hefty moss-covered posts. The jetty's worn timbers creaked and groaned under the men's antics. From their dress, and their being in their late teens, early twenties, she guessed they had been partying all night and, on their way home, had invented a game for some last-minute fun. Unfortunately, the game seemed extremely one-sided.

Another pebble hit the lake's limpid waters. It skipped once, twice, three times and then…

Honking erupted once more.

Ducks near the far shore honked and squawked and quacked as the missile skimmed the surface between them and then plopped into the depths.

The three guys whooped with disappointment tempered with delight.

With a brown pug in a red dog coat ambling alongside her, an old lady approached the men. Tess couldn't hear what she said to them, but she didn't need to. The men turned towards the lady, grimacing.

The nearer one, a tall, gangly guy with a leather jacket, gave her the finger. "What's it to do with you, you nosey old cow? Fuck off!"

At the end of the jetty, a short, fat guy skimmed another stone across the water. Frantic quacks suggested something had been hit.

The fat guy shouted, "Score!"

All three guys cheered and laughed.

The old lady must have said something else, because the gangly guy pulled his arm back and aimed a stone at her dog. "You gonna fuck off? Or do I have to make you?"

The lady scurried back along the path, almost dragging her poor little dog off its feet in her hurry to get away.

Tess huffed. She had to be somewhere. Urgently. The only reason she'd stopped off here was to mentally prepare herself for the ordeal to come. She should really walk away from this. But could she?

One sunny afternoon years ago, Tess had lounged in the shade of a cherry tree playing Xiangqi on a wobbly oak table with Cheng Chao-an. With sunlight dappling the Chinese chessboard and a cool breeze gliding up the valley to the ridge on which they were

26

sitting, she'd felt peace. True peace. The kind of peace people dreamed about after seeing it in a feel-good movie but never truly believed existed outside Hollywood fantasy.

But there was a problem with peace – it never lasted.

Cheng moved one of his canons and captured her last elephant.

Staring at the pieces scattered across the board, Tess realized she was just two or three moves away from losing yet another game to the master of Wudangshan Temple.

Her shoulders slumped and before she knew it, she blurted out, "Oh, I hate this stupid goddamn game."

Cheng didn't understand English, but he obviously recognized her anguish from her tone and body language. As he moved one of his chariots across the river to threaten her general, she was sure the tiniest of smiles flickered across his craggy face. Not that he enjoyed winning. Teaching, however, was a different story.

In Mandarin, he said, "We each create our own versions of heaven and hell through the choices we make."

Almost everything Cheng said had many layers, a point she'd quickly picked up during the two months she'd been studying philosophy under him. This remark was no exception. If she'd won the game, she'd have congratulated herself for being a skilled player and making all the right moves. However, having lost, similarly, she had only herself to 'congratulate' for making all the wrong moves. Likewise in life, a person chose all the moves they made so they alone were responsible for the resulting predicaments in which they found themselves.

Tess neared the jetty which stretched out over the park's lake. Today, would her students appreciate the beauty in the teaching she was about to share?

Breathing hard, the old lady patted her pale face with a cotton handkerchief, all the color having drained from her complexion.

An ordinary person looking on would have recognized this loss of color as fear, even cowardice. Something to disdain. But that person would be wrong. Under stressful situations, the brain released adrenaline to aid with any necessary fight or flight, one side effect of which was the blood draining from the extremities to boost the supply to vital organs, which meant the skin looking pale. It was simple biology.

And that was why most people fell apart in stressful situations – they didn't understand their own bodies, their own reactions, so they couldn't grasp what was happening to them. The result was they either froze or panicked because they'd let their rational mind be replaced by a basic survival instinct. And an inability to make a reasoned decision seldom led to a favorable outcome.

Again, it was all down to choice. How the world crumbled without it.

Now Tess had a choice of her own to make: to walk away from men abusing people and animals unable to defend themselves, or…

Watching the three men tormenting the ducks, Tess felt her heart start to race. She knew if she let it, her adrenaline would spike, her heartbeat would skyrocket, she'd lose motor skills and rational thought, and… her world would come crashing down.

Tess drew in a deep breath for four seconds, held it for another four, and then blew it out over four seconds. Slowing her breathing would slow her body's reaction, slow the release of adrenaline, slow the onset of panic. It was a simple technique with which to face hazardous situations. A simple technique that could see you walk away with a spring in your step instead of being carried away with a sheet over your face.

Tess stopped in front of the old lady. "You okay?"

"Oh Lord, I can't hold my hand steady. Look." She held a trembling hand up.

"Do you have a cell phone?"

"Yes, but I come here every day. If I call the police, heaven knows what they'll do to me and Charlie." She looked down at her pug, which looked as upset as she did, though that being the breed's normal expression, it was somewhat misleading.

"Don't call the police. Call an ambulance."

"Thank you, but I don't need an ambulance. I just need to go home and sit down."

"Trust me. Call an ambulance." Tess walked by her toward the jetty. And the three delinquents.

"Don't go down there," the old lady called after her. "It's not worth it."

Chapter 04

AS TESS STROLLED toward the jetty, her heart pounding, her mind a whirl of scenarios each ending with her in a pool of blood on the ground, she used her four-second breathing technique to steady her heartbeat and her mind. Clarity. She needed clarity if she was to survive a dangerous situation without injury.

Out in the lake, a lump of bloody feathers silently bobbed on the water. Walk away? As if that were a choice open to her.

Today, it was ducks. Tomorrow, it could be dogs. Next week, it could be kids. Not worth it? Man, was it worth it.

From the grassy lakeshore, she picked up two stones. Without looking, she rolled them around in her hand to know their shape and weight.

On the jetty, the gangly guy pulled his arm back to skim another pebble at the ducks.

A stone cracked into the side of his head.

"Ahhh, fuck!" He hunched over, his hand naturally cupping his wound. When he took it away and looked at it, he swore again. He turned, scowling.

Tess stood at the start of the jetty, just looking at him. She tossed her other stone a few inches into the air and then caught it.

He shouted, "You fucking mental bitch!"

"You know" – she gestured to the birds on the water – "the ducks were right – this is fun." She smiled.

He stalked towards her. "You'll pay for that, you crazy bitch."

"Hey, don't be like that. They really want to play with you guys. The thing is they think the teams are unfair, so they've asked me to play on their side. That okay?" She threw the second stone at the gangly guy.

He twisted away. Too late. The stone hit him square in the back.

He growled like an angry animal.

Spun.

Stormed toward her.

His face twisted with rage, he said, "I'm gonna break your fucking legs, bitch."

She waited. Unmoving. He must have thought it was his birthday it was going to be so easy.

The auburn-haired fat guy at the end of the jetty shouted, "Do her, Gazza. Fucking do the bitch."

Gazza grabbed her jacket's lapel with his left hand and heaved his right fist far back to his shoulder. It was obvious what he was intending to do – smash her face to a bloody pulp with a heavy right cross.

This was when an ordinary person would be scared. This was when an ordinary person would run like hell. This was when an ordinary person would soil themselves.

She threw her hands up. "Whoa, whoa, whoa, whoa…"

He hesitated.

She said, "You really wanna do this?"

Tess didn't need to hear his answer. She felt his grip on her jacket tighten. Saw his right fist pull back a couple more inches. Sensed his body tense for action.

Yes, choices. It was all about choices.

He growled. Unleashed a crashing punch toward Tess's head.

She snapped her right arm up, bent, elbow jutting straight out in front of her face.

Gazza's hand smashed into the point of her elbow, one of the hardest parts of the human body.

He yelped like a dog that had been stomped on.

He pulled back. Cradled his hurt hand in his other.

Tess slammed a kick into his gut.

With a great wheeze, he doubled up. Staggered back.

With barely an effort, she shoved his shoulder.

He toppled into the lake.

The jetty was only five feet wide, so she knew they could only come at her one at a time. She slunk forward.

In a red shirt, the skinny guy who'd been in the middle of the three shuffled toward her. Fists at chest height. Knees bent. Body angled diagonally with his left leg forward. It was a trained fighter's stance.

When just a pace away from her, the guy shifted his weight onto his front leg and twisted that foot inwards.

He might as well have held up a placard declaring his intentions.

The guy spun backwards.

Shot a kick straight up at her head.

And a damn fine kick it was. It would've looked great in a movie. But for a real-life street fight?

Tess's head was no longer where he'd aimed. Already dropped to one knee, she slammed the heel of her right palm into the most exposed part of his body – his groin.

He gasped, eyes wide.

As the guy crumpled, Tess bounced up. Her elbow slammed up into his jaw. Bone crunched.

Arms splayed, the skinny guy crashed backwards into the water.

Tess swung her gaze over to the fat guy at the end of the jetty.

Mouth agape, the fat guy stared at her. His face was so pale, his auburn hair looked all but fluorescent in comparison.

She stalked toward him.

Face twisted with panic, he backed up. Inched closer to the end of the jetty. Teetered on the edge.

Tess crept forward. Watched his hands. His feet. Where his gaze fell.

Even the most inept of fighters could land a lucky punch if their opponent was inattentive. There was no room for arrogance or complacency on the street.

Probably looking for escape, the fat guy spun to his right – water. To his left – water. Behind him – water. On three sides there was nothing but water. On the fourth, nothing but pain.

Tess feigned punching him.

He dodged.

She feigned another shot.

Again, he needlessly dodged.

Obviously exasperated, he lunged. He didn't so much punch as merely flail an arm in her general direction.

She sidestepped. Twisting her hip to get her full weight behind it, she slammed her open hand into the side of his head.

He staggered right.

Regaining his balance, he flailed his other arm at her.

Again, she dodged. A mighty slap cracked into the other side of his head.

He staggered left. Teetering on the jetty's edge, he caught himself just before he fell into the water.

He held his head and then shook it as if to clear it.

Gulping great breaths, he glanced at her, at his two drenched friends, and then back to her.

Tess drilled her stare into him. "The way I see it, you've got two choices." She clenched her fists, raising them into a guard position similar to that of a boxer.

Again he spun for escape – to his right, left, behind him.

He turned back to her.

"Fuck this." He spun.

Leapt from the end of the jetty.

Crashed into the lake.

Tess said, "Smart choice."

She looked at the three guys in the water. They stared up at her, pale faced, whimpering, clutching their injuries.

She nodded. "Good game, guys. Shall we say same time next week? I'm always here."

She sauntered along the jetty and back onto the asphalt path. She'd have liked to have thought the three guys would reflect on this encounter and, through deep empathy, develop a greater appreciation for life – all life. But she didn't live in la-la-lu-lu land. Still, at least, they'd think twice before abusing anyone or anything else for fear of who may be lurking in the shadows, watching.

Goggle-eyed, the old lady stared as Tess approached. The woman's mouth gaped so wide, Tess could all but see the filled cavities in her lower teeth.

But the woman didn't smile. Didn't thank Tess. Didn't congratulate her for seeing justice done. Holding her white handkerchief to her face, the woman's hand trembled even more than when Tess had first met her.

The path was wide enough for five people to walk comfortably side by side, but the old lady stepped off it and onto the grass to let Tess pass. It was as if she'd seen a vicious beast. A monster run amok.

Around the world, most women were caregivers, nurturers, child bearers, victims, healers, homemakers, followers, mediators… Women were many things, but the one thing they were not was predators.

Psychologically, sociologically, and physiologically women had evolved to be the gentler sex. Both voluntarily and because it had been demanded of them. They turned mere places to live into homes; they dedicated their lives to the good of their social group; they sacrificed their goals for the sake of others.

Most women did not seek vengeance.

They did not reap justice.

They did not kill.

So was it Tess who was the monster?

She glanced back. The old lady hadn't moved. Except to turn and watch Tess leaving. Tess would've liked to think the lady was simply curious, but it was far more than that. The old lady had been more afraid of her than of those three delinquents.

So was she a monster?

Today, Tess hadn't killed anyone. Hadn't even maimed anyone. Those guys would suffer for a few weeks, but make a full recovery. All she had done was be present to witness the choices each of them had made.

If they had chosen a different path – chosen to be home in bed instead of terrorizing animals in a park – there would have been no violence. The violence had only occurred because of the path each of them had chosen to walk. Even up to that last few seconds before the violence erupted, they'd had the opportunity to make a different choice. They had chosen not to. Every path reached an end. The violent encounter with Tess had been at the end of theirs.

Tess shook her head. No, she wasn't a monster. She'd done the right thing. And she'd do it again. And keep on doing it until there was no longer the need. But when would that be?

Everywhere she went she found injustice. Found the greedy exploiting the vulnerable. Found scum abusing the innocent.

It was endless. What would she find next?

Who would she find deserving of the justice only she could bring?

Chapter 05

WITH YELLOW CRIME scene tape closing off the alleyway between two apartment buildings, the police might as well have sent out invitations to every busybody within a five-block radius. Not that there was anything to see; the crime, whatever it was, was hidden around the corner, where protruding scaffolding suggested some form of renovation was underway.

From the front of the crowd of people, Tess stared at the graffiti on the side of the right-hand building. In blue, black and red letters five feet tall, the main element spelled out ISAAC.Z. The second *A* completely blacked out one of the building's windows. Either someone didn't live there or was too afraid of Isaac Z to scrub his tag away.

She looked at the young male officer guarding the perimeter. "Excuse me?"

Nothing.

She waited a moment, then tried again. "Excuse me?"

With a slight squint, the cop looked at her and then meandered over. "Can I help you, ma'am?"

Ma'am!? Since when did she stop being a miss? Was that what happened as you approached thirty? The worst part was he looked no younger than she felt she did.

She smiled. "Who's the detective in charge, please?"

"That would be Detective McEleroy, ma'am."

"Pete McEleroy?"

"Yes, ma'am."

"Could I speak with him, please?"

"As you'll appreciate, he's kind of busy right now."

"Can you tell him Tess Williams is here?"

"Do you have information about the crime, Ms. Williams?"

"If you just tell him I'm here, please."

The officer studied her eyes for a second.

"Just a moment." He turned and said something into his radio that she couldn't hear. A moment later, at the other end of the alley, a portly man waddled out from behind the building and waved for her to join him. The young officer lifted the tape to shoulder height. "There you go, ma'am."

"Thank you." She ducked under and marched up the alleyway. The portly detective waddled a few steps toward her. A noticeable smile crept across his face. He tried to hide it by rubbing a hand over his face and then back through his graying hair.

On reaching him, she smiled and shook his outstretched hand. "I see the cheeseburger diet is working its magic, Mac."

He laughed and proudly rubbed his gut. "Gained six pounds so far this year." He turned for the back of the building again. "So how are things with you?"

"Oh, you know. We'll have to have a drink sometime soon and catch up."

"That would be, er, nice."

She saw him try to stifle a smirk again. No surprise, really – it wasn't every day an overweight fifty-five-year-old cop got to secretly lay a woman half his age with the toned physique of an Olympic swimmer.

"'Nice', huh?" She raised an eyebrow.

He glanced around for who might be listening. "Yeah, you know…"

She smiled to let him know she was messing with him. She didn't want his colleagues learning of their relationship as it would cramp her style, and he couldn't risk it – if his wife learned of it, she'd take his kids, his house, and most of his paycheck.

But she liked that he'd squirmed. It meant she still had access to what she needed: information. And access was all that mattered if she was going to do her job.

Approaching the corner of the alley, she said, "So what have we got here?"

"Put it this way, you ain't gonna be rushing to eat anytime soon."

She turned the corner. And there was the victim. Unusually for Tess, she gasped and stopped dead.

As if reading from a somewhat bland menu, Mac said, "Amelia Ortega, twenty-one, local resident. Found by some kids playing hide and seek. We have no time of death and we're still trying to establish cause. From the blunt force injuries, it looks like she was beaten with something – maybe a rock hammer or some similar tool – so death could be from that or..." He gestured to the body. "This is one real sicko."

At a glacial pace, one forensics officer hovered around the body, taking photos from a variety of angles, while a colleague crouched examining some kind of marking on the asphalt which Tess couldn't make out. A bald man hunched over the body, scrutinizing the face and throat.

Tess winced as she looked at Amelia. Lying face up, Amelia 'hung' in midair. Impaled through the crotch on a horizontal scaffolding pole, her arms and legs dangled down to either side behind her. To support her, the pole obviously extended deep into her body cavity, so must have caused massive internal damage. Not only that, but from where her mouth and lower jaw should have been burst forth bloody pulp and jagged white bone, as if someone had tried to impale her the other way around to start with but only succeeded in mashing up her face.

"Jesus." Tess stared at the body dangling in the air like a dead bird a child had picked up with a stick.

This was not just a straightforward murder. This was something else entirely. But what?

"How deep does the pole go?"

Mac shrugged. "We don't know yet. But it must be quite a way. I tell you, whoever did this was either real strong or real pissed."

In times of extreme stress, natural strength wasn't necessary: rage could turn an ordinary person into an absolute Goliath. She knew that from her own experience. And, luckily, she knew how to harness such power.

With the majority of homicides being committed by a person the victim knows, there were the usual suspects to consider. Tess said, "There a guy in the picture?"

"And that's where it gets interesting – live-in boyfriend Ethan Michael Dumfries has conveniently gone AWOL."

"Priors?"

"Two years ago, his girlfriend at that time made a complaint for assault, but then refused to follow through, so it was dropped."

There was someone else at the scene, though. Someone Tess didn't recognize. Someone taking notes while crouched beside the bald ME. She knew who should've been there, and though she couldn't get a good look at this guy because he had his back to her, it was definitely not who she was expecting to see with Mac.

She tossed a glance toward the stranger. "Old Horowitz finally get his year-round fishing vacation?"

"Sadly." Mac nodded. "This guy's a transfer from uptown. He's doing okay."

But a newcomer wasn't the important issue here. Tess looked at the victim.

From what was left of Amelia's face, and from her slender limbs and Hollywood-flat stomach, Tess could tell Amelia would've been very popular. Maybe too popular.

There was an obvious question just begging to be asked, so Tess asked it.

"Was she raped?"

"Hard to say." He shrugged. "But I guess that could be one reason for doing that to a body – trying to hide crucial evidence. The lab results should clear that up."

From beside the ME, the transfer-from-uptown guy meandered toward them, his gait slow but solid, upright, purposeful. With a full head of thick black hair and a muscular build, he looked like Mac must once have looked before the ceaseless cases and endless junk food took their toll.

Tess cringed. Oh, God, she knew this interloper, alright – the pompous dick from the Pool Cleaner job who had all but advised her to take up flower arranging on the grounds that she was a helpless woman.

On catching Tess's eye, the transfer-from-uptown guy looked equally thrown, though she guessed it was for a different reason. He scanned Tess, obviously wondering why she, a mere member of the public, deserved access to their inner sanctum.

Chapter 06

FOR A MOMENT, Tess and the new guy stood facing each other like rival gunslingers in a Wild West saloon, each warily sizing-up the other. Luckily, the local sheriff was on hand to ensure the encounter remained peaceful.

Mac gestured to each of them in turn. "Tess Williams, meet Detective Josh Hardy. A transfer from uptown."

Not wanting to let her body language give away her displeasure, she resumed her jovial demeanor as quickly as she could.

Smiling, Tess held out her hand. "Hello again."

Josh shook it. "Miss Williams."

"You two know each other? Have you worked together?" asked Mac.

"No, no," said Tess. "It was just in passing." She could kick herself. Would it have hurt her to phone Josh after he'd been kind enough to offer to coach her in self-defense all those months back? She'd known he might be useful at a later date, so why the hell couldn't she just have gritted her teeth and let him play the hero by giving her some free pointers. Hell, she'd scalded her mouth on the coffee he'd bought her she'd been so eager to get away.

Josh frowned at her. "So what? You're a cop? You never said anything."

"No, I, er…" Tess fumbled for the right words.

Mac said, "Tess has proven invaluable in the past. She has a knack for digging up information we can only dream of finding."

Obviously suspicious, Josh scrutinized Tess. His slate-blue eyes stared intently. Cold, yet strangely drawing. He said, "Some kind of consultant?"

Mac shock his head. "It's complicated. Don't bother about it. Just feel free to speak openly in front of her."

Josh still studied Tess. "If you say so."

"I do," said Mac.

Tess gestured to the dead body. "So, any signs of foul play?"

Josh's jaw dropped. "Excuse me?" He pointed back at the suspended body. "You don't think—"

A huge belly laugh burst from Mac.

Josh looked at him, then back at Tess. She stood, unflinchingly serious.

"Ohhh." Josh nodded, smiling. "Okay. Yeah, I'm the new guy. You got me. I can see now why you keep getting your ass kicked."

Tess winked at Josh. Making a good impression now could serve her well in the future if he was Mac's new partner, and humor was a great icebreaker. A quick wit could quickly and easily endear you to a complete stranger. Or to someone you'd inadvertently offended.

"Am I missing something?" Mac looked from one of them to the other for an explanation.

Tess smiled. "No, Detective Hardy bumped into me one day after a bad sparring session at my self-defense class, is all."

"Oh, okay." Mac beckoned for Josh to reveal what he'd noted. "So, what we got?"

Josh glanced at his notes. "From the temperature of the body, the M.E. estimates the time of death to be between one and three thirty this morning, though he's hopeful he can narrow that down later. The blood pattern suggests the victim was killed someplace else, possibly with a single blow to the throat, and then dragged here."

"Any insight on why the elaborate display?" Mac asked.

Josh shrugged. "Maybe it's gang related."

Tess shook her head. "Unless she's some gangbanger's girl and been caught banging someone from a rival gang, this isn't gang related. It's way too personal. To be so brutal, the killer was either punishing her and sending a message to someone else, or he's insane and believes he's an artist with this his masterpiece."

Sweeping his hand from Josh toward Tess, Mac said, "What did I tell you?"

She knew Mac would've had that same thought, but she appreciated the vote of confidence he'd just shown to quell any concerns the younger detective might have harbored about her.

Tess scribbled all the other available details in her notebook and then dropped it into her backpack. To say her goodbyes, she touched Mac's forearm. She noticed Josh's gaze flick down to follow what she'd done. Good: keeping Mac on edge would ensure he stayed nicely compliant and amenable.

"I'll check back with you later," said Tess. "Maybe arrange that drink."

Ambling back down the alley toward the street, Tess thought about the old lady in the park who'd been so horrified by Tess's aptitude for violence that she'd looked at her as if she were a monster. Tess could understand such a viewpoint – it was too unusual for a woman to be able to do what she did. More crucially, it was too unusual for a woman to use such brutality with such calmness. That was the crux of the problem – Tess's calmness. The calmness of a psychopath. Someone who had no empathy for others and so saw no problem in inflicting unbelievable suffering upon them. A monster.

In the old lady's world, there were ordinary people and then there were monsters, with no gray area blurring the distinction between the two. A serial killer was a monster. A rapist? A monster. A pedophile? A monster. A monster was simply a monster. No gray area. No questions. No doubts, only fact. That logic meant the old lady saw Tess not as an ordinary, decent person like herself, but someone more akin to the monster who'd killed Amelia.

Those three guys in the park, on the other hand, weren't monsters. They were just ordinary guys, like hundreds of guys in hundreds of cities. Cruel, yes. Irresponsible, yes. Unthinking, yes. But explainable, understandable, even relatable.

Tess?

How could people relate to her, to what she was, to what she did?

To the old lady, indeed, to the majority of the population, a woman who could inflict such carnage, without even flinching, could be nothing but a monster.

Tess sighed. Was she a monster? Could so many people really be so wrong? Would the world be a better place without her?

Tess pictured Amelia impaled on the metal pole.

A better place without her?

The only time the world would be a better place was when it no longer had a need for her and what she could do.

That time was not now.

On the contrary, now, it was time for her to do what she did best – be what some might call a monster.

Chapter 07

AT THE BOTTOM of the alley, the police officer lifted the yellow crime scene tape and Tess ducked under it again.

She fished her cell phone from her backpack and slipped it out of its little pouch. Made of RF shielding materials, the pouch meant no one could trace her through her phone like they did in the movies. It irritated her how often some James Bond-wannabe saved the world from total obliteration by managing to trace the bad guy through his phone. Hell, all the villain had to do was blow a whopping seventy bucks on one of these little pouches and he could stand on top of the most powerful cell tower in Manhattan and even the NSA's biggest supercomputer wouldn't spot him. Talk about handing it to the hero on a plate.

She scanned the numbers in her phone. Where to start?

She half-heard someone say something but was too engrossed in her phone to pay any heed.

A gentle voice disturbed her. "I said, 'excuse me,' dear."

She glanced up. "Hmm?"

A little old man stood before her. "Do you happen to know what's going on, please?" He gestured to the alleyway.

"Oh, er, sorry. Miles away. Yes, it's a crime scene. There's been a homicide." She went back to her phone.

"It's not someone from around here, is it?"

"I'm sorry, but I'm not at liberty to say."

"I run the local neighborhood watch, so maybe I can help."

She looked up. Maybe he could help. She smiled, putting her phone in its pouch and into the inside pocket of her black leather jacket. "I'm sorry. You were saying?"

He said, "Are you with the police?"

"No, but I'm looking into this case."

"A reporter?"

"Not exactly. Now, about your neighborhood watch."

"I actually started it nearly thirty-five, no, I'm lying, nearly thirty-seven years ago this fall. Back then it was so different around here. I tell you, you wouldn't recognize the place. There was a real sense of community, you know. Folks helped each other. Cared about each other."

She wanted to tell him to get to the point, but often, especially with lonely older people, if you gave

52

them the chance to talk, feigned interest in their lives, they'd be far more forthcoming. "Is that so?"

"Oh yes, dear. In its day, this was a wonderful neighborhood. A place you could raise a family and know your kids were going to come home from school in one piece at the end of the day."

She nodded. "But it's not like that anymore?"

She looked at his brown wool blazer. It was buttoned up as if it was not now in the low seventies, but was a chilly autumn morning. Five would get you ten, under that jacket, he'd have a sweater vest. What was it about getting old that meant you were never warm?

He said, "You know as well as I do, the world isn't changing for the better."

"So you know most of the families around here?"

"Lived here all my life. If there's anything you need to know, I'm your man."

She held out her hand. "I'm sorry, I'm Tess Williams."

The old man tucked his walking cane under his left arm and then shook her hand, cupping it with his left hand, as if wanting to savor that tiny bit of human contact as fully as possible.

"Nathan Ridley. Everyone calls me Nat."

He smiled at her. The skin around his eyes crinkled, meaning the smile was genuine, friendly. Understanding body language helped her with her work, so little things other people might overlook she consciously analyzed. It sometimes meant the difference between knowing whether a gunman was going to pull the trigger or burst into tears over what he'd done. A useful trait. But, sadly, not infallible.

She smiled back. "So did you hear anything last night, Nat?"

He rested on his cane again. "Well, I walked around the block as usual, nine p.m. I call it my patrol, but it's more a leisurely hobble with this old thing." He patted his right leg.

"Hear anything later?"

"Only when I went to the store later on. My leg was aching like nobody's business. It's rare I get a good night's sleep these days. One of the problems of getting old. Not that you'll have to worry about that for a long, long time, dear." He smiled.

"So you went out to the store and…?"

"Yes," he continued, "I figured I'd make myself a hot milky drink but I had no milk, you see. Darned if I know where it all goes." Despite his thick jacket, he rubbed his hands together. "Boy, is it me or is it a cold one today?"

There was often great value in agreeing with someone, even if you didn't hold to their viewpoint, because it helped to establish a kinship which encouraged them to open up to you.

"Yes, it is a little chilly," said Tess. "So what did you hear last night exactly?"

"If you're cold, dear, we can chat in my old place. It's only across the street." He pointed to a nearby building and a ground-level apartment.

She looked at her watch.

When he saw her hesitating, he tried to seal the deal. "I can make us some hot tea in a jiffy."

So this guy heard something last night, knew everyone in the neighborhood, and could virtually see the crime scene from his living room window.

"Tea would be lovely. Thank you."

Statistics proved most murder victims were killed by someone they knew. That meant those people who knew the victim invariably also knew the killer. Who did Nat know? Which suspects could he point her to?

Chapter 08

NAT'S APARTMENT WAS much how she'd expected it would be. When she sat on the couch the protective plastic cover squeaked and all but glued her in place, while, despite the large windows, the room's dark wood, leather, and brown furnishings made it unnaturally gloomy.

On the ebony mantel stood an arch-shaped wooden clock. It ticked louder than any clock she'd ever heard. And it seemed to tick more slowly too. As if time were tired in this house. As if it were biding time, with every day the same, just waiting for death.

"Nice place," she said, wanting to endear herself to him to get the information she needed.

He turned from pouring boiling water and smiled.

"Wouldn't live anywhere else," he said. "I know everyone and everyone knows me. It's my little plot of heaven."

She gazed about the dingy mausoleum he called home. She'd bet if he had five visitors a year, it would be a busy year.

On a five-foot table beneath the biggest window was a miniature diorama consisting of countryside dotted with tens of tiny model soldiers. Squeaking as she prized herself off the plastic, she meandered over to look while Nat was brewing tea.

"The Battle of Ball's Bluff, Virginia, 1861," he said. "I like to re-enact and study strategy."

"Uh-huh."

She studied the old man. Was he really so old and decrepit? Or did prematurely gray hair, a naturally haggard hangdog expression, and a limp make him appear far older than he actually was? It was hard to tell. He looked like he was on the wrong end of his seventies but could easily be ten or fifteen years younger.

She said, "So, you were saying you heard something late last night."

"Oh, yes. But you never said why you're here, dear. Why you were at the crime scene."

"It's part of what I do." She ambled back to the couch.

"Which is?"

She was going to have to give him something. Share so he'd do likewise.

"I write. Freelance. Sometimes I uncover things that help the police."

He hobbled over with two cups of tea on saucers. He placed them on coasters on the dark wood table in front of the couch and then sat.

Nat smiled. "So, who is it we're investigating today?"

We? So far, *we* had zip.

And the clock ticked slowly on.

"You were telling me about last night," said Tess, hoping he had more to offer than a hot drink she didn't really want.

"Oh yes. Well, it's my leg, you see. I tell you, never get old, dear. You won't believe the problems. I've got a cupboard full of pills and potions, the strongest painkillers and the most powerful sleeping pills known to man, but can I sleep? So, anyway, I decided I'd make myself a hot milky drink, see if that would do the trick, but I had no milk. So, since I wasn't doing anything else, I went to the convenience store around the block to buy some."

"Around...?"

"Just around the block, dear. You can't miss it."

"Sorry, I mean around what time."

"Oh, around two fifteen, dear. And that's when it happened."

"Yes?"

"Well, I saw young Amelia from next door having a blazing argument, first with a taxi driver and then with her boyfriend."

"Amelia? You mean Amelia Ortega?"

He gasped. "It's not Amelia, is it?" He obviously saw something in her face. "Oh dear Lord, no. Oh, the poor child."

"I'm sorry."

"Oh my. She was such a lovely girl. Led a little astray of late, but a lovely girl. Do they know who did it?"

"Not yet."

"Any clues?"

"There will be."

His expression dropped even further. "She wasn't…" He looked at the gaudy brown-and-gold-patterned carpet, no doubt a popular design three or four decades ago. He took a breath as if mustering the strength to say what he needed.

Finally, he got the words out. "She wasn't violated?"

Tess gave a slight shrug. "I'm sure the forensics team will find something to help catch the person responsible."

"Forensics, eh?" He nodded to himself. "I hope they catch them. My God, what I'd do to them if I could."

Maybe talk them to death?

"I can imagine," said Tess. "So Amelia argued with her boyfriend Ethan?"

"Yes, dear. Ethan Dumfries. They've been together around nine months."

"Did you catch what they were arguing about?"

"I'm sorry, no. I don't like to snoop."

"So how about the taxi driver? Any chance you got a good look at him?"

"Middle Eastern… maybe." He shrugged and shook his head. "I'm sorry. I'm not being much help, am I?"

"Oh, I wouldn't say that – knowing Amelia argued with someone could be crucial."

He smiled and then pulled out some scraps of paper from his sweater vest's right pocket.

"I did note the taxi's medallion number, if that's any use."

Any use? Every cab had to have a medallion to be able to pick up fares in Manhattan. Every medallion number, or cab number, was unique to a specific cab, so if she got that, she'd find the cab Amelia had taken, no problem. Thank God for busybodies and people with too much time on their hands.

He picked through the various scraps, notes scrawled on each.

"No, not that one… That one…? Nope… What's this? Oh, I mustn't lose that. Heavens, no." He looked up and smiled. "I'll have it for you in a second, dear."

She smiled.

He patted her arm. "It is so nice to have company." He went back to his notes.

Finally, he scrutinized a paper. "Hmmm… is that a five or a six? I think it's a six." He handed it to her. "There you go, dear."

6Y11.

"That's terrific. Thank you, Nat."

"My pleasure, dear. Anything to help."

"There's just one thing. Er, it might sound a little strange, but the police will be canvassing door-to-door soon. Would you mind not letting on I was here, please?"

"Well…" He scratched his head.

She knew giving people what they wanted would get her what she wanted. She laid her hand on his arm. "It would be a huge help, Nat."

He cupped her hand with his. "For you, dear." He smiled.

She stayed with Nat for another ten minutes, long enough to drink her tea and to make him feel good, useful, important, so he'd be eager to help her again should the need arise.

When she left, he waved through the security bars at his window.

She waved back. What a strange little man. Pleasant, kindly, but strange.

And deeply, deeply lonely.

Was that what was waiting for her in forty years?

That was a question for another day. Now it was time for the hunt to begin.

Chapter 09

STRIDING ALONG THE sidewalk, Tess wondered what her first move should be to find the killer.

There was absolutely no point going to Amelia's apartment as Ethan was missing. Why had he run? Either because he'd killed her or because he was afraid no one would believe he hadn't. Whichever it was, tracking him down could prove problematic.

Amelia's family? If they hadn't been involved in her death, they'd be such a mess of tears they'd be no use. On the other hand, if the family had been involved, they'd be so full of lies, it would be easier for the police to uncover the truth than for Tess to struggle with it.

Amelia's friends? Again, same problem as her family. Plus, if they did know something, and it involved a mutual friend, they may feed Tess false information out of false loyalty. She could waste hours, even days, chasing down leads only to find she was further from the truth, and the killer, than she was right now.

No, for now, her answers lay elsewhere. She needed time to formulate a plan.

A taxi having a medallion meant either it was owned by an individual, which was getting rarer nowadays since a medallion could cost hundreds of thousands of dollars, or it was one of many owned by a corporation from which drivers leased it. Either way, there'd be a record of who drove Amelia last night.

That was the good news. The bad news was that anyone could hail a yellow cab on any street, without having to go through the company's dispatcher, so to get the details of Amelia's journey would mean talking to the driver himself. That was vital anyway as Amelia had had some sort of altercation with him.

Cab drivers got irate if they didn't receive the tip they thought they deserved, so if Amelia had tried to stiff him on the fare, it could easily have led to trouble. The key could be in discovering from where she'd taken the cab and what hefty fare she'd racked up. After all, a driver wouldn't turn all Vlad the Impaler over a twenty-dollar ride, would they?

Twenty bucks? Well… People had killed for far, far less.

Once in a heightened emotional state, people did the most outrageous of things for the most ridiculous of reasons. No, she had to keep an open mind about the whole fare issue until she'd gathered more facts.

Feeling hunger gnawing at her, it approaching lunchtime, she wandered into A Taste of Napoli. She ordered a black organic tea and a small mushroom pizza, then sat at a round green table with her back to the wall and made sure she could see all the exits.

Having removed her phone from its RF shielded pouch, she scrolled through its apps until she reached Dental Schedule. That being the most boring title she could think of, she hoped if ever she lost her phone, anyone finding it would think such an app too boring to investigate. Looking directly into the camera lens on her phone, she photographed her right eye for her iris recognition software to unlock all her phone's sensitive files and features. She hadn't been able to help but feel very James Bond the first few times she'd used this security software, but these days, it was as exciting as logging in to Facebook.

Google took her to the NYC Taxi and Limousine Commission. A few clicks later, she confirmed the owner of the taxi medallion number was not an individual, but a company: Get-U-There Taxis. A trip to the dispatch office would hopefully provide the name and contact details of the driver. She continued her research.

When her order arrived, the pizza crust was chewy and the mushrooms lightly charred. She looked up at the picture of the Leaning Tower of Pisa above the counter. She sighed. That should have warned her: Pisa was a completely different town in a completely different part of Italy to Napoli, the town after which the café was named. Attention to detail was obviously not something the café's owners embraced.

Still, the tea was decent. But what kind of an imbecile would you need to be to screw up a black tea?

With music videos playing on a television suspended high on the wall toward the back of the café, she flicked through her contacts. She stopped at Bomb and hit dial, satisfied the music would mask her conversation.

Chapter 10

AFTER ONLY ONE ring, a male voice said, "Yo, Tess."

"Hey, Bomb. I need a Level Four workup on one Amelia Ortega. Priority contacts, communications for the last forty-eight hours, affiliations, images – the full gig. I'll send you the details I have. How long?"

"Corporate, government, or individual?"

"Twenty-one-year-old nobody."

"Give me an hour."

"You're going to come across Ethan Michael Dumfries. I need the same on him. Plus location updates. How long to trace his cell phone?"

"Is it turned on?"

"Don't know."

"He using Wi-Fi hotspots or a paid service?"

"Don't know."

"I'll get back to you on that when I deliver the first package."

"Great," said Tess. "How's the new housekeeper working out?"

"She didn't."

Tess sighed. That was the third in two months.

Bomb said, "Hey, she moved my keyboard. Okay?"

Hell. And she'd only been fired, not flogged? "You mean in those sixty seconds per day you pry yourself off it for a shit, shower and shave, she crept in and dusted it?"

"Funny, Tess. Real funny. As funny as if someone moves my gear and dislodges a cable, so I can't get the info you need when you need it and you end up bleeding face down in an alley."

Ah, maybe he had a point. "You could've just explained it to her."

"She got the manual. Just like all the others."

Bomb's *Housekeeper Dos and Don'ts* was indeed a 'manual' – thirty-two double-sided pages of single-spaced text. He might as well have given them the Japanese version of *War and Peace*.

She said, "Do you want me to help you find someone?"

"Thanks, but if I need help, I'll ask."

Yes, because that was what guys were renowned for – asking for help.

He said, "I'll get back to you when I have something. Ciao, Tess."

She sighed.

Just because Bomb was a genius with a computer he expected everyone else to be a genius at their chosen profession. Why couldn't he get that most people didn't pursue a calling to change the world, so much as endure a job to cover their bills? For a smart guy, he could be incredibly dumb. But hey, since when was she Little Miss Tolerance?

She left her phone out of its pouch so Bomb could reach her when he needed to. It left her susceptible to being tracked, but only if someone was actually looking for her, and looking for her at that moment. Plus, they'd need her information on the online telephone exchange Bomb had created and hidden so deep in the Deep Web, she didn't even know where it was.

She and Bomb had tried her checking in half-hourly, so her phone was only unshielded for a few minutes at a time, but it had proven unworkable. Any longer than thirty minutes would mean vital information couldn't be acted on as quickly as possible, which could mean someone ending up in the morgue – maybe her. That left only one option – the immediate job taking priority over the risk of her being tracked. It was one of the hazards of the job. Anyway, who was to say she wasn't just being paranoid?

After a couple more bites of pizza, she slung a piece of crust back onto the plate and pushed it away. Tess looked at Amelia's Facebook page on her phone.

Family rarely knew the truth about a loved one's life.

Close friends often knew more, but still had gaps in their knowledge.

Why?

Because every individual was a roiling mass of blatant contradictions, dark secrets, and impossible dreams. If you knew one person intimately over your whole lifetime, really intimately, you were truly blessed.

But secrets weren't always as safe as people liked to believe they were. Those websites people visited in the dead of night, when there was nothing around them but darkness, so they knew it was private, knew they were alone, knew they were safe… The reality was they couldn't be more vulnerable. To skilled hands, those little mouse clicks bared people's secrets as clearly as a full-page ad in the *New York Times*.

A person's true life, their true feelings, their true needs could be put together like a jigsaw puzzle if you just had enough pieces. Did they surf any unusual websites? Who were their most messaged contacts? Which groups did they look at but not join? What forum questions did they read? Which words did they google? Yes, if you knew how to mine for data, and how to recognize patterns, a person's online history could give a truer picture of their life than their parents, partner, and friends combined.

Luckily for Tess, Bomb was a jigsaw genius.

She left the café and found the nearest subway station. Moments later, she was rocketing through the bowels of the city towards the most brutal killer she'd ever encountered.

She hoped.

The Thompson job had been exhausting. Mentally and physically. It would be great if she could end this job quickly and get some time to relax, away from a world of endless exploitation and savagery. Even if just for a few days.

And that looked like a distinct possibility, with only three suspects: Ethan, who'd done it in a jealous rage; the cab driver, who'd done it after an argument had escalated; a third, as yet unidentified, individual, who'd done it because they were a psychopath looking for media attention, which was obvious by the way Amelia's body had been displayed.

Lover, driver, psycho. Which one would it be?

Chapter 11

LIVING IN NEW York City was like living in a land where everyone and anyone could be a cannibal looking for their next meal – in public, no one made eye contact in case that one person you connected with had polished their silverware that very morning.

Obviously unaware it was supposed to be invisible on the subway train, an auburn-haired baby didn't see anything wrong in bawling, making itself the center of attention. The center of attention for all but its mother. Looking over the top of it at her ereader, she gently rocked her child, but paid no heed to the fact that her maternal efforts were achieving absolutely squat.

The kid wailed. And wailed. And wailed.

Christ, Tess hated that sound. And she hated that kind of parent – they never seemed to give a crap about how many people their kid irritated as they blissfully went about their lives. Despite her meditation practices, this was one of those noises she just couldn't tune out. Which made it even more irritating.

The kid's scream turned into a guttural squeal, but still the mother was oblivious.

God only knew why there weren't laws against traveling with kids under five years old. Especially in such confined areas as trains and planes. Oh, man... planes. On her flight to Shanghai, she'd had to ask the old guy next to her for one of his sleeping pills because of the spawn of Satan wailing in the seat behind her. It was either that or risk killing every passenger onboard by opening the emergency hatch to pitch the squealing brat into the clouds.

The flight attendant had suggested Tess couldn't ignore the baby's distress cries because of her maternal instincts. After Tess had stopped laughing, she'd given the idea some consideration. And then burst out laughing again.

Maternal? Yeah, she was as maternal as a great white shark with a seal pup.

Back in the daylight on the street, surrounded by the serene cacophony of the city's honking, revving, bustling life, Tess strolled into Get-U-There Taxis. It was only a small company, so she hoped she wouldn't have much trouble getting the information she needed.

With the stench of gas and oil hanging heavy in the air, she stepped over a soggy black patch on the concrete floor and headed for what looked like the office. In the doorway stood a scrawny man with a moustache that jutted out from his face as far as his nose.

As she marched over, Moustache Man eyed her head to toe.

She couldn't have hoped for anything better – a horny guy well below her league. She smiled at him.

He smiled back. "Can I help you, miss?"

"Hi. I'm looking for a driver."

"And where do you wanna go?"

"I'd like to know who was driving cab 6Y11 between midnight and five a.m., please." The time of death estimate and Nat's memory could both have been inaccurate, so best to play safe with a wide time frame.

"Ah, see, we don't give information like that to members of the public."

She glanced to the back of the garage, where two cabs had their hoods up but no one working on them while a third stood on blocks.

She looked back at the mustachioed dispatcher. On the front of his white shirt he'd sponged a ketchup stain to save wasting a fresh garment when there was still wear in that one.

When a taxi medallion could cost upwards of a million bucks, any company that didn't have its fleet on the road 24/7 was a failing company. This was a guy going nowhere in a company on the ropes.

She smiled. "Fifty bucks for a name."

"If it's worth fifty, it must be worth a hundred." He smiled. Smiled like he knew the game they were playing and how he could win.

He didn't.

She said, "It's worth forty-five. Or I walk."

"You said fifty."

"Now it's forty."

"Okay, okay." He threw his hands up and trudged into the office. "Jesus. A guy's gotta make a living, you know." He leaned over his desk and hit a couple of keys on his keyboard. "Yeah, it's Amir Suleman."

Tess spelled the name out to check she'd gotten it right, then said, "And where will I find Mr. Suleman?"

Moustache Man folded his arms, put on a stern expression, and then held out a hand, rubbing his thumb over his fingertips for the money. This was his idea of hardball? Awww, bless his heart.

Tess handed him forty dollars.

"This time of day, he'll be at the corner of Baker and Richmond. Look for Eastern Promise food truck. He's working two jobs since his wife took the house and most of his paycheck."

Money. As was so often the case, was money at the root of this crime?

Getting stiffed on a fare wouldn't directly lead a cab driver to impale a woman on a metal pole. No, but one person in effect stealing from another invariably led to a verbal attack, which invariably led to a physical assault, which invariably led to one hell of an escalation where rationality disappeared and all that mattered was payback. In the eyes of the person who'd been wronged, the sum in question became inconsequential. It could be twenty dollars as easily as twenty thousand. Now, it was all about payback. Payback at any cost.

Could Amir have killed Amelia over less than the average Joe would pay for a decent pizza?

Chapter 12

SITTING ON A fire hydrant outside Manning's Bikes, Tess looked over at the bright green food truck with 'Eastern Promise' emblazoned across it in black and gold letters. Fifty yards diagonally across from her, a couple of customers waited for food. The lunchtime rush ending, she'd wait a few more minutes until Amir was doing nothing but wiping down his counter. Make her approach in private.

Tess returned to browsing files on her phone.

She read through another of Amelia's private Facebook messages that Bomb had emailed her. So far, there was nothing concrete to suggest any lover except Ethan. Neither did her Internet browsing reveal any gang-related talk, sexual deviancy, or Internet dating – any of which could have led her into a dangerous situation.

In green Kawasaki leathers, a biker grinned at Tess on the hydrant. "You're sitting in the wrong place, baby, if you want something big and hard between your legs." Grabbing his crotch, he nudged his black-clad friend. They both laughed.

She ignored them. Banter would lead nowhere and confrontation would alert Amir to her abilities. She returned to her files.

To a female friend called Becks, Amelia made occasional references to TG, as though it was someone's name. As Tess trawled back through the messages to find where this story started, she found multiple references first to 'that guy' and then further back to 'that guy in the bar'. Had 'that guy in the bar' morphed into 'that guy' and then into simply 'TG'? Without giving details, the texts referred to something Amelia had done, innumerable times and in a variety of public places, which she didn't want Ethan to discover. Was TG a nameless fuck buddy Amelia sometimes ran into? Did she revel in an element of danger? If so, exactly how much danger did she enjoy?

Unfortunately, there'd been no direct communication with TG and no photo. Amelia was probably wary of Ethan gaining access to her account and seeing something incriminating. Finding TG was going to be a problem. A bar at which they'd regularly met, however, was mentioned.

Shades.

Another phrase also captured Tess's attention. A month ago, Amelia had made a 'huge mistake' after TG had finally said he loved her. Amelia's messages concerning him had become much darker after that.

There was far less hope. Far less sense of fulfillment in the danger. Far less sparkle.

What had Amelia done that was such a 'huge mistake'? Or, more likely, what had TG made her do? And what had that incident led to? Was TG that third unidentified suspect – the psychopath? Had he turned into a jealous lover? Or had Ethan discovered Amelia's secret and sought to punish her for her betrayal?

Tess needed answers.

She looked up. A lone customer was being served at the truck. Time to grill a taxi-driving chef.

Chapter 13

AMIR SULEMAN, THE taxi driver, looked down at her through the hatch in the side of his green truck. "What I can do for you?"

From his accent, his dark skin, and the name of his food truck, Tess guessed he was from the Middle East. Lebanon, Syria, maybe Turkey.

"Your chili special – is that hot?"

"Is hot."

She smiled. "I love hot."

"Is very hot."

"Can I get four portions? To take home, please?"

"Will take a few minutes."

"That's okay." She watched him put a large saucepan of chili on his stove and turn up the heat. "This an old family recipe?"

He didn't turn. "No."

"Is it Turkish?"

"No."

She sighed. Talk about hard work. Finesse would obviously not win this battle.

"You're a taxi driver, aren't you?"

He still didn't turn from cooking. "Yes."

"Could you tell me about one of your fares last night?"

He stopped what he was doing and turned. Holding a large knife, he said, "Police?"

"No."

"Then I say nothing." He turned back to his cocking.

"You picked up a young woman. Slim. Twenty-one. You dropped her—"

He turned around again, gesturing with the knife. "You don't speak English? I say 'I say nothing.' Now you go. I don't cook for you."

"She was killed last night."

His mouth dropped open. His eyes glazed for a moment while he processed the information. Then he stabbed his knife towards her. "And you think I did it?"

"I need to know what you know."

"I know nothing without lawyer." He stabbed his knife down the street. "You go."

She looked at the middle-aged man before her. Looked at his greasy hair, the dark rings under his eyes, his slumped shoulders. Life hadn't been good to this man. Whether that was deserved or not didn't matter. What mattered was such a man would grasp any chance to feel, even for the most fleeting of moments, like a winner.

And she knew just how to make any guy feel like that.

She slammed banknotes down on his counter. "I've got fifty bucks… or a warm, soft mouth."

Her gaze fell to his crotch.

Chapter 14

GOING DOWN ONTO her knees in the food truck, Tess's hand stuck to the greasy floor. No way had a health inspector visited this thing recently. God only knew what she'd catch if she didn't wash her hands after this.

She peeled her palm off the floor, snagged a couple of paper napkins from a shelf under the counter, and wiped her hands. She looked up at Amir Suleman towering over her. He double-checked the shutters over the truck's serving hatch were locked. And then unzipped his pants.

Thank God he'd picked this option. She was struggling to make all her rent payments this month as it was, so she couldn't afford to blow too much of this week's budget on bribes.

Using both hands, she eased out his pecker.

The smell hit her instantly. A smell most women have encountered and each dreads encountering again – like rotting meat a dog has pissed on. It was no wonder his wife left him. Such a smell alone was tantamount to domestic abuse.

That was the bad news.

But there was good news – it wasn't the biggest dick she'd ever had to cope with, so it wouldn't give her jaw-ache. And despite the smell, it did look clean.

She took him into her mouth and sucked.

What was it about men and personal hygiene? Hell, most guys took better care of their car than their pecker: they wouldn't stick their beloved vehicle in any old place but only in places they knew and trusted; they were obsessive about having it not just in functional condition, but as impressive as possible; they were particular about who even touched it let alone drove it. But their pecker? An actual piece of their own body? Hey, who cared what sleazy neighborhood that had to venture into and who got their hands on it?

Where was the logic?

Still, who was she to talk? She'd had worse things than a grimy dick in her mouth – living and dead, and cooked and raw. The worst must have been China. Their markets stocked packets of frozen dog meat, deep-fried starfish on a stick, snake skin – not snake meat, that was another dish entirely, but just the skin. How the devil could you make a meal out of skin?

Amir making guttural moaning sounds, she wondered if passers-by could hear. So what if they could – they weren't her customers.

To speed things along, she got to work with her hand.

Scorpions, wild birds, insects… The Chinese diet seemed to leave no species off the menu.

Oh, seahorses!

That had to be the worst 'food source' she'd found there.

As respite from her brutal training regiment, she'd spent many an hour sitting on the floor of Shanghai Ocean Aquarium, basking in the gentle world of the seahorses as they glided about their tank. Outside, only a leisurely stroll away, grilled seahorse was on sale at a local food market. How could the Chinese do that? Marvel at a creature one minute, then slap it on their dinner plate the next? And seahorses truly were wondrous. Such beautiful, peaceful little creat—

Amir groaned. He grabbed the counter edge to steady himself.

Something hit the back of her throat.

Pulling away, she flung her free hand over the end of his pecker and caught the rest of his gunk in a clean napkin. She continued pumping with her other hand to empty him into the tissue paper.

Feeling him softening, she let go and looked up, nodding to the napkin. "Don't want the health inspector shutting you down, do we?"

She knew she should feel some sort of revulsion over what she'd just done, or guilt, or shame, but she didn't. She didn't have the money to buy what she wanted so she'd traded what she did have for it. It was a simple transaction. Nothing more. Sex could get her pretty much anything she wanted – the favors she got from her many cop fuck buddies was proof of that.

Maybe it would be different if she enjoyed sex. Or if she was in a relationship. But she didn't and she wasn't. So why not use sex as a simple commodity? When other people prized it so highly, that gave her an instant advantage.

Amir distracted, dressing himself, she stuffed the napkin into her pocket and then swiped a can of cola from a storage shelf. "I'm sure you won't mind."

She took a good swig and swished it around her mouth, but grimaced. "Urgh… warm."

She looked at Amir, "Now, about last night."

"I think… I wait for lawyer."

Chapter 15

TESS JABBED HER cola at him. "Hey, whoa there, cowboy. We had a deal."

"Deals change. Here, I give you free chili." He moved toward his saucepan, still on the stove beside her.

"Like hell." She pushed him back. "You're going to tell me what I want to know. Now do you want to do it standing up smiling, or lying on the floor bleeding?"

He laughed. "You threaten me?" He pointed at her. "You?"

She grabbed his finger and bent it back toward him.

He winced.

She bent further.

To stop his finger from breaking, Amir bent his knees and leaned backwards.

With her foot, Tess swept his feet from under him.

He crashed to the floor.

"Just remember: I tried to play nice." She whipped the saucepan of simmering chili from the stove. Threw it into his lap. With her foot, she held the upended saucepan on him.

Amir screamed, the boiling chili soaking through his clothes onto his crotch.

She said, "Tell me what happened and I'll move my foot."

He grabbed the pan, obviously thinking he could pull it away, but cried out and pulled his hands away instead, the pan was so hot. He wrung his hands in the air.

"Tell me!"

In between gasps, he said, "Her boyfriend." His face screwed up in pain. "They fight."

"And?"

"An old man."

"What about an old man?"

"They fight also."

"She had an argument with an old man?"

"Yes. Yes. Yes." He whimpered. "Now, please."

Tess pressed down with her foot on the pan. "When you've told me everything."

Amir let out a gargling cry. He said, "Old man with stick. Old man with stick."

Nat? Surely he couldn't mean Nat.

She said, "And then what?"

"She went to store. She buy something. She leave."

"But why were you at the store? Why didn't you leave after you dropped her?"

"I buy cigarettes; I smoke cigarette."

"You didn't see the boyfriend or old man again?"

"No." His face twisted with pain and despair. "Please, please, I beg you!"

She kicked the saucepan away. He curled over. Grabbed his crotch. Whimpered.

So that was why he didn't want to confess to seeing Amelia later – other than the killer, he was likely the last person to see her alive. People had witnessed him argue with her and threaten her, so who could blame him for withholding information to avoid a lot or sweaty hours under police interrogation?

Tess turned to leave, but huffed. She stamped her foot into the floor a few times to test it, then bent her leg to see the underneath of the sneaker that had held the boiling hot pan on Amir. A crescent shaped groove from the saucepan's base had melted into the sole throwing out the balance when she stood on it.

"Oh, for God's sake." She glared at him. "Would you look at what you've done?"

She looked around. "Well, don't think this is coming out of my pocket." She hit No Sale on his cash register and snatched seventy dollars.

As she opened the door at the back of the truck to leave, she turned.

Still curled on the floor, Amir splashed a bottle of spring water over his crotch. He sobbed.

Tess shook her head. "Think that's pain? Try getting a Brazilian with hot wax. Pussy." She slammed the door behind her.

Back on the street, Tess placed the soiled napkin in a plastic bag and into her backpack. You never knew when DNA evidence could come in handy.

Heading toward the subway, she wondered why Nat hadn't told her he'd had a run-in with Amelia. What was he hiding? And, more to the point, what could they have argued about? He was boring, yes. But if that were a crime, the majority of the population would be behind bars. Apart from that, and though she didn't like to admit it even only to herself, she actually quite liked the guy.

She liked his understated control, his meekness, his concern for those around him, his inherent goodness. While each passing year colored her memories more, and there had been more years than she cared to remember, she could see her deceased grandpa in Nat.

Oh, her grandpa hadn't been boring, but he'd been soft-spoken, polite, had interests that both insulated and isolated him from other people.

Yes, maybe that was why she liked the little old man.

But why would anyone fight with Nat? He was what he was – an absent-minded, lonely old man. Pleasant, polite… harmless.

Or was he?

Around the dinner table, some of history's most notorious killers had been charming and entertaining.

Every single person had at least one secret. A secret they ached to take to the grave. What was Nat's?

Chapter 16

AS TESS DESCENDED the narrow subway steps, people bustled left and right, each lost in their own little world of importance, dreams and fears.

Equally distracted, Tess drifted down the steps. She couldn't help but wonder about Nat. Did he harbor a dark secret or was he just the amiable, if pitiable, figure he appeared? More crucially, why was she struggling to tell which was the case? She could usually read people well. Was his similarity to her grandpa coloring her judgment? She needed answers. Needed clarity.

Halfway down the steps, her phone rang. "I hope this is good news, Bomb."

"I think I'm homing in on our boy Ethan. Unless something changes, I should have a location sometime within the next hour. Ninety minutes max."

"Great. Thanks, Bomb."

"Good hunting. Ciao, Tess."

She climbed back up the steps and marched along the street toward a bus stop she'd spotted. If Bomb could call anytime within the next ninety minutes, she couldn't get caught deep underground with no cell phone signal, miss his call, and thus miss Ethan because she reached his location too late.

To be better able to discuss options with him, she'd once asked Bomb to explain how he did what he did. She'd even started recording the session to review the more technical aspects later.

Review the more 'technical' aspects? Who was she fooling?

Aside from the software he'd coded himself, it was all to do with Google dorks, open ports, shellcode, brute force password crackers, IP addresses, Skipfish, ZAP, trojans, worms, Burp, bots, and backdoors. Talk about hi-tech wizardry only a NASA scientist could appreciate.

Luckily, her battery had died, so they'd had to stop long before he'd run out of details or enthusiasm.

If he'd lived in Silicon Valley in the 80s, he'd have been hailed as a genius. But born a decade too late and three thousand miles away in a rundown apartment building controlled by a loan shark, Bomb hadn't been blessed by serendipity.

But fate had a weird way of choosing your path at times. As she knew only too well. You could do all you could to make the right decisions, but sometimes, even in hindsight, you could never see how you could've done anything differently for things to have turned out any better. But then, wasn't that what made life so interesting? A utopia would be fun. For a while.

But if there were no more challenges? Well, humanity would just fade away. Die of boredom.

Yeah, there was something to be said for hardship. It pushed you. Made you work for what you wanted. Made you resourceful. Made you better. Stronger. Most of the time.

Other times, it twisted you into a perverse image of humanity. Doing to a person's soul what a Hall of Mirrors did to their body – warping and corrupting, turning the beautiful into something hideous.

It was a fine line between being a good person and a bad one. Between hero and monster. A fine line that every single person had to choose, all by themselves, on which side they wanted to stand. It was easy to be a hero – you just chose to do good things.

The problem was it was even easier to be a monster.

Put your toe just a fraction of an inch too far over the line… and there you were: cheating on your partner; skimming off a few dollars from your boss's takings; backstabbing your friend for a promotion. Little things. Yes. But little things were never enough. Not once you'd started. Not once you'd seen how ridiculously easy it was. And that was when the monster inside everyone came a-calling.

The strange thing was, the slide from hero to monster was so, so easy. Yet the climb back from monster to hero? Like climbing Mount Everest. And she should know.

En route to Nat's, Tess received the full workup on Ethan, so she took a minor detour. Examining multiple files on her phone wasn't fun, because, ideally, you needed to have as many open as possible to make cross-referencing easier. Her tablet was okay, but with two Level 4 workups, a full-size screen was the best option.

In school, while the other kids had all been dreaming of being a wizard learning magic in a mystical castle, she'd dreamed of being a librarian. With thousands and thousands of books at your fingertips, every day all day, what more could anyone possibly want?

Like an ancient queen entering the temple to her gods, Tess climbed the stone steps to the white marble building fronted by grand porticos and Corinthian columns – the public library. She glanced at the huge marble lions on either side, Fortitude and Patience, guarding the entrance. No matter how many times she came here, it always filled her with wonder.

For her, as a small child, this had been a magic castle. Or as near to a castle as she'd ever seen. It had been her favorite place in the whole city. The Statue of Liberty, the Bronx Zoo, the view from the top of the Twin Towers... All too small. Too limiting. Too unadventurous. The library, on the other hand, housed the whole world – and how she'd globetrotted.

Stories from every age, country and culture. Facts from every discipline, hobby and sport. Wisdom from every thinker, religion and philosophy. She'd devoured it all.

And thank God. If it hadn't been for her appreciation of books, appreciation of learning, appreciation of how others had faced impossible odds yet triumphed, the path her life had taken would surely have seen her as a junkie stealing to numb her pain. Or a suicide victim. Both of which pretty much amounted to the same thing.

Sitting at a wide wooden desk in the third-floor Catalogue Room, beneath one of the four-tier circular chandeliers, Tess fired up one of the computers. After inserting her USB drive to have available the array of apps Bomb had created for her, she logged in to Bomb's darknet.

Using AES-Twofish-Serpent cascaded three-cipher encryption, Eastern European servers, and domains registered in the Far East, Bomb had created a website Tess could access on the move while making it virtually impervious to detection. 'Virtually impervious' – as with everything online, it was a trade-off between security and functionality.

She followed Bomb's instructions to establish backdoor access to both Amelia's and Ethan's social media and email accounts. Going in through a backdoor meant, firstly, the police wouldn't be suspicious about a dead girl accessing her account and, secondly, that Ethan wouldn't be frozen out and, therefore, suspicious by there being two simultaneous logins to his accounts.

More importantly, it meant no one would be able to track Tess's cyberspace movements.

Bomb's software had already completed basic pattern recognition and cross-referencing of the accounts for names, places, dates and other preprogrammed criteria within set parameters, so Tess began digging.

From the photos she'd seen on her phone, she'd already memorized Ethan's face, but a larger screen meant she could see more detail. Now, she saw a crescent-shaped scar on the left side of his jaw that she hadn't earlier – an excellent unique identifier. At least now, whether she saw him in a bar or on a mortuary slab, she'd know he was the guy she was looking for.

Or one of them. How about TG?

There was no such reference in any of Ethan's online messages.

His phone records, however, proved far more interesting. After an initial phone call that morning which had lasted just one minute forty-seven seconds, Ethan had bombarded Amelia's friend Becks with messages.

Tess counted the entries: twelve phone calls and twenty-seven texts. He'd tried to contact her more than three times as often as any of Amelia's other friends.

Opening the attachment sent with one message, Tess found a shadowy photo of a woman talking intimately to a man at a bar. The woman looked like Amelia, while the club could've been Shades, which

Ethan referenced elsewhere. As for the man? Could that be the elusive TG?

The message with the photo simply said, *'tell me who so i can kill him.'*

Tess zoomed in to the photo for a better look at TG, but with a low-resolution image taken in a dark club, his face was just a shadowy, pixelated mess. She ran the photo through their site's image-enhancement software. It reduced the number of artifacts, but, with the source image of such low quality, the face was little but a blurry oval blob. She'd never identify TG with this.

Other than the first, all Ethan's calls to Becks had gone unanswered; most of the texts had gone unread.

Hardly surprising. Most contained threats. All very blunt. All very graphic.

Ethan sounded like an incredibly nice guy. Tess couldn't wait to meet him.

One phrase was common to many of his messages: *'i didnt do it.'*

Becks had only sent one SMS reply: *'I DON'T BELIEVE U!!!'*

At the crime scene, Mac had said Ethan had a record of violence against women. Becks obviously knew he was a violent man, while his messages gave every indication he saw violence as an acceptable solution to his problems. It was easy to see how a fight with Amelia might have got out of hand.

But why was he so desperate to talk with Becks? Did he want her to provide an alibi for the time of the murder? Did he think she knew he'd abused Amelia and was worried she'd tell the police? Was he innocent and simply trying to trace the man in the photo talking to Amelia, either to clear his name, or to seek vengeance, believing this stranger to be the killer?

As Tess scanned the texts for more clues, Bomb posted Ethan's latest message to Becks. It left little doubt about his intentions: *'tell me who it is or after i've found him i'll find u.'*

Tess checked Becks's profile: she waited tables at A Taste of Napoli, where Tess had eaten earlier. A black woman with straightened shoulder-length hair and a smoldering look, all Becks's photos screamed 'sassy'. She and Amelia obviously had an active social life and appeared to share everything. Maybe Becks held the key. Scanning through the photos Becks had uploaded to her Facebook account, Tess came to a number of interesting ones. She sent them to her phone just as it vibrated.

Gesturing to the librarian that she'd be back after taking a call, Tess removed her USB drive and then ducked out. She strode through the immense Reading Room as quickly as she could and into the McGraw Rotunda, a 'hallway' more suited to a European palace than a city public library.

Surrounded by French walnut and pink marble, and beneath a gigantic ceiling mural of Prometheus stealing fire from the Gods, Tess answered her phone.

"I located your boy," said Bomb.

"Great. How close is he?"

"He's on the move. Has been for an hour now. Seems to be just hopping on and off the public transit system. Probably thinks if he keeps moving no one will find him."

"Let me know when he stops in one place for longer than twenty minutes. Or if you find a pattern."

"You got it."

"Thanks, Bomb." She hung up.

There was no point in trying to chase Ethan around the city. If he was taking random routes, it was impossible to guess where he was going to be at any one time. But if it was random, he wouldn't sit tight for more than a few minutes, but just take the first bus or train that came along. If he stopped for twenty minutes, it was a fair bet he'd reached where he wanted to be and would be there for much longer.

They say a criminal often returns to the scene of a crime. The dumb ones, yes. Or the really smart ones who believe they can throw a wrench in the works for the investigators. Most, however, just run. Was Ethan running because he had something to hide? Or running because he had someone to find? And if the latter, what would he do when he found them? If he wasn't guilty of murder now, would he be guilty come morning?

Tess phoned A Taste of Napoli and asked for Becks. The man who answered said she was busy with a customer so asked if Tess could hold a moment. "That's okay. I'll send her a text. Thanks."

The phone call being simple enough not to arouse suspicion, Tess returned to the computer and gathered

99

up her belongings. Becks was at the restaurant. She'd be distraught about the death of her best friend, but probably felt safe surrounded by other people, so she wouldn't be rushing to go home.

Ethan had ceaselessly denied any involvement in Amelia's death, but what else would anyone expect of a murder suspect? He had also endlessly demanded the name of the man Amelia had been with in Shades. And constantly threatened untold violence. He needed stopping. But to stop him, Tess needed answers.

And then there was what Amelia had called her 'huge mistake.' What was that and had it led to her death?

This sordid little saga was like some cheap daytime soap opera. Except, in this one, no amount of imaginative scriptwriting would bring the heroine back from beyond the grave.

With the early evening's shadows creeping across Fifth Avenue, forewarning of the imminent demise of another day, Tess left the library and strode toward the subway station at the far side of Bryant Park.

Enjoying the last of the day's sun, New Yorkers lounged with friends on rickety green metal chairs scattered along the tree-lined South Promenade.

At the intersection of two paths, beneath a towering London plane tree, a black guy in grubby denims played saxophone. Eyes shut and seeming not to care whether anyone was listening or not, he swayed to the music of his own private world.

All around, people chatted and laughed and smiled and chilled.

Meandering through them, Tess couldn't help but notice one glaring thing – they all made it look as if life was so easy.

If only.

But then, she'd chosen her lifestyle. And while her work might be as difficult as it was dangerous, no job she took was ever impossible. Someone always knew something. Always. The secret was in finding them.

With no way to identify TG or to locate Ethan, Tess had one choice, one slender hope: find Becks. Amelia's best friend would know the full story on Ethan and TG, and as she was being threatened herself, would be eager to help anyone who could protect her. Hopefully. The theory was logical, but unfortunately, people invariably weren't.

Becks was the key. Tess was sure. But was there something else? Something vital she was overlooking?

Tess's mind lost, struggling for answers to impossible questions, she drifted through her fellow New Yorkers.

A chubby power-walker panted her way up the path toward Tess. Red-faced and puffing as if she was running the New York Marathon, not merely ambling around a football-field-sized lawn, she glared at Tess for being in her direct path, despite there being ample room to pass on either side.

Tess barely registered it. She couldn't shake the feeling she'd missed something.

Like straining to reach a pen on the floor only for it to flick away under the pressure of her fingertip, a thought lay just out of reach of her grasping mind, both there and not there.

She squinted with the effort as she struggled to dig out that one thought from the midst of the mire that was her mind. The turmoil of thoughts, each jostling for pole position, clouded everything.

What the devil was it? Or was she just imagining it?

Having exited the park, Tess descended the subway steps on Sixth Avenue, still lost in thought.

People bustled all around her. Workers, shoppers, tourists, daydreamers, moochers… Everyone seemed to know exactly what they were doing and where they were going. It was as if they were all privy to some grand plan.

Everyone but her.

She had an idea for what to do next, yes, but something felt… felt off.

As they passed, someone bumped Tess's shoulder.

It didn't hurt.

Didn't even throw her off her stride.

But she gasped.

Tensed.

A chill scraped down her spine as if someone had dragged a dagger made of ice across her bare flesh.

She grabbed the metal handrail. Gripped it tight.

"Oh, Jesus." That was him!

She was sure of it.

Him!

Chapter 17

IT HAD BEEN seventeen years since she'd last seen *him*, but she was sure the guy who'd just bumped into her was the killer who'd ruined her life when she was just a child. She'd only caught a glimpse of him today, but it had been so much closer than those other times.

She clutched her chest, her heart pounding so hard it felt like it might burst out at any second.

Oh, God, it really was *him*.

The blood drained from her face just as the energy drained from her body. Hyperventilating, she clung to the cold metal rail, confused thoughts skittering through her mind.

With her legs shaking like those of a newborn lamb, she gripped the rail so hard her knuckles whitened as she desperately tried to steady herself.

It was him. She was certain.

Wasn't she?

Of course she was. How could she ever forget *him!*

She dragged a trembling hand over her brow. Realized it was shaking. Stared at it.

Calmness. She needed calmness. If she intended to face the sadistic killer she'd just seen, she needed total focus. Any other state would and she'd be the one lying motionless in a pool of blood.

Forcing her breathing to slow and deepen, she felt air flowing into her and expanding, then radiating through her like the glow of the sun on a blissful summer's morning. A calmness gradually swept over her, a calmness that gave her mastery of her thoughts, her body, her life.

After a few moments, she again held her hand up before her. Rock steady.

She spun. Scrambled back up the steps to the street. Stared through the crowd for the man she hadn't seen for seventeen years, the man who'd ruined her life by robbing her of her family.

Where was he?

Wriggling her way through the people swarming toward the subway, she scanned for the killer.

Where the devil was he?

She spun. Stared. Spun again. Scoured the packed street and the sea of faces. So many faces. But not the one she wanted. Again, her heart started hammering as if someone long dead had just breezed past her.

Where the—

There!

Way ahead, an average-height man in a black hoodie meandered down the sidewalk. Him!

Though she couldn't see his face, that was the same man who'd just bumped into her. No mistake. That was her target.

Adrenaline shook her body with nervous energy.

Finally, after seventeen years, she had him.

Tess stormed along the crowded sidewalk.

She'd always known this was how it would go down – just a chance encounter when she least expected it. But here? Right now…?

She'd waited for seventeen years. Prepared for seventeen years. Yet fear and anxiety swamped her system. Even after all that time, she wasn't ready. But it wasn't like she had any other choice but to grab this chance.

A skinny woman with shopping bags in either hand dawdled along the busy street. Tess barged by her, knocking her into a display of magazines outside a newsstand.

Two chubby guys in suits waddled toward Tess, laughing about God only knew what, but taking up way too much of the sidewalk. She crashed straight through the middle of them.

She didn't see any of the angry glares.

Didn't hear any of the angry words.

Her world consisted of one thing and only one thing: him.

Like a salmon fighting its way back upstream to find the point at which it had been spawned, Tess fought through the swarming pedestrians to reach the man who had turned her world into a nightmare and set her on the path to being the killer she was today – the monster who had created her.

Weaving in and out of the surging wave of people, she struggled to fix her gaze on him as endless bodies seemed to delight in blocking her path, as if determined to hide him and to cheat her out of her justice.

Again, she lost sight of him.

And again, she agonizingly scoured the sea of faces.

Where was he? Where the hell was he? Where—

There!

Tess ripped her backpack off her back as she tore through the crowd. She was not geared up for combat, but if she caught him by surprise, that wouldn't be too much of a problem. Still, having witnessed his brutality, she needed an edge if she was going to tackle him out in the open. Especially if she hoped to do it so fast that she could be little but a blur in the crowd and thus get away with it.

She whipped out her armored black leather gloves. With her eyes fixed on the man sauntering along some distance ahead as if he didn't have a care in the world, she pulled on the left one. The one-tenth-of-an-inch-thick titanium alloy plates cocooned her hand in metal – a lethal gauntlet for the twenty-first century. But with her gaze nailed to the man, as she bustled past a woman pushing a stroller, she dropped her right glove.

"Goddamnit." She bent to snatch it up. A teenager in jeans dashed by and kicked it.

Tess scrambled back along the pavement. She thrust out her hand just as some guy glued to his phone was about to step on her glove. The guy's peripheral vision must have caught her, because he sidestepped without even looking up.

Tess grabbed her glove. Yanked it on. Spun. Stared ahead.

The killer had disappeared.

She tore back through the hordes of pedestrians, clawing her way through the meandering wall of flesh. Frantically, she scoured further up the sidewalk.

He had to be there. Had to be.

But there was no sign.

This couldn't happen. She couldn't get so close and then lose him. No. Please, no. Not again.

She battled against the river of bodies rushing down the sidewalk, desperate to sweep her up and carry her away in completely the wrong direction, carry her away into despair and loss and darkness.

She wove and twisted and barged and...

Her eyes popped wide and she gasped.

There!

Barely twenty yards ahead, the killer nonchalantly waltzed into a department store.

Tess scrambled straight through the middle of a family of burger lovers who enveloped the entire sidewalk from side to side. She raced after him.

She had him. She goddamn had him.

Tess flew to the entrance. She glared up at the electronic sensor as the doors crawled apart with all the speed of a glacier. As Tess tried to squeeze through before the doors had fully opened, a chubby woman blocked her way, appearing to be arguing with a balding man over how much she'd just paid for some scent.

"Excuse me." Tess tried to squeeze between them.

"Do you mind!" The woman glared at Tess and shifted to purposefully obstruct her all the more. "Can't you see we're having a conversation here?"

"And can't you see you're blocking the fucking doorway?"

Tess barged through and into the store.

Women sniffed fragrances on their wrists, clerks smiled with lips so glossy it was as if they applied fresh lipstick every few seconds, cash registers chinged and card readers beeped.

Tess pulled up. Gasping for breath. Even though she could run a mile and barely break a sweat, her mind had sent her body into overdrive. Gulping air, she wiped her brow and peered across the huge sales area.

Tess's gaze shot from one side of the room to the other, one perfume counter to the other, one face to another.

He was here. He was here. He was here. She'd seen him. But where?

A pudgy security guard sporting a bushy moustache plodded over.

"Are you okay, miss?"

She barely noticed anyone had said anything.

There he was!

Tess sped along the main aisle toward the inner depths of the store and a section dedicated to male cosmetics and grooming.

She had him. She goddamn had him.

And hell, was he going to bleed.

Tess hurtled by a woman at one of the display counters and knocked a glass bottle from her hands. It crashed down onto a display, sending other bottles flying. The woman shouted something, but Tess was already past her and way too close to the killer to care.

She had him.

Two young girls ambled along, laughing and smelling a new scent they'd bought. Tess barged between them.

She flew through the store.

Then…

She was there. Only ten feet from the man who'd destroyed everything she'd loved.

With his back to her, he stared at a display of electric shavers. As he perused the rows of products, he turned, which allowed anyone behind him to see part of his face.

Tess caught her breath.

It was him. *It was him!*

She trembled with nervous energy. She'd dreamed of this moment for so long. Dreamed of it. Ached for it. Prayed for it.

And now it was here.

Finally, the man who'd ruined her life was going to die. In a surprise attack like this, she'd need only a few seconds, then she'd run like hell and go to ground. Or escape on a plane back to China. Or end up in Sing Sing. It didn't matter. All that mattered was that she'd finally found him.

The man held up one of the shavers and said something to the immaculately groomed male clerk. They both laughed.

Tess sneered. He had no idea that that was the very last thing he was ever going to say.

She stared at him.

All she had to do was reach out.

Reach out and end the nightmare.

End it by ending him.

Chapter 18

THE CLERK BEHIND the male grooming counter eyed Tess warily.

And the killer noticed it.

He turned.

Tess had suffered for seventeen torturously long years. But the nightmare was going to end, because she was going to have her justice. Right this second.

She surged forward.

Knocked the killer over backwards so he sprawled on his back over the counter.

Pulled her fist back to hammer into his throat and pound the life out of him that very instant.

She ached to see his blood. Ached to hear his screams. Ached to know true justice.

But she gasped. Froze.

The face staring back at her, with mouth agape and eyes wide with fear, was not *his* face.

The same kind of high cheekbones, yes. The same jawline. The same pointed nose. The same eyes. Just not *him*.

The man threw his hands up and twisted away, cowering from the impending beating.

Tess let go of him and staggered back, holding her hands up submissively.

"It's okay. I…" She slumped, completely exhausted. "I—I thought you were someone else."

"Asshole." He glowered at her as he pushed off the counter.

Panting as if she'd been sprinting all day, she said, "I'm so sorry. Really. I honestly th—"

Hands grabbed Tess from behind.

The pudgy mustachioed security guard and a gray-haired colleague pinned her arms and bundled her further back from the innocent man.

Pudgy Guard said, "Are you okay, sir? Would you like us to call the police so you can press charges?"

Tess fell limp. Let the guards restrain her, even though she could take them both out with a single hand.

The innocent man waved her away with the disdain of swatting away an irritating bug. "Just get the whack-job away from me."

She stared into space. Part dazed. Part drained. How had she let this happen? Again? What kind of a cruel joke was it that the universe kept playing on her?

"You're sure, sir?" said Pudgy Guard. "Because we'll have the whole incident on CCTV."

"I appreciate the help," he said, "but please, just get her out of my sight."

The two guards hauled Tess back through the store. A mother pulled her young daughter to her as Tess was bustled past. Shoppers stared. Staff gossiped.

The guards dragged Tess right out through the doors and onto the street. Finally, they released her.

Without being supported by the guards, she staggered, but caught herself.

As if half asleep, she said, "Sorry. I didn't mean to cause any trouble."

"Yeah, well just see you don't come back anytime soon, because the next time, I'll make damn sure that the store presses charges even if the customer won't."

Her legs wobbled and almost gave way. Tess grabbed a lamppost for support. Mentally and physically spent, she slumped against it.

Pudgy Guard sneered and shook his head. "Get a grip, lady. And get yourself clean."

The guards went back into the store but hovered inside the entrance watching her, ensuring she didn't try to enter again.

Tess hung her head and rubbed her brow.

How many times was her mind going to play this cruel trick on her? How many times was she going to see that killer, only for it not to be him? Seventeen years ago, he'd ruined her life; seventeen years later, he was still ruining it.

But she couldn't relive this. Not again. Not now. She had to focus. Had to concentrate on the job she and Bomb were now working on. Distractions could kill just as surely as a bullet in the head. If she let ghosts from her past cloud her mind, the killer she was hunting today would see her long before she saw him. And that could only end one way.

She drew a series of long, slow breaths to help clear her mind and reenergize her body, then tottered away from the lamppost.

Her legs still unsteady, she stumbled back the way she'd come.

Focus. She had to focus.

But how?

The city blurred. She passed people, buildings, vehicles, but she might as well have been alone in a desert for all the sensory information she absorbed.

Finding herself back in Bryant Park, Tess all but collapsed onto one of the green metal chairs scattered along the tree-lined promenade. The chair rocked and almost toppled over, but Tess flung her arms out and spread her feet to keep from crunching into the ground.

Once steady, she leaned back and closed her eyes. Breathed long and slow. Let the fresh air, stillness, and saxophone music transport her to a world of calmness and stability.

Tess shut out everything but the music, the wind gusting through the trees, and her breathing.

Bit by bit, she banished all the chaos that had created such confusion inside her head. Blanked it all out as if her mind was a brand-new canvas. Once her mind was clear, she started filling it with thoughts again, painting ideas on it once more.

Her thinking still unsure, she forced herself to look at the cold hard logic of what she had to do to find Amelia's killer. Logic would ground her. Logic would save her.

But where to start?

Becks. Becks was the key.

Get to Becks. Get the facts. Get the killer.

Simple. Just as logic should be.

Her mind steady once more, her thoughts started to flow more fluidly.

She tensed her leg muscles and readied to push herself up, but sank back onto her seat. She rested her hands on her thighs and gasped another couple of breaths, then tried again. Finally, as if a 200-pound man was pushing on her shoulders to pin her down, Tess heaved herself up off the chair.

She trudged back toward the subway on 6th Avenue. After she'd talked with Becks, she'd go to see Nat. She still needed to know why he'd had an altercation with Amelia, not to mention why he'd felt the need to hide it.

But that was only a minor point. More importantly, as head of the neighborhood watch, Nat might know if TG had been spotted loitering in the area.

She started down into the subway again.

Even after seventeen years... She could've sworn that was him.

"Goddamnit." Tess hammered the side of her fist into the tiled subway wall. Seventeen years and still he was haunting her. Seventeen goddamn years. When would she ever find peace? When would she…

Clawing its way through her questions, a thought dragged her back to the moment.

Tess quickened her pace down the steps.

Nat's 9:00 p.m. neighborhood watch patrols involved him staring into the shadows. Had he seen someone lurking there? And, more crucially, had that someone seen him?

Maybe Nat had been threatened with violence if he said anything.

That meant Becks wasn't the only one who needed protecting.

But who was in the greatest danger?

Who should Tess run to protect first?

Chapter 19

WHETHER IT WAS the stress of Amelia's death, or that she simply needed to tell someone – anyone – what she knew, once Becks sat down opposite Tess in the café, she spewed forth the whole sordid saga of the dangerous double life Amelia had reveled in leading.

"Why haven't you spoken with the police?" asked Tess.

Nursing a coffee at the green table at which Tess had eaten earlier, Becks didn't look up. "I ain't got nothing to tell 'em."

Becks swirled a drop of coffee around and around in the bottom of the cup as if finding the circling liquid soothing, and then said, "I ain't got no proof. I ain't got no lawyer. Last time I tried to help with an investigation, I was the one that got busted."

She looked up from her cup. Her eyes red and swollen, she stared deeply into Tess's eyes as if she believed if she looked deep enough she'd find answers. "Why are all guys worth shit?"

If she expected Tess to give her that answer, hell was she going to be disappointed.

Tess tapped her phone on the table between them. It displayed a photo from Becks's Facebook gallery that Tess had downloaded at the library: Becks, Amelia, and a man all squashed up together to squeeze into a photo taken at arm's length. Each of them grinning, they looked like the best of friends.

Tess said, "And this is him? This is TG?"

Becks said one word. It wasn't *yes* but it couldn't have been a more positive identification. "Bastard."

"But you have no idea where he lives because it was always in public?"

"Up an alleyway, in a bathroom stall, behind a dumpster… It was like if it wasn't in public, he couldn't get off on it. You know?"

"But if he showed no interest in Amelia other than for sex, why did she continue seeing him?"

"Said she loved him. You know? Said he loved her and was gonna take her away from here." Becks shook her head. "Hell, asshole wouldn't even give her his real name so how's he gonna give her a new life?"

"And you told her that?"

"Only every time he showed up. But would she listen?" She swirled the coffee around the cup again. "After one time with his friend Jimmy, I said, 'Girl, that there guy's gonna be the death of you' and even though she knew she done wrong, she still went back for more."

"Jimmy? That was the friend TG persuaded her to have sex with while he watched?"

Becks looked up again, tears in her eyes. "Is that love? 'Cause it sure as hell don't sound like love to me."

So when dangerous sex – sex in public places – lost its novelty, TG upped the stakes. Tess sighed. With violence at home and abuse in public, in what kind of hell had Amelia been trapped?

"Was he ever violent towards her?" asked Tess.

"Hell if I know. After I ragged on her over the Jimmy thing, she stopped telling me a lot of stuff." She looked up. "But one time, I seen him with a knife."

"And she was with him last night?"

Becks hung her head. Nodded. Sobbed.

The man in the photo, who they'd christened TG because, as part of his game, he'd refused to give his name, had regularly met Amelia. Wanting a better life than the violent one she shared with Ethan, Amelia had seen TG as her escape route, so she'd pandered to his craving for exhibitionist sex. Sadly, she was merely being used by a sexual predator.

Tess eased a thumb and forefinger into the secret pocket inside the waistband of her trousers, a pocket similar to the one she sewed into all her clothes. Inside, she kept an emergency stash of cash: one thousand dollars. In her line of work, she never knew when she might have to go to ground and get rid of her bank cards to avoid being traced, or be trapped and need to buy her way out of trouble.

It was emergency money.

Strictly emergency.

She'd do absolutely anything to avoid tapping into it.

But emergencies came in many guises.

Tess slid three hundred dollars across the table.

With a deep frown, Becks looked up at her, cheeks streaming with tears.

"Take it," Tess said, "Keep out of sight for a few days. Go see your mom or get a room in Queens. Anything. Just get away from here. You'll be safe and I promise you, when you come back, all this will be over and the person responsible won't hurt anyone ever again." She stood.

Becks peered up through eyes so red, so teary. "Really?"

Tess rested a hand on her shoulder. "I never break my word."

If Ethan hadn't intended on killing TG when he'd gone on the run that morning, he would surely be intent on it now if he'd learned the truth of how this man had so abused *his* woman.

As for TG? Was sexual abuse the worst aspect of Amelia's relationship with him? Or could someone who craved ever greater and greater thrills see murder as the ultimate high?

Chapter 20

ON THE STONE stoop to Nat's apartment building, Tess paused. In what way was Nat involved? She hoped she was about to find a perfectly reasonable explanation for Nat to have had an altercation with Amelia in the dead of night. But… Though other suspects had loomed to the fore, with far stronger motives for violence, sometimes it was the most placid of folk who perpetrated the most horrendous of acts.

Had Nat's similarities to her grandpa clouded her judgment? Could there be a dark side to his sweet nature? Or was he really just a little old man who'd been threatened so needed protection?

She drew a deep breath. She needed answers.

Having to be buzzed in, Tess looked at the names associated with each apartment. All of those listed under the buzzers were scrawled on scraps of whatever paper must first have come to hand. All except one. 'Nathan Ridley' was typed on a piece of crisp, white paper which fitted its slot perfectly.

Her thumb hovered over the buzzer. She hoped she'd find the quiet little man, living the quiet little life, that she'd met just that morning, and not a man with a dark secret he'd do anything to hide.

She pushed the buzzer.

A few seconds later, Nat's voice came through the little speaker. "Yes?"

"Nat? It's Tess Williams. I'm sorry to disturb you again."

"It's a little late, dear."

She glanced at her watch: 7:54 p.m. "I'm sorry, but I need to ask you something, please."

He let her in and immediately busied himself in the kitchen.

"Would you like some tea, dear?"

"No, thank you."

"Coffee?"

She shook her head. "No, thanks."

"Juice?"

"Thanks, but no."

"Oh, I know. I've got some lovely organic carrot cake. Absolutely beautiful with a glass a milk." He smiled at her, eyebrows raised with expectation.

"Nat, really, I'm fine."

She couldn't help but smirk to herself. Her grandpa had been just like that – gracious to the point of irritating. Not just with her, though, but with everyone, because he loved people and loved playing host.

Well…

Maybe she'd received special treatment occasionally.

Okay, often.

Truth be told, nothing was ever too much trouble for her grandpa's little princess. She still occasionally felt pangs of guilt remembering the times she'd played on that. But then, she'd only been a kid. Wasn't that what kids were supposed to do?

But it wasn't the 'special treatment' she missed.

No, it was… the sense of belonging.

Yes, that was it. It was being able to close the door on all the coldness in the world and relax in a home where love lived.

She watched Nat hemming and hawing to himself over whether to put coconut or chocolate chip cookies on a white porcelain plate. She smiled again. Her grandpa hadn't been quite the ditherer that Nat was, but the similarity was uncanny. Bathed in a warm glow, she watched him arrange three coconut cookies on the plate.

Finally, Nat hobbled over to the couch. He walked so slowly his gait was almost in time to the ticking of his deathly slow clock on the mantel.

Sitting beside her, he said, "So, what is it that's so important? Have we caught someone?" He nibbled a cookie.

"Have you seen this man around the neighborhood?" Tess showed him the close-up photo of Becks, Amelia, and TG.

"Oh, there's Amelia, bless her. And her friend Rebecca. Oh, such a lovely photo."

"Yes, but have you seen the man?"

"Hmmm..." Nat scrunched up his face, scrutinizing the photo. "Well... I'd like to say yes, but..." He rubbed his chin. "No, I couldn't swear to that." He looked up at her. "Why? Is that who did it?"

"Let's just say he's someone I'd like to talk to."

He pulled her phone closer. "Let me have a better look, dear."

She let him lift her hand right up to his face.

There was more chin rubbing and muttering.

And the clock ticked on. Unbearably loudly in the mausoleum of a room. And the ticking got slower and slower and slower as she waited, and waited, and waited for Nat to reply. It really felt like waiting for death.

Finally, he said, "You know... I wouldn't be able to say hand on Bible, but..."

Nat stood and wandered over to a wooden rolltop desk. He rummaged inside. Not finding what he was looking for, he pulled open one of the drawers. He took out a manila wallet file and thumbed through the loose paper contents, and then took out one of the letter-size papers.

He nodded. "Yes. Yes, it was last weekend. Not on my patrol, but later when I couldn't sleep – those darn good-for-nothing sleeping pills again – I saw someone lurking around outside Amelia's building. When he saw me, he crossed the street and disappeared

125

down that alleyway." He pointed through one of his living room windows.

"The alley in which Amelia's body was found?"

"That very one, dear. Yes."

She held her camera up toward him. "And it could've been this man?"

"The more I think about it, the more I believe it was."

That was a major breakthrough: TG had not been just someone who used to meet Amelia for no-ties sex, he'd been a stalker. He liked to push boundaries; he liked to control others; and most importantly, he liked danger.

What if he really had wanted to take Amelia away from Ethan?

What if she was having second thoughts after the voyeurism incident?

And what if he'd decided that if he couldn't have her no one could?

"Is there anything else I can help you with?" asked Nat.

There was. But could she bring herself to ask?

Chapter 21

TESS FUMBLED FOR words and looked away so she wouldn't catch Nat's eye. "Er… there, er, might be something you can help with, yes."

"Well, spit it out, then, dear. As my old grandpa used to say, you can't grow turnips without sowing turnip seeds."

Nat was such a kindly old man, she didn't want to put him on the spot. Neither did she want to look foolish to him by asking what would appear to be a truly dumb question. But she needed answers.

Finally, Tess said, "When you saw Amelia, was everything okay? There wasn't any unpleasantness between the two of you?"

"Heavens no. Why?"

"The taxi driver—"

"Oh, you found him. Oh, good. Was it my information?"

"Yes. Thank you. It was very helpful. So, anyway, he said he saw you argue with her on Chiltern Avenue."

"Argue? With Amelia? No, I'm afraid he's taken you a bit of a ride there, dear."

The driver had been in no position to indulge in any dancing with a saucepan of scalding chili broiling his crotch. Why would he lie about that?

Tess said, "He was quite adamant."

"Well… to be fair… Amelia was a little, shall we say, colorful with her language when I saw her. But she was only blowing off steam after her fight with Ethan, dear. It was perfectly understandable." He smiled. "Water off a duck's back."

"But why didn't you say anything about it?"

"Because it was of such little consequence it wasn't worthy of bringing to anyone's attention."

She noted he didn't say 'to your attention', but 'to anyone's attention'.

Tess said, "Have you spoken to the police yet?"

"An officer came by this afternoon."

"And you didn't tell him either?"

He laughed. "Oh, my word, Ms. Williams, you'd make an outstanding prosecuting attorney."

He was right – where was the payoff in grilling Nat over something so insignificant to the bigger picture? She'd already discovered that TG had the motive and means for attacking Amelia, and now Nat had confirmed he had been lurking in the area, probably looking for the opportunity. Though the justice system was broken, as a set of criteria, means, motive and opportunity was one thing it had gotten right.

She smiled at Nat. "I'm sorry. I just need to check everything and that nothing's been left out."

"That's perfectly alright, dear. Now" – he winked – "what about that carrot cake?"

Her phone rang.

"Excuse me." She checked caller ID. "I'm sorry, but I have to take this."

"I'll leave you to it, dear."

He picked up his plate and padded over to the kitchen area.

Tess wandered over to the corner of the room farthest away from Nat.

"Hi, what you got?" She purposefully didn't use a name in such a quiet environment. Especially around such a busybody as Nat.

"Your boy," said Bomb.

"Where?"

"The scene of the crime – or at least one of them – Shades."

"Thanks." She hung up and turned to Nat. "I'm heading off, Nat. Thanks for all your help."

"Oh, it's nothing. I'm only doing what any decent person would do."

"You be careful on your patrols. There're a lot of sickos out there."

"Don't you worry about me, dear. You just catch whoever did such an awful thing to poor Amelia."

"You can be sure I'll give it my best shot."

Walking to the door, she couldn't help but ask one last question. "There's nothing else I need to know, is there? It might seem unimportant to you, but it could be vital."

He gazed away into space for a few seconds.

Finally, he said, "I don't believe so, dear. But I'll be sure to let you know if I think of anything."

She pulled the door open as he was walking over to see her out, "Thanks again, Nat."

"Any time, dear. You know where I am if you need me."

As she walked down the stoop onto the street, she looked back. The drapes pulled aside, Nat again waved to her through the security bars at his window. She smiled and nodded to him.

Once this job was over, she'd pop back and have that carrot cake. Maybe buy Nat a book on the strategy of war as a thank-you present.

She smiled to herself. Every moment she spent with Nat, she couldn't help but feel she was with her grandpa again. And how she'd ached for that feeling for so very long. Ached to spend just a few more minutes, just a few more seconds with him. To feel… To feel as if the world wasn't filled only with pain and hardship and deceit, but filled with… with love and with someone who'd smile just because she was there.

She sighed. Yes, he might be boring, might use fifty words where one would do, and he might have the most horrendous taste in décor, but she'd enjoy visiting him again.

At the junction with Chiltern, she hailed a cab – she didn't have time to waste using public transport.

Ethan had obviously decided to stake out Shades and wait for TG. She had to be there. Between them, Ethan and TG were the only people who knew the truth about what had happened to Amelia.

But Becks had said TG carried a knife. Ethan might be mean and muscular, but against a blade, even the biggest biceps sliced like butter. If Tess got there too late, she might discover nothing but a bloody corpse and even more questions.

This could be her one shot at finding the killer.

Finding him and punishing him.

But could she get there in time?

Chapter 22

HARSH SPOTLIGHTS AND headache-inducing strobe effects creating an ambience only matched by the distorted rumbling of the subwoofers, Shades greeted Tess with all the finesse of a wife finding her husband in bed with her sister – raucous, ugly, yet strangely compelling.

At the bar, she bought a bottle of cider and then scanned the room for Ethan, panning across the assortment of smiling, laughing, lonely, frowning, bored, desperate faces.

No sign.

Tess ambled over to a table opposite the main door, where she took a seat with her back against the wall.

Her gaze flicked around the club. She could see the bar, entrance, emergency exit, and restrooms.

After doing this job for so long, deciding where to sit in a public area was no longer a matter of choice but of an almost Pavlovian response – she needed to be in the position where no one could surprise her from behind and from where she could easily reach the doors to get out, or reach whoever had gotten in.

Leaning back, she cradled her bottle. Now it was just a case of waiting.

She took a swig of cider. Cold, sweet and as golden as the morning sun, it was so refreshing it was like downing a glass of Nature itself. When she was on a job looking to befriend someone for information, she drank domestic beer so she would blended in. That not being necessary in this instance, she could enjoy her drink of choice, a drink she'd come across in Europe and loved ever since. She took another mouthful. How easy it would be to kick back and forget about Amelia, sexual abuse, and homicide.

Tess put her bottle on the table. Unfortunately, this was work, not a night on the town. There had been enough distractions already, now she had to prepare for the encounter she was sure was going to come.

She already had on her body armor. At a tad under a thousand bucks, it was the most stealth bullet- and knife-proof vest on the market, but she couldn't risk removing her jacket. While almost invisible under her shirt to the average Joe, the armor might still be visible to those with an eye for such things. She couldn't risk rumors spreading through the club that she was an undercover cop – nothing would spook Ethan quicker.

She scoured the faces again. Only a few minutes earlier, Bomb had confirmed Ethan was still in there, so where was he? It was a good thing it was still early so it wasn't packed tight and she could see most of the clientele.

With no target in sight, her mind wandered back to Bryant Park, back to the subway, back to him.

She could've sworn that was him. Even after all these years.

Eighteen months ago, on the corner of Broadway and West Forty-Second Street, she'd last seen 'him'. She'd been standing waiting to cross the street and he'd casually cruised past her on a bus hanging a right. She'd chased the bus two blocks as it lurched through traffic till it stopped at lights and she got a clear view of the man sitting four seats down by the window. That hadn't been him either. It never was.

On that occasion, it had been the best part of a week before she'd been able to think of anything else and stop reliving the nightmare he'd thrust her into.

She banged her bottle down on the table.

Focus.

She had to focus.

In her line of work, being distracted was like crossing a busy road with your eyes shut – it wasn't a case of if you'd make it across, it was a case of how quickly you'd be nothing but a bloody mass of splattered flesh.

Forcing her mind to quieten, yet again, she scanned the bar's clientele.

But, yet again, that niggling question clawed its way from the back of her mind – what was she missing?

She couldn't even remember now when she'd first had this feeling. Maybe it was merely the subway incident that had so rattled her it was skewing her thoughts. Was there something she wasn't seeing? Or was it just her mind playing tricks?

A tall man strutted toward her. He flicked his long brown bangs out of his face by throwing his head backwards.

She knew that cocky arrogance. Great. This was all she needed.

Resting his hands on her table, he leaned down to her. "I haven't seen you in here before."

"No." She leaned to her left to try to look around him so she wouldn't miss Ethan.

He leaned to his right to remain in front of her. "Let me buy you a drink and give you three reasons you should sleep with me tonight."

Did lines like that ever work except in male fantasies?

She smiled. "Can we start with a kiss?"

He grinned. "Sure." He leaned in.

"You got a breath mint first? I blew a Syrian taxi driver earlier, and I bet I don't have to tell you how that taste lingers."

He pulled back, face twisted in disgust. "Jesus, what's your problem?" He scurried away to his friends.

For a moment, she closed her eyes.

Forget the subway incident. Forget 'him'. Forget dumb niggling questions.

Focus. Get Ethan. Get answers. Get the job done.

Simple.

Opening her eyes, she took another swig of cider.

Again, she panned face to face to face.

Ethan had to be here. Had to be. Unless he'd had his phone stolen, which meant Bomb was tracking the wrong person. Or he'd seen too many cop shows, so wary of someone tracking him through cell towers, he'd dumped it. Either way, she'd be screwed.

But was Ethan either that lucky or that smart?

Briefly removing her backpack, she retrieved her black leather armored gloves.

The custom-made gloves looked innocent enough except under the very closest of scrutiny, yet, secreted within, ergonomically crafted titanium alloy inserts cocooned her hands. Only one-tenth of an inch thick, the inserts were barely discernible through the leather.

She examined them. Surreptitiously, under the table, just to be safe.

Running her fingertips over the metal and the thin inner layer of latex foam rubber inside which provided a modicum of cushioning, she checked for damage to the plate that covered the back of each hand and wrapped around the pinkie side of it before spreading across the palm.

She then felt along the segmented sections that lay over the knuckles and partway down each finger to ensure there were no sharp edges and the segments hinged freely.

All the while, she scanned the bar's drinkers for any sign of her target.

People came, people went, people milled and mixed, chatted and posed. But nowhere was Ethan.

Under the table, Tess continued examining her gloves. Flipping the hinged section across the heel of the palm of the left glove, then the right, she checked for unrestricted movement for her thumbs, so giving her complete freedom for which techniques she wanted to use.

Everything seemed okay.

Tess had broken bricks with her bare hands. But that was in a dojo in Kyoto where the bricks weren't moving, let alone trying to hit her back. Hands were surprisingly delicate. If a fighter misjudged it, a simple punch could break their knuckles or fingers, leaving them one-handed and vulnerable. That was why boxers taped up their hands and wore padded gloves – protection.

But titanium alloy being harder than steel, her gloves didn't only protect her – they gave her hand strikes the stopping power of a hammer.

She slipped on her gloves. The metal inserts cocooned her hands perfectly.

She was ready.

But ready for what?

Again, she scanned the bar. Scanned the doorways, scanned all the tables, scanned all the people reveling in the joys of night life.

Nothing.

Absolutely nothing.

Maybe Bomb had been wro—

137

There!

Across the far side of the bar, Ethan strode toward the men's room.

Chapter 23

NONCHALANTLY, SHE STOOD and followed Ethan.

The prospective confrontation causing her stomach to quake, Tess calmed herself with her four-second breathing technique.

A small man with a cheeky smile stepped in front of her. He grinned. "Can I get you a drink?"

"No, thanks." She sidestepped to her right to move around him.

He moved left to stay in front of her and held up three ten-dollar bills. "I hear you like BJs. Wanna fit me in some time?"

He obviously thought if it was true she was blowing taxi drivers, it was because she was short of cash, and if it wasn't true, it would be a good laugh at her expense.

"Thanks." She snatched the money. "I'll pencil you in for a week from Tuesday."

She barged him out of the way with her shoulder and stormed toward the restroom.

He turned. "Hey!"

Easing the restroom door open, Tess peeked in.

Grappling on the floor, Ethan struggled with another man.

Limbs flailed, smacked, pushed, and clawed.

Bodies gasped, grunted, cursed, and groaned.

Flung onto his back, the other man's face became visible – TG. Why hadn't she seen him? He must have been in here already, or had snuck in while one of those two sleazeballs was trying to romance her.

Tess watched. If they exhausted each other, it would make her job much easier.

Sprawled on the gray slate tiles, Ethan pinned TG in a headlock. TG bit his forearm.

Ethan swore and pulled away.

TG rolled across the floor. Whipped out a switchblade.

They both slowly clambered up, warily watching each other.

Ethan stabbed a finger at TG. "You're gonna bleed, you fuck. I'm gonna stick your knife in your fucking neck."

TG sneered. "The bitch was begging for it. If I hadn't done her someone else would have."

Ethan lunged at him.

TG slashed his knife.

Tess ripped Ethan out of the way by his arm so the blade passed harmlessly by. He tumbled against the sinks and crashed to the floor.

She turned to TG.

TG waved his blade at her. "You want some, bitch?"

She had on her body armor, but if he sliced an artery in her leg or arm, she'd bleed out almost as quickly as if he slit her throat. Blades were a danger that had to be closed down as quickly as possible.

She stared at him. Her voice calm, unwavering, she said, "Try it. If you're man enough."

TG slashed at her.

Tess blocked his knife arm and trapped it close to her body to immobilize it.

She smashed her palm heel into his face.

Tightened the lock on his elbow joint.

Stripped the blade from his loosened grip.

He struggled to pull free.

She kneed him in the thigh to deaden his leg.

Head-butted him in the face.

He cried out. Staggered back. Hands covering his nose.

She kicked him in the gut.

He gasped and reeled into the middle stall. Fell over the toilet. Collapsed in a heap.

Music blared as the restroom door opened.

Tess whirled around, wary of another threat.

The two guys who'd propositioned her stood in the restroom doorway, mouths agape.

Tess pointed. "Get out!"

Scrambling, they fought with each other to get out first.

She saw Ethan clambering to his feet. She grabbed his hand, twisted to lock the wrist, then spun him around. He twirled, almost balletically, into the white porcelain urinals and crashed to the floor.

Whipping two nylon zip ties from her pocket, she grabbed TG. Still holding his knife so no one else could use it against her, she yanked him out of the stall and strapped his left hand to one stall door's handle, then his right to a handle two stalls away. On his knees facing her, he hung, suspended.

Tess turned to Ethan.

Groggy, face down in the urinal trough, he floundered as he tried to push up.

Tess stamped on his lower back.

He sprawled across the floor.

With one knee, she knelt on his back to pin him and yanked his head back by his hair.

She slammed his face against the porcelain. "Tell me what happened last night."

"Get off, you crazy bitch."

"Jesus, if I had a dime for every time someone's called me that." She slammed his head against the urinal again. "You were seen fighting with Amelia. Tell me what happened."

His cheek and mouth squashed against the porcelain, Ethan said, "*He* happened. *He* fucking happened."

She hammered her fist between his shoulder blades.

Ethan groaned and arched back.

With the pain distracting him, Tess slipped a zip tie around his ankles before he even knew it.

She shoved Ethan aside and made for TG.

Music blared again. She looked around. In the doorway stood a black dude in a purple shirt.

She shouted, "Get out."

The dude in the entrance said, "Everything alright, miss?"

She pointed the knife. "I said, 'out'!"

The dude held his hands up defensively as he backed away. "Hey, no worries."

Tess turned back to TG, his face running with blood from a gash on the bridge of his nose.

She pressed the switchblade against his cheek. "How about we see just how sharp this is?"

TG smirked.

Tess leaned closer. "You will tell me what I want to know."

But he snickered and shook his head. He was either really dumb and had a death wish or really brave and had a cunning plan.

The hairs prickled on the back of her neck at the thought that it could be the latter.

Chapter 24

TESS'S FEET FLEW from under her and she crunched into the floor. The knife skidded across the tiles.

TG shouted, "Kill the bitch, Jimmy. Kill her."

A heavy kick smacked into her ribs.

Tess yelped, but fought her instinct to curl into a defensive ball. Doing that, she might just as well stick a sign on her back saying 'please kick me.'

She twisted.

Grabbed Jimmy's foot.

Rammed her shoulder into his shins.

Jimmy crashed to the floor.

She rolled onto his legs.

Hammered her elbow into his crotch. And again. And again.

He squealed so high-pitched it was like a small animal.

He leaned forward to try to protect himself.

She slammed a backfist into his jaw.

His head flew back and smashed into the floor. He lay still.

So that was Jimmy. TG's comrade in voyeurism. Why hadn't she thought of him showing up? Talk about a rookie mistake.

She climbed to her feet. Looked around.

"Goddamn it."

Ethan had disappeared. In his place lay the knife and a cut zip tie.

Now she'd have to contact Bomb. Start the whole hunt over again. Except this time, it would be ten times harder because this time Ethan would know he wasn't paranoid: someone really was after him.

She scowled at TG.

He pulled back into the middle stall as far as his binds would allow, the nylon cutting into his wrists. "Please. I'm sorry. I don't want trouble."

She prowled over to him. "Too late. Trouble's here." She pounded her steel-clad fist into his gut.

He wheezed and doubled over.

She bound Jimmy's hands with another zip tie and then checked his wallet. James Iverson had fifty-six dollars and change. She left the coins.

TG tried to pull back into the stall when she turned to him. "My wallet's in my back pocket. Take it. Please. Take everything."

"Thank you." She did. Henderson 'TG' Sumpter donated ninety-two dollars towards making the world a better place.

Henderson smiled feebly, probably believing that his money had placated her.

How wrong could someone be?

She grabbed him by the throat, her fingers clawed around his windpipe. He made strange gargling sounds.

Tess stared deep into his eyes, eyes that were screwed up with pain. "Why did you kill Amelia Ortega?"

His eyes opened. Opened wide.

She relaxed her grip.

He spluttered, then spoke, his voice rasping. "What…? Amelia… Amelia's dead?" He struggled to swallow.

His eyes widened again as his mind worked out why this was happening to him. "And you think I had something to do with it?"

She released her grip on him. Strolled away. Under such circumstances, you couldn't fake a reaction like that: he wasn't the killer.

She ripped open the restroom door, but stopped.

A simple beating wasn't enough. Even if it had been by a woman.

She paced back.

Henderson's voice rasped still. "Please, please. I didn't do it. I didn't even know."

"This is for humiliating a woman." She hammered her steel fist into his groin.

He gasped with barely a sound, his eyes so wide Tess thought his eyeballs might fall out of his head.

"This…"

She slammed a fist into his face.

His head flew back.

Blood and broken teeth fell to the tiled floor.

"… is in case you're ever tempted to try it again." With a crooked nose and missing teeth, he'd find it much harder to manipulate women.

Reaching around his waist, she unfastened Henderson's trousers with little effort, him groggy from her headshot.

"And this…" She pulled them down only to find tighty whities. "Really? Your mom buy you those?"

She shook her head, hoping that once she'd removed his underwear there'd be something inside that would've made it worthwhile for a woman in a long-term relationship to risk losing everything. There wasn't.

Him now half-naked, she said, "This is for every woman you've ever lied to just to get laid."

How much would he like humiliation games and exhibitionism when he was the one abused? Especially when it would be all over YouTube within minutes for everyone he knew to laugh at.

Tess leaned right down to his ear. "If you don't want us to meet again, learn to respect women."

She took a quick photo of each of their driver's licenses on her phone, chucked the licenses in the urinal trough, and then stalked out.

Okay, things hadn't quite gone to plan, but even though she hadn't caught the killer, at least she'd identified him – Ethan. Now, how the hell was she going to find him again?

Chapter 25

DESPITE KNOWING IT was pointless, she searched the faces in the crowded bar for Ethan's as she dashed for the exit.

God, the world was twisted. Well, no, the world was just fine – it was the goddamn people who infested it that were twisted. This job was all about obsession. Twisted obsession. In a jealous rage, Ethan had killed Amelia and now he'd tried to kill the man who'd dared to lay hands on his prize possession.

Choices. How easily people let emotion cloud their judgments. And how easily misjudgments ruined lives.

Amelia had chosen infidelity in the hope of bringing joy into her miserable life.

Ethan had chosen violence as a way to control a disintegrating relationship.

TG had chosen exploitation to gain what he believed would make him happy.

Choices. People chose their own paths so only had themselves to blame for the hell to which those paths led. How easy it would have been for Ethan, Amelia, or TG to have made a different choice so this dire situation would never have arisen.

Outside Shades, Tess glanced up and down the street.

Ethan was nowhere in sight. She scoured the faces of the pedestrians enjoying their night on the town. Where the devil was he?

She grabbed her phone for Bomb to get a new location on Ethan, but stopped. "Oh, hell." What was it she'd said to Ethan: 'You were seen fighting with Amelia.'?

She stamped her foot in frustration "Shit!" God, she could be so stupid.

Nat had witnessed the fight. Past 2:00 a.m., he was likely the only one to have done so. What if Ethan figured that out? Especially if he feared being arrested and facing a trial?

It was obvious what he'd do. She might as well have painted a target on Nat's back.

Worse still, Ethan had a head start on her.

Whipping her head first to her left, then to her right, she scoured the street for a taxi.

Nothing.

"Come on. Come on."

She stepped off the curb for a better view around a number of parked vehicles.

Nothing.

"Oh, for Christ's sake."

She peered both ways along the street again, praying for a taxi to magically materialize.

Could she get there in time to catch Ethan?

Could she get there in time to save Nat?

Chapter 26

"**YES, I KNOW** how late it is, but…" In the back of the yellow cab, Tess held the phone away from her ear. Nat wouldn't stop babbling about how late it was and how discourteous a phone call was at such an ungodly hour, even from a friend.

She rolled her eyes and muttered, "For the love of God."

Putting the phone back to her ear, she tried again. "Nat…"

Still talking.

"Nat…"

Still talking.

She raised her voice, "Nat!"

He stopped.

She said, "Please, just listen to me: don't open your door to anyone until I get there. Promise me."

She shook her head and rubbed her brow. She wanted to strangle him herself.

"Yes, I know I'm being very dramatic," said Tess, "but just do it, please. Okay?"

The taxi driver glanced back. "Everything alright, lady?"

Some guys could pull off the unshaven look. Rugged handsomeness oozing from every pore. Others just looked like they lived on a park bench. Unfortunately for him, the driver lay firmly in the latter category.

With a wave of her hand, she gestured everything was fine.

Still on the phone, she said, "Okay, thank you, Nat... Yes... Yes, I'll be there just as quickly as I can." She hung up.

She groaned with frustration. God, it was like trying to get through to an awkward child. She wouldn't mind, but she was sure he wasn't really that old. He was likely one of those guys who'd already appeared middle-aged when he'd barely graduated college.

But thank God he had security bars at his windows. On the first floor, he'd have been a sitting duck without those. And it would make her job easier – there'd be only one point of entry Ethan could exploit.

Scrolling through her phone's address book, she called Detective Pete McElroy.

A man answered. "Detective McElroy's phone, Detective Harding speaking."

"Can I speak to Mac, please?"

"I'm sorry, he's just stepped out for a moment. I'm his partner. Can I help, ma'am?"

Tess took a slow breath. Did she really want to get involved with yet another cop?

"Ma'am? Are you still there?"

No, she didn't want to get involved. But if she wanted access to privileged information to be able to do her job, she had no choice.

She said, "Hello, Detective Harding. This is Tess Williams. We met at the crime scene this morning."

"Oh, the comedienne, yeah. What can I do for you, Ms. Williams?"

"I've got information on two suspects whose DNA you'll want to eliminate from the Amelia Ortega case."

"Er… okay." He sounded thrown. "We do have a number of unidentified samples, yes. Do you have their names? A description?"

"Henderson Sumpter and James Iverson. I'll send their photos to Mac's phone."

"Great. Thanks. And can I ask how you came by this information?"

"Sure." She hung up. He could ask whatever he wanted. Didn't mean he'd get an answer.

Apart from banging a number of detectives to obtain privileged information, it helped if she threw them a bone every so often. This Josh Harding might be useful at some time in the future – now that he knew she could provide quality information, he'd be more forthcoming if that time ever came.

She glanced at her watch. Every second that ticked by was one second more Ethan had to reach Nat before she did and torture him for ratting him out.

154

She leaned forward. "Can we go any faster, please? This is an emergency."

"Lady," said the driver, "I don't know what drama you got going, but I got a wife and kids. I ain't getting pulled over."

Pulled over 'for nothing' was what he really meant. Money had a way of swaying the judgment of even the most steadfast of people.

Holding up banknotes, she leaned right up to the plexiglass divider that protected the driver from aggressive passengers.

She said, "There's an extra fifty if you put your foot down."

The driver snorted a laugh. "This ain't no movie, lady. I ain't putting my foot nowhere for fifty bucks."

Protecting his livelihood was fair enough. After all, not all drivers were as desperate as Amir. But she had to reach Nat. Had to reach him before Ethan did.

This was no time to quibble about money.

She pulled off her right armored glove and reached into the secret pocket inside her waistband. She whipped out the remaining bills from her emergency stash and shoved them through a gap in the plexiglass divider so they fell beside the driver.

She said, "Seven hundred bucks. You going to put your foot down now, or do I have to put my foot somewhere?"

The driver said nothing. But a burst of speed threw her back into her seat.

Tess gazed at the buildings flying by. Gazed out, but saw nothing. Too many nightmares were crammed into her mind for her to see anything.

She had to reach Nat. Had to.

Usually, she was little more than a clean-up crew – arriving after a crime, her only option was to punish those who'd hurt an innocent victim. It was rare she got the opportunity to actually intervene; to not merely take a life, but to grant one and make a real, tangible difference. Such occasions were precious.

Of course, punishing the guilty was rewarding. But knowing she'd given someone a life they wouldn't otherwise have had… Well, that was how a surgeon must feel cutting out a tumor that everyone else believed to be inoperable – unbelievably gratifying.

Plus, this particular life wasn't just any old life. This was Nat's. This was a life that had touched her more than most. This one, she was determined to save. This one, she was going to save.

But the buildings and the pedestrians on the sidewalk stopped speeding by.

She frowned through the passenger window.

The taxi was slowing down.

She looked ahead.

"Oh, for God's sake."

Red stop lights reared out of the darkness.

She rubbed her brow as the taxi slowed to a crawl.

Leaning forward again, she said, "Can we go a different way?"

"You want a rental to drive yourself, lady, feel free."

With such a pleasant demeanor, she wondered how often the driver received tips. But he was right – he knew the city streets far better than she did.

Snorting with resignation, she leaned back.

This was taking too long. Ethan's head start wasn't big, but it was big enough for a burly young guy to cripple a little old one.

No matter how she tried, she couldn't stop her mind conjuring horrific images of what Ethan might be doing to Nat that very second. She struggled not to think of Nat's blood on that hideous brown-and-gold carpet of his. Struggled not to think of his heart slowing to a dead stop just as was her taxi.

Trying to clear her thoughts of an old battered body laying at an unnatural angle on an old battered carpet, she pulled off her other glove to inspect them both.

She ran her fingers inside them to check for damage. Even though she knew there was none.

But still the images of blood and pain and a lifeless body haunted her.

She glanced up. Ahead, the light was still red. Like some sick joke.

She glared at the light.

It mocked her.

"Come on."

One blazing red eye gazed back at her, as if it had all the time in the world.

"Oh, for the love of God."

The light all but laughed at her predicament.

And suddenly…

Green.

The people and streets once more flew by.

She gazed ahead through the windshield.

How much farther was it?

The taxi sped on.

It swung out wide and passed a bus. Cut back in front of a red SUV.

The SUV blared its horn.

But the taxi was already swerving around a black sedan.

The taxi hammered down the street.

Weaving in and out, in and out.

It screeched around a hard left turn. Flung Tess against her door.

She pushed herself upright. Peered at the buildings.

Where were they? How close were they?

She had to get there. Had to save Nat.

On her right, the subway station she'd exited that morning to reach the crime scene shot by.

Oh, thank God. She was close now. So very close. But was she close enough? Had she been quick enough?

Under her breath, she said, "Come on."

Her gloves fine, she pulled them back on. Balled both fists.

She was ready.

Moments later the taxi pulled up to the curb. Finally!

Tess leapt out.

She shot down the street.

Her guards bounced in her backpack. She'd have to strap them on in Nat's bathroom. Even though she'd always intended on leaving the taxi a block away to hide her destination from the taxi driver, she couldn't have risked putting them on in the car and having him witness her preparations in case something went wrong later and the police traced him.

In the distance, the glowing red neon sign for A Taste of Napoli taunted her about how far away she was still.

She sprinted toward it.

Nearing the corner to Nat's street, her heart hammered. Not with the exertion of running, but with what might be lying in wait: police cruisers, crime scene tape, the coroner's truck...

She prayed she wasn't too late.

Rounding the corner, she found nothing but a quiet, dimly lit street. Not that such a sight stopped her heart from thumping.

Nat's building reared before her, black and foreboding. Other than the checkered pattern of lit windows, nothing suggested anyone stirred inside.

Anything could be happening in there.

Anything. Right now.

Arms pumping, heart pounding, Tess raced along the sidewalk.

What would she find at Nat's?

A smiling old man and carrot cake?

Or a bloody corpse and endless self-recrimination?

Chapter 27

"SO YOU HAVEN'T seen or heard anyone?" Tess peered through the barred window into the lurking darkness outside. In the background, Nat's clock ticked as slowly and as ominously as ever.

"No, dear. No one."

As usual, Nat stood at his kitchen counter fussing with drinks and baked goods as if the Queen of England had dropped in for a spot of afternoon tea. Still, if it kept him busy it would distract him from the impending threat.

Considering the predicament he was in, he was surprisingly calm. The resilience of old folks always amazed her. People always thought of retirees as helpless, infirm buffoons who needed mollycoddling like children, but often in times of crisis, old folks stepped up and really surprised you.

Nat limped over and set a tray of tea and carrot cake down on his table.

"Come. Sit down, dear. You look exhausted."

There was little point in doing anything else right now so she joined him.

Sitting down to tea and cake on the couch, she pulled off her armored leather gloves and stuffed them into her backpack. She still had on her stealth body armor, but hadn't yet donned her shin and forearm guards – as Ethan hadn't broken in before she'd arrived, it looked like he was biding his time until there were as few potential witnesses awake as possible. He likely wouldn't show before midnight. Maybe he was smarter than she'd thought.

Nat said, "I brewed a full teapot, dear. If you've been on the go all day, you're probably dehydrated."

He was right: to remain mentally alert, with muscles supple and ready for action, she made a point of drinking at every opportunity. She picked up the tea and drank.

She said, "Earl Grey. Hmmm." There was nothing as refreshing as a good quality tea.

"At my age, what am I saving up for?"

So buying quality tea was Nat's idea of high living? She smiled.

It always puzzled her why tea wasn't more popular in the USA. She couldn't live without it. But that was likely because she'd spent so long in the Far East, where tea could be not merely a drink but an occasion. She'd loved tea ever since. Except first thing in the morning: she loved a strong coffee as a mental and biological kick start.

"Tell me, dear, why do you believe Ethan will come looking for me?"

"I'm almost sure he's responsible for Amelia's death. And you're the eyewitness who saw them fighting in the street."

The clock ticked on. It seemed even louder than before.

He slid a plate across the table to her with six slices of carrot cake arranged in a fan.

"Almost sure? Why only 'almost'? Don't you have enough evidence?"

She placed a piece of cake on a little porcelain plate, beside the delicate pink flower painted just off-center.

"The police have a number of DNA samples from the scene. Hopefully, they'll nail Ethan by matching his to a sample taken from one of Amelia's wounds." She bit into the cake. "Hmmm, this *is* nice."

"So why can't we just call the police and tell them to arrest Ethan, dear? Isn't that what they're there for?"

These days, the police department was just as susceptible to economic instability as every other business and organization. Not to mention incompetence, corruption, and disinterest. What good cops there were didn't have the time to babysit every single witness to every single crime for fear that the suspect just *might* show up to silence them. Understaffed, underfunded, and crippled by bureaucracy, it was amazing they solved the number of crimes they did.

"They're doing their best," said Tess, "but they're spread pretty thin a lot of the time."

Considering a brutal killer could be lurking outside his door that very second, Nat was remarkably unflustered. She watched him pour her more tea. His hand was steady. Breathing calm.

He said, "So if *you* don't catch Ethan, he might never be caught?"

"I don't want to paint things as bad as that, but…" Tess shrugged.

"So you're Amelia's best hope for justice."

"Well…" She drank her tea to wash down the cake. "You have to try, don't you? It's like you trying to make the world a safer place with your neighborhood watch – every tiny bit helps, doesn't it?"

"It does, dear. But for me, come nine twenty at night, after my patrol, I'm safely here at home and can get on with my life. But I get the impression you see this more as a calling. Something you have to see through to the bitter end, no matter what?"

"If I can stop a crime, or catch the person responsible for one, but choose not to, doesn't that make me just as bad as the criminals themselves?"

The clock ticked. Ticked as if it were waiting for someone. Or something.

"So you won't stop until you catch Ethan?"

"One way or the other, he's going to pay for what he did to Amelia."

"And what if he didn't do it?"

"Then I'll find whoever did." She ate the last mouthful of her cake.

He gestured to the plate on the table. "More cake?"

"You're right – it's lovely, but no. Thank you."

If Ethan hadn't done it, she was back to square one: no clues, no suspects, no options. If he was innocent, there was a chance forensic analysis could turn up something else. But that relied on databases like IAFIS and CODIS, so if a person's fingerprints or DNA weren't on file, they couldn't be identified no matter how much evidence the police had.

She stared down at the little pink flower on the white porcelain plate in her lap. Such a delicate flower. Such a delicate plate.

But who else could the killer be? If not Ethan, TG, or Amir, who? It was way too brutal to be a senseless killing. An opportunistic killer wouldn't go to all that trouble of impaling a body for no reason. And who carries a rock hammer just on the off chance they'll find someone to beat with it? No, Amelia hadn't just been murdered, she'd been punished. It was not an opportunistic killing.

So was it a psychopath? Someone deranged? Someone just starting out on a crusade and this would be the first of his many victims?

But why smash in Amelia's face? It was almost as if he wanted to silence her. Even in death. That suggested he knew her. You only silenced those who knew you and who knew something about you that you didn't want others to discover.

Nat stood and picked up the empty plates on which they'd had cake.

Tick... Tick... Tick...

"Nat?"

"Yes, dear?"

She watched him hobble over to the kitchen area to wash his dishes. The only thing standing between Nat and a brutal killer who impaled his victims was a young woman he'd known less than a day. Yet here they were enjoying tea and cake. Why was he so calm? Why wasn't he frightened? It was almost as if he believed there was no danger. He was an intelligent man so why would he think that?

Tess said, "Are you sure you didn't see anyone else around last night?"

"Not that I remember. Why?"

She looked at him standing at the counter. Looked at his bad leg.

"If I catch Ethan, but he turns out to be innocent, that means the killer's still out there. And we have no idea who it is."

He hobbled to one of the cupboards. "I suppose so, dear. But that's hardly likely, is it?"

She watched him, how his body was like hinged wood, not supple and elegant the way a body should be, but awkward and restricted. Her gaze glided over to his cane, standing propped against the side of the couch.

Tick... Tick... Tick... Tick... Tick—

"What time did you say you got home from the store after fighting with Amelia?"

Nat laughed. "Oh, you could hardly call it fighting, dear."

Tess studied Nat's cane. His black wooden cane with a large polished chrome handle. A T-shaped handle. A handle shaped kind of like a rock hammer.

"No?" she said. "So what would you call it?"

Hands on the edge of the sink, he hung his head.

"I knew you were never going to stop. Just knew it." He shook his head. "I gave you Ethan as a suspect, the taxi driver, that man from the photo you showed me – why couldn't you just pick one of them? Or pick none of them and decide the case couldn't be solved? Why couldn't you just..." He threw one of his china cups into the sink. It shattered, bits flying out. "... just let it go?"

"What are you saying, Nat?"

"What am I saying?" He sniggered. He looked around at her. "Do you know how long I've lived here? Sixty-six years. That's how long. Sixty-six wonderful years. And that vicious little bitch was going to take it all away from me."

"Oh God, no."

"She left me no choice, did she? I wasn't going to lose everything because some cheap slut spread gossip about me. A pedophile. *Me!* She said she was going to put my photo on Facebook. Said she was going to spread her lies all over the Internet."

"So you killed her?"

He slumped against the counter. "It was an accident."

"An accident!? Nat, you impaled her on a goddamn pole."

"I only meant to smash her phone with my cane. But she turned, didn't she? Got it full in the throat and stopped breathing. So I had to do something. And what better way to make the police believe it was a jealous lover, or a whacko rapist, or a serial killer? Anything but an ordinary person. Anything but me."

She looked at Nat. Feeble old Nat.

He was Sixty-six years old – ancient to Tess, but hardly decrepit in reality. Amelia was such a tiny thing, if she'd weighed 110 pounds it would only have been after a heavy meal. Still, could he have lifted her?

Rage could give a person extraordinary strength, strength to overcome all manner of threatening circumstances. But such strength came at a hefty cost. In moments of extreme stress, the brain reacted by releasing adrenaline to boost strength and endurance. Unfortunately, a side effect was this reaction sapped the mind of balanced thought, transforming a rational person into a primal creature of dark needs and savage actions. It was no mistake that a state of rage was also called 'blind fury.'

"Oh God, Nat… Look, maybe we can claim extenuating circumstances."

Tess stood, but fell back to the couch, her legs wobbling and unable to support her. What the hell…?

"We? Since when is it we? Will you be in the next cell?"

Her head felt thick, like soup you could stand a fork in. The room started to spin. She shook her head to try to clear it, but that just made her feel woozy. She laid her head back on the couch, blinking her eyes to try to focus on the ceiling.

Nat appeared beside her. "I didn't mean to hurt her. Really, I didn't. Only to smash her phone. But someone like me can't go to prison. I wouldn't last a week."

Tess tried to push up but barely had the strength to talk.

"Nat... what... what have you done?"

Chapter 28

A WOMAN SCREAMED.

Lights flickered in front of Tess. She heaved her heavy, heavy eyelids half open, but they fell shut again. She struggled again. Gradually, they fluttered open. The world slowly sharpened into focus.

Nat hovered around his reenactment model muttering to himself. On the table in front of the couch lay an odd selection of objects, amongst them a meat cleaver, an ice pick, a bottle of pills, a glass of milky fluid, a leather belt, pajama bottoms cord, a foot-long screwdriver, and a hammer.

On the TV in the corner, a shadowy figure crept up behind a teenage girl and ran his knife into her back. She screamed. So loudly. And blood splattered everywhere.

Despite the movie, Tess could still hear that damn clock. Each tick pounded in her head like a mallet. She tried to raise her hand, but it caught on something. She looked down. Seated on a wooden dining chair, she'd been tied around the elbows to the back uprights with what looked like her own nylon zip ties, while her legs were bound to the chair legs.

"Nat…" She managed no more than a whisper. "Nat." Louder.

At his window, he stopped muttering and looked over. "You just couldn't let it go, could you? Just couldn't let it go. All you had to do was walk away and say the case was unsolvable. You said yourself the police are stretched – why did you have to decide this case had to be one of those they solved?"

Tied at the elbows, Tess could still move her forearms. But not enough to escape. She tested her binds. Talk about stupid – she wouldn't have bought the ties if they were easily snapped.

Her legs were equally well secured. Tied at the knee, she could probably stand, but she wouldn't be able to run or fight. She needed time.

Tess looked across at him. "Stop, Nat. Please. Before it's too late."

"It's already too late. Do you think a man like me would survive prison?" He shook his head. "I'm a good person. I don't deserve this."

"So if you're a good person, let me go."

"Because you promise you won't tell the police? Promise they won't come and rifle through all my private things. Won't take fingerprints and DNA? Won't ruin me, innocent or not?" He shook his head again.

His 'private things'? 'Fingerprints and DNA'? Everyone had a past. Was there something in Nat's he was eager to keep buried?

That made him all the more dangerous.

Her only hope was to not play the victim, but to play the woman who'd befriended him – humanize herself so she wasn't merely an object he could dispose of, but a living, breathing person, just like him.

"Nat, think what you're doing. A good person wouldn't do this. I've got a life. People who love me. Dreams I—"

Marching over, he shouted. "Shut up! Just shut up and let me think."

He looked at the objects on the table. He must have collected everything in his home that he figured would make a decent implement with which to kill her.

He picked up the ice pick, but put it down immediately.

Next, he weighed the hammer in his hand and took a practice swing, but put that down too.

How long had she been out? How many times had he practiced the death blow? And more to the point, why wasn't she already dead?

For an ordinary person, it wasn't easy to take a life. Especially up close. It was one thing to pull a trigger from a distance, but within arm's length? You could see into your victim's eyes, see their hopes and dreams dying right before you when they realized there was no escape. Killing so coldly was a mighty big thing.

A hammer, a knife, a rope…?

In a blind fury, or in a life-or-death struggle, yes, a person could kill with such weapons. But beating, stabbing, or strangling someone to death while they were bound in a chair? That took a tremendous strength of will which few people could muster. Few normal people.

"Please, Nat… think about what you're doing."

He stood for a moment and took a deep breath, eyes closed.

"Nat. Talk to me. Please."

When he opened his eyes again, his voice had that usual calmness and innocence.

Nat said, "You want to talk? Okay, let's talk. But don't think of screaming. Upstairs is vacant" – he pointed to his right – "and there's a storage room. And anyone walking by in the hall will hear that." He pointed to the slasher movie.

Smart thinking. In fact, it was a technique she'd used herself. But then his hobby was studying the strategy of war; he obviously had a very logical mind. He must have. The way he'd played her. Told her about Ethan, about TG being in the area, about the taxi driver. Hell, she couldn't have screwed this one up more if she'd tried. And all because he'd reminded her of her grandpa so she'd had feelings for him. That was where having feelings for someone got you! Hell, talk about dumb.

He pulled another dining chair across and sat before her.

"So…" Unblinking, he locked her with an intense stare. "Let's talk."

Chapter 29

NAT THREW HER armored gloves into her lap. "What are these?"

"I rollerblade. They're protectors for my hands for when I fall."

He nodded. "And these?" He flicked the tie holding her left arm.

"I grow tomatoes in my kitchen. I got these to tie them to stakes."

He nodded again. "Okay."

Without a word, he ripped open her shirt. Buttons scattered across the floor.

While its stealth design allowed her to discreetly wear it under her clothes, it was nonetheless obvious what it was – a bulletproof vest.

"I'm a writer. I told you. I was supposed to be going for a police ride-along tonight."

He leaned closer. Not threatening in any way, but calm. Terrifyingly calm.

He said, "Do you really think I'm so stupid, dear? Who are you? Who knows you're here?"

Tess whimpered. "Okay, okay. Please. Don't hurt me. I'll do anything you say."

"So tell me who knows you're here."

Tess's face screwed up. Her chin quivered. "My editor. My editor knows I'm here."

"You said you were freelance." He held up her cell phone. "Show me your editor's name and number."

Tess's face scrunched up. She sobbed.

"No one knows, do they, dear? You haven't told anyone?"

He stood. Walked over to his arsenal of killing implements. He returned with the glass of milky fluid. He leaned down and held it to her lips.

"Drink this, dear, and it will all be over soon."

Poison: the coward's weapon of choice.

She pulled away. "No. Please."

"It won't hurt. I promise. You won't feel a thing. You'll just drift off to sleep like you did before. But this time... for a little longer."

So that was how he'd knocked her cold earlier – some concoction of his superstrong painkillers and sleeping pills in her tea.

She whimpered again. Slowly shook her head. "Please." Her voice squeaked, the way women's voices go off the scale in times of deep emotional stress. "Please. Don't kill me like this."

He moved the glass to her lips again. "Please, dear. Don't make me fetch the hammer."

Her voice rose even higher in pitch.

He leaned closer. "I can't hear you, dear. Say what you need to say and then we'll get it all over with."

She shook her head. "I can't die like this. If I don't confess, I'll go to hell."

"But I'm not a priest, dear."

She squeaked something unintelligible again. Hunched over. Sobbed.

"Okay, okay. Say what you need to say." He leaned down even closer.

She squeaked.

"I can't hear, dear, you'll have to speak up."

She squeaked again.

"What was that?" He leaned even closer.

Too close.

She clamped her teeth right over his nose. Bit. Hard.

He screeched.

She grabbed each of his arms. Pushed up with her legs. Lurched forward.

He fell over backwards and crashed onto his muddy brown carpet. In her chair, Tess landed on top of him, still clamped to his nose and each arm.

He screamed and flailed.

She bit harder.

Ground her jaws together. Like a wild dog savaging a rival.

Harder.

Harder.

She snatched her head away.

He screeched. Blood spurted from the middle of a jagged mess of flesh in his face.

Tess spat. A hunk of nose hit the carpet. She let go of Nat's arms. Let his bucking help her roll away from him.

She clawed at a leg of the table on which Nat waged war between his tiny Confederate and Union armies. With the chair tied to her arms and legs, she couldn't move. Couldn't fight.

She glanced back.

Nat rolled on the floor clutching his face, blood seeping through his fingers. He wailed.

She pulled herself to her feet. She didn't have time to find a knife and try to cut herself free. Not that she'd have been able to reach any of the ties to cut them the way she was bound. She had one option.

As best she could, she leapt into the air, up and backwards. Her chair hit the floor at an awkward angle, but its legs didn't break.

She struggled up again. Glanced over again.

Nat flailed about on the carpet trying to get up.

"Bitch. You fucking bitch!"

Hell, if he got to the table and came at her with a knife now, she was dead.

Again, she jumped backwards.

Again, she crashed to the floor.

Loud cracking sounds bit the air and Tess sprawled amid splintered bits of wooden chair.

She shook her right hand free of the broken chair back. Kicked her feet and shook her left leg loose, but the ties were tight and held her right leg and left arm to the chair's skeleton framework.

She yanked on the wood to try to free herself so she could stand. How could she fight with a three-foot chunk of tree trailing alongside her?

But Nat came at her. Blood streamed down his face, drenching his sweater vest. He looked like a frenzied zombie.

"You fucking bitch! You fucking bitch!" He stormed toward her. Meat cleaver held high to slice into her.

She didn't have her armored gloves. Didn't have her forearm guards. Didn't have a moment to think.

So she didn't.

Like water flowing naturally into a channel, unable to follow any other path, her body reacted.

On her back on the floor, she kicked Nat's legs from under him.

He crashed to the carpet.

But unlike in a third-rate movie, he did not impale himself on his meat cleaver.

On his side, he swung the blade at her.

With a piece of splintered chair leg, she knocked the cleaver from his hand.

She twisted over.

Slammed a kick into his gut.

He clutched his stomach.

Gasped for air.

She rolled towards him.

Smashed the jagged wood down into his bloody face.

On his back, Nat flailed his limbs. They flapped and flapped and flapped.

One by one, his arms and legs dropped.

He gurgled. Spurted blood.

Then lay.

Still.

The broken chair leg stuck up out of his mouth.

Chapter 30

TESS LAY ON the floor for a moment, panting. Her body trembled with nervous energy.

She closed her eyes. Took a long breath in for four seconds, held it for four, then blew it out for four. She repeated the process. She needed to be calm, to have a clear head to formulate an exit strategy.

While she'd been the victim of a crazed killer and had acted in self-defense, she could never admit to what she'd just done. A police investigation might unveil her 'private things.'

Not that doing time was a problem. Unlike Nat, with her skill set, she'd not only survive prison, but thrive there. But how many victims would go unavenged while she was busy being transformed into what the authorities believed was a decent person who made a valuable contribution to society?

She stood and freed herself of the bits of broken chair.

Having grabbed her backpack from the couch, she slipped on a pair of nitrile gloves. She preferred nitrile to latex because of its superior resistance to wear, tears, and chemicals – the ideal prerequisite for clean-up jobs.

Having located the TV remote control, she lowered the volume. The last thing she needed was an irate neighbor banging on the door complaining about the noise. At that moment in the movie, a teenage girl pushed the villain back onto a conveniently placed spike in a wall. Tess snorted. "Yeah, right."

Time for the clean-up.

She walked over to Nat. Stared down at his bloody body. Heaved a weary breath.

That had been too close.

Way too close.

But it wasn't like it could've gone down any other way – she'd done everything she could to identify the killer. When a job took such a sudden, unexpected twist, there was nothing she could do but try to ride it out and pray she struggled through to the other side. Thank God such situations didn't happen often.

Maybe if she hadn't been thrown such a loop by the Bryant Park subway incident, she'd have picked up on something earlier. But there could be no contingency plan for such a fluke encounter and how it had shaken her up. She should just thank her lucky stars she was getting to walk out of here tonight.

Tess snickered.

Luck?

LUCK!

For fuck's sake, what was wrong with her!

'A sudden, unexpected twist'?

Yeah, right. That was what she needed – excuses to make her feel better about herself after screwing up in the most outstandingly dumb way imaginable.

Her gut instinct had warned her something was off. If only she'd listened instead of sentimentalizing this whole ridiculous situation, this predicament would never have arisen.

She glowered at the corpse.

Like her grandpa?

Like her grandpa her ass!

How many times was it going to take before she learned her lesson? Getting close to people got you killed. If nothing else, Shanghai had taught her that. Or so she'd thought.

Yet here she was nearly flat on a slab in the morgue. Again.

And why?

Because some loser reminded her of someone from her past. A past as dead as the person being remembered. Hell, with the tricks the mind played in coloring memories, she wasn't even sure she'd ever lived that life, ever had a grandpa so loving and nurturing.

She heaved a sigh.

When would she learn? It wasn't like it was difficult. In fact, it couldn't be simpler.

No feelings.

Ever.

For anyone.

How many more times would she needlessly have to fight her way out of a deadly situation? This time had been too close. You only got so many chances. Only so many times the cards fell in your favor. The next time she might not be so lucky. And that was why there couldn't be a next time.

No feelings. Ever. For anyone. That had to be her mantra. If she wanted to keep on breathing.

The chair leg made a slurping sound as she pulled it out of Nat's head. While over the body, she took his wallet to let the scene suggest it was a robbery gone sour. An extremely gruesome robbery.

Using Nat's cheese grater, she scraped his face and the piece of bitten-off nose to obliterate the chances of any dental molds being possible.

As the stainless steel teeth chewed up his face, Tess looked into Nat's dead eyes. How wrong had she been. And to what ends people would go to survive.

His facial muscles relaxed, no longer twisted into a raging grimace, he looked like the sweet old man she'd met only a few hours earlier.

Apart from the blood.

Blood she'd spilled.

She gazed at him. She almost felt sorry.

Almost.

With one less monster, the world was a better place. She would close her eyes and sleep well tonight.

She tidied away Nat's arsenal, washed the dishes they'd used for tea and cake, and then collected the broken pieces of chair. She'd dispose of all those later.

In the closet, she found Nat's cleaning supplies. Taking the chlorine bleach over to the body, she doused Nat, head to toe, with pure bleach. That would kill the DNA in any of her hair follicles, saliva, blood, and anything else left behind. She also doused the piece of bloody nose and everywhere else she felt might compromise her situation.

Fingerprints weren't an issue. She'd freely admit to interviewing Nat if need be.

For extra insurance, she pulled a small plastic container from her bag. She glanced around. The couch was as good a place as any – she tossed a broken fingernail onto it that she'd ripped off Marvin Thompson's dead hand two days ago on the Carson kidnapping job. That would give the police something to occupy them and keep them away from her. Especially as they'd never find Thompson's body.

Snagging her wet wipes from her backpack, she popped into the bathroom to clean up so she'd look presentable on the street. Wiping her face in the mirror, she couldn't help but wonder about Nat having a secret. Should she search his apartment for his 'private things'? Why bother? Whatever he'd done in the past, he'd more than paid for it tonight.

Having collected up anything else that might be incriminating, she strolled toward the apartment door, but stopped. She went back to the mantel. Picked up the ticking clock.

She turned it over in her hands. The wood looked like ebony. There was fine engraving on the face. It was probably one of the oldest things Nat owned. Maybe antique. She'd take it. Pawn it. After the expenses of the day, she needed every penny she could lay her hands on to cover all her rents.

She left.

At some point, the neighbors would complain about the smell. The door would be broken down, and Nat's decaying body would be found.

Forensics would process the scene.

Police would interview neighbors.

Suspects and motives would be examined.

Would anyone come knocking at her door?

Chapter 31

EYES CLOSED, TESS bowed her cello, lost in a world of sound and the colors conjured in her mind's eye. Zoltan Kodaly's Solo Cello Sonata Opus 8 enveloped her apartment. The contrasting counterpoints both clashing and delighting in equal measure, the music danced and fought at Tess's command.

A knock at her door almost breached her world but was too far distant to be real.

She played on.

A second knock came louder.

Tess stopped.

Silence.

She strained to hear something. Had she heard a knock? She couldn't have. Had she?

A banging on her door answered her question.

She froze. Why would anyone ever knock on her door? *Who* could ever knock on her door? Other than Bomb, who almost never ventured outside, and the landlord, who was paid direct from her bank so he had no reason to call, no one knew she lived here.

187

She leaned her cello against her chair and walked through her spartanly furnished living room. Other than the cello and, on a drawer unit near the door, a small glass bowl in which a red Japanese fighting fish swam, there was little to suggest anyone lived here at all.

Keeping it on the security chain, she opened the door two inches and peeked out.

"Oh!" She felt her eyes widen in surprise. And her heart start to pound.

The man said, "I'm sorry. I haven't come at a bad time?"

"No, no. What can I do for you?" If she was going to start getting visitors, she'd have to insist on a peephole in the door in her next place.

He said, "Detective Josh Harding? We met two weeks ago during an investigation into—"

"Yes, I remember. Hello, Detective Harding." She felt her heart slowing, her mind calming. Police officers did not ask if they'd come at a bad time just before reading you your Miranda rights.

He smiled. It was a nice smile. Boyish, yet strong. And those slate-blue eyes drew her even more as the skin crinkled around them.

He said, "Well, since you showed such interest in the case, and actually helped us eliminate certain DNA evidence – you must tell me how you did that, by the way – I thought you might like to know we've apprehended the boyfriend, Ethan Dumfries."

"Oh, that's great." She realized she might not appear to be acting quite normally, so she removed the chain and opened the door eighteen inches.

She said, "Sorry, I'm just a little surprised – I didn't know the police were now doing house calls to fill in reporters on case details. Maybe you'd like to finish writing my article while I put my feet up with some Ben and Jerry's and *Murder She Wrote*." She loathed the show, but such a comment bolstered her image of being an unthreatening, gentle woman.

"*Murder She Wrote?* Okay." He laughed. "And here I had you pegged as a *Kill Bill* kinda girl."

She laughed. "All that blood? No, thanks!" She looked at him. He showed no sign of leaving. She was not going to invite him in. Why didn't he get that from the fact she was peeking through a half-closed door? "Was there something else?"

"Well, er... Ha." He shifted his weight awkwardly, like a naughty schoolboy not wanting to confess to what he was up to. "I was kinda hoping you might like to go for a drink some time."

"Oh, er..."

"If I'm stepping on someone else's toes..."

"No, no. Sorry, it's just... talk about a curveball."

He nodded. And waited. "So...?"

"So..." She took a breath. "Sure. That would be nice."

"Fantastic."

"Let me give you my number."

"That's okay." He patted his breast pocket, where many cops kept their notebooks. "Already got it."

"Great. So feel free to give me a call sometime." She smiled and waited for him to leave.

He didn't.

"You know," he said, "if you're not busy now, there's a great little blues bar only two blocks away."

What the hell? Tess stared. "You want to go on a date *now*?"

"Hey, it's just a suggestion. I mean, it's Friday night – you're not out; I'm not out, so…" He shrugged.

"Tell me, Detective Hardy, have you ever dated a woman before?"

His forehead knitted. "Excuse me?"

"A woman. Have you ever dated a woman?"

He smirked. "Yes, I've dated a woman. In fact, more than one. You might say I've dated" – he made air quotes – "women." His cockiness faded. "Though, not at the same time, of course. I'm talking individually. Separately. Er… Monogamously. I don't, er, you know..."

While his bumbling vulnerability was somewhat attractive, she remained silent to let him dig himself a hole and maybe end this here and now.

His face reddening, he said, "Believe it or not, I'm usually quite good at this."

"At screwing up dates?"

He snorted a laugh and then held up his ringless ring finger. "Actually, I, er, guess so."

He locked her with his slate-blue eyes and roguish smile.

That was one hell of a smile.

"Okay," said Tess, "so drawing upon this vast experience of dating women – all separately, with absolutely no crossover – exactly how many seconds did each of those women need to prepare for those dates?"

"Ahhh." He hit himself on the forehead with the palm of his right hand. "Sorry, that's guy mentality for you." He rolled his eyes. "Let me try again – if you aren't busy tonight, would you like a drink at the little blues bar along the street? If so, I can go grab myself a beer and whenever you're ready, you can join me."

This guy just wasn't going to give up.

She said, "I'll tell you what, give me an hour, and have a bottle of cider waiting. Okay?"

He frowned at her. "Cider?"

"It's a drink made from apples."

"Yeah, I know, but—"

"Do you want me to write it down for you?"

"No, it's just, you know, cider…? Who drinks cider?"

She cocked an eyebrow at him. "You're sure you've been quite good at this in the past?"

His face even redder, he flashed a sheepish smile. "Sorry." He tapped his watch, turning to go. "I'll see you in an hour."

She said, "Just one thing."

He turned back, his raised eyebrows asking what she wanted.

"I didn't know I'd given anyone this address." She knew she hadn't. "How did you find me?"

"Hey, I'm a detective. I detected. That's what I do."

She nodded.

"See you in the bar. With a nice cold cider." He waved and blasted that smile at her one last time.

Man, that was a smile.

"Bye." She closed the door. And took the knife from behind her back and replaced it in the small drawer unit upon which Fish sat next to the door.

Tess was always prepared for having to disappear at a moment's notice, so an hour was fifty minutes longer than she needed.

Time to change apartments. And change phone numbers.

The End.

Continue the pulse-pounding *Angel of Darkness* adventure. Flip the page now and jump into the thrilling *Mourning Scars* (book 05).

Free Library of Books

Thank you for reading *Midnight Burn*. To show my appreciation of my readers, I wrote a second series of books exclusively for them – each Angel of Darkness book has its own *Black File*, so there's a free library for you to collect and enjoy.

A FREE Library Waiting for You!

Exclusive? You bet! You can't get the *Black Files* anywhere except through the links in the *Angel of Darkness* books.

Start Your FREE Library with *Black Files 04-06*.
http://stevenleebooks.com/tfbm

Make Your Opinion Count

Dear Thriller Lover,

Do you have a few seconds to spare?

It is unbelievably difficult for an emerging writer to reach a wider audience, not least because less than 1% of readers leave reviews. Hard to believe, isn't it? Of one hundred readers, maybe - that's 'maybe' - one reader will post a few words.

Please, will you help me by sharing how much you enjoyed this book in a short review?

It only takes a few seconds because it only needs a handful of words. I'll be ever so grateful.

Don't follow the 99% – stand out from the crowd with just a few clicks!

Thank you,

Steve

Copy the link to post your review of *Midnight Burn*:

http://stevenleebooks.com/zlj1

Free Goodies – VIP Area

See More, Do More, Get More!

Do you want to get more than the average reader gets? Every month I send my VIP readers some combination of:

- news about my books
- giveaways from me or my writer friends
- opportunities to help choose book titles and covers
- anecdotes about the writing life, or just life itself
- special deals and freebies
- sneak behind-the-scenes peeks at what's in the works.

Get Exclusive VIP Access with this Link.

http://stevenleebooks.com/wcfl

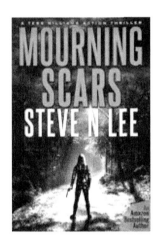

Mourning Scars

Angel of Darkness Book 05

196

Chapter 01

SLOWLY REACHING ACROSS the shelf under his cash register, fingers knotted with arthritis found something cold, hard, unforgiving – his revolver. Chiang had never fired a gun, but no lowlife scum was walking out with his money. Not again. Three robberies in twelve months was just too much.

At his side, Bashe growled. The German shepherd was no fool – he knew there was something wrong too.

Dragging his gaze away from the convex mirror hanging in the far corner of his convenience store, and the shadowy figures reflected in it, Chiang tousled the thick brown fur on Bashe's head.

"Easy, boy."

The big dog shifted restlessly and whined.

Chiang eased his hand back from the shelf. His gun was within reach if he needed it. That was all he needed to know right now.

Standing in front of the register, an old woman with a bulbous nose fussed in her purse. "I'm sorry, Mr. Chiang, I know I've got it somewhere."

She counted out more of her loose change, the skin so thin on her wrinkled hands, the veins stood out like spaghetti under wet tissue paper.

"Is okay, Mrs. Hills. Take your time." Chiang smiled a quavering smile at her and then at her little granddaughter beside her. Sucking on a candy bar she'd only had a few seconds, the little girl already had a ring of chocolate hugging her mouth as if a drunk had applied brown lipstick.

Chiang's gaze returned to the reflection in his security mirror. Three men huddled next to the baking products. Tattooed necks and loping swaggers did not cry 'chef'. What were they doing?

While Mrs. Hills was busy, Chiang surreptitiously slid his hand under the counter to his gun – again – just to check it was within easy reach – again. It was.

Praying he'd never have to use the movement he'd practiced, his gaze shot back to the mirror. He drew his hands down the back of his slacks. When his mouth was so dry, why were his palms so wet?

He stared at the three men. He'd purposefully placed all the baking ingredients at the end of that third aisle, the hardest area in the store to protect, purely because those were the products no one would ever bother stealing. What were those guys doing? What were they waiting for? Did they really believe anyone thought they were discussing which was the best flour to bake cupcakes?

"Well, I'll be darned," said Mrs. Hills. With a laugh, she shook her head. "If I didn't have a twenty-dollar bill in here this afternoon, I'll be a monkey's uncle."

He'd been serving Mrs. Hills for well over ten years. Probably closer to twenty. He'd normally tell her to take what she needed, and give him the money next time, but that wasn't an option today. Today, Chiang needed her to stay as long as possible.

If those guys meant trouble, they'd have caused it already if they didn't care about witnesses. As they were still huddled at the back, they obviously wanted privacy to see through whatever it was they were planning. The longer Mrs. Hills was in the store the better the chances were these guys would get bored and move on.

"Ah!" Mrs. Hills beamed a smile and held twenty dollars aloft. "I knew it was in there somewhere."

His hand trembled as he reached for the money. "I get you anything else, Mrs. Hills?"

"No, that's it, thanks."

Taking his time collecting her change from the register, he glanced up into the mirror. Those men hadn't moved. He needed to buy more time. He held the change out, but didn't drop it into her waiting hand.

He said, "And Mr. Hills? He's good? I don't see him now for nearly two weeks."

She rolled her eyes. "Oh, now there's a tale. Three months he's been waiting to see a consultant about his back. Three months. Well, wouldn't you just

199

know it, no sooner—" She snickered. "Oops, here I am gabbling on and forgetting all about this little one here." She stroked the little girl's head. "Time we should be getting you off to bed, isn't it, sweetheart?"

The girl looked up, but just continued silently sucking her candy bar.

Mrs. Hills looked at Chiang expectantly. He did nothing, so she glanced at his hand holding the money, and then looked back at him, arching her eyebrows.

Chiang dropped the money into her hand. "Thank you, Mrs. Hills."

"We'll catch up tomorrow, when Janie here's back with her mom." She smiled and bundled her granddaughter out of the store.

Chiang watched her every inch of the way.

He wasn't the only one.

The three guys at the back of the store watched too.

Then their gaze swung over to him.

His heart pounding, he hovered his hand over the shelf on which lay his gun. Three robberies in twelve months? There would not be a fourth.

Yes, he could hit the store's panic button and have the police there in minutes, but that wouldn't solve the problem of so many people thinking he was an easy target. As long as they thought that, they'd keep coming back. Well, those people were wrong – he was *not* an easy target.

He kept his hand near his gun. But he had to wait. Had to stay calm. They could be legitimate customers. What would happen to his business if word spread around the neighborhood he'd pulled a gun on three customers just because he didn't like the way three black guys looked?

The three men stalked down the aisle towards the front of the store.

He stared in the mirror. Were they carrying anything? Flour? Sugar? A .45? He couldn't see.

His mouth unbelievably dry, he swallowed hard.

He'd never seen them around here before. So there it was. Proof. Word had spread that he was an easy mark, so now thugs were coming from another neighborhood. Well, were they going to find how wrong they were.

He peered at them over the tops of the shelving units, but could only see their heads.

Hovering over the shelf with his gun, his hand trembled.

The three men sauntered around the corner of the aisle to face him. All tattoos and attitude.

With almost a rehearsed fluidity, each of them reached into their clothing.

Chiang reached onto his shelf.

In a heartbeat, four handguns shot out into the open.

Pushing up on his hind legs, Bashe thumped his huge front paws onto the counter. He fixed his dark eyes on the three men. He snarled.

Chiang aimed at the closet man, a guy with a goatee. "You no take my money again!"

Chiang saw his own gun shaking, so he gripped it in both hands. Still it shook.

"You leave," he continued. "Now! Or I fire. I do. I fire!"

He aimed at the next of the three, a man with a bird of prey tattooed on his chest, visible under his white undershirt. The man planted his foot against the bottom of the door to stop any other customers gaining entry. From outside, no one would see him for a full-length banner advertising an energy drink.

Goatee spoke out of the side of his mouth. "You said he didn't have no piece."

The tattooed guy said, "Yeah, according to Stretch. Don't be laying no blame on me."

Chiang saw them floundering. He shook his gun at them. "No money! I fire!" His thoughts so muddled, he struggled to get English sentences out.

Goatee smiled. He took his aim off Chiang and pointed his pistol at the ceiling. "Hey, we're all cool, man. Ain't no reason for nobody to bleed here tonight, so there ain't."

Goatee waved at his two friends to lower their weapons. They frowned, but they followed his lead and lowered their aims.

The leader smiled at Chiang. "See, everything's cool. Just lay your piece down and everyone will get home safe tonight."

Bashe barked. Chiang dared not even glance at him. But he was thankful he wasn't facing this ordeal alone.

Chiang still trained his trembling gun on them. Before one of them shot him, he could shoot one, maybe even two of them, but no way could he shoot all three. If he wanted to survive this, shooting wasn't an option.

If he played this right, everyone could walk away from this. Everyone. And once word spread about how he'd faced down three goons with guns, people would respect him and leave him alone. Yes, everyone could walk away.

Slowly, he let his gun drop.

The third man smiled. But it wasn't a smile of relief. A sneer of contempt slid across his chubby face.

Chiang whipped his gun back up. Aimed at Chubby Face. Something wasn't right here. He didn't trust these men.

Maybe he was wrong. Maybe fighting was an option. Bashe was so named because of his ravenous appetite – Bashe's mythical namesake was renowned for devouring whole elephants. If Chiang turned Bashe loose, he'd rip one of these men wide open. Could he shoot the other two before they shot him?

What should he do?

His heart hammered.

His breath came in huge gulps.

His gun felt slippery in his sweaty hands.

He couldn't think. Couldn't make sense of the situation. It didn't feel like this was happening. It was as if he were a bystander watching it happen to someone else. And being a bystander, he had no control over it.

What should he do?

"You leave!" He kept his gun up. Shaking. But up.

Goatee kept his smile aimed at Chiang. "Yeah, we'll leave. Just put your piece on the counter so we know no one ain't gonna be shooting no one else in the back."

Chiang's gaze whirled from man to man to man and then back again. What should he do?

He felt a bead of sweat running from his temple down the side of his face.

It was no good. He couldn't fight off all three. Not even with Bashe's help. At least one of them would get a shot off. And if anything happened to Bashe, he'd never forgive himself.

No, if he fired, he'd die. And Bashe too. It was that simple.

So what could he do?

He could press the panic button. Let the police deal with these goons.

But how long would it take for them to arrive?

And that would mean taking a hand off his gun. Fumbling for the button. Waiting and waiting and waiting.

No. He couldn't let the police 'save' him again and have people believe he was weak. He needed to prove he was strong. He needed to prove they had to respect him and never come back. He needed to deal with this alone.

His gaze once more wheeled from face to face to face, looking for a trace of humanity, of honesty, of regret.

Apart from the smiling one with the beard, they looked anxious. Maybe they didn't want to risk shooting any more than he did. Maybe it was all show. Maybe now they respected he was strong too.

So what was he going to do?

Well, their guns were all down. If he put his gun down, there was a good chance they'd leave. Maybe, finally, he'd done enough that word would spread and no one would ever come here looking for easy money ever again.

But could he trust them?

This was a standoff. The four of them couldn't stand like this all night, so mutual trust was the only option.

Chiang looked at the leader again, who smiled and waved for him to lower his gun.

Almost without thinking, Chiang lowered his gun a few inches.

Goatee's smiled broadened. "That's it. No one ain't gonna get shot tonight. But no one."

Bashe snarled.

"Bashe!" Chiang couldn't risk Bashe causing chaos. And he couldn't risk losing him. Not Bashe. Not now. Not when this would be over and everything would be okay in just a few seconds.

Chiang said, "I put down and you leave."

Goatee nodded. "You got it – you put down and we leave."

Chiang put his gun down.

And Goatee whipped his back up.

He fired.

Chiang slammed back against the cigarette display, a red rose of blood unfurling on his chest, and then crumpled forward.

Bashe leapt onto the counter, teeth bared, ready to rip into soft flesh.

Chubby Face fired.

Bashe yelped and fell to the linoleum in a bloody heap.

"Fucking yapping fucking dog." Chubby Face kissed the chunky gold ring on his trigger finger. "Ain't never let me down yet, have you, baby."

Slumped over the counter, blood oozing out over pale blue laminate, Chiang reached a trembling hand toward his dog. He voice croaked when he spoke. "Bashe."

Bashe struggled to look up at Chiang. The effort forced another yelp.

Goatee nudged Chubby Face. "Get your phone. People gotta see what happens when they fuck with me. But no faces!"

"You think I'm stupid?" With his free hand, Chubby Face snagged his phone from his pocket and filmed the unfolding action.

Goatee stalked toward Chiang, gesturing wildly. "Think you can point a gun at me, motherfucker? Who the fuck d'you think you is dealing with?"

Bashe snarled and tried to stand, tried to defend his master, his friend.

Chubby Face kicked Bashe.

The big dog yelped again.

"Fucking dogs. I hate fucking dogs." Momentarily, Chubby Face trained the camera on his gun and then swung his gun over to aim at Bashe.

Chubby Face said, "Bye bye, doggie."

He fired.

Blood splattered across the linoleum floor and up the side of the counter.

Chubby Face whooped. "Fucking cool, man!"

Chiang shouted, "Bashe!"

Goatee shoved the muzzle of his gun against Chiang's head. "Ain't no slanty-eyed fuck gonna point no piece at me!"

Gasping for breath between words, Chiang's voice rasped. "I ... curse ... you!"

Chiang spat.

Goatee's gun boomed.

Chapter 02

SHADOWS LURKING IN the darkness all about her, Tess Williams clomped along the asphalt path which led to the Lake and Bethesda Fountain, her usual athletic grace purposefully replaced by the clumsy meandering of someone seemingly worse for drink. As she neared them, some shadows formed recognizable shapes – trees, bushes, fountains, benches – while others were still so mired in gloom they remained forever shrouded in mystery.

She glanced at the flower beds on either side of the path – just a mass of dark blobs. And they looked so lovely by day.

The wind whistled through the trees and swirled some of the fallen brown leaves about her feet.

She clomped on. She'd chosen these shoes especially because of how loud they made her footfalls on hard surfaces, but alone in the dead of night, she was amazed at just how noisy they were.

Patches of dark cloud hanging motionless in the sky, Tess struggled to see the moon or any stars.

While the park was a glorious place to visit during daylight hours, it was a nightmare place to be at night. Why would any of those women have been here alone after sunset? Stupidity. Ignorance. Intoxication. Whatever the reason, you could almost say they'd got what they deserved. Almost.

A chill wind forced a shudder from her. Instead of zipping up her black leather jacket, as she would've liked, she unzipped it fully. She looked down at her cleavage bursting out of her little white top. Surely that was enticing enough.

She dawdled, dragging her feet so they scraped on the path to make even more noise and alert anyone in the vicinity to her presence. She threw in a little stumble and then giggled at having tripped – let anyone spying from the shadows think she was drunk and even more vulnerable than she'd at first appeared.

The wind rustled the leaves in the heavy trees lining the path.

Tess shivered. She didn't know if it was the cold or anxiousness. Probably a little of both.

At night, the park offered way too many places from behind which someone could attack the unwary. And they had. The proof was all over the media. But not just attacked them. No, this guy was twisted. Even by New York City standards. His story certainly wouldn't feature in one of those cozy police procedural shows the TV corporations loved to set in the city. No way. He was way too sick for primetime.

A big dark blob loomed on her left. Seven feet tall and pear shaped. Probably a bush. Probably. But even if it was, who lurked behind it: a mugger, a rapist, a psycho with a meat cleaver…?

The wind howled through the darkness.

And the shadowy blob moved.

Tess gasped, her heart pounding in her chest as if it were trying to break through her ribcage and run for safety.

Even though she was expecting to be attacked, wanting to be attacked, it didn't stop icy dread crawling up her spine.

She squinted, trying to see more clearly, trying to put form to that which was shrouded in blackness.

Was it a bush?

Really?

Or was it…?

It moved again as the wind once more howled down the tree-lined avenue.

Her pulse raced as she neared the blob. She breathed slowly to try to calm herself. She couldn't afford to let adrenaline flood her system and cloud her thinking.

If only she'd been able to wear her body armor. But while it would've protected her against attack, bulletproof vests weren't designed to emphasize cleavage.

And still she moved forward. Forward into what could be a nightmare far worse than the one she was picturing in her mind.

The dark blob loomed ever larger. Yes, it was a bush. But that didn't mean some whack-job didn't lurk behind it.

Her fists clenched.

Her body tensed.

As nonchalantly as she could, she strode alongside the bush.

Who was watching?

Who was ready to pounce?

Who dreamed of the nightmares they could inflict upon the innocent?

She took another step. And another. Walked past the bush.

All the while, she waited. Waited for someone to grab her. To hit her. To wrestle her to the ground and thrust their hand between her thighs.

She took another step.

And another.

And another.

But no one leapt from the shadows. No one.

Where the devil was he?

This was her fifth night of traipsing around these secluded paths on her own. If he didn't strike soon, she'd start getting paranoid – twenty-eight, nice boobs, great ass, pretty face... What the hell was wrong with her that a rapist wouldn't even attack her in the pitch black?

She took a left fork and meandered down a gentle incline. Ahead, with a gaping mouth of darkest black, a tunnel crawled under one of the main park walkways.

She sauntered straight for it.

Pretending to trip, she giggled at herself, as if she was drunk.

She strained to hear the faintest footstep, to see the slightest movement in the darkness.

Nothing.

Oh, come on. Talk about an easy target. Hell, what did this pervert want – an embroidered invitation on some soiled panties?

As she ambled deeper and deeper down towards the tunnel, the grass banking on either side walled her in, while above, the black trees clawed at the sky.

The tunnel's dark stone mouth swallowed her. On the uneven flagstones, her clomping footsteps made the tiniest of echoes.

She kicked her feet again. Sighed loudly. Ruffled her purse against her black leather jacket.

Surely, if someone was close by, they couldn't fail to know she was there.

Ahead, the shadows moved.

She gasped.

Her stomach fluttered.

Her heart rate rocketed.

Had something just ducked into the blackness at the far-right side of the tunnel?

Chapter 03

TESS PEERED INTO the blackness. Squinting, she tried to make out any kinds of shapes, identify what they were, and guess what it could be that had moved. But it was impossible – the darkness ate everything.

So had she seen movement?

Or was it her imagination playing tricks?

Spending too long in the gloom could do that. Your imagination conjured all manner of demons lurking in the darkest of corners, just waiting to attack. In reality, that demon was a branch, a stray dog, or a plastic bag blown on the wind.

Her heart pounding at the nightmare images flooding her mind, she controlled her reactions with her breathing technique: breathe in for four seconds, hold it for four, and breathe out for four seconds. She had to control the fight-or-flight response. If she didn't, adrenaline flooding her system would cloud her capacity for rational thought, push her into making panicked decisions, and she'd end up nothing but a battered lump of bloody flesh stuffed under the bushes.

Calmness was the only way to survive a potentially deadly situation. And calmness, no matter how skilled a fighter you were, took supreme discipline in situations like this. Only a fool wouldn't feel afraid here.

She neared the far side of the tunnel. She was sure she'd seen someone duck in behind that right-hand wall. Would she be lucky this time? Would some sick psycho yank her into the bushes and into some twisted sexual nightmare?

If only she could be so lucky.

Her inner voice screamed at her to run. To run and not stop until she reached her apartment and slammed the door shut.

She slowed her pace.

No matter what her inner voice screamed, this was not a time to run, but a time to dawdle. She needed to be a nice, slow-moving target.

As she strolled out of the tunnel, she fixed her gaze straight ahead, resisting the urge to glance to either side – she didn't want to spook her rapist, but to give him every opportunity to sneak up on her.

But again, no one pounced.

She huffed. What the hell did a girl have to do to get raped around here?

She marched up the path. Enough was enough. Her warm bed was beckoning.

Talk about a wild goose chase. Had even a single woman *ever* been accosted in this park, or was it all just media bull to keep the people hooked? Fear was a great tool to boost sales and rocket ratings. Spook people enough and they'd pretty much buy anything you wanted them to. Hell, the country had gone to war because of just such scare tactics, hadn't it?

At the top of the path, she took a left to head for the nearest park gate.

Someone leapt from behind a bush.

An arm locked her around the chest.

A hand jammed a knife to her throat.

She gasped. Froze.

Leaning right in to her ear, a man said, "Don't scream."

His voice was calm and unwavering. His grip strong and steady. This was obviously not his first time.

He said, "Do as I say and you won't get hurt."

Tess said, "You took the words right out of my mouth."

"What?"

She could literally hear him frowning with surprise and confusion. His momentary struggle to process such an inappropriate response broke his concentration.

With both hands, she ripped away his knife hand.

She slammed her head backwards into his face. A split second after she stamped on his foot.

With the shock of being attacked and dazed by being hit, he relaxed his grip on her.

Twisting around, she held the knife at bay with her left hand while the side of her right fist hammered into his groin.

Arcing her fist up, a backfist crunched into his nose.

Blood splattered across his cheeks.

He staggered back.

But she still held his knife hand. His right arm now outstretched, she punched right into the bicep muscle, ripping it away from the bone.

He cried out.

Dropped the knife.

She clawed his throat.

Sank her fingers into the flesh.

Latched around his windpipe.

His face contorted in pain and he made strange gargling noises.

As if ordering a slice of pizza in a café, Tess said, "Now, where were we? Oh, yeah – do as I say and you won't get hurt." She snickered. "Well, we both know I mean that as much as you did, don't we?"

Clawing his throat with one hand and locking his right wrist with her other to render him nonthreatening, she pushed him backwards and over to a wooden bench.

He clawed at his throat with his free hand.

"I can't—" Choking, his voice was guttural. "I can't... breathe."

Tess ignored him.

Having pushed him behind the seat, she head-butted him.

The rapist dazed and struggling to function, she shoved him and bent him over the bench. She bound his hands to the wooden laths with zip ties. But when she tried to bind his legs, he'd come around enough to kick out at her.

She crashed her elbow down into his right kidney.

He yelped.

She bound his right ankle to the bench's metal base and then heaved his left leg wide and bound it to the seat back, locking him spread-eagled.

"Pl... Please..." he gagged, his throat injured, "I—I haven't done... anything."

She sniggered. "Yeah, right."

Patting him down, she found his phone. She hit speakerphone, dialed and then held the phone to his face. "Tell them where you are."

It rang.

A chirpy woman said, "Becky Walters. WPPK News 24."

"Help!" His voice croaked. He swallowed hard. "Help me. Please. I'm in Central Park. Someone's trying to kill me. Help!"

She snatched the phone away and ended the call. "Good boy."

Now, before she saw justice done, she needed to know just how much justice needed to be inflicted.

Many psychos liked souvenirs to remember their triumphs. Knowing this sicko's particular penchant for having fun with women, a pair of pantyhose wouldn't cut it. With what he did to his victims, he'd need something visual. She checked the media stored on his phone.

Scrolling through the files, she found a video dated for the day and time of the first reported attack. She played it.

Naked from the waist down and bound over the back of a bench, a woman struggled. Shadows drenched everything else in blackness.

A gloved hand slapped her bare buttocks, her flesh deathly pale in the dismal light produced by his phone.

Through her tears, she gasped. "Please, don't hurt me. Please."

But other than his heavy breathing, he remained silent. He slipped his hand between her thighs.

She squirmed. "No... No, please!"

He ignored her. His breathing deepened, quickened.

The woman sobbed.

He pulled his hand away.

Her voice breaking as she cried, she said, "No... Don't... Please."

With a steady voice, he said. "This is glass. If you struggle, it will cut you."

The camera's viewpoint lowered. From being high enough to give a person's eye viewpoint, it followed a two-inch-wide glass tube down and between her thighs. The tiny light source revealed all.

He inserted the tube.

She shrieked.

Tess stopped the video. Talk about twisted. No wonder the media had christened him the Midnight

Gynecologist. Well, this sicko's reign of nightmares was over. Now, he was going to learn what it was like to be vulnerable, to be overpowered, to be a monster's plaything.

But how much pain and degradation would see justice served?

She snatched a hefty stick from the shrubbery, grabbed his glass tube from his pocket, and then whipped his trousers down.

How much justice? Well, that was the good thing about justice – you could never have too much.

Chapter 04

STANDING AT THE dark blue door to apartment 316, Tess took a deep breath. She didn't really know what she was doing here again. It couldn't possibly go anywhere, so what was the point? *And* he was a distraction to her work. But then, was that such a bad thing?

Her cello served no purpose in tracking down the city's scum, yet she enjoyed that distraction without feeling guilty. Yes, but her cello wouldn't slam her in Sing Sing if it learned of her secret life as would good old by-the-book Detective Josh Hardy.

She turned and trudged back towards the stairwell, gazing along the pastel blue hallway but seeing nothing because she was so lost in thought.

It would've been so easy for her to have avoided this situation. Eleven minutes after he'd surprised her by turning up on her doorstep that night, she'd been standing on the sidewalk with her cello, rucksack of clothes, backpack of work tools, and Fish in a plastic bag of water. Why hadn't she just kept on walking instead of going back inside?

Why?

Why? Because she wasn't stupid, that was why.

Going on that date with the guy had been the most logical course of action. Because Josh was Mac's new partner, she'd inevitably bump into him again, so she needed the guy on her side if she wanted to continue obtaining quality information from Mac.

Plus – and it was an enormous plus – he'd proven how resourceful he was by tracking her down. She didn't want someone so smart and so tenacious to be so curious about her that he started digging into her life.

Yes, going on the date had been the wisest choice.

Besides, like her cello, he was a pleasant distraction from her work.

But, if the relationship wasn't going anywhere – it couldn't go anywhere – why risk everything just because she enjoyed his company? After all, a rule wasn't a rule if you didn't follow it – no feelings, ever, for anyone. It was simple enough.

Yes, she was right – this couldn't go anywhere. Couldn't!

She slumped forward and rested her forehead against the wall.

Every time she'd dared to let herself get close to someone – every single time – it had all turned to shit. Su Lin, Elena Petrescu, Nat Ridley. Every goddamn single time.

If she dared to let Josh in, it would be no different. Oh, it would be the romance of the century for a while, but then he'd leave her because she didn't want kids, or he'd leave her because he found out about her other life, or he'd leave her because… because she wanted to follow her dream and live in China. Whatever the reason it would be the same result – he'd leave her.

Wait…

No. No, it wouldn't be that. She'd got that completely wrong. He wouldn't leave her. No, that would be way too easy. Whatever ruled her life, be it God or fate or goddamn aliens, it wouldn't let her get away so easily. It never had so it sure as hell wasn't going to start now. Hell no.

She and Josh would have a wonderful life – they'd move to the suburbs, get a dog, maybe – maybe – even talk about kids. Then, she'd be in a bad mood one day for no reason, they'd argue and he'd storm out and stay on a friend's couch. One night apart would turn into a week, then a week would turn into a month. To forget his problems, he'd throw himself into work, maybe even go undercover for a while to lose his life completely. Yeah, that would be it – undercover so he could create the perfect life he couldn't have with her.

But then she'd realize how much she missed him. She'd phone. Beg him to talk. Arrange a day when he'd come over. As nervous as a teenage girl who'd decided to give herself to her boyfriend for the first time, she'd sit at the table, gnawing her fingernails and watching the clock.

But he wouldn't show.

She'd sit staring at the food she'd prepared as it slowly got colder and colder. And she'd curse him more and more.

Then the doorbell would ring.

Without being able to help it, she'd dart to the door with a beaming smile, her eyes sparkling, her heart aching.

But it wouldn't be him.

No, it would be his partner Mac. And Mac's eyes would be sparkling, only not with joy, but with tears.

He'd tell her all about what they thought had happened after they'd found Josh's bullet-riddled body, but she wouldn't hear any of it. She'd be too busy reliving some picnic in Central Park, or the time they went to the Kandinsky exhibition at the Guggenheim, or that last bust-up they'd had which was all her fault. Yes, she'd relive every second of that last bust-up. Every damn second. Over and over and over.

No, this relationship was going nowhere. Nowhere but to a shitload of pain.

She pushed away from the wall.

"Oh, for Christ's sake!"

She enjoyed his company.

That was the problem – she simply enjoyed his company.

She'd banged so many guys she couldn't even count them, let alone remember names or faces, but this guy was different.

"Goddamn him."

Why couldn't he have been just like all the rest – out to use her for whatever he could get? Why the hell did she have to meet a goddamn decent guy?

She buried her face in both hands and groaned. What was she going to do?

Hell, after five nights of risking her life tramping around that dark, windy park, she'd caught that rapist. Didn't she deserve just a few moments of pleasure to take away the taste of all the blood and brutality she suffered every moment of every day of her life?

Damn straight, she did.

She marched back to the door. Before she could change her mind, she hammered her fist on apartment 316.

She cringed, instantly regretting it, but it was too late – she'd done it.

Chapter 05

SMILING, JOSH OPENED the door. "Whoa, I thought that was SWAT breaking in." He ushered her in. "Bad day?"

"Not especially. You?"

He gestured to his striped couch. "Same old same old. Got a case that's not looking good for a conviction, and that always pisses you off." He held up his glass of beer as a way of offering her a drink.

"Any wine?"

He smiled and turned toward the kitchen area. "I knew you'd ask so I grabbed a box on the way home."

Tess sighed. Great, if anything said quality it was wine that came in a carton. Her gaze drifted down to his buns. Still, it wasn't all bad. Especially considering her usual choice in men. Yep, Josh wasn't balding, overweight, married, or pushing retirement. Except that meant he was no use to her – he didn't have to be so grateful, or so fearful of any secrets getting out, that he'd share classified case information with her.

But that was work with those other guys and, while she hated to admit it to herself, this was... well, this was pleasure. And hadn't that been in short supply for... hell... forever?

Pleasure? She smiled. She'd almost forgotten what that felt like. Yeah, she'd stick with him for a few more weeks, then get out before things got messy.

Music playing low, she moseyed over to his music system and picked up an isolated CD case. It gave the group as *The Silver Mt. Zion Memorial Orchestra and Tra-La-La Band with Choir*. It was a ridiculous name, but she couldn't fault the off-the-wall music.

Josh appeared with a glass of red wine. He pointed to his rack of CDs. "You can change it, if you like."

"No, it's okay."

"It's no problem."

"No, it's interesting."

"'Interesting', huh?" He reached for another CD. "I'll change it."

She grabbed his arm. "No, really – it's refreshing to hear a rock band using a cello."

"Okay." He chinked her glass.

She sipped her wine and then smirked. "This isn't out of a box."

He grinned. "You think I didn't learn my lesson after last time?"

They meandered over to the couch. He splayed out at one end, and she kicked off her shoes and sat cross-legged in the middle, angled diagonally to look at him.

She had another sip of her wine. "So, what's this about the case that's going sour?"

"Oh, just some shooting we're getting nowhere with. No witnesses, no DNA, and the ballistics sent us on a wild goose chase today."

She nodded. Sounded interesting.

"Oh" – he pointed his beer at her – "but there is some good news. We caught the Midnight Gynecologist."

"Yeah?"

"Yeah. Early hours of this morning. Well, I say 'we' – some vigilante really went to town on him and then just left him there for us to find."

"I hope they beat the crap out of him?"

"Well..." Josh laughed. "Put it this way, he's going to be crapping oak splinters and glass shards from now until Christmas."

She winced. "Ouch."

"The strange thing is, only four women had come forward, but we found videos of another six on his phone. Sick bastard."

"So do you know who stopped him?"

He grimaced. "See, that's the weird thing – he swears it was a woman, but…" He shook his head. "I don't know. To overpower a guy and then do that to him, she'd not just have to be stronger than he is but sicker than he is too. I just can't see it."

That was good news. "No?"

227

"No, I'm hoping it's a male relative of one of the victims. I mean, it's bad enough having this sicko on the street, but some nutjob vigilante as well? Hell, that's all we need."

"Some people might say it's poetic justice." If she was going to continue spending time with the guy, she really needed his take on this.

"Nah-huh." Taking a swig of his beer, he shook his head again. "Do you know how often vigilantes get the wrong guy?"

"But she didn't. She got the right one."

"That's not the point. See, the law is there to protect the innocent. If someone attacks someone else just because they *suspect* them of a crime, where's it going to end? I tell you where – with a store clerk blowing a kid's head off just because he's black and has a suspicious bulge in his pocket."

"But say they have proof?"

"How are they going to have proof without conducting a legal investigation? The problem is, these people think it's the goddamn Wild West out there. They see being a vigilante as something romantic, as heroic, because that's what movies and comic books make it out to be. The truth is, they're just criminals who should be behind bars. Simple as that."

Yep, this relationship was destined for success! She sighed.

His shoulders slumped. He put a hand on her knee. "Oh, hey, look I'm sorry. I didn't mean to bring my work home, but sometimes, you know, it just gets to you."

She smiled. "It's okay." She gestured to the music system, the CD having finished.

He jumped up. "Sorry. Not being a very good host, am I?" He glanced over his rack of CDs. "Anything you fancy?"

"More of that Silver Zion Tra-La-La…?"

"Silver Mount Zion? *Really?*"

She grinned. "Really."

"Great. Later you've got to hear some *Godspeed you! Black Emperor*, you'll love it."

She ogled his butt as he bent over to look through his rack of CDs.

The relationship was going nowhere. Could never go anywhere. It would either end with her in prison or dead. Or Josh dead. Or both of them dead. Or both of them in prison.

Hell, what a fantastic selection of options.

The smart thing would be to simply walk out. Walk out right this second, not say a word, and never look back.

She dragged her eyes from Josh's butt to the door.

She should.

But would she?

Chapter 06

HER BREASTS BOUNCING as she rode him, Tess tensed her pelvic muscles – years of drilling combat kicks had given her muscles that other women thought were nothing but fantasy propagated by male pornography.

Josh groaned as she gripped him harder.

"Go on, baby," she said in a husky voice, "Give it to me. Go on."

He grabbed her breasts. Squeezed.

Thrust harder.

Deeper.

"That's it." She pushed down to meet him, grinding her hips. "Go on, baby."

He heaved up and tensed. In the morning light filtering through his bedroom's gold drapes, his face contorted as if someone had just kidney punched him. He groaned again, long and hard.

And then he relaxed.

She blew out a heavy breath. "Oh, yeah." She grinned down at him and ran her hands over his hairy chest. She liked a hairy chest. Maybe it was a primal thing, but she liked her men to be men – rough, earthy, strong. Smooth, manicured, coiffured? Oh, please! If she wanted that, she'd go lesbian again.

He pulled her down to him and kissed her.

Wrapping his arms around her, he squeezed her close.

She felt warm. Safe. Wanted.

Jesus, what was she – some sixteen-year-old who'd just had her cherry popped by the star quarterback? She pulled back and rolled away from him. No way could she afford to get comfortable with this. Time to get up. Leave.

He caught her around the waist and rolled her onto her back. "And where do you think you're going?"

He kissed her shoulder. Caressed one of her breasts.

She rubbed his arm. "Much as I'd like to do this all day, I've got work."

"It's barely seven. Stay a little longer."

"I wish I could."

He sighed, looked into her face, down her neck, and over her body. "You know, we've been doing this for going on three months now, but I still know, literally, nothing about you."

His hand caressed her neck and down her shoulder, over the scar she'd picked up in Shanghai, but which was now all but invisible thanks to cosmetic surgery. He stroked her chest and smoothed his fingertips lightly over the three faded circular scars on the underside of her left breast.

"There's not much to know."

He snickered. "Well, there must be something."

"Nope. I'm about as boring as they get."

"So we can screw, but not talk? I'm supposed to run your prints to get to know you, am I?"

He'd said it with a smirk, but that didn't stop her stomach clutching into a knot. After their first encounter, he'd used his detective skills to find her. What if he couldn't stand knowing nothing and really did investigate her?

Okay, he wouldn't find anything. And therein lay the problem – he'd find so little, that might raise even more questions which she wouldn't want to answer. Was it easier to just give him a little now? Give the dog a pat before it howled the house down?

He caressed the three small scars again, "Okay, so… these. How about telling me how you got them."

She hesitated. Let out a deep breath. Finally, she said, "Let's just say foster care isn't as fun as it sounds."

As soon as she said it, that knot tightened in her stomach.

Hell. Why hadn't she just kept her mouth shut? That was what happened when you started getting too comfortable around people – you got guilt-tripped into being sloppy.

Sharing information about herself was dangerous. It left her vulnerable. And not just her – whoever she shared it with.

His smirk faded to a look of sympathy, he said, "You were fostered?"

She said, "For a short time."

"Why? What happened?"

She smiled. "Hey, do I need to have my attorney present?" Banging this guy was one thing. Getting intimate? Hell, no. She'd given away too much already.

"Sorry. I'm interested, is all."

"It's okay. But I really have to get to work."

"But you're freelance? At least let me make you breakfast. You could even write here, if you like."

She pulled away and sat on the edge of the bed with her back to him. "Thanks, but I have a routine, and if I don't stick to it, I don't make my word count for the day, and if I don't make my word count, I don't make my rent. Besides, all my research is at home." It was a well-practiced lie that never failed.

He touched her arm. "Hey?"

She turned. "Hmm?"

He propped himself up on one elbow. "We're doing okay, aren't we?"

"Whoa, there cowboy. Not thinking of getting down on one knee, are you?"

He laughed. "Oh, yeah. What gave it away?"

"Well, there you go, then." She moved to stand up, but he pulled her back by her arm.

"Look, I, er... I was just wondering, er..." He looked down at the white cotton sheet.

She turned and fixed her stare on him. "What? If it's time to use the L word? No. If we should move in together? No. If this is going somewhere—"

He pushed his right index finger against her lips to shush her. "No, I didn't mean that. I..."

"What?"

He heaved a sigh. "Is it just... *me*?"

"Is it just *you* what?"

"Look, I can tell, you know."

She turned around to face him. "Tell what?"

He drew a long breath. "Okay... Er... Let's see... Hmmm, how can I put it? Er... Okay, when I was a kid, I loved baseball and, like all kids, I always wanted to be the hero, you know. I always wanted to be the one to hit it out of the park and score that winning home run."

"And?"

"And..." Another deep breath. "And I think you're lobbing easy pitches so I always hit a home run, but, occasionally, it'd be nice if I could lob it for you so you could hit a home run too."

"Ohhh." She nodded. "You're thinking my batting average isn't what it should be compared to yours."

"No, but... well, kind of."

"Relax. It's not you." She leaned down and kissed him. "Maybe I just need a little time, you know, to get used to the feel of a new bat." She winked and ran a hand over his crotch.

He was right: she didn't enjoy sex. Not surprising, considering her childhood.

Childhood? That was a joke.

Once she'd been caught doing Mikey Drummond in the equipment closet at the back of the biology classroom. She'd admitted it was only because he'd promised to complete her physics homework for a month. One of the quacks she'd been sent to – that balding, beady-eyed Iqbal – had said she'd have problems establishing healthy relationships if she didn't adopt a different attitude to her body and to sex.

So he had letters after his name and a certificate hanging on his wall while she didn't, that didn't mean his diagnosis was correct.

She hated physics; she didn't intend to be an engineer; she had a pussy. Surely the elegance of her solution deserved merit, not condemnation.

But, oh no. Her attitude was all wrong. *Her* attitude. *Hers!* If Iqbal had suffered her childhood, Tess would be amazed if the good doctor ever got wood without bursting into tears.

Her attitude? Her attitude was just fine.

Yes, all it took was a little disconnection and she had no problem at all with sex. Though it was hard to understand people's fascination with it. Barring time in China, she'd never gotten much out of it. Seemed a big waste of a lot of effort. Oh, she enjoyed what it could get her, just not what it actually did for her. Sex merely fulfilled a purpose – it was an ideal commodity to trade.

But Josh? To date, no one had ever complained she was pleasing them too much. Josh was a first. Weird, but in a warm way. In the future, she'd have to try harder to fake genuine pleasure. It couldn't be that difficult – women all over the country got away with it every night.

She stared into his eyes. "Don't worry. We're good."

He smiled. "I just needed to check I wasn't doing anything wrong, you know."

She caressed his cheek. "That's sweet." She pushed off the bed.

He frowned. "Sweet? I'm *sweet?* You do know I carry a gun for a living?"

Pulling on her shirt, she said, "And I'm sure it's a damn big one."

"It is."

She laughed.

He sat up. *"It is!"*

"So who you going to be pointing it at today?" She needed to deflect the conversation away from her. The job he loved was the ideal patsy.

"Hopefully some lowlife scum in Harlem."

Her jeans in a heap on the floor, she picked them up and shook them. "That shooting you mentioned last night?"

"Yeah. A convenience store owner. And his dog."

She stopped. Looked at him. "They shot him *and* his dog?"

"And put it on YouTube to show the world what big men they are."

She sat back down on the bed. "So why can't you catch them if you've got video?"

"No faces." He shrugged. "Just a few voices. We've got a partial plate for the vehicle they *might* have driven away in, but nothing that's gonna give us an ID."

She nodded and stared away into space.

He tugged on her arm. "You sure you can't come back to bed? Just for an hour?"

"They shot his dog?"

"Twice. A big German Shepherd. Looked a magnificent animal too. Must've tried to protect its master." He caressed her shoulder. "You're sure you don't want any breakfast?"

She shook her head. "What kind of sick fuck shoots a dog?"

She was going to find out. And then those responsible were going to find out what a huge mistake it was they'd made.

The police couldn't find them. But the police had neither her resources, nor her resourcefulness. Plus they were hamstrung by having to follow the letter of the law.

But a convenience store owner? She felt her heart start to pound as images flashed through her mind.

Images she'd buried. Images she constantly prayed to never ee again… but always did.

Josh leaned over. He stroked her face. "You okay?"

She pulled away. "Sorry, I have to go. Now."

She *had* to go. She had demons of the past to tame so she could slay the demons of the present.

Chapter 07

CROSS-LEGGED ON THE ground, her back against her lazy willow tree, Tess gazed at the world.

Two ducks floated by on the lake before her. No sound. No movement. Just effortlessly gliding through a still world. She watched them, until a bush obscured them from her view. That was what she wanted – to effortlessly glide through a still world. Here, during her meditation, that's what she found, but the moment she left the haven of her park…

She sighed. How she wished her mind could be still. Not just in this place, but everywhere, all of the time. Maybe then, she'd find peace. Maybe then, she'd find a life.

On a rock out on the lake, two turtles lay basking in the sun. In the water, a third struggled to gain enough purchase on the slippery stone to pull itself up. It kept sliding back in, no matter how many times it tried to get out of the cold water and into the warm sun. It tried again and again. And failed again and again.

Drawing a slow, deep breath, Tess stretched both arms way over her head. Stillness and a life was a nice dream, but reality beckoned.

She pulled her phone from the black backpack she'd packed during a brief trip home, and then she photographed her eye. Iris recognition unlocking her phone's hidden features, she placed a call.

"Yo, Tess."

"Morning, Bomb. There's, uh…" She'd practiced this conversation in her head, but each time it had gone just the way she hadn't wanted it to go.

"Yeah…?"

She tried again. "There's a partial plate I need and, um…" She swallowed hard. "And a video online I need you to trace. It's been deleted, but that's not a problem, right?"

"Was it uploaded to a real account that's used regularly or a dummy opened just for this one video?"

"A dummy." Using the account only to upload one video meant there was less than usual for Bomb to trace. That made the job more difficult but, she hoped, not impossible.

"If it's a recent deletion, it's probably just been hidden from public view waiting to be reviewed, so it'll still be on the server. If not, it'll probably be on a server somewhere – if it was popular, someone will have uploaded it somewhere else claiming it's theirs. What is it?"

"It's, er…" He wouldn't like it no matter how she said it, so it was best to just get it out there. "It's of a shooting at a convenience store two nights ago. The Web says it was—"

"Kim Chiang and his dog, Best Bargains, Harlem. Yeah, what about it?"

"I'm taking this one, Bomb."

He said nothing.

On the lake, the little turtle tried yet again to clamber out of the cold water. It heaved with its forelegs. Pushed with its hind legs. Tess willed it to succeed. She could see its body shaking with the effort. It almost cleared the water. Just one tiny bit more and—

It fell. Sank into the cold, dark depths.

Bomb had still said nothing.

Tess waited.

And waited.

Until she could wait no longer. "I need to take this one, Bomb."

"No, you don't, Tess."

She drew a deep breath. He was only trying to look out for her. Only trying to pay her back. But he was wrong. She was right. So she was finding those killers. End of story.

She said, "You know why I have to do this."

"And that's why we should walk away from it."

"Bomb, I need you with me on this one."

He sighed. "Last night in the Bronx, a guy was stabbed over a parking space outside a bar; three nights ago, a woman was shot in a gang dispute in Brooklyn; four nights back, two black kids shot another over God only knows what... Tess, it's not like we're stuck for

241

choice – there's a homicide in this town every single day of the year, so why in the name of God do we have to go after this one?"

"Simple: the police can't; I can."

Out on the lake, the little turtle once more lost its grip and splashed back into the cold water. Why didn't it swim away? Find an easier rock? Hunt fish?

"Tess, we both know how hard you searched last time. And we both know how that almost killed you. But what did you get at the end of it? Squat. *Absolutely squat.* You were chasing ghosts. Do you really want to dredge all that up again?"

This time, it was Tess who remained silent. He was right. She'd spent the best part of a year either beating the hell out of every guy she met, or screwing their brains out to get information. In the end, she'd sunk so far into the human sludge in the darkest part of the city, she'd thought she'd never claw her way back out. Somehow she had. But there was no way she could do it again.

Finally, she said. "There's one big difference – last time, I didn't have you."

"Oh, shit!"

After a moment, he sighed. "Okay. But one condition – I see things getting too crazy, I don't care who's seen what, said what, or done what, if I give the word, you're out of there. Deal?"

She'd clawed her way out of the human sewer once, but she didn't have the strength to do that again.

If she got sucked in too deep this time, it was game over.

Bomb knew that.

Just like he knew all her secrets so he could help her protect them. He knew about her shell accounts in the Caribbean; about her collection of passports and gun permits; about all three of her safe houses. As easily as phoning for a pizza, he could end her life. That's why she trusted him with it. So could she trust him now?

"Deal," she said.

"I've got a few hacks in place that could give us a lead, plus I can run a search – see if the video is still live anywhere else. There's bound to be a digital footprint somewhere we can trace to get a source."

"Thanks, Bomb."

"Don't thank me yet, because I mean it – if I think everything's going south, we're out of there. Is that straight?"

She didn't like to commit to anything she wasn't positive she could see through. More importantly, she didn't like the idea of lying to Bomb. But sometimes, life didn't play fair, so she couldn't either.

She stared at the turtle climbing up the rock yet again. And yet again, it fell.

Tess said, "Just say the word."

Chapter 08

IN JAPAN, A convenience store was called a konbini. According to Ayumi, Tess's jiu jitsu instructor in Okayama, when the Japanese imported the shopping concept from the States, 'convenience store' was such a tongue twister for them, they modified the name to be less of a mouthful.

Tess had had no problem visiting konbinis – Lawson, 7-Eleven, Family Mart. No problem at all. Yet just looking at Best Bargains of Harlem – here in her own backyard – her heart raced, sickness rose from her stomach, and her breathing came sharp and shallow.

Standing on the opposite side of the street from the store, a light drizzle dampening a warm day, Tess stared at Best Bargains. She stared at its bright red sign which ran the length of the store's frontage and proclaimed 'Best Bargains' in giant, black-bordered yellow letters. She stared at the security-grille-protected windows, behind which lay all manner of treasures such as tea, bread, even beer. And she stared at the door, the

244

store interior secreted behind a promotional banner for an energy drink.

The door.

She stared at the door the most.

She knew she didn't have to open it. Knew she didn't have to walk through it. Knew she didn't have to close it behind her and on her life up to that very moment.

There were eight million people in New York City. Eight million. By necessity, it was majority rule. Those with the loudest voices, with the strongest wills, with the greatest power, created society's rules to, supposedly, serve the majority – the average joe.

But only up to a point.

If old Joe became too much of a problem, he moved from being part of the majority to being part of a minority – no longer part of the herd, no longer someone for whom the system worked, no longer someone who mattered. Just one person among eight million others had no voice to do anything about their predicament. They were totally invisible.

With regard to the shooting, the police had no leads, no evidence, no witnesses. For whomever Kim Chiang had left behind, there would be no justice. Not unless Tess walked through that door.

Yes, she knew she didn't have to open that door. But she knew she was going to.

Tess knew what it was like to have no justice. Because she knew what it was like to be on the other side of that door. She knew what it was like for the police to say they were sorry, but that there was nothing more they could do. Knew what it felt like to be abandoned, as if you were invisible. Knew what it felt like to look out at the world and see no color, no joy, no kindness, only darkness and pain and savagery.

The person on the other side of that door was suffering, feeling so many horrendous emotions – disillusionment, confusion, loneliness, desperation. These emotions sapped away their life just as surely as the bullet that had ripped Chiang's life away from him. The person was invisible. Everyone else just walked on by, getting on with their own lives as if that person wasn't even there. That was what would be happening behind that door right that second. Just as it had happened in the past. Just as it would happen again in the future.

For most people, being invisible would be a gigantic problem. For Tess, it was an absolute godsend. If she wasn't invisible to as many people as possible, she'd never be able to do what she did. But Kim Chiang? Did he want to be invisible? Did his family want him to be?

Tess wouldn't let him be invisible. Tess was only one person among eight million, but she had a voice. And, man, could she scream.

Her heart hammering, she marched into the street.

Oh God, she was really doing this.

Again.

Images swirled about her mind, whirling faster and faster as her heart pounded harder and harder. She used her four-second breathing exercise to try to control her physiology, but thoughts of blood and guns and pain engulfed her.

Tess marching through the slow-moving traffic, a red Buick blared its horn at her.

She didn't even look.

She had one goal. One hurdle. One tiny step. After which, no matter how hard she tried, like a row of toppling dominoes, her life would be set on a dangerous path which had only one inevitable conclusion – everything was going to come crashing down.

The one thing fixed in her sight was that door.

She crossed the sidewalk to it.

Reached for the handle.

Ripped open the door.

Marched inside.

And the first domino fell.

Chapter 09

TESS SLAMMED THE store's door shut behind her. Slammed it shut on the safe life she'd spent years building around her and, more importantly, within her.

She didn't even look at the clerk at the cash register that her peripheral vision told her was on her left – she wasn't ready for that yet. No, that she'd build up to, once her heart slowed, and the images spinning through her mind settled enough to allow clear thought.

She strolled straight down the middle one of the three aisles, the one directly in front of the entrance. It was a store layout she knew so very well. She glanced at the shelves as she sauntered by: microwaveable meals, cereals, cookies. Slowing her breathing and forcing herself to study the product labels, she gradually calmed her mind.

At the end of the aisle, she didn't look left. She couldn't look left. Not yet.

Turning right, she trailed her hand inside a chest freezer of frozen pizzas, letting the cold air bathe her skin – something she'd done on particularly hot days in

Okayama, where every opportunity to cool down had demanded to be exploited.

As she passed beneath it, her peripheral vision caught a convex mirror up on the wall in the corner of the store. There'd be a reflection of the register in that. Still not ready to face that yet, she lowered her gaze to study the shelves.

Strolling past shelves of baking ingredients and cleaning supplies, her heart started to hammer again. Her palms felt clammy, so she wiped them on her black jeans. She couldn't put this off any longer. She needed to do this, so she did. Her fists clenched as she looked over the top of the shelving unit at the register.

She froze.

And stared.

On the spare space beside the register, all around the floor at the base of the counter, and completely engulfing the cigarette display behind the young female clerk… were flowers. Beautiful, beautiful flowers. From a handful of just five or six blooms, to flowing bouquets that must have cost tens of dollars, that whole corner of the store was an explosion of petals.

Tess stared. Was that what it had been like in her store? Was that what it had been like after they'd taken away the body and washed away the blood? Was that what it had been like after her life had been ripped inside out?

Shuffling to the front of the store, Tess gawped at the rainbow of blooms. They hadn't let her see her store afterward. They'd said she was too young. Said it would be too distressing. Said it was for her own good.

She crawled around the end of the aisle, across the front of the store, and up the aisle nearest the register. Her gaze remained glued to the shelves of snacks and soft drinks and never – never – looked further along the aisle, especially not toward the far-left corner at the back of the store.

Midway along, she stopped and looked back.

From there, Tess had a clear view of the area behind the counter and of the clerk with straight jet-black hair flowing right down to her waist. Tess looked at the floor where the clerk stood. In her grandpa's store, that was where he'd fallen. That was the last place she'd seen him. That was the first place she'd seen so much blood. So, so much blood.

She'd held him. Held him so tight. And she'd pressed on the holes in his chest, in his stomach. So, so many holes. Pressed just like they'd taught everyone to do with lacerations in that first aid class in fifth grade at *Jefferson Elementary*.

She'd pressed and pressed and pressed.

But there was so much blood. So, so much blood.

She'd been so caked in blood that, when it had dried, a nurse had had to cut her out of her clothes – that pretty white dress with the thin pink stripes that everyone had said made her look so grown up. Grown up? Hell, she grew up that day.

So, so much blood.

The hairs prickled on the back of her neck at the thought of turning around, at the thought of looking at the end of the first aisle and the far-left corner of the store. Her stomach churned. She thought of her willow tree, of the tranquil lake, of the ducks effortlessly gliding through a still world…

She turned.

Looked to the end of the aisle.

Froze.

In her grandpa's store, that was where she'd fallen.

Her legs trembling, she grabbed the top shelf on her right where canned meat lay cold and silent.

She dropped her head and closed her eyes. She drew a slow breath for four seconds, held it for four, and then exhaled for four.

Slowly, she turned back toward the register and took another long, easy breath.

Her gaze crept up the flowers.

So they hadn't let her see the tributes to her grandpa for her own good?

For her own fucking good?

This would have been for her own good – to see how well-loved her grandpa had been.

This would have helped to ease the trauma of an eleven-year-old girl.

This would have proven there was still goodness left in the world, not only brutality and hatred.

Why didn't they let her have this, have *her* moment? If she could've seen this… everything could have been so different. Maybe… If only they'd—

"Are you okay?"

Tess snapped back to the moment.

The store clerk stood before her. About Tess's age, an East Asian woman with red puffy eyes looked into Tess's face, the way a person looked into the eyes of a sick animal – wondering how much the poor thing was suffering, yet unsure of just how much it truly comprehended.

Tess didn't know how long she'd been rooted to the spot, staring at the flowers.

She looked at the clerk. "Sorry." She strained a smile. "Just drifted away there for a moment."

The clerk's eyes became teary. "Yes, I… I still can't believe this is really happening." She gestured to the flowers. "But everyone's being so kind and thoughtful. It helps – a little – knowing he was so loved. Did you know my grandfather well?"

"No, it's not—" She looked at the clerk. She knew exactly what this woman was feeling. Exactly. "Yes… Yes, I did."

The clerk smiled. "No hurry. You just leave when you're good and ready." She ambled back to the register.

Tess drew a long slow breath. Steadied her body. Steadied her mind. The time for mourning was over. Now was the time for action.

She strode to the register.

Leaning on the counter with both hands, the clerk smiled.

Tess clasped the clerk's left hand with her right. "Whoever did this will pay."

The clerk shrugged. "I wish I could be so sure, but..." Her chin trembled.

Tess stared deeply into the clerk's eyes and squeezed her hand. "They'll pay. Believe me."

As if struggling to hold back her tears, the clerk gasped a broken breath.

Tess smiled. "You take care."

She left.

The Chiangs deserved payback.

Tess would take it for them.

In blood.

Or die trying.

Chapter 10

BECOMING JUST ANOTHER face in the herd, Tess strode along Harlem's store-lined 125th Street. Way ahead, a massive sign with red vertical lettering said 'Apollo'. One of the biggest landmarks in the area, the Apollo Theater was where many black artists had made their name, including Billie Holiday, Diana Ross, and Mariah Carey.

Tess marched past a beat-up boombox sitting on the curb and pumping out R & B, beside which a fat black guy struggled to protect his stock of bootleg CDs from the rain with a ten-foot sheet of plastic. He struggled with the wind making the sheet flap, but finally managed to tuck it over his assortment of boxes. He then lurched back to his fold-up wooden stool.

Tess rubbed her chin as she scoured the street. She'd already decided what she was going to do, she just needed a place from which to start and for that, she needed a key. She studied Harlem's shoppers, hoping to spot the key to that starting point.

Struggling to put her red spotted umbrella up, a woman in black stilettos strolled towards her.

No, not the key.

A skinny black woman with a gold ring through her left nostril sidled over to walk alongside Tess.

The woman said, "Want your hair braided, honey? I'll make you beautiful."

Tess snubbed her.

The woman didn't take the hint. "I'll give you my best price. Cheapest on the drag."

Walking on, Tess didn't even look at the woman. She didn't like being rude toward strangers, but engaging a hawker, even if it was to refuse their offer, only encouraged them to try harder.

The woman lost interest and went back to leaning against the wall of an electronics store.

Tess actually liked having her hair braided. It didn't only look cool, but she found the tactile sensation of the process relaxing. Unfortunately, she could rarely let her hair grow long enough to warrant such styles. Long hair could too easily be grabbed in a fight – one yank and your balance went, and before you knew it, you were on the ground getting stomped on.

She'd love to have hair right down her back like Chiang's granddaughter, but she routinely had it cut so it barely reached her shoulders. Even that was too long. But combat practicality had to be off-set against desirability. In order to manipulate men, she had to look the part, and today's porn stars and supermodels would look very different if crew cuts were a turn-on. Luckily for her, the hair could stay.

A balding man paced by Tess, his newspaper over his head to shield him from the rain, despite the drizzle having all but stopped.

No, he wasn't the key to her starting point, either.

Two teenage girls ambled toward her, chatting and smiling.

There. The key.

Kim Chiang's granddaughter didn't think his killers would be found. As most people did, she had placed her belief in the authorities – she'd staunchly believed that, in a time of crisis, they would not just offer her help, but give her answers, deliver her justice.

And then came the day when she actually needed those in whom she'd placed all her faith.

Talk about a wakeup call.

She'd found herself staring into emptiness – they couldn't offer her hope, couldn't offer her answers, couldn't offer her justice. They could offer her nothing. The police *might* catch her grandfather's killers; the courts *might* sentence them to a lengthy prison term; the correctional system *might* see they served out the full term of their sentences and not receive early parole.

Or everything *might* all go to hell.

Tess knew which she was laying her money on.

In a country of 316 million people, Chiang's granddaughter was, just like Chiang himself, just 0.0000003% of the population – just one tiny, insignificant statistic that thought she was a person, and a person who mattered, at that. She had no power, no influence, no wealth. If the police caught the killers, great. If they didn't, would the entire city grind to a halt? Or would it go on as normal as if nothing had ever happened?

The Chiangs were invisible.

Luckily, Tess was invisible too. Most people didn't like being invisible. Hence the runaway success of 'look at me!' social media. For Tess, however, invisibility was a godsend. Being invisible allowed her to reap justice in the darkest corners of the world and yet saunter away leaving barely a trace.

She smiled at the two teenage girls ambling toward her. "Excuse me."

They looked at her expectantly.

"Is there a skate park around here, please? You know, skateboards, BMX, things like that?"

The girl on the left, a stud through her left eyebrow, pointed back the way they'd come. "Yeah, take that left, then right, then, um... second left?"

She looked at her friend, who nodded.

"How far altogether?"

The girl shrugged. "Five, ten minutes maybe."

Tess saw a fast food joint sitting on the corner of an alley. "Okay, so left at Dylan's Diner, then right, then second left. Yeah?"

"Uh huh."

The other girl said, "You can't miss it."

"Thanks."

Tess quickened her pace.

A skateboard park was an ideal situation: lots of kids; zero adult supervision. It was an excellent environment for predators to spot easy prey and then stalk them to a more isolated location where they could launch an ambush. That's what she was going to do, but with a unique twist – the predators would be her prey.

Chapter 11

A **TEXT ARRIVED** from Bomb as Tess meandered down the sidewalk. It provided only a tiny clue, but a clue all the same: the partial license plate for the car the killers were suspected of having used. Tess made a note of it in her little notebook. She found the act of physically writing something down helped her not only to remember it more easily, but to process it better. As if she wasn't only making marks on paper, but engraving details in her mind. In the past, even the tiniest of facts had sparked something that had led to a breakthrough, so she regularly embraced the tactic.

As she passed Dylan's Diner, she glanced in.

A balding guy stared out at her as he chomped on his burger. A glob of ketchup squished out and splattered on the pale blue Formica tabletop, but he either didn't notice or didn't care, so he just went on munching.

After the diner, Tess hung a right. A few parked cars were dotted along the length of an alley, while fire escapes climbed up the graffiti-strewn buildings like lizards zigzagging up a wall.

Quite a distance ahead of Tess, a scrawny guy with shaggy hair shuffled along in the same direction in which she was going. He stopped at a Ford pickup, raised a tablet, and pointed it at the truck as if taking a photograph, then he looked down at the device and appeared to enter details.

As she watched, the guy shuffled toward the next vehicle. From his shaggy jet-black hair and lean build, he looked young, and yet he moved as if he had lead weights sewn into his clothing, so every movement was awkward and labored.

Trudging on, he glanced back. He was late teens, early twenties, but had a dusky complexion, suggesting he was Asian, maybe Thai. He then continued shuffling toward the next stationary car.

There didn't appear to be any parking restrictions in the area, and she couldn't see a single No Parking sign hanging anywhere, so the man's behavior was a little strange. Especially as he wasn't wearing a security guard uniform or anything like that, but a mismatched wardrobe of purple slacks, not jeans or sweats, and a lime cardigan with a blue shirt, not a T-shirt or hoodie. If the colors had harmonized, he would have looked quite smart. Old-fashioned, yes, but presentable enough. However, as it was, he looked like a color-blind geriatric. Talk about an oddball. But crazy wasn't illegal unless it was hurting someone.

Crazy Dude stopped at a Toyota and took a photo of it. Again, he peered down at his tablet as if entering information, then shambled on.

An old yellow Chevrolet Camaro was parked halfway along the alley. Even at the distance she was from it, Tess could see the battered vehicle had been driven into the ground – the fender was lopsided, and where the left-hand headlight should have been was just a gaping black hole.

Crazy Dude stopped right in front of it, lifted his tablet, and took a photograph.

There was movement inside the car.

"Oh, crap," said Tess.

She didn't have time for this when she was on a job. But… like she'd ever been able to just sail on by when someone was in need. And unless she was seriously mistaken, Crazy Dude was going to be in desperate need about three seconds from now.

She quickened her pace. And her heart started pounding at the prospect of who was about to climb out of that car. Of course, there was a chance it would turn out to be a perfectly innocent and amicable encounter, but since when did Life ever give her a break like that?

Chapter 12

THE DRIVER'S DOOR of the Camaro creaked as it swung open while Crazy Dude was still standing and peering down at his device.

A tall black man lurched out, doing up the fly of his trousers. His glare drilled into Crazy Dude and he shouted, even though the scrawny man was only a few feet in front of his car.

"What the shit, motherfucker? Was you just videoing us?"

Crazy Dude didn't even look up. It was as if he didn't appreciate that the question had been posed at him.

The lack of response seemed to incense the driver. Camaro Guy marched over, chest puffed out and arms splayed in an aggressive gesture to make himself look bigger than he was.

"Hey, was you peeping on me getting blown, you freaking fuck?" said the driver. "Or was you angling to jack my ride?"

Finally, Crazy Dude reacted. But instead of running, or cursing, or screaming, or preparing to fight like any normal person, he simply cowered and froze. With his head down and turned aside, he seemed to look at Camaro Guy from under his brow through his bangs.

Camaro Guy loomed over the slender Asian man and glared down at him.

"Hey!" He jabbed Crazy Dude in the chest. "Don't you be disrespecting me, fucker." He jabbed again. "Look at me when I'm talking."

The little man hunched over all the more, as if believing that making himself smaller would save him. He clutched his tablet to his chest.

Camaro Guy shoved him on the shoulder. "You got a death wish, motherfucker? Because I'll slap you up like your daddy never did. You just see if I don't."

Still the man didn't raise his face, as if he was trying to hide behind his dangling bangs, believing they somehow shielded him.

"Look at me!" Camaro Guy shoved him harder.

Crazy Dude staggered back. But he still didn't raise his gaze. Hunched up, he clutched his tablet to his chest as if it was something precious.

"You like messing with folk, huh? That your game?" Camaro Guy snatched the tablet away. "You ain't the only one as can play games."

"Gil's!" Crazy Dude cried out like a child and clumsily reached for his device with both hands.

Camaro Guy punched him in the face. Crazy Dude spun away and sprawled into the dirt.

Crazy Dude cowered on the ground, hiding behind his raised arms, obviously fearing a beating.

Again, Crazy Dude shouted, "Gil's!"

"What the…?" Camaro Guy frowned, then slapped his forehead. "Oh, you're shitting me – you're a fucking retard, ain't you? Jesus, they should keep freaks like you in a goddamn cage."

"Hey," Tess shouted as she approached the scene. "Leave him alone and give him back his stuff."

"This retard with you? Get his ass out of here, or I'll report you for letting him off his goddamn leash."

Camaro Guy kicked Crazy Dude in the side, and he cried out in pain. "Go on, get, you freak!"

"I said leave him." Tess twisted and shot her right leg out sideways.

Her foot slammed into Camaro Guy's ribs.

The driver reeled away and crashed onto the hood of his car.

Tess glanced at the man on the ground. She was half right about his ethnicity - it looked like one of his parents was Asian while the other was probably Caucasian.

"Don't panic," she said, "you're safe now."

Crazy Dude had a little blood on his lip, but it looked like a very minor injury. However, the moment she looked him in the face, he turned away as if frightened of making eye contact. He yelped and hid behind his arms all the more.

Did he think she was going to attack him too?

The little oddball had just gotten a whole lot odder. He wasn't reacting the way a normal victim did, and he didn't seem to understand that she wasn't a threat but was trying to help. Something was off here, but what? Was he disabled in some way?

However, Crazy Dude wasn't her immediate priority.

She looked back at the car and its driver, who was lurching up off his hood. He hammered his fist into the metal and cursed.

Tess's heart rate rocketed. She knew this wouldn't be the end of it – a woman and a disabled person were easy targets for this kind of thug. She prepared herself for the onslaught that would inevitably come by slowing her breathing, which would help her to control her body's physiology. She needed to remain calm and refuse to let fear take hold if she was to survive a violent encounter without injury. Her breathing technique would allow that.

The Camaro's passenger door clunked opened. A black woman heaved herself out, a bulbous belly hanging from her like she was shoplifting pumpkins.

"You gonna stand for that, Tyrone?" Fat Girl said. "Slap the white off that bitch's goddamn ass."

"I ain't standing for nothing."

Tyrone glowered at Tess. "You're gonna regret letting your retard stick his nose in my business. Fuck if you ain't."

He hurled the tablet against the graffiti-strewn brick wall of the nearest building.

Tess didn't flinch but stared him down.

She said, "Walk away."

She hadn't been expecting a combat situation, so she didn't have on any of her body armor, not even her armored gloves. That meant that when things escalated, which experience told her they were about to, she'd have to choose her strikes wisely to avoid damaging her hands. People didn't appreciate just how delicate the bones of the hand were – even a skilled fighter, with the most immaculate of punches, could easily lose a fight purely because he broke one of his knuckles on his opponent's skull, thus reducing him to fighting one-handed.

As her adrenaline surged like a gas pump with the valve stuck open, Tess forced herself to breathe slowly, keeping her fight-or-flight response under control.

Nonchalantly, she angled her body to around forty-five degrees, creating a narrower target, and raised her rear hand to chest height, while the one closest to Camaro Guy hung by her hip. To the average Joe, she looked to be standing quite casually, but to a trained fighter, she was a coiled snake.

"Walk away?" Camaro Guy sneered. "Seriously?" He laughed. "Oh, I'm gonna walk alright. You're gonna be wiping Nike off your goddamn ass till Christmas."

"Walk away now," said Tess. "Or crawl away later. Your choice."

Tyrone snickered and turned to Fat Girl. "Get the balls on this bitch!"

He looked at Tess. "You wanna play, little girl, then let's play."

He snatched something from the back pocket of his jeans and flicked out his hand. A blade glinted in the sunlight.

Worrying about breaking the bones in her hands had suddenly taken a backseat. Way, way back.

Her heart pounding, Tess bent her knees, tucked her chin in, and raised both her fists to chest height, adopting a fighting stance similar to that of a boxer.

She studied Tyrone as he leered at her, swishing the knife threateningly through the air so the light flashed off it. He held it not like an ice pick, but so the blade extended from between his thumb and forefinger. His choice of grip gave her an idea of from which angles a slash or a stab would come.

He sneered. "So, who's gonna crawl away now, bitch?"

A seasoned fighter would have hidden the blade until the last second, knowing a surprise attack would be much more devastating. Added to that, Tyrone's lolloping gate and exaggerated hand movements were not those of a trained fighter preparing for combat but those an imbecile getting a kick out of the fear knives instilled.

However, any confrontation with a blade, even if the knife was in the hands of a total incompetent, could easily become lethal if not approached with the deadliest of respect.

Tess forced herself to breathe slowly, thus reducing her oxygen intake, which in turn would reduce her fight-or-flight response. She needed to stay calm if she was to think clearly enough to take on some knife-wielding goon.

Tyrone feigned lunging at her and flashed the blade out.

Tess didn't move. Her years of combat experience told her he was at the wrong distance and his weight distribution was way off for him to actually reach her.

"Ooo." Tyrone slashed the blade again, reckoning to cut her as if playing a game. He laughed, then snaked it out again. "Ooo."

Tess didn't flinch. Just stared at him.

Tyrone's eyes narrowed. He obviously knew something was off here but hadn't cottoned on to what. Instead of imagining she might be a trained fighter, he'd probably judged that the kick that had sent him crashing into his hood had been a lucky shot she'd gotten in when he wasn't looking. Big mistake. He was going to pay for underestimating her. Pay dearly.

His eyes wide with fake surprise, he flicked out the knife again. "Ooo, ooo."

Grinning, he turned and winked at Fat Girl.

Hell, he was loving the power he believed he had. Unfortunately for him, it was time for Tess to take it away.

When Tyrone looked back at Tess, she shot her right hand out toward him.

Startled, he flinched, then immediately slashed at her arm. But she was already pulling that hand back, and shooting out her other.

Having lured Tyrone into positioning his knife hand just where she wanted it, her left hand caught his forearm and latched onto it hard. She pulled it to her, locking it under her arm to securely pin the knife behind her back so he couldn't pull it free or twist it. At the same time, she fired her palm heel into Tyrone's face.

His nose exploded and blood spurted across his face.

Tess clamped his knife arm with both hands.

Slammed her knee into his crotch.

Headbutted him in the face.

Hooked his legs out from under him.

Tyrone crunched into the unforgiving ground.

Still holding his arm to control the knife, Tess hammered a kick into his armpit.

He howled as the joint ripped apart, dislocating his shoulder.

Tess stripped the knife from his feeble grip and tossed it aside. With her adversary writhing on the ground, a crumpled heap of agony, Tess glared at Fat Girl.

Tess said, "Get this piece of crap out of here. Or do *you* want to slap the white off my ass?"

Chapter 13

FAT GIRL COWERED behind the car's passenger door, her eyes wide and her knuckles white as she gripped the top of it. Warily, she straightened up.

Without taking her gaze off Tess, she skulked around the back of the car to make her way to Tyrone. It was by far the longer route, but it was the route that kept her the furthest away from Tess for the longest time.

Because of her girth, the woman groaned as she reached down and grabbed Tyrone's arm.

She pulled. "Come on, baby, let's get you back to my place."

He twisted away, grimacing and clutching his shoulder. "Get the hell off me, bitch. I ain't no cripple needing no goddamn help."

She jerked back, as if worried he was going to take his anger out on her.

Tyrone struggled onto his knees, holding his right arm awkwardly across his chest. Sucking through his teeth, he fought to clamber to his feet but squealed and sank back down. He hunched over on the ground, clutching his busted shoulder.

Wincing, he glared at Fat Girl. "So, you gonna goddamn help me or what?"

She waddled back. With her assistance, he hauled himself to his feet. He slung his good arm around her shoulders for support, while she held him around the waist, and together, they lurched toward his car.

"Can you drive, baby?"

"Are you shitting me?"

They hobbled around the back of the car, taking the long way around to the passenger side. Once he was standing beside the open door, he scowled at Tess.

"I'll be seeing you again, bitch. Just you see if I don't."

Tess took the tiniest of steps toward him.

He dove through the doorway, then cried out in pain as he crumpled into the passenger seat.

The threat now neutralized, Tess turned away from the car. She reached a hand down to the root cause of the confrontation.

Crazy Dude looked up at her from under his brow, still hiding his eyes behind his bangs.

"It's okay," said Tess. "No one's going to hurt you."

He tentatively reached up a hand, but then jerked it back, like an abused dog wary of taking free food from a stranger for fear the morsel would be snatched away and be replaced by a stomp.

She kept her hand out and smiled. "My name's Tess. I'm a friend. I can help, if you'll let me."

Again he peered at her without really peering at her.

He said, "Tablet."

Tess looked around as the Camaro backed down the alley.

Tyrone hung his hand out of the window and flipped her the bird.

Yeah, real big man.

She ignored the childish retaliation and fetched the tablet.

"Ah, hell." It was covered in scratches and was considerably heavier than hers, suggesting it was old and very well used. However, the crack in its screen was brand-new.

She wandered back to Crazy Dude, still lying on the ground.

"I'm sorry, but it's—"

He grabbed it and cradled it against his chest.

The guy wasn't crazy but obviously had some mental disability.

"If you let me give it to him, I've got a friend who can fix that for you."

Bomb probably couldn't fix the screen, but he could certainly rescue the data and transfer it to one of his older tablets that he no longer used, a device that would be infinitely better than that old piece of gear.

Crazy Dude squinted at her. "He knows computers?"

Three words? Wow, that was one hell of a breakthrough – for Crazy Dude, three whole words was the equivalent of the State of the Union Address.

"Yes," said Tess.

"Can he make it faster?"

"Like lightning."

He held it up to her.

Another breakthrough.

She took it, then reached down again.

"Now," said Tess, "how about we make you faster too?"

This time, he took her hand and let her pull him up, but hung his head away when he caught her looking him in the face.

But she'd seen what she needed to see – he'd have a swollen lip for a few days, but his injury looked far worse than it actually was, which was often the case when the tiniest of bleeding was involved.

She gestured down the alley the way they'd both come. "Let's get you cleaned up in the—"

But he obviously had other ideas – he toddled off in the opposite direction.

"Oh, okay" – Tess sighed as she stood watching him – "we're going that way, are we?"

She trudged after him.

He took a scrap of paper from his pocket and wrote down the registration plate and details of the next parked car. Once he'd done that, he looked ahead to a Ford sedan.

Tess barred his way. "How about a drink? It must be thirsty work recording all this data."

His head bowed, he glanced at her for a moment from under his brow but then looked down again.

Of course! This guy wasn't crazy; he was autistic. Recording details of cars had to be his 'thing.'

"The diner at the end there does a mean burger and a fantastic milkshake with chocolate ice cream." She didn't know if it did, but she needed some form of inducement.

"Strawberry," said Crazy Dude.

"What?"

"Not chocolate. Strawberry."

"Oh, the strawberry is even better. Good call."

She reached out to guide him around to point in the right direction, but he jerked away from her as if he'd just received an electric shock.

No touching – was that another of his 'things'?

Tess ambled back toward the diner slowly enough for him to comfortably keep up. It was like walking beside a geriatric. Like how her grandpa had made her walk when she was dressed for church on a Sunday morning, when all Tess had wanted was to be scampering any which way to investigate something over here, check out something over there...

She smiled at Crazy Dude. "My name's Tess."

"I know."

"Oh, yeah, I already told you, didn't I"?

He said in a monotone voice, "My name's Tess. I'm a friend. I can help, if you'll let me."

Had he just quoted her word for word? If he had, that was a cool trick considering the stressful situation he'd just suffered. How many more 'things' did he have?

"So what's your name?" asked Tess.

He shot her a sideways glance from under his bangs.

"Gilmour Bach."

Well, if his autism or ethnicity hadn't gotten him bullied at school, that name sure as hell would have. His parents hadn't made life easy for him.

"Oh, Bach like the composer?" asked Tess.

He shot her a sideways glare. "No. Bach like Dad."

Looking away, he shook his head as if finding it incredulous that someone had gotten something so simple so wrong. But then, considering the number of times he must have heard that question over his lifetime, maybe it wasn't surprising it had become irritating.

He said, "It means white."

Tess frowned. "What does?"

He heaved a sigh and rolled his eyes. "Bach."

"It does?" She only knew a handful of German words.

"In Vietnamese."

"Ah." That explained his complexion. "Sorry, I get you now."

He raised his arm to show her the back of his hand. "This isn't suntan."

276

Tess glanced away for a moment so she could smile without him noticing. She didn't want to offend him but couldn't help but see the funny side of their conversation, especially when he was so deadly serious and not trying to be witty in the least.

Turning to him, she said, "Well, it's very nice to meet you, Gilmour."

Tess put her hand out to shake his, but then remembered his touch 'thing' so she pulled it back.

"Gil," he said.

Tess cringed. She didn't want to appear even more stupid, but…

"Sorry, you've lost me again."

He said, "It's not Gilmour. Tess is a friend, and friends say Gil."

"Ah. So it's nice to meet you, Gil."

"Nice to meet you, Tess."

He ambled along. He seemed completely oblivious to the humor in their exchange, yet content that he'd made a new friend, even if that friend did appear somewhat dim.

Shuffling down the alley beside Gil, Tess glanced at her watch. Before getting back to work, she'd make sure he got home safely. The last thing she wanted was for that asshole with the Camaro to circle around and find Gil alone and vulnerable. She glanced back to make doubly certain that they weren't being followed.

Chapter 14

IN THE DINER'S pale green bathroom, Gil stood like a Ken doll while Tess posed him this way and that to clean him up, starting with his busted lip. It was strange that he was so averse to physical contact, and yet when it came to hygiene like this, he'd happily stand and be poked and prodded every which way necessary. Maybe it was something to do with the way he'd been mothered, and as Tess was a surrogate, her touching him in this way was perfectly acceptable.

She plugged the drain in the stainless-steel sink with paper towels and then ran the faucet, pushing the lever as far over as possible to get hot water, but when she tested it, it was barely even lukewarm. Using a damp towel, she sponged the back of his lime cardigan around the shoulders. The green top couldn't have clashed more with the purple slacks and blue shirt.

Maybe it was his mother who bought his clothes because of his condition. A very staid, color-blind mother. One who'd never seen MTV, read a fashion magazine, or shopped in a mall, but who ordered clothes out of a 1950s mail-order catalogue that only had black-and-white photos. Such a pity. As if his general demeanor wasn't enough, his wardrobe made him appear even more of an oddball.

She finished sponging and looked him over.

There was still a tiny smear of blood on his lip, so she dabbed that away with a clean corner of the towel, then looked at him again.

"Well? We good to go?" She glanced in the mirror at him.

"The button."

"Huh?"

Gil didn't point but merely stared into the mirror. She followed his eyeline and looked at his cardigan.

"Oh, sorry." Tess fastened the second button from the top, which had come undone.

"We good now?" she asked.

He nodded.

"So, burger, strawberry milkshake, then call your mom, yeah?"

"Mom's dead."

"Oh, I'm sorry."

"Why?" asked Gil.

"What?"

"Why is Tess sorry? Tess didn't give her cancer."

Tess snickered. "No, I don't believe I did, but that's what people say when they hear something sad like that."

He shot her one of his sideways glances as if questioning her.

"Really." She nodded. "So your dad, then?"

"Dad's not here."

"So did he say when he'd be back?"

"Mom said he'll be back when hell freezes over."

"Oh, I'm— er..." She smiled at him in the mirror. "So, that burger, huh?"

It looked like getting this lost puppy home might be harder than she'd bargained on.

A few minutes later, sitting on the blue vinyl bench in the fourth booth along, Tess watched Gil eating his burger.

Well, not so much eating it as dissecting it.

She'd never seen anyone eat a cheeseburger with a plastic knife and fork before. Especially when each piece had to be cut to as near as possible the same size and shape as the last. She studied him, shaving off a fraction here and a fraction there, until a chunk looked as square as he could make it with the implements at hand.

He popped it in his mouth. Then chewed twenty-two times before swallowing. Not twenty-one, nor twenty-three, but twenty-two. Just like the last mouthful, and the one before that, and probably the one to come. Then, he returned to hacking up his burger with all the ferocity of a surgeon operating on his beloved only child.

Tess sipped her strawberry milkshake. She hadn't known the diner would serve them, but her guess had paid off – it was wonderfully creamy and fruity.

With Gil's eating regimen making his meal last for days, Tess tested his tablet. It booted up, but the screen had a spiderweb crack right across it, and the image flashed and distorted intermittently like an old-fashioned television that suffered from very bad reception.

She said, "So do you often go around collecting license plates?"

He didn't look up from squaring off his chunk of food with the precision of an architect.

"Yes."

With a napkin, she wiped the dirt off the device.

"Why?"

"Because that's what the spreadsheet asks for – duhhh!" He shook his head as he shaved a tenth of an inch off the right side of the chunk.

She was certain he wasn't intentionally being impolite, but that he simply didn't have any sort of filter that turned his raw thoughts into something more socially acceptable when he spoke. She could no sooner blame him for being rude than blame a wheelchair user for being slow to climb a flight of stairs.

But attitude aside, in his mind, that was obviously all the reason he needed – something asked for a piece of information, so he provided it. However, someone must have set up the spreadsheet to set these events in motion.

She tried again. "Why do you do it?"

"It's Gil's job."

"Your job, huh? And who gave you such an important job?"

"Dad."

His father had left. Or had he? Maybe Gil wasn't just autistic, but seriously confused. Or maybe the bump on the head had been far more serious than Tess had believed.

"Didn't Dad leave?" asked Tess.

"Yes."

"But when he was here, he asked you to record license plates?"

"He was tired of people taking his parking spot. Gil's job was to record who did it so Dad could give them a piece of his mind."

"Ahhh." So this 'job' was probably part to solve a problem and part to keep Gil occupied and to help him focus his mind. But why was he still doing it if his dad had moved out? Maybe simply because no one had ever told him to stop.

While that seemed logical, one thing didn't – the alley where she'd found him was not a residential area.

"So you live around here?"

"No."

"Oh?"

"You say 'Oh' a lot."

"Do I?"

"Six times."

"O—" Tess caught herself. "Really?"

He didn't look up from his cutting. "Six and a half."

Tess smirked. For someone who many people would openly call slow, he was amazingly fast.

"But if you don't live around here, why are you collecting plates?"

"Gil got bored seeing the same cars everyday."

Tess nodded. "That's fair enough. So do you cover a specific area or just wander about wherever you fancy?"

He rooted in his pocket and pulled out one of the free tourist maps of the district. Without looking, he handed it to her.

Tess laid it out on the table. A large network of streets had been traced with red highlighter, another of comparable size had been traced in blue, while a smaller network was in green.

"And you do all these areas?"

"Red Monday. Blue Tuesday. Green Wednesday. Yellow Thursday. Black Friday. Rest Saturday. Church Sunday."

"Well, it's good to plan ahead."

"Next week is Brooklyn."

"Brooklyn, huh? And the week after…?"

He held his hand up for her to wait while he completed his latest chewing marathon.

Tess said, "Queens? Staten Island? The Bronx?"

New York City had five boroughs; if he was gathering data in Manhattan and Brooklyn, it was fair to assume he'd look at the others too.

She watched him as he chewed. He didn't speed up or appear to reduce the number of times, but plodded on to his usual twenty-two. Finally, he swallowed.

"The Bronx," he said.

Tess knew this was one hell of a long shot, but she pulled out her notebook anyway. She paged through, then, sounding as nonchalant as she could, she asked the question she was praying would bring her a one-chance-in-a-million answer.

"I don't suppose you've seen this plate on your travels?"

It could narrow her search tremendously if Gil had seen the killers' car parked somewhere, so she slid her notebook across the pale blue Formica tabletop so he could see it.

He barely glanced at it. "No."

"Don't you want to check?" She gestured to his tablet. The screen was messed up, but zooming in to the spreadsheet would surely make things legible enough for a simple search.

"No." He didn't look up from his cutting.

"Can you at least check, maybe? It would mean a lot to me." She smiled, even though she knew he wouldn't even look at her. "Please."

"Gil hasn't seen it."

"But…"

Tess frowned at him. She stroked her chin while she watched him eat. Was he being awkward, despite how she'd helped him, or was he simply stating a fact?

Tess pushed her notebook a tiny bit closer. "You *know* you haven't seen this number?"

"Yes."

"So you don't just write the number down, but you remember it too?"

"Yes."

"All of them?"

"Yes."

"You remember every single plate you see?"

"Yes."

"Wow."

"And everything people say."

Tess sniggered. "Whoa." Had she heard that right? "You remember *everything* that anyone says to you."

"No."

"Yeah, I didn't figure that was possible."

"Not just what people say to Gil. Everything Gil hears."

She laughed again. "No way."

He neatly placed his knife and fork down side by side on his plate. Then nudged the knife a fraction to make sure the ends of the two pieces of cutlery were perfectly aligned.

In a monotone voice, he said, "Tess, 'Get this piece of crap out of here. Or do you want to slap the white off my ass?' Black woman, 'Come on, baby, let's get you back to my place.' Black man, 'Get the hell off me, bitch. I ain't no cripple needing no goddamn help. So, you gonna goddamn help me or what?' Black woman, 'Can you drive, baby?' Black man, 'Are you shitting me? I'll be seeing you again, bitch. Just you see if I don't.' Tess, 'It's okay. No one's going to hurt you. My name's Tess. I'm—'"

"Okay, okay, okay." Tess chuckled. "I believe you."

"Because Gil always tells the truth."

"Man, that's one hell of a memory. I wish I could do that."

He frowned. "Tess can't?"

Again, she sniggered. "God, no. I don't know anyone else that can. That makes you damn special, I can tell you."

"Gil is special. Gil was tested."

"You better believe it. Hell, you'd clean up on something like *Who Wants to be a Millionaire?* You ought to apply."

"Yes."

He picked his cutlery back up and went about dissecting another piece of his burger.

He didn't appear to have a sense of humor, and he'd already said he always told the truth, so was he merely agreeing with her, or could his amazing memory really earn him a million bucks for just a few minutes' work?

"So you've thought about applying?"

"Yes."

"But you haven't because…?"

"People don't like Gil, so Gil doesn't like people."

Oh, poor guy. Tess wanted to lean over and hug him, but she knew that would be as well received as a kick in the crotch. Instead, she did the next best thing.

She said, "I hear you there, buddy. Believe me. But listen…" She couldn't touch him, so instead she rested a fingertip on the edge of his plate to get his attention. "Tess is people, and Tess likes Gil."

He stopped cutting and looked at her from under his brow. Looked at her for at least three or four seconds, the longest he'd ever looked at her. Then, he stared into space for a few moments. Finally, he went back to cutting up his food.

Had he just judged whether she was a nice person or not? Someone who he really could call a friend? If so, what had he decided?

She could hardly ask. And he probably wouldn't understand the need for the question anyway. His world seemed totally binary, the most black-and-white world she'd ever encountered. It was kind of refreshing. Especially considering the length of time she'd lived in the shadowy underworld, where rules and ethics were endless shades of gray.

But time was getting on, and no matter how pleasant and interesting it was passing time with Gil, she was getting no closer to tracking down Kim Chiang's killers.

"Listen, I'm going to have to make tracks." She pushed up out of the booth as she pulled on her black leather jacket.

Picking up the tablet, she said, "Like I said, I'll give this to my friend who's a magician with tech stuff and meet you here in two days. Okay?"

He stopped eating and just stared down at his plate.

"Are you going to be okay?" she said. "Or do you want me to get you that cab?"

He still stared down.

"Gil?"

He nudged his knife to be level with the fork. Finally, he shuffled out of the booth and then guided her around by the arm so she was standing directly opposite him.

He flung his arms around Tess and hugged her. Except it wasn't a hug. He draped his arms around her as if to hug her, but they were completely limp, as if he'd seen the action performed, but had never grasped the nuances or the emotional content.

Fearing she'd upset him if she broke his No Touching rule too much, she lightly put her arms around him.

He said, "Gil is people, and Gil likes Tess."

Strangely, considering she'd only just met the guy and he was one of the weirdest little dudes she'd ever come across, Tess got a lump in her throat. She couldn't help it. It was something about being appreciated by someone with no agenda, no pretence, no ego... just someone who couldn't help but be honest-to-God genuine. This simple act reached in and touched something deep down in her.

"Thank you, Gil."

He let go and retook his seat as if nothing special had happened.

Tess couldn't help but smirk – she was so unbelievably touched, while he didn't even appear to have registered the incident.

She double-checked. "Here. Two days. Okay?"

"Here. Two days. Okay."

Tess left. As she retraced her steps back down the alley, she smirked, the image of Gil shuffling along down there having flashed into her mind. Her smile broadened as she pictured him shambling about the streets and documenting every parked car he came across, day after day, month after month. What a funny little dude. But what a remarkable brain he had to be able to 'record' conversations like that.

Her brow wrinkled.

He remembered every word he heard. And he trailed the length and breadth of the city. Every day, every month, every year.

Maybe there was far more to all this than just a chance encounter with a guy with a 'thing'. As Gil tramped around the streets, he'd overhear an incredible number of conversations, 99.9% of which would be meaningless crap, but every so often… Maybe she hadn't just saved a vulnerable guy from getting a beating, but made a valuable contact. It was lucky she'd arranged to meet him again.

After taking the second left, Tess saw the skate park ahead. She hoped she'd made the right play here.

Tracking someone completely unknown was always a hell of a problem. Was this place going to provide her first solid lead?

Chapter 15

AT THE PARK, Tess stepped through a hole in the fencing where the wire mesh had been peeled from the metal supports. Thankfully, the rain having stopped and the sun drying light gray patches on the swathes of concrete, kids were out being kids. Tess doubted drizzle would have mattered to the hardcore boarders, but the more that were here the better.

Wedged between two buildings, the park looked like it had been a wasteland the authorities had converted in a bid to help regenerate the neighborhood. Such initiatives were often suggested. Few were implemented. Even fewer met with success. This one appeared to be aimed at giving kids something to do, something that might distract them from the lure of crime and gangs and drugs. Not a bad plan.

All concrete ramps and curves, the park held around fifteen youngsters spellbound. It obviously hadn't been open long as there was only the odd small clump of vegetation sprouting through cracks in the concrete, while the walls on either side had been painted black but weren't yet caked with graffiti.

Avoiding a biker jumping his bike along on its front wheel, like an old-fashioned pogo stick, she made for the crest of the biggest upward concrete arc. At the top, three teenage boys whooped and hollered as their two friends repeatedly tried to pull off a particular stunt.

With twice as much hair as Tess had, a teenage boy sped up the ramp. As he neared the top, he crouched. Both board and boarder soared into the air. In flight, he flipped his board while spinning himself around horizontally. But his timing was off – he crunched into the top of the arc, while his board clattered to the concrete and rolled away without him.

It reminded her of the hundreds of hours she'd spent perfecting her jumping kicks in a Tae Kwon Do dojang in Kyoto. Despite flights from Japan being relatively cheap, she'd only trained in Korea, the home of the art, for a few weeks. She'd regretted that at the time, but it had been the right decision.

In martial arts movies, fighters often performed fancy kicks that made their audience gasp, rewind, and then view in slow motion to fully appreciate their gravity-defying artistry. Tess had mastered such kicks, mainly for her own amusement, but also as an aid in perfecting her balance and body awareness. Acrobatics like that were great for show, but for a real fight? Hell, they were the easiest way to the emergency room. Or the morgue.

But then the martial arts were plagued by misinformation, some verging on the myth – like being able to learn the Dim Mak death touch by sending a few bucks to an address in the back of a comic book.

Self-defense was about simplicity, speed, and accuracy. Not about how high you could kick, or how flashy a move you could pull off. The more you overcomplicated things, the more room you left for error. And if you made an error on the street against a skilled fighter, that could be the last mistake you ever made.

After clambering to his feet, the skateboarder didn't even dust himself off. He trudged across the concrete, retrieved his board, and took off on it again. She had to applaud his commitment.

Tess knew all about getting knocked on her ass and having to get back up and try again – invariably with the same result. Her years in the Far East had oftentimes seemed just one long session of doing nothing but that.

But her techniques had finally come together.

As her grandpa had used to say: *'Get the right tool for the right job and the job almost does itself'.* That was how it was with fighting. Get a simple strike, performed at speed, hitting the right target, and you couldn't lose. And therein lay the rub – to get that combination of simplicity, speed, and accuracy took years of dedication. This was why, be it piano, painting, or palmistry, 99.9% of the population were never more than adequate at anything they did, instead of being complete masters of it – it was simply too much effort.

On the top of the curved concrete slab, Tess approached the group of three boys in their early teens. The frowns and staring said they didn't understand why she was there. She showed them.

She held out a twenty dollar bill. "Can I get a few minutes of your time, guys?"

They glanced at each other, both obviously wary of taking the cash for what catch might be involved.

She smiled. "Hey, I just need a little information on the neighborhood, that's all."

The fat kid nudged his friend, the nearest one to her, a geeky-looking kid with long, gangly limbs. She doubted he shot around the curves here, pulling acrobatic stunts, but you never could tell. He slowly reached out, as if he expected her to pull the bill away any second and say 'Ha ha!'

She didn't.

He took the cash. "Okay…?"

Tess said, "There's another if you give me what I need."

"Okay."

"When you're walking home, who is it you have to see that makes you either hide your cell phone or cross to the other sidewalk? Or maybe even turn back and go a different way? Who are the local thugs?"

The fat kid said, "Are you the police?"

She laughed. "Do I look like NYPD?"

"So why d'you wanna know?"

"I'm a journalist. I'm writing a piece on gang violence, so to do it properly, I need to actually talk to some gangs." She smiled. "Like I said, there's money in it if you help."

The geek held his hands up defensively. "Whoa, I ain't getting beat up as a snitch just so you can do your job."

"Hey, no one's going to get beat up," she said. "Haven't you ever seen a cop show where some journalist gets into trouble because they won't reveal their sources? Well, that's true. Think about it – if everything wasn't confidential, why would anyone ever tell us anything?"

The fat kid leaned across to the geek and, behind his hand, whispered in his ear. The geek shook his head and then whispered back. The fat kid replied. The geek nodded. Finally, the geek turned to her. "Fifty bucks."

Tess said, "Okay. I can go another thirty." She'd already given them twenty. She'd figured on forty bucks for the information, but an extra thirty wouldn't break her.

"No. The price is an extra fifty."

Tess smirked. "You're obviously smart kids, so I'm not going to give you any BS – I'll give you thirty bucks, or I'll give you nothing and ask the next kid I see on the street."

The fat kid whispered to his friend again. The geek nodded, then said, "Thirty bucks."

Tess held up a twenty and a ten. The geek reached for them, but she pulled them away. "Information first."

The geek looked at the fat kid, who nodded. He pointed left down the street. "Three blocks down, one over on the left, there's Livingstone's courtyard. Check out the guys on the benches." He held out his hand for the money.

Tess turned to leave.

"Hey! Our money!"

She turned back. She could tell by their outrage that they felt they'd been cheated. You only felt cheated if you'd given away something of value but received nothing in return.

She smiled and held the notes out to the geek. "Just testing you weren't making it up."

He snatched the money before she could snatch it away. "Try being a wiseass with them, lady, don't blame me when you get cut."

She walked away. Yep, these courtyard gentlemen sounded just the kind of guys she was dying to meet. But a measly fifty bucks wouldn't work with them. What would be the easiest way to get them to talk? Well, it had to be one of the three things that made the world go round – money, sex, or violence. Which one should she pick?

Chapter 16

DESPITE THE SUN having cracked the clouds, its shafting light did nothing to brighten the gigantic mass of concrete which was set back from the street, like a vicious dog that needed to be tethered well away from the sidewalk.

Livingstone Project.

After being away for the best part of a decade to master the Far East's deadliest fighting skills, Tess had finally decided she had all she needed, so she'd headed back to the USA. Except, instead of simply flying east across the Pacific, the quick and easy way, she'd taken the long route – worked her way west over land.

Tess had seen ghettos in Indochina, in India, in Eastern Europe. She'd seen human waste running in the streets; seen houses that were little more than shacks; seen people surviving by scraping through landfills for lost treasures like discarded bottles they could sell, old sneakers they could wear, or moldy bread they could eat.

With power, water, and heating, the Livingstone Project was not a ghetto. No matter what its residents thought. But it was probably the closest thing to one in the city.

Tess ambled into the complex of giant concrete slabs.

To her left, in a gloomy alleyway cutting straight underneath one of the buildings, something small and brown scurried over an upended sofa. It was not a cat, not a dog. In a real ghetto, that would've made some lucky family a tasty meal.

She gazed up at the gray building, which oozed depravity and depression. Bomb had grown up in just such a project not far from here.

Black and impoverished, if Bomb hadn't been imprisoned in his wheelchair, would he have turned out the decent guy he had, or would he be running with a gang like the one she was now hunting?

Maybe his disability had made him. Just as the trauma in her past had made her.

But what if he wasn't in his chair?

She didn't want to think about that. Bomb was the closest thing to a friend she had. The closest thing to a family. She didn't want to imagine how their paths might have crossed for an entirely different reason – she craving justice for the sins he'd committed.

Venturing into the courtyard, Tess scanned the endless gray concrete walls strewn with layer upon layer of spray paint from talentless artists who'd felt the need to announce their existence. Invisible people trying to be visible.

In the middle of the courtyard sat a group of benches. On the benches sat those she'd come to visit.

They also did not believe they deserved to remain invisible.

"Hey, chica, you come to party?" Sitting on the back of the bench, with his feet on the seat, a moustachioed young guy grabbed his crotch.

On the next bench sat a man wearing a white undershirt to show off his muscles and an abstract sleeve tattoo. He waved at the mustachioed guy. "Manny, you ain't doing shit with that worm." He looked at Tess. "You want a man, chica" – he held his arms wide – "You ain't got no further to look."

"Fuck you, Jesus," said Manny. "Your maggot ain't seen no pussy since you last fucked your mother." He laughed and bumped fists with the guy next to him on top of the bench, a kid so fresh-faced he looked barely out of high school.

Tess pointed at Manny and the kid. "People have to sit on that bench. Do you want to get your dirty shoes off it, please?"

The laughing stopped. They glared at her.

She grinned. "Hey, I'm just yanking your chain."

Manny smiled. "That's a good job, chica. I'd hate to have to smack up something pretty as you."

Three things made the world go round: money, sex, and violence. Bed the right person, pay the right person, or kill the right person, and you could pretty much get anything you wanted. The secret was in finding that right person, and in learning exactly which of the three things was needed to deliver your favored result. So what would it be with these guys – money, sex, or violence?

Tess made her choice.

She glanced over the five guys sprawled over the benches. Which one was the leader? The two loudmouths obviously weren't – a savvy leader wouldn't have propositioned her like that and risked the humiliation of being rejected in front of his men. Also, Jesus wasn't the leader because he wouldn't have stood for backtalk like that.

The fresh-faced kid was also out because of his age, and because he'd sided with Manny against Jesus.

That left just two out of the five. It might have been a cliché, but it was usually true so she went with it – she spoke to the guy second from the right, the one so handsome he wouldn't have to rely on cheap sexual innuendo to attract women.

She said, "I need some information about the shooting at Best Bargains."

The guy merely shrugged. He held her gaze – defiant, without being threatening. Yes, she'd made the correct choice.

Manny jumped down off the bench. "You wanna talk shooting." Again, he grabbed his crotch. "I got a full load to shoot here, chica!"

He turned and laughed at his own hilarity to his friends. The kid laughed. The leader didn't.

Tess ignored Manny and carried on addressing who she thought was the gang's leader. "I'm sure you've seen the video. I want to find the person who shot it."

Again, he remained silent and simply shrugged.

And again, Manny felt the urge to run with the ball. "You wanna shoot video? I got a zoom gonna split you in two." He motioned having sex doggie style.

Tess shook her head. "I was told you had a mean bunch of guys here, but this?" She pointed at Manny. "Seriously?"

Manny stalked toward her. "You disrespecting me, bitch? Who the fuck do you think you are?"

The leader held up his hand to Manny.

Manny threw his arms up. "What! Disrespect gets a pounding, Emile. Them's the rules."

The leader, Emile, finally spoke, his curiosity obviously aroused by a woman who had the nerve to act like that on his home turf. "Before I let Manny teach you about respect, tell me, you ain't a pig and you ain't a chink, so why are you bothered about old man Chiang?"

"That's my business," said Tess.

He waved his hands. "Then who made the video is my business." He looked away, as if bored.

These guys obviously sat here day after day, terrorizing the weak, preying on the vulnerable. They probably lived by dealing drugs, ripping off kids' phones, maybe demanding some protection money. Small stuff. But they didn't do it just to 'earn' a living, they needed it to kill the boredom. Abusing others was entertainment that helped them cope with their dismal existences, to give their lives some sort of meaning.

If they wanted entertainment, had she got a blockbuster feature lined up. She pressed 'play'.

She said, "You a gambling man, Emile?"

He didn't even look at her.

"I bet you I can knock any guy here on his ass with one strike, but none of you can put me on the ground."

Manny, Jesus and the kid all shouted and gesticulated at her.

Emile finally turned. His gaze crawled up and down her. "And what exactly you got to bet with?"

"You put me on my back" – she cupped her crotch – "I'll stay there and let you take turns."

Most of the gang whooped.

Manny and the kid high-fived each other.

Emile remained calm. He said, "And, if you win?"

The gang hooted with laughter.

"You tell me who shot the video and where to find them."

With Manny and the kid desperately goading him on, Emile considered. "You say this now, but later you're gonna run to the pigs screaming rape."

She pointed to his phone resting on his thigh. "May I?"

He gestured it was okay.

She picked it up. She knew the model so, in an instant, she was recording video. She panned the camera across the gang. "These are my friends." She turned it on herself. "Completely of my own free will, I give Emile and his four friends permission to use my body in any sexual manner they choose." She tossed the phone back to him.

The predictable members of the gang whooped with delight and anticipation.

She folded her arms and arched an eyebrow at Emile.

This was a slam dunk. She'd given Emile absolutely no choice – how could a gang leader turn down what appeared to be guaranteed sex for his men and still retain their respect? Emile would never imagine he could lose such a bet to her, just a woman who'd walked off the street, so he had to accept it.

He said, "One hit?"

She nodded.

He pointed to the cracked paving stones. "Just put you on the ground."

She nodded again. "Let's say for a count of five."

Manny laughed. "Five seconds or five days?"

Emile said, "We go first."

She gestured for him to do so.

Emile turned to the guy on the bench next to him, a guy who splurged over most of the bench by himself. The guy stood up.

Manny, the kid, and Jesus chanted, "Luca. Luca. Luca..."

303

Having already noted that the ground was smoother there, Tess took a couple of steps back, so, when she had to move, her feet wouldn't catch on anything. While tripping would be disastrous when executing a high kick, it could be equally calamitous when stepping forward and twisting your body into a strike to generate maximum power.

Luca waddled over. His arms didn't hang vertically at his sides, but out at an angle over his gigantic girth. Tess looked up into his smirking face, a face well above her head.

She looked back at Emile, who'd stood up to watch. "He gets one hit to put me on the ground for five seconds. One."

Emile nodded. "One. But you move out the way, you lose."

Tess said, "Tell you what, you win and I'll even throw in a blow job each too."

Manny clapped and danced a little jig.

While Luca swung his massive arms back and forth to limber up, he blew her a kiss. He then adopted a fighting posture, akin to a boxer's stance.

Manny shouted, "Not the face, Luca. I don't want no busted-up teeth mashing my dick!"

That was what she'd been gambling on. She couldn't have taken a direct hit to the head. And the guy obviously wouldn't hit her in the crotch because that would ruin all the fun they were banking on afterwards – you didn't bruise a peach right before biting into it.

She'd left him very little choice – it would be a straight shot to the torso.

But Luca was an immense guy. Even with all her years of training, could she withstand being hit by a fist like a sledgehammer?

Having left them little choice for a target area, she prepared herself.

Luca looked at Emile. Emile nodded.

Outwardly, Tess strained every muscle to tearing point, making her body as hard as possible.

Inwardly, she pictured her lake. She pictured the ducks. She pictured a still world of color and beauty and tranquility. She pictured a world where there was no such thing as pain because there was no such thing as her physical body.

Luca swung his club-like arm back.

His lip curled into a snarl.

He screamed.

His fist crashed into her gut like an out-of-control SUV.

Slammed off her feet, Tess crunched into the cold, unforgiving paving stones.

She lay.

Unmoving.

Chapter 17

IN THE COURTYARD, the gang applauded and cheered Luca's devastating blow. Triumphant, he held his arms aloft in celebration, a wide grin across his fat face.

In unison, they all chanted. "One…"

Gasping for air and hunched over, Tess clutched her stomach.

"Two…"

She strained to straighten up, but pain ripped through her abdomen. She had to get up.

"Three…"

Still clutching her midriff, she rolled onto her elbows and knees. *She had to get up.*

"Four…"

She cried out.

Heaved through the pain.

Pushed up to her feet.

Everyone gazed openmouthed.

Manny muttered, "Five."

Wincing, Tess stretched. She rotated her shoulders and arched her back to stretch her abdomen wall muscles.

She patted Luca on the arm. "Not a bad shot, there, buddy."

He stared at her, mouth agape.

Emile said, "You ain't won nothing yet. You still gotta down Luca."

Tess gazed up at the giant before her.

Luca leered at her. He stuck his chin out towards her to goad her.

"One hit!" Emile reminded her. "And he has to be down for a five count."

Tess pulled her right foot back.

Brought her hands up.

Loosely clenched her fists.

Shifted two thirds of her weight onto her back leg.

In her mind, she pictured her strike, pictured Luca buckling, pictured him crashing into the stony ground like a withered tree felled by a mighty axe.

She pulled her right arm back ready to strike.

Within the skull, a layer of cerebral fluid around the brain acted as a shield. Should the head be impacted upon, instead of the sudden force slamming the brain into the hard bone of the skull and damaging it, this fluid cushioned it – a natural 'air bag' inside your head.

However, because no one could build muscle up around it to protect it, the point of the chin was one of the most vulnerable parts of the human body. What competitive boxers learned through years of training, and some street fighters picked up on through trial and error, was that a powerful strike to the chin hammered the head with such force, the cerebral fluid could not stop the brain from slamming against the inside of the skull. Such a devastating shock to the brain could cause it to shut down – it was a knockout punch.

Luca smiled and stuck his chin out even further. He tapped the tip of it with an index finger.

Tess had her target.

Had her body wound up for maximum torque.

Had already seen the outcome in her mind's eye.

Time to strike.

Whipping her torso around as she stepped forward, Tess dropped to her right knee. With her full body weight behind it, she slammed her right elbow into the side of Luca's left knee.

Bone crunched.

Ligaments snapped like a handclap bang.

And the mighty redwood of a man fell.

A powerful strike to the point of the chin could be a knockout blow. *Could.* But shatter the trunk, and even the mightiest of trees could do nothing but fall.

Turning to face Emile as she rose to her feet, Tess didn't even watch Luca crash to the ground. She didn't need to. Like hitting the perfect shot off the back of the perfect swing in baseball, the connection, the sound, the gut instinct all told you the result before the result became a reality – home run.

"One…" Tess said.

Emile gawked at her. Then his gaze drifted down to Luca, now rolling on the ground, squealing in pain.

"Two…"

Manny stumbled over. "Get up, man!"

"Three…"

She heard Luca scuffling in the dirt, but knew a man of his size would never be able to put weight on a broken knee. She didn't even turn.

"Four…"

His voice more urgent, Manny said, "Come on, Luca. Come on, don't let no bitch—"

"Five."

Manny spun around to her, "You've done busted his leg, you dumb bitch."

She looked at him. He was going to be a problem. Good.

Chapter 18

MANNY GLARED AT Tess. "You don't mess with the Courtyard Kings." He pulled out a blade.

Tess had tried to play fair. Tried to play nice. But pulling a knife? She wasn't only going to disarm this imbecile, she was going to give him a life lesson. Plus, as this motley gang might still believe her downing Luca was a fluke, she needed to prove she wasn't someone to be screwed with.

Manny sneered. "I'm gonna cut you good, bitch."

He slashed at her.

Instead of stepping away from danger, away from the blade, she stepped toward it. She slammed both hands into his swinging arm. The impact hurting muscle and nerves, the knife flew from Manny's hand.

Grabbing and twisting his forearm, she levered his arm backwards to lock the shoulder joint. Then ripped it further.

He screamed as ligaments in his shoulder snapped.

He a plaything in her hands, she whipped his arm forward. Snapped the wrist back on itself. It broke with a crack.

He yelped.

Lifting the arm high, she spun under it. Yanked his elbow down the wrong way over her shoulder.

The joint crunched.

He screamed.

She released the arm.

Manny crumpled to the ground behind her, a sobbing heap of trembling manliness.

He wouldn't be grabbing his or anyone else's crotch for a long time.

She didn't even look at the carnage behind her, she just stared at Emile. "That's two down. How many more you got?"

In silence, a stunned expression on his face, Emile simply stared at her.

The kid looked away when her glare fell upon him. Jesus held her gaze for a few seconds – long enough for him not to appear too weak, but not so long as to appear threatening – then he looked down.

She looked back at Emile. "Telling me what I want to know isn't squealing to the pigs. No one can accuse you of that. Plus, you'll get a rival gang's men off the street, which can't be bad for you and your merry little band. Especially considering a couple of your guys appear to have had something of a mishap."

Emile glanced around at his men. No one met his eye. He looked back at her.

She glanced around the courtyard. "You know, I kind of like it here." She looked at his bench. "Yeah, I could see myself spending many a happy hour sitting there."

This gang was strictly small-time. Its turf probably didn't extend beyond a block or two. What would happen to Emile's little empire when everyone saw them getting beaten up by a woman day after day after day? Tess could make their lives utter hell. And they knew it.

"Word is" – Emile heaved a breath – "to roll with Sharky's Crew, you've got to off someone."

That explained why the killers had felt the need not just to shoot Chiang, but to film it – it wasn't just a souvenir, it was proof, a badge of honor, a VIP pass into an exclusive club.

Emile looked around to see if anyone outside the immediate vicinity was listening. No one was within earshot.

He said, "I heard a guy in Paco's over on Juniper was shooting his mouth off about being involved. That's all I know."

"Paco's?"

"A coffee shop. Cheap and free Wi-Fi."

A free Wi-Fi connection would be ideal for anyone wanting to upload video of a criminal act without incriminating themselves through their Internet service provider.

"See," said Tess, "that wasn't so hard, was it?"

She held out her hand. Gestured with her fingers for him to give her something.

"That's it. God's honest truth," said Emile.

"Phone," she said.

Emile handed her his phone. She deleted the video of her authorizing them to use her for sex.

Sidestepping to be in front of Jesus, she said, "Phone."

"What? I didn't video nothing."

She gestured for him to give it up. He did.

She did the same with the kid, who caved without a word or even making eye contact.

Tess glowered at him sitting on the back of the bench with his feet on the seat. "And get your feet off there. People have to sit on that bench after you've had your dirty shoes on it."

"Yes, ma'am." He slunk off and sat properly.

She sauntered over to Luca and Manny, still both on the ground, still both rolling in pain. "Phone."

Cradling his destroyed right arm with his left, Manny glared at her. He struggled to extricate his phone from his right-hand jeans pocket, but he managed.

Luca tossed his at her without being asked.

She looked coldly at him. "Didn't anyone ever tell you – it's wrong to hit girls."

She walked away.

Someone called out. "Hey!"

She turned.

Standing in front of his bench, the kid pointed. "My fucking phone!"

Her pointing finger swept across each of them. "If any one of you can show me just one store receipt, I'll give them all back."

She waited.

No one said anything. She headed for the street.

The kid said in a low voice, "That bitch ever comes back, man, will I fuck her up."

But it wasn't low enough.

Tess turned. Meandered back.

The kid slunk back to sit on the top of the bench. He gazed away into space.

"You say something?" Tess asked.

"Hmm?" He innocently looked at her. "Me? No."

"Well, okay, then."

She glared at his feet on the bench, then up into his eyes.

He slid back down to sit on the bench properly.

Tess strolled away.

Having removed the SIM cards for fear of what illicit material might be on them, she handed out the phones to the kids at the skateboard park. They'd probably have them stolen again inside the month, but they'd see there was a little justice in the world and seeing that could sway them to stay on track and not go the way of the gangs when they got older.

As she was leaving, she got a phone call.

"Hey, Bomb."

"Tess, I found a copy of the video."

314

"Great. And I've something for you – I need you to check out a possible upload location."

"Don't tell me – Paco's on Juniper."

So it looked like Emile's information was sound if Bomb had traced the source there too. But how could they find those involved even if they knew where they had uploaded the video from?

She said, "Any faces, tattoos, scars?"

"You'll see for yourself – it's all tight shots. Nothing much to see other than the victim's getting it. I don't know if it'll help, but I've included blow-ups of the weapons, plus one of a gold ring one of the killers was wearing."

"But other than it possibly being one of the customers at the coffee shop, you can't narrow it down any further?"

Bomb said, "There's one thing, but I don't know how much help it will be – from what metadata I could dig out, plus the video's codec and resolution, it's likely it was shot on an iPhone."

"If you come up with anything else, get back to me. Thanks, Bomb."

"Ciao, Tess. Good hunting."

So, she was looking for a guy who might have an iPhone and who might or might not drink coffee. Well, that narrowed it down to a few hundred thousand New Yorkers.

There was only one thing to do…

Chapter 19

SITTING WITH HER back to the wall, equidistant from Paco's front entrance and the emergency exit at the back, so she could see and reach both easily, Tess sipped a steaming cup of green tea. With a sideline in soul food, the coffee shop was an eclectic mix of food, furniture, and garishly painted walls, perfectly mirroring its clientele – mismatched, budget, colorful.

Tess took another piece of fluffy, sweet waffle and juicy, crispy chicken, a cord of maple syrup dangling to the plate before snapping. The sweet and savory combination danced on her taste buds. Tanner, a big black detective from the Sixty-Seventh, had introduced her to the dish, which had sounded utterly revolting. How wrong could you be! Now, whenever she was in Harlem around lunchtime and needed to refuel, she couldn't resist indulging herself.

While munching on another mouthful, she scanned the ordinary bunch of people before her – a Latino man in his twenties, alone with a book; three young women – two black and one white – laughing about the previous night's adventure; a graying man reading a newspaper; two black dudes comparing tattoos; an old woman with a young child. They were just people. They could just as easily be schoolteachers, nurses and bus drivers, as pedophiles, rapists and serial killers. How could she ever pick out the person she was hunting?

But then, just like chicken and waffles, that was the beauty of people – they had surprising uniqueness. On a species level, each and every one of them was physically identical, but on an individual level, every single one was utterly unique. Even identical twins weren't *identical* – they might have identical faces, identical physiques, identical skin tone, but they had different fingerprints.

But it was on an intellectual and psychological level where people got really interesting. And really disturbing. The schoolteacher who sexually abused a pupil; the nurse who raped a coma patient; the bus driver who snapped and went on a killing spree at their local mall. Yes, looks could be extraordinarily deceiving – you never knew what was really going on behind a person's mask of sanity.

Tess took another sip of tea. So, how could she spot a dog killer in this crowd of 'ordinary' people?

After rooting in her backpack, she removed her tablet from its RF shielded pouch which protected it from being traced or cloned. Then, using her onion routing software so her Internet surfing would be untraceable, she browsed to her and Bomb's darknet. She put in her earbuds, retrieved the video file Bomb had found, and played it.

She winced when the dog was shot. A defenseless animal lying on the floor, probably already dying – and this scum shot it. Yes, she'd enjoy meeting him.

Likewise, Kim Chiang stood no chance.

These were brutal, psychopathic killers. They took what they wanted, irrespective of the cost to those they took it from. Like many people these days, they obviously felt a sense of entitlement – that the world owed them something, despite them never having done anything of value to deserve better than they had. Taking them off the streets would not only see justice done for the Chiang family, it would be a service to mankind.

From what was said in the video, even though there were only two voices and only four shots were fired, there were three gang members. But, other than the color of the hands holding the guns being black, there was little to work with. Because the killers had had the smarts to take the security camera footage, it wasn't surprising the police had nothing to go on.

She opened the supplementary files Bomb had created of the weapons and the gold ring.

One pistol looked to be a Glock, but it was hard to tell from the angle. The other was a Sig Sauer. In close up while shooting the dog, the Sig looked like a

P226 – a popular pistol favored by some law enforcement and government agencies.

Tess studied the dog shooter's gold ring. She held her tablet closer for a better look, to try to make out any engraving or scratches, but it was simply a plain, chunky gold ring.

The coffee shop door opening, Tess's gaze shot to the customer entering, just as it had on every such occasion. A middle-aged woman shuffled in, putting down a pale green umbrella. It must have started raining again.

Tess returned to her tablet and clicked on a link Bomb had supplied. It took her to a video-sharing site. Still live, the video of the shooting had 158,692 views. God, there were a lot of sick bastards in the world.

She scrolled down to the 136 comments.

The video had elicited outrage from most commenters. Sadly, not all. Some delighted in its bloody spectacle.

NinjaWolf_42 had written, *'i hope the cops got the dog in an evidence bag before the family got it in a saucepan. you know what slopes are like for eating anything they can get their hands on! LOL'*

Not far below, VidMonsterPete had said, *'Oh, boohoo. So there's one less chink in the world. Big f***ing deal. Like there ain't another billion ready to take his place. I say blast a few more of the slitty-eyed bastards. You rock, guys!!!'*

Tess followed the profile links to check out their other comments. She found more of the same cruelty and disregard for the suffering of others.

NinjaWolf_42 and VidMonsterPete sounded like really nice guys. And typical of so many assholes that prey on the innocent online. It was so easy to be vicious when you were only a 0.0000003 percent statistic and invisible to the entire world.

Yes, scum like this thought they were untouchable because they believed they were completely anonymous. No one could ever trace them. No one could ever discover their real names. No one could ever exact the justice they deserved.

No one?

Tess placed a call.

"Yo, Tess," said Bomb.

"Hey, Bomb. I need a couple of Web Kills."

She knew he was smiling from the tone of his voice. "Like I didn't know that was coming. Way ahead of you, Tess – NinjaWolf_42 and VidMonsterPete have both seen the light and come clean on their social media accounts about their private lives. I figured good old VidMonsterPete had cranked it up a notch, so I gave him a Level Two Web Kill instead of just a One. Hope that's okay?"

A Level Two? Man, that would be good.

"Any problems?" she asked.

"Ha. Yeah, right. VidMonsterPete is a real star. Aside from his comments, anyone who uses 'password' as his password deserves what he gets. It'll be a valuable life lesson for him."

People thought they were being smart using 'password' for their password. They figured it was easy for them to remember but that other people would think it was way too obvious for anyone to ever use as a real password, making it secure.

Way too obvious?

The only thing 'way too obvious' was just how dumb some people were. '123456' and 'password' were the first two options Tess tried whenever she had to crack an account on the fly without Bomb. According to data encryption analysts, millions of people used these and similar terms. Tess had memorized the top twenty most common passwords the analysts had found, one of which, statistically, was used by one in fifty people. Despite the statistics and her success rate at accessing accounts, she was amazed each time she hacked a site using such a simple technique.

"We got graphics for VidMonsterPete?" asked Tess.

"We got the whole shebang. I'll send you the links. Any joy with our boys?"

Tess sipped her tea as she once more gazed around the coffee shop.

"Nah-huh. But I've got a good feeling about this place."

"Okay. Good hunting. Ciao, Tess."

"See you, Bomb."

No sooner had she hung up than a text message appeared from Bomb. She followed the enclosed links. The second – the Level Two Web Kill – went to the Facebook page of VidMonsterPete, one Peter Adrian Monteith, a thirty-six-year-old accountant from Encino, California.

A profile picture greeted her – a man with a drawn face and receding brown hair, cropped short. She could easily imagine how he'd know his way around a balance sheet but be completely lost at a social event.

In today's update, as if he were proud of his accomplishments, he'd listed a number of the ugly comments he'd made as VidMonsterPete, complete with links to each one, including that about Kim Chiang.

Below these, good old Peter had announced that when he wasn't scouring the Web for people to hurt simply because he could, he liked to blow dogs.

Tess smirked as she sipped her tea. Bomb had a real vicious streak. You had to love it.

Complete with an infographic entitled *'My Top Ten Doggie BJs'*, Peter confessed – *'I always keep a little bacon in my pocket, then if I see a stray or a dog off a leash and there's an alley or clump of bushes nearby... hey, it's Xmas come early!'*

Tess clicked through to Peter's gallery. A collection of photos revealed Peter blowing dogs of all shapes, sizes, and breeds.

She grimaced at the pictures, the cream-covered waffles churning in her stomach. Bomb's Photoshop skills were just plain scary.

She clicked away from the gallery.

With his password and email address changed, Peter would find it almost impossible to alter any of this information. Tess wondered what his accountancy firm Turner, Paget and Fumio would make of its junior partner. Not to mention what his wife would think.

He already had one comment posted by Chris J. Just two words – *'Dude, WTF!!!!!!!!!!!'*

Tess would visit his profile again later. See what comments other people had left. There was nothing so sweet as poetic justice.

But that was only a very minor wrong they'd righted there. A little respite from the heinous crime for which true justice still had to be exacted. Tess returned to the video of Kim Chiang's murder.

Instead of playing the video on the website, and helping to boost its rating and, thereby, promote it further, she played the MP4 file of it Bomb had sent.

Even though she knew it was coming, she winced again when the dog was killed. Hell, she hated these people, and yet she'd never even seen them, let alone met them.

Again, she studied the footage. But this time, she studied with her eyes shut and the volume turned up to try to drown out the sounds of Paco's customers – dishes chinking, chairs scraping, waitresses bustling.

Unlike many classical musicians, Tess enjoyed learning to play pieces on her cello by ear, instead of simply sitting in front of the sheet music. By discovering the music herself, she found she felt a greater connection to it. A bonus was it developed her ear for pitch and timbre.

Listening repeatedly to the video, she bathed in the killers' conversation. She let each nuance of their voices, each quirk of their accents, each vocabulary choice and contraction bleed into her mind, lodge in her subconscious, root in her memory. As long as she had the music of their voices, she didn't need to see their faces.

She took out the earbuds and finished her tea.

Unfortunately, stakeouts could be interminably long.

To pass the time, she experimented with the MP4 in her video-editing software, before finishing off an admission essay for a West Coast college and then writing an assignment exploring the contrasts between the three narrators of Faulkner's *The Sound and the Fury*.

She caught the waitress's eye and ordered another tea while she uploaded her writing assignments to the company's website for them to be accepted for payment and passed on to the two clients.

Thanks to the English student waiting until the last minute to order his essay and so having to pay a premium to be able to hand it in on time, all in all, that was an easy two hundred bucks in the bank for just a few hours work. Looked like she might make all this month's rent payments, after all.

She didn't mind helping kids game the system. However, even if she could, she'd never write technical or medical papers – she liked the bridges she crossed to remain standing, and the doctors she saw to know which part of her body it was they were examining. But in which line of work would having cheated on a study of Faulkner's character development leave a life hanging in the balance?

With bright red lipstick and enormous round silver earrings, a waitress plonked a tea on Tess's table. Tess smiled at her and put her tablet down.

Arching her back, Tess tried to surreptitiously adjust her body armor, which had ridden up from her hours of sitting. She'd have liked to have taken it and her jacket off, not least so she wouldn't sweat so much, but she couldn't risk encountering her target, a known killer, without a bulletproof vest.

Most people would never spot her body armor under her shirt, the vest being as stealth as they came, so keeping her jacket on may have been overly cautious. However, it only took one person with a trained eye to spot it and raise questions, and hours or days of work could be blown in a second.

She leaned back in her chair with her tea, just as the coffee shop door opened. Tess had counted the first twenty-two times that had happened, but she'd lost track of how many customers she'd watched come and go now.

Walking between the tables, a chubby-faced black guy with a shaven head nodded to a couple of guys who she'd earlier heard discussing a basketball game.

"Hey, Leroy." Her bright red lipstick emphasizing a glorious set of teeth, the waitress smiled at the chubby-faced guy.

Leroy nodded. "Darla."

As he'd passed in front of Tess, she saw a gold ring on his right index finger – what would be, if he ever chose to shoot a gun, his trigger finger. But being black and wearing a gold ring wasn't enough. She needed proof he was the prey she was hunting. And she knew just how she was going to get that.

Chapter 20

LEROY SAT AT a table two along from Tess, near the emergency exit at the back of the coffee shop.

Innocently glancing around while blowing on her fresh tea, Tess watched Leroy slouch in a tan easy chair and put his feet up on the blue seat opposite. He pulled out a phone and started scrolling through his text messages. A phone that looked like an iPhone.

She picked up her tablet again. She needed him to speak more than a word – she needed at least a full sentence to hear his voice, its inflexion, its rhythm. Twisting around in her chair to lean back as close to him as she could without arousing suspicion, she surfed to a fashion website. She didn't look at the clothes, but at the small round mirror, the size of a quarter, she'd stuck in her tablet's top left corner. In the reflection, she had a perfect view of Leroy.

Darla sashayed over, chunky hips wiggling, chest out. "What you hungry for today, Leroy?" She grinned.

He smirked up at her. But didn't say a word.

She said, "Coffee? Black? Three sugars?"

"Uh-huh."

Tess stared into her mirror. Yes, stakeouts could be long, wearisome, and frustrating. But also challenging, satisfying, and exhilarating. The payoff of a hunt wasn't only in the kill, but in the stalk. Like a guy getting a rush out of hitting a home run, a grandma getting a kick out of finishing a sudoku puzzle, a schoolgirl getting a buzz out of collecting pictures of a boy band, it wasn't just those last few seconds of success that made it such a joy, but the entire buildup – the anticipation, the wait, the effort.

Tess felt the hairs on the back of her neck prickle. She was sure this was the guy, sure her hunt was coming to the payoff. She just needed him to say a few words.

Darla returned with a coffee. She placed it on Leroy's table. He didn't look up from his phone, or even mutter a thank-you.

"So, you doing anything fun tonight, Leroy?" Sticking her chest out, Darla wound a lock of her straightened black hair around her finger.

"Uh-huh."

"So, what you doing?"

Finally, he looked up. "Baby, I'm doing you is what I'm doing."

It was him!

The iPhone, the ring, the voice. Him!

Tess was 99% sure. But 99% wasn't good enough. She couldn't risk punishing an innocent man. No, she had to nail that last 1% of uncertainty. And then get him all to herself to exact the justice Kim Chiang deserved. Luckily,she knewjusthow to dothat.Itwas all about pushing buttons, and man, was she going to push his.

Chapter 21

STILL WITH HIS head down, lost in his phone, Leroy lifted his coffee cup to drink.

On her tablet, Tess hit *'play'* and then studied Leroy in her mirror.

With no earbuds connected and her tablet's volume turned up, its speakers blasted out a single line of dialogue followed by a sound: "Bye bye, doggie." *Bang!*

Shocked at hearing his own voice say the words he'd said during the shooting, Leroy spun around to her, then cursed as he spilled his coffee down his black T-shirt.

She could imagine how he felt. Over six billion hours of video is uploaded to YouTube every day. Six billion hours. What was the chance of a two-second clip being played by a total stranger in front of the person who'd filmed it, in the very place in which they'd uploaded it. If that didn't freak you out, it would at least arouse your curiosity.

Tess played the snippet of video again, just to prove she hadn't clicked something by mistake. And, if it hadn't already, to send a chill down the spine of the filmmaker.

Even though he could only see the back of her head, Leroy scowled at her.

Just to rub the message in, Tess played the clip a third time.

Leroy kicked away the blue seat he was resting his feet on and stormed through the coffee shop to the exit. He didn't even look at her.

Darla called after him. "Tonight, baby, eight thirty?"

He ignored her and slammed the door behind him.

Through the window on the left of the door, he glanced back in at Tess.

Expressionless, she stared directly at him.

He glowered. All but stabbing her to death with his glare.

She held his gaze. Didn't look away. Didn't blink. Just stared.

He spun. Marched away.

If he wasn't freaked out before, he sure as hell would be now.

Tess rammed her tablet into her backpack, grabbed her leather jacket, and flew out after him.

Yep, there was nothing like poking a rabid dog with a stick to provoke a reaction. Now all she had to do was avoid getting bitten.

On the street, she turned left and followed him down the sidewalk. But what was he going to do? Would he go running to his friends to tell them about the freaky incident and ask for their help and advice? Or, he being the big man and she being a mere woman, would he want to deal with this problem himself?

Chapter 22

THE SUN IMPRISONED behind heavy clouds, vehicle tires made a *shhhh* sound as traffic crawled along the wet asphalt outside Paco's, while pedestrians scurried under umbrellas, desperate to avoid the rain as if it were made of acid, not mere water.

Pulling on her armored gloves, Tess marched down the street after Leroy. She flexed her fingers and clenched her fists to check the one-tenth-of-an-inch-thick titanium alloy plating inside wrapped around her hands snuggly and hinged properly, so as not to impede any movement.

She could have tailed Leroy discreetly, like they did in the movies, and hoped he'd lead her to his gang, but she wanted some quality alone time with this big brave dog killer. Plus, she wanted him freaked out, anxious, confused. That way, he was more likely to make a mistake. After all, she was only a girl – what threat could she pose to a hard man like him?

Ahead of her, Leroy glanced back. He clearly saw her. But he carried on down the sidewalk. At

Lindy's Laundromat, he turned left down a narrow alley.

The alley slick with rain and noxious with fumes from umpteen washing machines all emptying into a single drain at the side of the building, Tess followed.

At a corner at which he'd turned right, she stopped. She peeked around the edge of the wall to make sure he wasn't waiting, gun drawn. He wasn't. She turned right, stepped over a pile of broken wooden pallets, and continued down the alley. Ahead, Leroy did not look back. He turned left at a blue dumpster.

Excellent. Far away from the bustling street, she'd be able to confront him without witnesses. She quickened her pace to catch him up in the concrete maze of alleys.

Reaching the corner by the dumpster, she stopped and peeked around. Only about ten feet wide, buildings towered over the alley on either side.

Leroy had vanished.

Around ten yards away, she saw a red wooden door swinging too. She darted for it. From the grimy, mostly cracked windows in the building, it was obviously derelict.

She eased open the door a fraction, its red paint scuffed and peeling. She peeped in.

Gloom greeted her.

Wet footprints led across dusty floorboards, heading diagonally across a room forty feet square with walls stripped back to the plaster.

With no immediate threat, she stepped in and quietly shut the door.

The place smelled stale. Tasted dry. As if this was where air came to die.

Pounding footsteps hammered from a room beyond as if ascending stairs.

Tess's heart hammered too. She felt adrenaline start to energize her. This was a trap. She knew that. Somewhere inside the building, he'd attack her. Maybe even try to kill her. Through releasing adrenaline, her survival instinct was trying to prepare her for fight or flight. The easiest, the safest option was flight – to turn and run. But she had no choice – she had to go on.

With a clear idea of why he'd led her here, she needed to be prepared. Tess dug into her backpack as she padded across the room alongside the footprints and retrieved a pair of nitrile gloves. She liked nitrile. Latex gloves were harder to pull on over her leather ones and weren't as hard-wearing.

Pulling the gloves on as she prowled through the room, she breathed in for four seconds, held that breath for four, and then breathed out for four. Controlling her breathing was the easiest way to control her fear response.

Fear was a problem. Everybody knew that. But most people believed it for the wrong reasons.

Most people saw fear as a bad thing. As something itself to fear. Not least because most people associated fear with cowardice. On the contrary, fear was perfectly natural and nothing whatsoever to do with a lack of bravery. Fear was to be welcomed – it warned you something was wrong. Only a complete imbecile ignored fear.

Pale with fright – that was a sure sign of a coward, wasn't it? Everyone knew that. Except it wasn't. Paleness was a natural reaction. It was caused by the body drawing blood away from the extremities, which had two distinct benefits. Firstly, if the person was cut, there'd be less blood near the surface of the skin so there'd be less bleeding. Secondly, by prioritizing the flow of oxygenated blood to the most vital parts of the body, the person could better handle the impending fight or flight.

Fear was not to be avoided, but embraced as a survival mechanism.

However, unchecked, fear could put you in more danger than being in the dangerous situation itself. The rerouted blood flow starved the brain of oxygen so rational thought was difficult, if not impossible. Yes, it often wasn't a dangerous situation that killed people, but their inability to handle their own reaction to that situation. Their fear killed them.

At the far end of the room, a doorway led into darkness. Tess hugged the wall beside the opening. She closed her eyes tightly for three seconds, so on opening them again, her pupils would be as large as possible having been starved of light and allow her to see further into the darkness. Quickly poking her head out, she peered into the next room.

Even gloomier than the present room, a short corridor led to a staircase up to the next level.

Squinting, she just made out footprints in the dirt trailing towards the steps. She crept after them.

Her heart pounded harder, knowing the further she went into the building, the closer she was to danger.

At the stairs, she stared up into nothing but blackness.

Oh God, and she had to go up there?

She eased her right foot down on the first step.

It creaked loudly.

Hell, so much for creeping – he knew just where she was now. But where was he?

She moved her foot to the far-right side of the first step and eased down again.

Silence.

With firmer support at the sides of each stair to hold her weight better, she began her climb. She struggled to maintain her four-second breathing exercise, but she needed to remain as calm as possible.

Climbing higher and higher, the blackness gradually swallowed her. The hairs on the back of her neck prickled at the thought of what was lurking at the top.

Chapter 23

TESS STEPPED SLOWER and slower – she couldn't see the steps to place her feet with any certainty, and didn't want to stumble and alert him to her location, or fall backwards and break her neck. She imagined it was what it must be like to be blind and in a strange house.

Probing the stairs in front of her with each foot in turn to ensure there was something to actually stand on, she painstakingly made her way up. At the top of the stairs, darkness engulfed her.

But no voice cursed her. No hands grabbed her. No gun fired at her.

Her mouth as dry as the dusty floor, Tess hugged the wall of another corridor. At the far end, light bled in from the next room on the left. But the windows were either very dirty, or shrouded because the light was way too dim to be direct sunlight.

As her eyes became more accustomed to the dark, she made out shadowy shapes and a possible path through them.

She slunk forwards.

Something crunched under her foot. She winced. Froze. That had given the game away to anyone lurking in the shadows.

She listened.

Strained to catch the footfall of someone else moving about the building. Too far from the street for traffic noise, surely she'd hear Leroy. If he was still in here.

She strained and strained for the tiniest of sounds.

A footstep?

A rustle of clothing?

A breath?

All she heard was deathly silence.

She padded forward. The light ahead was her best hope. She'd see his footprints again, if not because of the rain, because of the dust he'd kicked up.

Her left arm outstretched, feeling along the wall, she crept toward the light. She ached to use the penlight in her backpack, but knew that would not just give away her position, but give Leroy a target to aim at. Her heart raced at the images of horror and death stalking through her mind.

This wasn't how she'd imagined this going down. Catching the guy in an alley, yes, but skulking further and further into a creepy ruined building? Hell, no.

She stared into the shadows. The black shadows.

The darkness filled her mind with nightmares.

Where was he?

Who else might be hiding here that she couldn't see?

When would they jump out and try to end her life?

She tried to slow her breathing again. She had to stay focused, had to listen for the smallest sound, had to watch for the smallest flicker of a shadow. She couldn't afford to put her mind elsewhere and to picture her tranquil lake. But she couldn't afford to let her fear run rampant, either.

She felt a dire urge to pee, but it wasn't due to all Paco's tea. No, it was that dreaded fear again.

How often does some schoolkid get laughed at for years because he was so frightened of something he wet himself? That was a typical example of cowardice. Everyone knew that. Except, again, everyone was wrong. Eliminating waste was simply another natural reaction – the body wanted to make itself as light as possible to be able to move faster. It wasn't fear, it was simple physics.

Using her four-second technique, Tess forced her breathing to remain as slow as she could manage. Limiting her body's natural responses. Limiting release of adrenaline. Limiting the possibility of her thinking becoming impaired. She had to stay sharp. Had to be able to think. Had to be able to fight.

Peering down, she strained to see the floor.

Blackness.

With each footstep, she felt the floor ahead of her with her toes, just to ensure there was actually floor there and she wouldn't plummet to a basement and spear herself on some rusting machinery.

Another step.

And another.

As was obvious from the dust, people rarely ventured in here. It was the ideal place into which to lure someone and ambush them.

She crept on.

Another step.

The light crawled nearer.

A body would probably rot to nothing but bones before it was found in here.

From the lack of noises ahead, she was sure Leroy was lurking in the shadows somewhere, waiting to pounce. But where?

If he wasn't and he'd escaped her, then at the pace she'd been moving, she'd lost him and would be back to square one. But why would he lure her in here if all he wanted to do was disappear?

Another step.

Her foot slid over something that scraped on the floor. Hell, it was impossible to be quiet in this place.

Almost at the light, she took out a compact from her backpack to look around the corner using the mirror. She fumbled it. Dropped it. But caught it. She heaved out a breath as quietly as she could.

At the edge of the opening, engulfed in murky light, she held her mirror around the corner.

Nothing.

Not a person.

Not a gun barrel.

Not a footprint in sight.

She'd lost him. Barely audibly, she said, "Oh, shit."

She felt the unmistakable coldness of a gun muzzle press against the back of her head.

Leroy said, "Ain't that the truth!"

Chapter 24

"MOVE." LEROY SHOVED her in the back.

Tess staggered forwards.

Unable to see their assailant and unable to feel their weapon, a person would have to be crazy to attempt to disarm a killer. Controlling Leroy's gun was paramount, but that was impossible in this situation. Yes, she had her bulletproof vest on, but that would do squat against a head shot.

If only she'd acted the instant she'd felt the gun, when she'd known exactly where it was to be able to attack it safely, then he'd be the one at her mercy, not her at his. But even with her years of training, a sudden shock caused a momentary freeze while her brain processed the information. Her training had made that freeze as tiny as possible, but that moment had been all that Leroy had needed.

No, she had no option but to do as he said.

Her hands up, she shuffled through the doorway.

Another bare room with nothing but grime and dead memories engulfed her. It was as if raiders had broken into a tomb and stripped it of everything but the brick walls and the wood floor.

Leroy shoved her towards the middle of the room. A ghostly half-light crawled across the bare dusty floorboards towards her from three small filthy windows.

In her mind, Tess saw herself lying in a pool of blood up here, dead, rotting, forgotten.

Her heart hammered as if it was going to rupture.

She breathed slowly. Calming her body. Calming her mind. She couldn't panic. Couldn't let fear cloud her thoughts. If she did, she'd miss any opportunity for escape, or seize an opportunity that she shouldn't have and end up the bloody mess on the floor she'd imagined.

"Stop," Leroy said.

Tess froze in the middle of the room. With no physical contact between them, she had no real idea of where he or his gun were. She needed to know. If she couldn't see or feel the gun, couldn't see or feel him, she was helpless. If she made one wrong move, said one wrong word, she wouldn't see anything ever again.

"What game you playing, motherfucker?" said Leroy.

"Please, don't—don't hurt me." She panted for breath. "I'm—I'm a journalist. I want an interview about gang violence. I—I can pay. Please."

"You shitting in my ears, bitch!"

"Honestly, I'm a journalist." Her voice tremored. "I can show you ID."

"Turn 'round. Real slow."

Tess shuffled around to face him, hands still held high.

He glowered down at her.

"Give me one good reason I don't blow your fucking ass away right here."

Leroy raised his gun to aim between her eyes. At less than a foot away, if he fired, she'd be dead before her brain even registered the muzzle flash.

Her chin trembling and voice high-pitched, Tess said, "Please, I can pay. I have money. Please." Her hands up, she gestured to her backpack.

He adjusted his grip on his pistol. Probably more to frighten than for his comfort.

Leroy said, "How much you gonna pay, fucker?"

"Do you want two carrots and a pig?"

A look of surprise flashed across his face.

That momentary break in his concentration, while his brain struggled to process something so unexpected, was all Tess needed.

Her hands already at the same height as his gun, she simultaneously ducked, in case he got a shot off, and grabbed the pistol over the trigger guard. She twisted the gun up and back toward him. Using the mechanics of the hand and shape of the weapon, she broke his trigger finger and with it, his hold.

Before it had even registered with him, he'd lost his grip on the gun. And on the situation.

Tess stepped back, racking a round in case her disarm had jammed the weapon. Distance between them, so he couldn't pull a similar move to get his gun back, she aimed his gun at him. A Sig Sauer P226. The gun with which he'd killed Chiang's dog.

He smiled, backing away and cradling his finger. "Hey, whoa." He laughed. "You wanna interview me, that's cool. Ask anything you want. Any question you like."

"Thank you."

In her mind, she saw him shoot the dog.

Tess shot Leroy in the right knee.

He screamed. A cloud of dust rose as he crashed to the floor.

He clutched his leg, rolling in pain. "You fucking shot me!"

Tess smiled. "Question one: who shot Kim Chiang?"

"Fuck you, you crazy bitch."

She shot his left foot.

He screamed again.

"Question two: who shot Kim Chiang?"

He wailed, clutching his knee while reaching for his foot. Blood gushed into the dust.

He pointed at her. "You know who I am, bitch? Know who I am? You is dead, motherfucker." He stabbed his finger at her. "Dead!"

She shot his hand.

He rolled back and forth, and cradled his hand with his remaining good one. He sobbed.

"Question three: who shot Kim Chiang?"

346

He shook his head and muttered to himself in between sobs.

She shot his left knee.

He shrieked. Flailed in the dust. Blood spurted. Blood gushed. Blood seeped.

"Question four: who shot Kim Chiang?"

His face smeared with blood and tears, he shook his head. "I can't… I can't tell—"

She shot his right arm.

"Question five: who shot Kim Chiang?"

Bloody saliva drooling from his gaping mouth into the dust, he simply shook his head.

She aimed at his right leg.

Trembling, he raised his hand to beg for her to stop. "Pl—please… Please no more."

"You're going to tell me what I want to know or, in a month or two, some kids playing hide and go seek are going to find a rotting body with eyes that are just black pits of mold." She smiled. "No pressure." She shot him in the right foot.

He cried out.

Blubbering, he struggled to get the words out. "I—I can't tell. They'll kill me."

"Is it they holding a gun on you right this second?"

His breathing but broken pants, he said, "If—if—if I say… You'll, you'll quit shooting and call 911?"

She shrugged. "That would seem fair."

Struggling with the choice, his face twisted in pain – whether more physical or mental it was impossible to tell.

She took that opportunity to step to one side and snatch a piece of old sacking and a couple of shell casings from the floor, while still training the gun on him.

Finally, through gasped breaths, he said, "Jarvis T—Taylor and Eddie—Eddie Br—Brown."

"And where will I find Jarvis and Eddie?"

"You'll call 911?"

She stared at him, deadpan and unblinking.

"They got a wor— workshop." He gasped a couple of breaths. "They's pimping their ride. 2417 Wilmington."

Tess walked away, trailing the sacking behind her to destroy her footprints.

"Hey! … Hey!" Leroy shouted, "You said you'd call 911!"

At the corner of the darkened corridor from which they'd entered, she turned.

"Sometimes, good people just have real bad days. Ask Mr. Chiang."

She disappeared into the darkness.

"Motherfucker! Mother—" He whined in pain.

Whimpering like a shot dog and drenched in his own blood, he struggled to move a trembling hand to his coat pocket.

Sobbing, he fumbled.

He managed to pull out his phone.

Hands trembling, smearing blood all over the screen, he tried to make a call.

Tess appeared around the edge of the corridor.

"Bye bye, doggie." She shot his phone. His last hope for life.

He screamed, "No!"

Picking her way down the black corridor, she popped out a couple of rounds from the magazine. Like the casings, they'd have his fingerprints on them, so they'd be ideal as evidence decoys for one of her future jobs.

As she meandered back through the darkness, she disassembled the gun. She couldn't help but wonder about what had just happened. No, it wasn't that. It wasn't what had happened – it was her reaction to what had happened. She'd killed before. Many, many times. And each one of those people had deserved it, but she'd never killed in such a cold, calculated way – letting a man bleed out, alone, in a derelict building.

Should she feel remorse? Guilt? Even shame?

Why?

She'd have no qualms about swatting a mosquito – an insect that fed off the blood of innocents. Why should this be any different?

The human race was the highest species on the planet, but it was still only a species – people were merely creatures, organisms, beasts. It was mankind itself that bestowed people with superior rights to every other living thing on the planet, not God. Once a person caused too much pain and suffering to others, their 'superior' status deserved to be revoked. They became just the same as any other animal. And like dealing with any crazed beast, there was only one solution – you had to kill it. Had to.

And it wasn't like she'd got some perverse pleasure out of torturing Leroy. He should've given her the information she needed sooner. That was his choice. Just as surely as pulling the trigger in the store had been.

Shame? Guilt? Remorse? Please! Did anyone ever feel guilt over scraping dog shit off their shoe?

Dragging the sacking through the dust behind her, she crossed the first room in the building she'd entered and then looked back at the smeared trail through the dirt where hers and Leroy's footprints had once been.

From above, she heard feeble sobbing and whining, and the occasional pleading for help, for God, for Momma.

It wouldn't last much longer. Not with such blood loss. The world felt a better place already. And soon, it was going to feel even better. It just needed everything to play out as she imagined it was going to. She drew a deep breath. But did life ever make things that easy for her?

Chapter 25

BACK IN THE alley, she tossed the sacking away. Keeping the gun's barrel – the part with which ballistics could most easily prove if the weapon had been involved in any crime – she tossed the rest of the gun into a dumpster.

Nearing the street, she popped her armored gloves into her backpack, took out a cigarette lighter, and then torched her nitrile gloves. She dropped the remnants down the grate at the side of the Laundromat, where gray soapy water sluiced them into the drainage system. Should she be stopped by the police, for whatever reason, she couldn't afford to have gunshot residue on her or her clothing.

When she reached the street and saw people and cars and stores and sunlight and life, a rush surged through her body, filling her with hope. Yes, the world did feel like a better place already.

Tess might only be a 0.0000003% statistic, but something so small and insignificant really could make a difference. While she knew many people wouldn't agree with how she chose to live her life, how she chose to make the world a better place, those same people would be able to sleep a fraction more soundly in their beds tonight and walk a little more carefree on the street tomorrow. All because of what she'd done. What she devoted her life to doing. Because of her, the human race was one tiny fraction of a step further along its evolutionary path.

Shame? Guilt? Remorse? She smirked. She was doing okay. As long as she kept asking those kinds of questions she knew was doing the right thing, because she knew she was still human. Unlike the Leroys of the world, who never questioned what they did and if they had a right to do it. The day she stopped questioning her choices, whether she was right to take the lives she did, would be the day she hoped some lowlife scum put a bullet in her head.

She crossed the street and bought a can of cola from a vendor with a little blue cart. He was obviously one of those people who felt uncomfortable if people weren't smiling all the time.

As he handed her the change for her cola, he said, "Cheer up, it might never happen."

It had happened. Innumerable times. In more dire and diverse forms than this poor deluded soul could ever fathom. But she smiled anyway. Gave his world a gentle tip in the right direction.

She avoided sugar-laden drinks most of the time, despite enjoying them – an athlete's body needed premium fuel if it was to run at a premium level. When she was out in the field working a job, however, she needed to eat and drink regularly to keep her energy levels from flagging, so the odd fast food fling was something she could easily justify enough to happily turn a blind eye to it. If she hadn't been working, she'd have mentally chastised herself for hours over such a slip.

Sipping on her cola, she glanced up at the sky. The rain little more than a light drizzle again, a rainbow arched over the city.

Taking a moment to admire the glowing pastel shades, she smiled, its simplicity yet undeniable beauty soothing her soul, providing a brief respite from the gore and mayhem into which she so willingly walked so often. She squinted at the faint outline of a secondary rainbow, its colors inverted. It was unusual to see one of those. She took a deep refreshing breath and then looked back to the street.

Beside her, the headline of the newspapers in a sidewalk vending machine read *Child's Foot Found on Liberty Island*. Tess's smile faded. Her shoulders slumped. That was the third severed body part found in the last six months. All from young girls. Even more worryingly, DNA had proven the other two had been from different children. Would this be a third child who'd been butchered?

She glanced back up to the heavens.

The rainbow had disappeared.

The sky was once again but a slab of gray.

She sighed. The world felt a fraction emptier without those pastel shades casting color upon it. Just like the Chiang family's world would feel emptier without the color Kim Chiang brought into it.

Jarvis Taylor and Eddie Brown would pay for that. Such cold killers would never appreciate the beauty of a rainbow. Just like they'd never appreciate Jane Eyre, the Mona Lisa, or Mozart's Piano Concerto No. 23. If they didn't appreciate what it meant to be human – the wonders to be shared and the wonder of sharing them – there was no place in humanity for them. Superiority revoked. Payback due.

Oh, she'd play fair with Jarvis and Eddie. As she always did. Hell, she wasn't an executioner. She wouldn't sneak up on them from behind, the way they probably would, and blast away with a .45. Oh no, she'd give them the same chance she gave everyone – if they could beat her, they could live. No, she wasn't an executioner. More of a prize fighter. And the prize was life.

She dropped the empty cola can into a trash can, dropping the gun barrel in at the same time. If the police discovered Leroy's body, they'd search the building and the surrounding alleyways, but they'd never find this barrel to be able to compare rifling on any bullets retrieved. If they couldn't connect Leroy to the Chiang murder, they wouldn't be looking at a revenge killing but something gang related. That gave Tess more leeway.

She marched down the street. What would she find waiting for her at 2417 Wilmington? Would Jarvis and Eddie be as obliging as Leroy and provide the means for their own demise? She doubted it.

And anyway, she detested guns – the weapon of the inept. The only reason she'd used one on Leroy was because he'd all but jammed one into her hand. It would've been stupid not to have used it.

Any time, any place, she wanted to be able to walk into a room, deal with a situation with her bare hands, and if need be, legitimately claim self-defense. Walk into a room with a gun and the shit hits the fan, you're talking premeditated murder.

Before finding Jarvis and Eddie, however, she needed to find a restroom. Using the toilet was always a good idea before heading into battle, but she needed to secure her combat guards to her shins and forearms under her clothes too.

More important, though, she needed to remove her body armor and reposition it. Too many hours of sitting in the café had seen it ride up – if she was to face two killers with guns, she needed her vest perfectly aligned to her torso. A black eye would be easy to explain away to Josh – another accident at her self-defense class. A bullet hole? That would be considerably trickier.

That was odd. Her first thought wasn't about a bullet killing her, but about how she'd explain a wound away to her... To her what? Boyfriend? No. That suggested commitment, a relationship, a future. No,

boyfriend was too strong a term. Fuck buddy? Well...
Maybe that was closer, but... What the hell was Josh?

Whoa!

More to the point, what the devil was she doing
thinking about him when she was on the job? This
game was all about focus. Extreme focus. Her life
depended on it. If her mind drifted off into relationship
crap at the wrong time, hell, she'd be lucky to make it
out alive, let alone with just a wound.

Josh? What the hell was wrong with her?

Chapter 26

TESS SLUNK DOWN the sidewalk as the sun meekly shone through breaks in the gray slabs overhead. In the rain, with shafting sunlight, buildings like the Chrysler, the Empire State, and the One World Trade Center all gleamed. Their masonry, steel, and glass were vibrant when wet – their colors so vivid, textures so tactile, polished surfaces so glistening. Like all things, the rainwater seemed to imbue such buildings with life.

Tess ran a gloved hand over the warehouse wall beside which she walked, its brickwork blackened by decades of smog and neglect.

The city was bipolar. In one moment it could be vibrant and effervescent, while in the next, it could be riddled with cancer and close to death.

It was no surprise it was a battleground for the *haves*, *have-nots*, and *haven't-enoughs*. Unfortunately, that meant a swathe of innocent bystanders being targeted and victimized.

And who mourned the innocent?

If they were lucky – a handful of people. If they were unlucky – no one.

To the people who loved them, they were a person with needs, dreams, feelings – a life. But to everyone else? They were just a number: to their employer, they were a Social Security number; to their favorite stores, they were a loyalty card number; to the government, they were one in 316 million, just 0.0000003% of the population. Such a tiny statistic was as good as invisible. Which made it no surprise that, unless they were wealthy or influential, they were only a number, not a real person.

The Chiangs were just such statistics. The authorities said they cared, but the case would be buried if it didn't shed immediate results. Buried and forgotten. Just like Kim Chiang – except by his family.

Luckily, Tess liked being nothing more than a 0.0000003% statistic. She'd learned to like it the hard way, but now she actively courted invisibility. She needed it to safeguard her anonymity and make her life so much easier. Living in a shadow world one step outside the real one, she could move freely whenever and wherever she pleased. And do all manner of things that normal people would never believe possible.

In the next hour, for example, she was going to rid the world of two other tiny statistics and, in so doing, not just avenge some people, but probably save innumerable others.

She pulled her black wool hat further down over her forehead and adjusted her sunglasses. There were a number of operational surveillance cameras in the area that she'd spotted already, so there were probably ones she hadn't yet seen. If she was captured on tape in the vicinity, she wanted as little of her visible as possible.

Nearing her destination, she studied the photos of Jarvis Taylor and Eddie Brown that Bomb had found for her and sent to her phone. She needed to be able to recognize them instantly – Jarvis's drawn cheeks and goatee; Eddie's sharp nose and tattoo of an eagle spreading up his throat from his chest.

Skulking along Wilmington, she practiced her four-second breathing technique to stop an adrenaline dump from ripping rational thought from her mind and, as a result, ripping life from her body.

Passing another warehouse, she finally came to 2417, a one-story unit set back from the road, wide enough for maybe five cars.

Ignoring the closed rolling steel door used for vehicles, she approached the solitary black door at the far left of the building. Despite her relaxation techniques, her heart raced. Fear was good. But not too much. Adrenaline was good. But not too much.

She removed her dark glasses.

Breathed long and slow.

And reached for the door.

She wrapped her fingers gently around the knob, much of its cheap chrome-like finish having worn away to reveal dirty, coppery colored metal, making it look older than it probably was. Tess prayed it wasn't so old it would squeal as she turned it, or stick so the door needed a hefty shove to open. But as the thump of music came from somewhere within the building, she hoped that would be loud enough to hide any noise she made gaining entry.

She eased the knob around slowly, ready to pull back at the slightest noise just to be safe.

The knob's metal innards scraped and ground, but not so loudly that anyone would ever hear, unless they were crouching down at the other side with their ear pressed against the door, listening for it.

Maybe getting in was going to be easier than she'd figured.

The knob stopped dead. Locked.

Goddamnit, why did she have to tempt fate like that?

She looked over her shoulder. After her stealthy approach, she couldn't risk spending too long getting in and have someone either call the police now or when giving a statement later, remember her for having loitered in the vicinity.

Having unslung her backpack, she slipped a hand in and removed a small black leather wallet in which she kept her selection of lock picks.

Picking locks always looked easy in films. As easy as fiddling with a couple of wires to start a car. Yeah, right, like real life was ever that easy.

Well…

Okay, there was the odd exception. And man, would that be useful right now.

Most door locks worked through a simple tumbler system: a number of tiny metal pins slid up and down inside cylinders and if a person twisted the lock slowly enough while levering up each cylinder in a precise order, the lock opened. Magic!

Except, it wasn't magic, just simple mechanics. The problem was that those 'simple mechanics' took patience, a delicate touch, and time, only two of which she had.

Tess selected two tools from her little wallet. She inserted one end of a thin, L-shaped piece of metal into the lock, eased the lock around until it wouldn't turn any further, and then held it there under tension.

After inserting her second tool, which looked like a tiny flattened corkscrew, she quickly drew it back and forth along the full length of the lock. Tess repeatedly raked the tool across the bottoms of the tumblers. The raking technique didn't always work, but when it did, it could open a lock in a matter of...

The door's lock clicked open. That was less than four seconds. Amazing. Thank God for those exceptions to the rules!

While rap music blared from an MP3 player sitting in a dock with speakers, Tess crept into the gloomy end of the workshop. At the other end, tube lights revealed two men working on a black car raised on jacks, its windows tinted.

She crouched beside one of two green easy chairs, grubby chunks of white padding bleeding out of them from tears.

Peeking out, she saw welding equipment, rudimentary lathe and grinding gear, all manner of hand tools, and shelves of other equipment, much of which she couldn't identify.

She placed her backpack at the side of the chair and then crept over to behind a large workbench daubed with various colors of paint and gouged by countless tools.

For just five seconds, Tess closed her eyes. Five seconds to an ordinary person in this situation would've felt like a lifetime. To Tess, it was just long enough. This was what she'd been waiting for. This was when justice would be done. This was when she'd make a difference to the world by shining a light into its darkest shadows.

A sickness churned in her stomach.

Her muscles ached with the adrenaline charging them with power.

By embracing her fear, she focused on the calmness found in its depths.

She opened her eyes.

Peeked out from behind the bench.

This was it. She was ready.

Chapter 27

WORKING ON OPPOSITE sides of the car, the two guys were in the middle of a heated debate.

With the chest tattoo, the man nearest to her said, "They gotta swallow. Period. They ain't gonna swallow, might as well be a handjob."

At the far side of the car, a man with a goatee said, "You crazy, nigger?" He waved a wrench at him over the car's hood. "You is telling me you'd have Betsy Green's hand on your cock before those luscious red lips of hers?"

"If she ain't gonna swallow."

"Swallow be fucked, man. It's the suck as matters. They gotta suck it strong. Like they is drowning and sucking on air for their life. They don't suck good, they don't blow good."

"Just 'cause it's called sucking cock, don't mean they literally gotta suck, dumbass."

"What!? Where the fuck you been sticking your dick, nigger, 'cause I'm telling you the best ever—"

Tess stepped out from the shadows. "While I hate to interrupt the advance of the feminist movement, why don't you boys just sixty-nine each other and settle it?"

Openmouthed, they both stood and stared at her.

She walked towards them.

Goatee said, "Who the fuck are you?"

Recognizing him from the photo Bomb had sent, she pointed at him. "Jarvis Taylor?" She pointed at the other man. "Eddie Brown?"

Neither man denied their identity.

From the far side of the car, Jarvis pointed his wrench at her. "Like the man said, who the fuck are you?"

She stared into their eyes. Simply to be accepted into a gang, these two men had taken an innocent person's life. By abusing the rights of another individual, they'd forfeited their own. They had no more right to draw another breath than a maggot gnawing away a perfect apple. And there was only one solution to a maggot infestation.

She said, "Kim Chiang sends his regards." She jammed in her mouthguard. And then waited. Defiant.

The men glanced at each other, then, the closest, Eddie lunged at her, while Jarvis dashed around the front of the car.

She ducked under Eddie's haymaker.

Shot the arc of her right thumb and index finger into his throat.

Gasping, he staggered back.

She slammed a kick into his knee.

364

Bone crunched.

He screamed and crumpled to the floor.

Jarvis already on her, he swung his wrench.

Instead of moving away, she moved in. Blocking his weapon arm with one hand, she let the wrench whip past her.

Grabbing him, she twisted and threw him over her hip.

He crashed into the floor on his back.

Still holding his arm, she locked it against the elbow. Heaved back.

Accompanied by the sound of a breaking joint, Jarvis screamed.

She pulled her hand back to strike, but saw Eddie was back on his feet. Back on his feet and pointing a pistol.

She leapt up.

Ran.

He fired.

"Motherfucker!" Clambering up, Jarvis blasted his weapon too.

Bullets ripped through the air as she dove over the car's hood.

Shots peppered the wall, blasting paint cans, tools, and spare parts off the shelving.

Tess crashed to the oil-stained concrete floor at the other side of the car..

Jarvis stopped shooting. He held his hand towards Eddie for him to do likewise.

They waited.

The room stood silent. Still.

"Fucking A!" Jarvis said, turning to bump fists with Eddie.

"That's what you gets for busting up my knee, motherfucker," said Eddie.

Jarvis nudged him. "Check it out."

Dragging his hurt leg, Eddie hobbled around the front of the vehicle, around an oil drum and a column of piled tires, to view his prize.

Maintaining his aim at the car area, Jarvis moved closer, holding his right arm across his body as if wanting to protect it.

Eddie lumbered around the far corner of the car, gun ready.

But there was no body.

"Where the fuck?" said Eddie.

Tess shot a hand out from under the car. Stabbed a long thin screwdriver through his ankle.

He screeched.

Toppled over onto all fours.

She drove the screwdriver up under his chin.

Speared it into him up to its hilt.

Glistening, its bloody shaft burst out of the top of his head.

Eddie splattered into the floor. Motionless.

"You get the bitch, Eddie?" When he received no reply, Jarvis called with more urgency. "Eddie?"

Tess glanced over her shoulder under the vehicle.

Crouched to peer under the car, Jarvis's jaw dropped as he saw her and saw the blood pooling from Eddie's head. He jerked his gun up.

Tess rolled over Eddie.

Used him as a shield.

As Jarvis let rip with his pistol.

Shots slammed into Eddie. As if he wasn't dead enough.

"Fucking bitch. You is dead!"

Tess saw Jarvis's feet under the car as he stalked around for her.

She couldn't fight someone with a gun like this. She looked for Eddie's gun, as an equalizer. Nowhere around. Shit! She needed to play for time.

Jarvis appeared at the front of the car.

Tess rolled over Eddie again.

Jarvis blasted another round.

The shot hit the ground behind her. Concrete shards flew up, as she rolled under the vehicle.

Luckily, she heard the unmistakable clicking of an empty gun. Unluckily, she was already too far away to take advantage of that.

She rolled out the far side and crouched at the rear panel, gasping for air. Had Jarvis gotten more ammo? She couldn't risk trying to attack only to walk into a shower of 9mm lead.

She looked under the car but couldn't see Jarvis's feet anymore. He was probably standing behind the piled tires, or the oil drum, at the front of the car.

He'd be freaked out by a lone woman walking in off the street and, not just attacking them, but killing his friend. He'd be jumpy, anxious, trigger happy. She could use that.

For just a second, she poked her hand up for him to see it.

No gun fired.

Was he out of ammo? Or was he faking it to lure her out?

She leapt up, ready to fight.

A car tire slammed her in the chest. She crashed back against the rolling steel main door, and then crumpled to the floor.

Gasping, she pushed up onto all fours and shot a look sideways.

Jarvis stormed towards her with another tire. "I is gonna tear your fucking head off and shit down your fucking neck!" He heaved the tire overhand and hurled it at her.

Tess rolled toward him. The tire hurtled over her and bounced off the door.

As she rolled to her feet, Jarvis kicked at her.

She sidestepped. Kicked into the soft tissue of his other leg's inner thigh.

In the same fluid movement, she stepped closer and smashed her elbow straight up into his jaw.

He fell back against the car.

Grabbing his head with both hands, she heaved it down to crash her knee into his face.

But her feet slid on the oily floor.

She fell against him.

He grabbed her.

Kneed her in the stomach.

Punched her in the side of the head.

Flung her aside.

She slammed into the car door. Slumped to the floor.

Jarvis aimed a kick at her face.

A little dazed, she dodged to one side, but the foot still grazed the side of her head.

The kick banged into the door panel, denting it.

More through instinct from years of training than through rational thought, Tess saw an opening, so she acted. She hammered her armored fist into his exposed groin.

Jarvis gasped.

Clutched his crotch.

Staggered back.

Tess scrambled to her feet.

Kicked him in the gut.

He hunched over.

She slammed a right hook into his face.

Blood and teeth flew through the air.

He sprawled face first on the concrete, beside one of the tires he'd slung at her.

With one arm injured, he struggled to get up on his hands and knees. Tess snatched one of the tires. She slung it over his head so its bead, the reinforced rim that fitted to the wheel, caught under his chin, while the inner hollow completely engulfed his face.

She thumped down onto him, slamming her right knee into his back.

He crashed to the floor with her on top of him.

Hooking an elbow through the tire, she heaved back on it.

He clawed feverishly at it, the black rubber straining his head far back.

His throat gurgled and spluttered as the hardened rim bit into it.

Tess jerked her whole body over, ripping the tire back towards Jarvis's feet.

His neck crunched.

His clawing hands slumped to the floor.

The gurgling died to silence.

Chapter 28

DROPPING THE TIRE, Tess staggered forward as her adrenaline high subsided and the stresses of combat hit exhausted muscles. A few teetering steps dragged her to the workbench. Collapsed on her elbows over it, she breathed long and deep, letting oxygen-rich blood rejuvenate her drained mind and body.

After a good twenty seconds, she pushed herself up. She glanced over her shoulder. She hadn't bitten anyone, so there'd be no teeth marks; had worn her gloves, so there'd be no fingerprints; she hadn't been scratched, so there'd be no DNA under anyone's fingernails.

She huffed.

But hair? Had she lost a hair follicle or two which would leave behind her DNA for a forensics team to find? Bomb had once managed to delete files of her DNA from a law enforcement database, but it had been a hellishly complex and risky task, so it was best to play safe.

She could torch the place. But if the gunshots hadn't already alerted people something was amiss, a fire would have the authorities here in minutes.

She saw the barrel at the front of the car.

Almost full of waste oil, solvents, and heaven only knew what else, she drew a bucketful. She removed the cash from both their wallets, took Jarvis's gold watch and Eddie's thick gold neck chain and rings. Those would cover her many rent payments for a few weeks. She then drenched the two bodies in gunk from the bucket, before upending the barrel for the sticky gloop to smother the whole floor. It wouldn't kill DNA, but even the most tenacious lab technician would never find a viable sample in such a mess.

Retrieving a souvenir from the Pool Cleaner job, she slung a used condom onto one of the green chairs and stuffed it down between the cushions. The Nazi scum she'd encountered on that job would have a fun time explaining to the police why his DNA had been found at the scene of a crime involving black gang members. After all these months, there'd be no way he would connect her with what was happening, so he'd be as confused as the police. And it was that which was important – the confusion the evidence would create. The more confusion there was over these killings, the bigger the safety net she had.

She left.

It being rush hour now, traffic even crawled along this seedy side street. She pulled down her wool hat as far as she could and put on her dark glasses.

Marching toward the busiest street to once more be invisible amidst the herd, a sense of dissatisfaction gnawed at her. She'd done the right thing. There was no question of that. Society was safer; the Chiangs were avenged. But...

She'd believed killing these three thugs would change things, that it would be cathartic. She'd seen Kim Chiang as a surrogate for her grandpa and thought that seeing justice done for Kim would finally help her feel justice had been served for her family.

It hadn't.

In fact, not only hadn't it helped, but now there was a dark void where, just hours before, had been contentment, or what passed for it in her brutal world. She remembered this void – it had eaten at her, driven her, shaped her for enough years that she could never forget it. But she didn't want it to come back. The endless years of tormented visions, of self-recrimination, of the frustration of unanswered questions – she'd buried all that. So deep. She couldn't let it all be unearthed again. The whole point of taking this particular job had been to finally bury the past, not to reawaken it.

So as not to cause an incident which might lift her cloak of invisibility, Tess normally zigzagged her way through the city, walking around people too busy to watch where they were going themselves. Now, however, the sidewalk swarming with people, Tess bumped shoulders with a woman on her phone, then a man laughing with his friends. Both of them stared at her.

Tess realized she had to focus. Had to calm her emotions and get home without incident or causing anyone to remember her as having been in that vicinity.

Standing between a mailbox and a streetlight to shield her from the rampaging herd, Tess phoned Bomb, while the rush hour traffic slowly shunted by.

"Yo, Tess. We good?"

"It's done. But…"

Bomb sighed. "But it hasn't changed anything?"

"That's the problem. It has. And…" She heaved a breath. "I thought it'd make things better, not worse."

With a red stoplight ahead, a silver sedan sat in the street in front of her. In the back seat, with sharp cheekbones and a pointed nose, a middle-aged man eyed her up and down. She ignored it and looked away.

"That's the problem with old wounds, Tess," said Bomb. "I tried to tell you."

"But it was seventeen years ago. *Seventeen years.* What the hell do I have to do?"

"You don't *have to* do anything. You just live with it. Like you've been doing."

She heaved another breath. That wasn't what she wanted to hear. This was supposed to have been cathartic. By ridding the world of Kim Chiang's killers, she was supposed to rid her own life of the demons that had plagued her for the best part of two decades. She knew it wouldn't bring her grandpa back, knew it wouldn't take away all the pain and suffering she'd endured since, knew it wouldn't give her back her childhood, but… Surely it should have given her something. Anything!

"I'm—I'm sorry, Tess," said Bomb. "I, er, don't really know what else to say."

"I…" Tess hung her head.

"Listen, go home, get some rest, and eat a decent meal. Let what's happened today sink in and we'll talk later. Okay?"

"I just thought it would be different."

"I know. I'm sorry."

She hung up.

Now what? She hadn't built a good life, but she'd built a purposeful one. But she wasn't a machine: she couldn't only help others because it was the right thing to do, she needed something for herself. She needed some sort of fulfillment. She needed some sort of hope. She needed some sort of… closure.

Her gaze roaming the street, it fell back to the passenger in the car who'd eyed her up. He blew her a kiss, then smiled the kind of smile you only ever see in toothpaste commercials, wide, beaming, glorious.

Tess's jaw dropped.

She froze.

She knew that smile. It had been burned into her memory amid a hail of bullets.

Her phone trembled in her hand.

The guy laughed at her reaction as his car drove away.

She stood. Frozen in a memory of her own personal nightmare.

In her mind, she saw the blood; heard the screams; felt the clawing hands. The same blood, the same screams, the same hands she'd suffered so many times, for so very, very long. For seventeen endless and torturous years.

She stood. Her mind ablaze with horrific images and unanswerable questions.

And she stood…

She didn't know how long she stood, but suddenly something snapped. She gasped an almighty breath like a newborn child startled at being introduced to the world with a slap.

She spun to see the car, the smiling man…

But they'd disappeared.

She ran. Ran to the intersection. Ran into the road. Ran into the darting traffic.

A red sedan swerved, horn blaring. It swiped a silver SUV. A blue car hammered on its brakes, but skidded on the wet road and smashed into the two cars.

Tess didn't see the crash, didn't see the danger, didn't see the angry faces. Twisting around and around, she scanned the other three lanes of bumper-to-bumper traffic into which fed all the vehicles from the street on which she'd been standing. Where was he? Where was that silver car?

Around and around and around.

Staring and staring and staring.

She hit speed dial #1. Shouted. "Bomb! Bomb, I've seen him. I've seen the man who murdered my grandpa!"

The End

Continue the pulse-pounding *Angel of Darkness* adventure. Flip the page now and discover *Predator Mine* (book 06).

Free Library of Books

Thank you for reading *Mourning Scars*. To show my appreciation of my readers, I wrote a second series of books exclusively for them – each *Angel of Darkness* book has its own *Black File*, so there's a free library for you to collect and enjoy.

A FREE Library Waiting for You!

Exclusive? You bet! You can't get the *Black Files* anywhere except through the links in the *Angel of Darkness* books.

Start Your FREE Library with *Black Files 04-06*.
http://stevenleebooks.com/tfbm

Make Your Opinion Count

Dear Thriller Lover,

Do you have a few seconds to spare?

It is unbelievably difficult for an emerging writer to reach a wider audience, not least because less than 1% of readers leave reviews. Hard to believe, isn't it? Of one hundred readers, maybe - that's 'maybe' - one reader will post a few words.

Please, will you help me by sharing how much you enjoyed this book in a short review?

It only takes a few seconds because it only needs a handful of words. I'll be ever so grateful.

Don't follow the 99% – stand out from the crowd with just a few clicks!

Thank you,

Steve

Copy the link to post your review of *Mourning Scars:*
http://stevenleebooks.com/w3ft

Free Goodies – VIP Area

See More, Do More, Get More!

Do you want to get more than the average reader gets? Every month I send my VIP readers some combination of:

- news about my books

- giveaways from me or my writer friends

- opportunities to help choose book titles and covers

- anecdotes about the writing life, or just life itself

- special deals and freebies

- sneak behind-the-scenes peeks at what's in the works.

Get Exclusive VIP Access with this Link.

http://stevenleebooks.com/wcfl

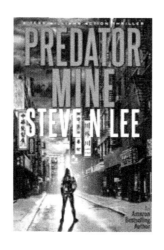

Predator Mine

Angel of Darkness Book 06

Chapter 01

WHEN WAKING FROM a nightmare in the dead of night, what would be the most terrifying thing a child could see? A shadow flitting across their room? Their closet door creaking open? Or Mommy gazing down at them?

The bedcovers pulled up over her head, just a few autumn-brown locks of hair laying across the pink cotton pillow, the little girl sobbed.

Her voice broke. "M—mommy."

"Mommy's here, sweetheart." As if caressing the rarest of Alpine orchids, Mommy stroked the covered mound that was the girl's head with her bony hand. "Shhh now. There's nothing to be afraid of."

The girl's breathing shuddered. She pulled her pastel pink sheet tighter about herself. "Mo—mmy—y—y—y."

Mommy rested her hand reassuringly on the girl's shoulder. "It's okay, sweetheart." She brushed her own graying brown hair behind her ear and leaned closer. "Everything will be just fine. You see if it isn't."

The girl shrugged away, pulled further down into the bed.

Mommy sighed. In the dim yellowy glow of the nightlight, she gazed at the window above the bed. No drapes hung to shut out the sun or the scary night. There was little point – the window wasn't formed of wood and glass, but of watercolor paints and brushstrokes. It had taken her days to capture the beautiful woodland scene, just as she remembered it, from the time her parents had taken her on that camping trip, the time they'd been so happy. She'd be darned if she was covering it up needlessly with drapes.

"M—mommy."

Mommy rolled her eyes. "Oh, dear Lord."

"Mommy."

As she stood, Mommy picked up the little pink baby monitor from the nightstand.

Michael scurried over. He probably suspected what she was thinking. He sat on the side of the bed and stroked his stubby fingers over the tiny body outlined by the bedcovers. "Christie, come on, sweetheart. Don't upset Mommy like this."

But the sobbing continued.

Standing in the middle of the room, Mommy shook her head. "This isn't working."

"Christie, sweetheart" – there was an urgency in Michael's voice – "be a good girl now. Be quiet and go to sleep."

Mommy buried her face in her hands. Heaved a great breath.

Shaking her head, Mommy said, "I can't do this." She raked her fingers back through her graying hair. "I've tried, the Lord knows I've tried, but…" She huffed.

"Christie… Christie." Michael peeled the sheet down to try to see her face.

The little girl shuffled further down the bed, further away from them.

Mommy said, "No, I just can't do this anymore. I give and I give and I give… And what do I get? This." She swept her hand towards the mound in the bed. "Where's someone who loves me? Where's someone who gives me everything? Where's my beautiful pink room filled with only the best clothes and only the best toys money can buy?"

Mommy kicked a little white table and sent a tiny floral-patterned tea set crashing against the wall.

"Christie, please," said Michael. "Don't upset Mommy."

The girl ignored him.

He turned to Mommy, sweat beading on his bald head. "Don't upset yourself, Helen, she'll settle down." He smiled a smile as fake as her window, but nowhere near as beautiful. "Just give her a minute. She'll settle, I know she will."

Mommy turned the baby monitor off. "She won't."

Michael screwed his eyes shut.

Mommy placed the monitor next to a bible in the drawer in the nightstand. "Things have to change."

"Again?"

Eyes wide, mouth open, Mommy spun to him. "What? *Yes, again!"*

"But, Helen—"

"But what, Michael? But what?"

He cowered, like a child who knew he'd riled his mother and was fearful of feeling the back of her hand.

"Yes, again!" she said. "And again and again and again until it's just right. Until it's perfect. Or do you think I don't deserve to be happy because I'm no good at being a mommy?" She didn't wait for an answer before jabbing her finger at him. "Because let me tell you, I'm a wonderful fucking mommy!"

Michael threw his hands up defensively. "You are, honey. You're a wonderful mommy, but—"

"But you don't love me anymore? Is that it? So you don't want to see me happy, to see me have the life I deserve? Huh? Because that's sure as hell what it sounds like."

"Of course I love you, Helen." He stood up. Reached for her. But she pulled away. "You're my world. You know that."

She stabbed her finger at the little girl. "Then shut that damn thing up. It's giving me one of my headaches." She flounced away, rubbing her brow.

At the door, she reached around the jamb, picked something up from outside, and then trudged back across the dimly lit room.

She said, "Do what needs doing, but make it quick. I need a neck rub after all this." She handed him a bloodstained axe.

He hung his head. "You're sure this one won't work out?"

"Was I wrong about the others?" She shook her head. Why did she have to make all the decisions? Why couldn't he ever think for himself?

She said, "You know what you have to do. Make it look good." With a scowl, she added, "But try not to enjoy it too much."

Mommy took one last look at the mound under the bedclothes and the autumn-brown hair splayed across the pink pillow. She'd felt so sure this one was going to be the right one. So sure.

She huffed and slouched out of the room. Outside the door, she leaned against the wall in the dark. This was always the hardest part. But like ripping off a Band-Aid, it was best to get it over with fast. Unfortunately, that didn't stop it from hurting.

She didn't like sharing him with someone else. Especially someone whose skin was the way hers used to be – smooth and soft and taut. Over the years, friends and family had often commented on her stunning complexion, but, no matter the lotions she applied or massaging she tried, it was a long, long time since she'd received such a compliment. Time was so cruel to people like her. Far more cruel than to ordinary folk who'd never had looks to lose.

The child screamed. A throaty scream that worked its way up from the gut and burst out as if the world were ending.

Mommy didn't flinch. She had the first time a child had cried out like that. It had really shaken her. And the second time. But then... Then it had just become noise. Meaningless noise. Like the panicked bleating in a slaughterhouse.

She made for the stairs. She'd make darn sure Michael scrubbed himself later. Who knew where that whining creature had been?

Chapter 02

"MOMMY, MOMMY, MOMMY!" Her blond hair wafting in the breeze, the little girl waved. "Look at me! Look at me!"

She leaned back against the black metal railings, a beaming smile on her face. Behind her, in the enclosure beyond the moat, an elephant trumpeted. The girl laughed and clapped with glee.

Fifteen feet away, a man lowered his phone from chest level and flicked his sandy hair out of his eyes. "Okay, Em, honey." He grinned. She was at that wonderful age – the whole world was a playground of treasures and miracles. It made him feel young again, too.

"Let me see." Her face aglow in the crisp autumn sunshine, the girl dashed over and grasped his hand to pull the phone closer.

He played the video for her. She giggled and clapped again.

"That good enough?" he asked.

She nodded as deeply as her neck would physically allow.

"So we'll send it to Mommy now?"

"Uh-huh."

"Okay." He did what needed doing to send the video on his phone, then showed her the screen. "Press the green button."

She pressed it.

"Okay, that's sent."

"Yeah!"

"Now what do you want to see?"

"Unicorns!"

He laughed. "I don't think the unicorns are here today, darling. But there are some baby tigers waiting to say hello to you just around the corner." He pointed. "Will they do?"

She gasped, grabbed his hand, and set off running in the direction in which he'd pointed. He scurried to keep up.

His phone rang. He answered. "We're still at the zoo, babe." He glanced down at the little girl. "Yeah, she's here." He held the phone down to her. "Em, it's Mommy."

"Mommy, Mommy, did you see me with the elephant? Did you hear it?" She listened, giggled, and then looked up at Daddy. "Mommy says that's the noise Daddy makes when he's sleeping."

He whispered, "And it's the noise Mommy makes when she's sitting on the toilet."

Eyes wide with shock, the little girl covered her mouth with her hands trying to stop herself from laughing at something she obviously knew was naughty. Naughty, but incredibly funny. Yes, it was a wonderful age. If only they could stay so innocent, curious, and playful for longer. But how quickly she'd grow up. And, man, would things change then.

He took the phone back. "Listen, we should be home about five. Do you need me to pick anything up? … Uh-huh. … And I can get that there, too?"

The little girl pulled on his free hand. "Come on, Daddy, the tigers are waiting to say hello."

"Just a second, honey, Mommy's giving Daddy jobs to do."

"But they'll be upset."

"No, they'll be fine, honey."

She pulled his hand. "They won't. You said they were waiting for us."

He smiled. "You run on and tell them I'm coming. Okay?"

She darted down the path.

He called after her. "Not too far. Stay where I can see you."

He watched her running down the curving path alongside bushes and a bench with an old couple sitting drinking coffee, the steam making the drinks look particularly inviting.

He ambled down the path, a sign for Tiger Mountain pointing straight ahead. "Yeah, so maybe have dinner ready for six if I have to run these errands."

Em scurried onto a trail walled by high bushes which led to the building from which the tiger enclosure could be viewed. The bushes hid her from sight.

He quickened his pace to catch up with her. "No, we've still got the monkey feeding to see and she'll be heartbroken if we skip that. … I will. Just as soon as—"

A little girl screamed. His little girl.

He shouted, "Emma?"

He set off running. "Emma!"

In his mind, he saw pictures of his beautiful baby being trampled by buffalo, eaten by lions, squashed by a hippo.

She screamed again. And someone else screamed. An older voice. A woman.

He sprinted along the wood chip trail, scrub brush on one side, bamboo on the other. The shadows deepened as the vegetation closed in.

Ahead, he saw a dark wooden building – the tiger viewing area.

Where was his baby girl?

What was happening to her?

He shot into the shadowy hexagonal building. On three sides, eight-foot-high walls of Plexiglas revealed a tiger-infested jungle just inches away.

His gaze whirled.

Where was she?

Where the hell was she?

Where–

There

Safe.

With a group of other people.

Oh, thank God.

He darted over. Swept her up into his arms. Squeezed her to him. "Daddy's here, baby. Daddy's here. What's wrong, honey?"

Beside him, a middle-aged woman retched. Vomit splattered the Plexiglas, then slid down to the ground.

Their mouths agape and eyes wide, an elderly couple stared into the enclosure.

A teenager aimed his phone at the animals inside.

Daddy followed everyone else's line of sight.

And that's when he saw it.

"Oh, dear Lord." He grimaced and twisted away, burying Em's face in his shoulder to hide the sight from her. "Don't look, honey."

Like dogs fighting over a bone, two tiger cubs had clamped their jaws around a severed human arm. A child's arm. They each yanked on the limb. With a sickening tearing sound, the one on the left ripped the flesh from the bone.

Daddy hugged Em tightly. So tightly he worried he might hurt her. But he couldn't let go. Just couldn't.

If anything like that ever happened to his baby girl, he'd...

He'd die too.

Why could no one catch this monster? Why?

He didn't like to question God's will, but how could He create such a monster and let it loose on this earth without also creating someone who could stop it? There had to be someone. Had to be.

But who?

And how long were they going to let this nightmare go on before they did something about it?

Chapter 03

"TEN, TWENTY, THIRTY, forty..." Ambling through the shadows under the trees, Tess Williams loudly counted off the bills from a bundle of tens. With the moon mired by black clouds and only a gloomy light bleeding through the tree branches from nearby street lights, the tree-lined avenue was the ideal cover for a mugger.

The hairs on the back of her neck bristled as she moseyed farther from the light. The dark slowly engulfed her. But no one leapt out.

She walked on. Deeper into darkness.

Buried beneath shadows, the children's play area on her right, a place usually filled with such life, harbored only monstrous shapes lurking in blackness. Like a playground in a ghost town.

Still Tess pushed on.

"... one hundred. One hundred and ten..."

Arm in arm, a twenty-something black couple sauntered towards her. From the corner of her eye, Tess watched them pass. The guy glanced at her, but laughed at something the girl said and instantly looked away.

Turning right and leaving the trees, Tess meandered towards the circular fountain. On warm days, people dangled their feet in its cooling waters. Now, the water stood as cold as it was black.

Entering the open paved area, Tess glanced to her right.

A gigantic gray structure reared up out of the blackness. Colder than the water. Colder than the shadows.

Washington Square Arch, a white marble structure as tall as a seven-story building, stood uncaring before her.

Tess gazed up at it. If she hadn't seen the Arc de Triomphe in Paris, which was more than twice the size and displayed more ornate carvings, this arch would be very impressive.

Some knew Washington Square as the first ever place Bob Dylan performed; some as the location that inspired Henry James to pen the book of the same name; still others knew the square as a great place to make a fast buck from some unsuspecting mark. Tess hoped to meet someone from that latter category.

Sadly, so far, she was out of luck.

Passing through the shadowy archway, Tess continued counting her $360 aloud. She couldn't help feeling somewhat foolish, but that was what she needed to appear – a fool.

Having crossed the street, she reached the ATM. She feigned fumbling in her purse for her ATM card and dropped the bills on the ground.

"Shit." She crouched and snatched up her money. Thank God it wasn't windy or tonight would cost her a fortune. All the while, her peripheral vision scoured the darkness for the tiniest of movements.

She stood up and rested the money on the flat lip of the alcove in the wall into which the machine was set. Finally finding her card, she input her PIN, selected *'Deposit'*, and then followed the on-screen directions, pausing just long enough to re-count the money, aloud, again, before finally depositing it in the bank. She then immediately took the money back out.

That was her fourth deposit and withdrawal tonight. Now to complete the process yet again at one of the other ATMs on the list.

Counting, she trudged away into the gloom of narrow Waverly Place. Its darkened buildings seemed to close in, all but leaning over to spy on her, as if suspicious of her actions.

One hundred feet ahead, a hulking shadow lurched from the other side of the street and then stalked down the sidewalk straight toward her. The guy was so big he looked like a defensive tackle for the New York Jets.

Could that be him? He was definitely the right body shape. Yep, that could easily be the guy she was praying would attack her.

Tess fanned her money out in front of her and counted loudly. With each step, her heart pounded harder.

Though it was hard to be certain in the dark, the guy appeared to be black and shaven headed – he fitted the description perfectly.

Fifty feet away.

Assuming he'd had ample opportunity to become aware of her cash, not to mention her naivety, Tess clenched her fists. Her heart hammered at the prospect of an imminent confrontation, while adrenaline surged through her body, powering her muscles to be ready for fight or flight. Not that flight was an option.

Her head down, she quickened her pace. A full frontal assault wasn't ideal, but it was better than being surprised from behind. Plus, it was she who had surprise on her side: he wouldn't be expecting his victim to fight back. Such a shock would cause a momentary confusion while he processed how to react to the new scenario, giving her the ideal opportunity to put him down.

Wide as a door, he marched toward her.

Ducking under the punch of someone so big would be easy. Once close in, she'd slam him in the groin, rake his eyes to blur his vision, then take out a knee to get him down to her level. From that position, she could finish him any way she liked.

Pumped and craving blood, Tess strode straight at him. Under her breath, she muttered to herself, "Come on, let's do this."

Twenty feet away.

Here we go.

Her adrenaline spiked. Her muscles ached for release. The voice in her head screamed, *'Hit him. Hit him. Hit him before he hits you!'*

Tess angled her body, raised her hand on the pretext of smoothing down her hair, visualized him on his back on the sidewalk, bleeding…

Ten feet away…

He turned, waltzed up to a white door and rapped three times.

What the…?

Tess gawped. It wasn't him? Really? He was one hell of a ringer for the guy she was hunting.

She slumped as all her pent-up fury drained away. Oh, boy. That was one pre-emptive strike she was relieved she hadn't rushed into.

All the same, she stepped over to walk alongside the curb, as far from the doorway as possible. To ensure this wasn't a ruse so he could jump her from behind a moment later, she watched over her shoulder.

The door opened and light burst out. A young black woman grinned and kissed the guy on the cheek, then they went inside together.

Thank God she always held back until the last second, until she sensed impending danger and was 100% certain she'd found her target.

Tess sighed.This wasn't her idea of a fun night out. She'd have liked to have been curled up with her tablet and Fish, reading him the rest of *Wuthering*

Heights, but work was work. It was a pity because they'd just gotten to the good bit – where Heathcliff returns as a man of means which sends the story in a completely new direction. She didn't know how much Fish understood, but he came closer to the side of his bowl when she was reading to him.

Maybe he enjoyed nineteenth-century British classics.

Maybe he enjoyed the sound waves from her voice penetrating the water and gently massaging his body.

Or maybe he enjoyed simply gazing at her and trying to fathom why she loved making her life so unspeakably complicated instead of simply drifting along without a care as he did.

Who'd ever know?

Alternatively, she could have been lying on the couch to watch a movie with Josh.

Hmm… What would Josh make of coming second to Fish? Well, he couldn't complain – there was a time when he wouldn't have even entered into the equation at all, let alone have attained second place. Besides, Fish was Fish. He shared everything. Her whole life. He'd never abandon her, never begrudge her unloading her problems onto him, never demand more than she was willing to give. Would a man ever be prepared to do that? Yeah, right.

So, why exactly was she still with Josh? Good question. One day, she'd have to sit down and not get back up until she found an equally good answer.

She turned up the collar on her black leather jacket. The autumn nights had started to bite. Snow wouldn't be far off.

A silver sedan drove by. Tess slowed her pace. Scrutinized the driver. A black guy. Not *him*. She scoured the interior for a passenger. No one. She huffed. She half-wished she could break her new habit, but she couldn't. It was already too engrained. Over the last two weeks, since seeing her grandpa's killer glide by in a silver car, it had become a Pavlovian response for her to inspect every silver car she saw. Considering one in five vehicles on the road was that color, that was a lot of cars.

Tess emerged from the narrow shadows. Away in the distance, beyond the end of Seventh Avenue, the shimmering needle that was One World Trade Center reached up into the blackness, higher and higher than any other building on the entire continent.

Tess headed into the West Village. She took a right and then a left. Marching along the sidewalk, she made for the HSBC bank a block down on the left.

A police cruiser crawled by. A cop with a moustache peered out, turning his head to watch her, as he and his partner passed.

Going that slowly, they were probably looking for the same target she was – a mugger with a penchant for ATM-related crime.

Though preventing petty theft was way down on the list of priorities in a city with more homicides in a year than there were days, the mugger had cut his last victim. Sliced her cheek and scarred her for life, despite her emptying her checking account for him. And that had bumped him up the list of wanted criminals. Theft was one thing. But violence with a weapon just for the sake of it? That was something else.

For the mugger, it obviously wasn't just about the money anymore – now he was reveling in the rush of hurting his prey. Like a junkie in a constant struggle for an ever greater high, this guy would crave ever more violent fixes. There was no telling what he'd do just for thrills. That made him extremely dangerous.

But a single cruiser was a joke. A token gesture so the authorities could say they were trying their best. What they really needed was some operational security cameras to cover all the ATMs he'd hit. Or hadn't they figured out that was why he was hitting the areas he was?

Tess walked through the steam billowing across the street from the city's underground heating system.

Yellow cabs zipped by, transporting important people to important places; buses whisked passengers along to dinners and meetings and loved ones; pedestrians rushed here and there, all eager to delete another task from their hectic calendar. It was as if they didn't know they were stumbling from one inconsequential incident to the next, but actually thought they were following some structured plan. As if they honestly thought they were in control to do and be whatever fancy possessed them at that instant. How

401

strange were the things people believed to help them cope with life.

A person's fate wasn't the result of finely tuned decisions aimed at achieving their life goals. For most people, life wasn't about achieving their dreams, but only about putting bread on their table, or a new car in their driveway. Too many days like that and people stopped living and started merely existing. But whose fault was that? Most people were so fickle, had such changeable goals, followed such haphazard paths, they had little more direction, little more purpose in their lives than the steam blowing on the breeze.

Renovation cocooning the HSBC in a tubular steel skeleton and green mesh skin, Tess strolled between the scaffolding uprights and the bank's wall, following the building around the corner and into an alley. Below the wooden walkways, shadows engulfed her.

Her head down, seemingly taking no notice of what was going on around her, she strolled over to the ATM. She pulled out her card and clicked through for a $360 withdrawal. She slipped her card into her inside jacket pocket while the machine churned out her money.

A man grabbed her shoulder.

Tess gasped. A genuine gasp of shock at being grabbed by surprise.

Something hard and pointed jammed against the right side of her back – a knife.

A gruff voice spoke right into her ear, "Give me the fucking money."

Chapter 04

TESS'S HEART RATE rocketed.

The guy had been so quiet sneaking up on her that even though she'd been prepared for an assault, he'd caught her completely by surprise. An image flashed into her mind of her unmoving body in the gutter beside a great pool of blood. It was a natural reaction to an unexpected violent stimulus – no matter how *expected* it actually was. But she couldn't let fear turn into panic or that image would become a reality.

The initial shock over, she drew a slow breath to slow her heart rate, which would control her fear response. She'd been doing this job long enough to know how vital it was not to let her mind wander but to stay focused at all times, no matter how boring the case. Talk about dumb. But she could berate herself later. Now, she had work to do.

The mugger shook her shoulder. "I said, 'money', bitch!"

From the position of the knife, the way he had to hunch down to speak into her ear, and the size of the hand gripping her shoulder, she knew he was much bigger than she was – maybe six foot three and 250 pounds. This time, it was definitely the right guy.

In a timid tone, as if she was frightened, she said, "Okay. Okay."

Tess knew how to survive a dangerous mugging encounter. There were just three rules. Even though she knew them, she still worked through them consciously in her mind so the stress of the situation didn't push her into making another dumb mistake.

Rule One: Don't antagonize your assailant.

Tess didn't attempt to turn to look at the man, didn't attempt to struggle, and didn't do what most people couldn't help but do – give him an order by saying something like 'Don't hurt me'. She stayed where she was, facing the cold gray wall, not even raising her hands as any movement could be misinterpreted as aggressive.

Rule Two: Give your assailant whatever was needed to placate him so he wouldn't want to hurt you.

Tess said, "You can have anything. Anything you want."

She slowly reached back with her left hand to give him the wad of bills she'd just withdrawn.

"Damn right I can." He took his hand off her shoulder to snatch his prize.

Rule Three: When the opportunity presented itself, beat the living crap out of the piece of shit.

He having released his grip on her shoulder and being distracted by believing he'd struck gold, Tess attacked.

In one flowing movement, she twisted around, swept her right arm back to push the blade away from her and towards him, and headbutted him in the face to daze him.

Clamping her left hand onto the wrist of his knife hand, she immobilized his weapon.

She stepped out to be alongside him.

Ripped his arm out straight.

Applying a modified figure-four lock, she strained his elbow and wrist joints to breaking point.

Blood streaming down his face from his nose, he grunted in pain.

Tess cranked his wrist back.

Bone crunched.

He screamed.

His hold on the knife all but lost, Tess stripped the blade from his feeble grasp.

Holding the weapon like an ice pick, Tess hammered the hilt into his face. Once, twice, three times.

She kicked his legs out from under him.

He crashed to the sidewalk.

She crouched. Thrust the blade into his right leg. Jammed it under his kneecap and into the joint. It sliced through muscle, ligaments, flesh.

He screeched as blood gushed onto the sidewalk.

"Wallet," she said.

His face twisted in pain, he stared at her wild-eyed.

She pressed his own bloody blade to his throat. "Wallet!"

He fumbled in his jacket and handed it to her. She grabbed his money and his expensive-looking watch – someone had to cover all her rent payments while she was out avenging the innocent.

Without glancing back, she sauntered away.

She dropped the blade into an evidence bag and popped it in her pocket. A blood-stained knife would come in very handy for throwing the police off her trail at some point in the future.

At the intersection, she turned right and slunk away into the darkness.

Far behind her lay a body in the gutter next to a great pool of blood – a man with a newly lame leg, who'd never again be able to sneak up on a woman and disfigure her just for kicks.

Chapter 05

TESS KNOCKED JUST below the bronze number 316 on the dark blue door. A moment later, it opened.

Toweling his short black hair and with a nick on his square jaw just to the left of his chin, one of the most handsome men she'd ever seen smiled at her. How long would he be so eager to make a good impression that he'd shave and shower for her at a moment's notice?

Josh said, "Hey, I thought you were busy tonight."

She shrugged. "Fish didn't think Cathy lusting after Linton was a realistic plot development."

He frowned. "Excuse me?"

The truth be told, she couldn't sit at home without fixating on that silver car and its grinning passenger from two weeks ago. That guy had killed her grandpa and ruined her life – how could she sit alone and think of anything else, having seen him again after seventeen years? But she couldn't tell Josh about him. Couldn't tell anyone. Except Bomb.

Holding up a bag of takeout with the unmistakable smell of fish, she pushed past him. "Fingers, chopsticks, or forks? Get it wrong and I get all of it."

Josh sniffed. "Ahhh." He smiled again. "You traipsed all the way over to *La Fleur Belle*? Hell, it must be love."

She laughed. "Yeah, right."

His smile dimmed.

She winked at him. It wasn't nice to see anything in pain, so she had to give the guy something, and a wink said enough without actually saying anything.

Okay, she liked him, yeah, but love? She wasn't even sure there was such a thing. Affection, stability, sharing, interest, respect… you could have all the fun elements of a relationship without the need for love itself.

As for love itself?

A full-on attachment came with all those other wonderful benefits: vulnerability, need, dependence, weakness, concern… Oh, yeah, in her line of work, the first thing she wanted was someone to worry about, who could be held accountable for her actions, who could be threatened in order to control her.

Love? Yeah, right, that was just what she was looking for.

She rested the takeout on his Indian Rosewood coffee table and then sat on the striped couch while he went to get silverware and plates.

In a television news report, a woman with puffy red eyes and lank brown hair looked directly into the camera. Above a telephone number, a caption read 'Monika Ecker, mother of missing Josie Ecker'. The woman held up a photograph of a little girl with long straight hair so dark it was almost black.

"Please, if you've seen my little Josie, call the number on the screen. We just want her to come home." Her chin trembled. "We're praying for you, Josie. Mommy's praying for you, d—"

Josh clicked the television off with the remote control and put a bottle of wine and two glasses on the table.

"One of your cases?" asked Tess, gesturing to the TV.

Josh went back for the plates.

Over his shoulder, he said, "No, the guys over at the Twenty-Ninth Precinct have this one. But a major case like this, you want to keep up with it. This kid's gone missing and, because she fits the profile, everyone's worried it's the Bronx Butcher – you know, the guy who abuses kids then hacks them up?" He laid the dishes and utensils on the table.

The killer had been christened the Bronx Butcher by the media after pieces of the first two victims were first found in the Bronx. Since then, hacked-up body parts had been discovered all over the city, but the name had stuck.

"Yeah, I heard about him," said Tess.

She dished the food onto plates: black sea bass in a crisp potato shell with leeks and Syrah sauce – Josh's favorite French dish from his favorite French restaurant.

She said, "So you're nowhere near catching him?"

Josh laughed as he pulled the cork out of the wine. "They got DNA, they got prints, they got victims, but the one thing they haven't got is suspects."

"There's nothing in CODIS or IAFIS?" On occasion, she'd illegally accessed those for DNA and fingerprint matching, so she knew they were the go-to databases for law enforcement.

Josh arched his eyebrows as he handed her a glass of wine.

He said, "Oh, so is that from research for a piece you're writing, or from watching too many reruns of CSI?"

He sipped his wine.

"Pillow talk. After blowing the Chief of Police."

Josh choked on his drink. He spluttered, then laughed.

"Man," he snickered, "you've got a mouth like a loaded marine."

"That's what the Chief of Police said."

Josh laughed our loud and shook his head. "Jesus." He lifted the glass to toast. "The Chief of Police – his loss is my gain."

They clinked glasses and drank.

Tess said, "So how come you've got so much evidence but no leads?"

"The guy's too clever. There're never any witnesses when he snatches the kids, or when he dumps them. We have no idea where he takes them, or what he does with them – well, aside from the fact that he violates them and then goes at them with an axe."

"And the thing at the zoo. What was all that about?"

Josh shrugged. "Beats me."

"Well, if it had been eaten out of sight, I suppose it's a clever way to dispose of a body, but there must be more effective ways."

"It's like he's playing a game. Daring us to catch him." He sat and took his plate of food.

"You think?"

"Oh, yeah. The thing that gets me is I just can't figure why he holds on to them for so long, only to hack them up. There must be some trigger, you know. But what…" He shrugged.

"Guys are notorious for getting sick of the same woman and wanting someone new."

With a mouthful of fish, he nodded. "But…" He closed his eyes. "Ohhh… This is sensational. Yeah?"

"Hmm." Tess nodded.

With a flaky texture and a light, almost buttery taste, the sea bass was okay, but no way did it beat fish sticks and baked beans.

After swallowing, he said, "I know what you mean, but the longest he kept one of the girls alive was around three months, the shortest about three weeks. They're all the same age – give or take – same long hair, same blue eyes, same body shape. So, what is it one of them does to piss him off that gets her hacked up after just a few weeks while another keeps him happy for months?"

Tess said, "So it's psychological, not physical."

He nodded.

She continued. "There's some behavioral aspect that sets one girl apart from the next."

"Must be," said Josh. "So, the question is, will the new girl keep him happy long enough for the guys at the Twenty-Ninth to find him, or will she piss him off and turn up in a dumpster?"

How could a nine-year-old girl ensure she kept a grown man happy? She couldn't keep house for him, couldn't earn money for him, couldn't provide companionship. No, there was only one thing a nine-year-old girl could offer – a warm body too small to fight him off.

And there was all the proof Tess needed for there being no God. Why would an all-powerful being let something so innocent be abused by something so twisted?

If Josie had been taken by the Butcher, her family had better put their faith in more than just prayer. But in whom could they put their faith? The police?

413

Yeah, right. This was the seventh such abduction in two years, the third in as many months – the police were no closer to catching him now than they were after his first victim.

No, there was only one person in whom the Ecker family could place their faith – Tess.

Chapter 06

HER EYES CLOSED, one hand clutching Michael, the other feeling along the wall to steady herself, Mommy laughed. She could actually see through the scarf blindfold he'd tied around her head. Chiffon – that was men for you! But she didn't want to see – where was the fun in spoiling his wonderful surprise?

She stumbled.

"Oops." Michael caught her. "Nearly there."

She clung on to him and laughed again. "Heavens, Michael, you really are crazy. Do you know that?"

Mommy reached out to feel along the wall again. Michael hadn't been so much fun, so attentive for... Well, she simply couldn't remember the last time. Oh my, when was the last time they'd had fun together? Had they really let things slide so far? Not that it was any surprise after what they'd been through. Boy, many a weaker mommy would've reached for a handful of sleeping pills.

"Can you feel the door yet?" asked Michael.

She laughed again. "No."

"Here, let me help."

He gently swung her hand over to something cold and solid. She felt one of the four recessed panels in the door, just like the door she'd had as a little girl on her bedroom.

She said, "Yes. Yes, I can feel it."

She ran her hands down and found the handle. She turned it.

"Careful now." Michael guided her through the doorway.

She shuffled in, wary of colliding with something.

Once in, she heard the light switch click. Brightness lit up the inside of the scarf covering her eyes as Michael closed them in the room.

"Michael, take it off! I can't wait any longer. I can't stand it!" It was like Christmas. It honest to goodness was just like Christmas. She ached to see her present. Ached with all her heart.

Michael stood behind her. She felt his hands on the blindfold. "Ready?"

She giggled. "Yes! Please, just do it. This is killing me!"

"Ready. Three... Two... One."

She jigged up and down and made a tiny whining noise. She just couldn't help it. She just felt so young again. So happy again. It felt... wonderful.

He whipped the blindfold off. "Ta dah!"

Mommy gasped. She clasped her hands to her mouth. "Oh, Michael." She gasped again. Tears welled in her eyes.

She turned to him. "Oh, it's just…" She turned back to ensure it wasn't a dream.

She flung her arms around him. "It's perfect. It's just perfect."

Mommy glanced around again. She couldn't believe it. No, it was just like she'd always dreamed it would be, how she'd always pictured it in her mind.

Sitting on the pink bedcovers, wearing that beautiful white summer dress with the lacy bodice, a little girl with long autumn-brown hair gazed into space. A little girl silent. Still. Well behaved.

Mommy crept closer, frightened that, just like approaching a rare butterfly, one wrong move would see the beautiful creature vanish and leave her with nothing but a memory.

She looked back at Michael.

He waved her on.

She crept closer.

But the butterfly didn't flutter away.

She reached out a hand. Stroked the little girl's hair.

Mommy gasped. There were no screams, no tears, no scratching nails.

She stroked again. And again there was no upsetting reaction.

Mommy smiled. And wept. She couldn't help it. This was the happiest day of her life.

Gingerly, she sat beside the little girl. Slowly, she reached out and placed her hand on the little girl's arm. The girl did not flinch.

"Oh, Michael. It's... It's everything I dreamed it would be. Thank you." She gazed at the little girl and again stroked her hair.

Still no shrieking, no lashing out, no tantrums.

Mommy looked back to Michael. "But how?"

"It's a combination of antipsychotics, benzodiazepines, and tranquilizers. You could have met her days ago, but this time, I wanted everything to be just right, so I had to experiment with the dosages."

Mommy grinned. "It's perfect."

She turned to the little girl and gently removed the red band from her hair. "But this should be yellow, shouldn't it, Christie? Yes, it should. Silly Daddy. Mommy knows best, doesn't she?"

Michael moved closer and gestured to the girl's hair. With a timid tone, he said, "I'm afraid I had to dye that, but it..."

Mommy wasn't listening. She slipped open the nightstand drawer and took out a yellow band and a pink hair brush from beside a bible.

Michael whispered. "I'll leave you two to get to know each other." He left.

Mommy brushed the hair with her right hand and smoothed it down with her left. "Oh, what lovely hair you've got, Christie. And how many times do we brush it to keep it so lovely?" She looked into the little girl's face. "That's right – one hundred times. My, who's my clever little angel?" And she was. *Her* angel. *All hers.*

The little girl didn't flinch. Didn't say a word. Didn't move a muscle.

Mommy couldn't help but smile. Everything was perfect. Just perfect.

"Yes, of course we can read a story together. You're Mommy's little girl and Mommy's little girl gets anything she wants." She pulled the little girl's face around to her and kissed her on the forehead. She smiled. "Anything she wants." She rubbed her nose against the little girl's.

"Now, what shall we read? Oh… I know. How about a story about animals? Do you like animals, Christie? Of course you do. Every good girl likes animals."

Mommy reached into the nightstand drawer and took out the bible. She knew just which story would fit such a glorious occasion – the story of Noah and the fresh start God gave him.

Leafing through to Genesis Chapter 7, Mommy smiled. She couldn't help it. Everything was just right. Just as it should be. She'd prayed to the Lord and he'd answered.

But then, she'd always known He would.

If she waited long enough.

If she prayed hard enough.

Though bad things sometimes happened to good people, the Lord always made things right in the end. In

His wisdom, He'd seen fit to reward her for being such a good, deserving person.

Yes, everything was perfect. They were a family. A proper family.

Chapter 07

"YEAH, I'M LOOKING at that now," Tess said into her phone while scrutinizing her tablet, which was resting on her thighs. Sitting with her back to her bed head, so the morning sunlight wouldn't create glare on her screen, she scrolled down a file detailing the Bronx Butcher's story to date that she'd downloaded from Bomb's darknet.

"Don't forget this is only a preliminary report," said Bomb. "A lot of it has been drawn from what's already been made public."

"Okay. I wonder how accurate these stats are on the length of captivity of the victims?"

"I'm guessing they're pretty hit and miss. Because of how the guy dumps the body parts, and because I've found a report mentioning cell damage congruent with extremely low temperatures, it's impossible to judge time of death on criteria like decomposition rate and insect activity. I'm betting the Butcher keeps the pieces in a freezer before dumping them, so the ME has just made educated guesses."

Tess rolled off her bed and wandered across to Fish.

She said, "So, if he has taken Josie Ecker, there's no telling how long we might have to find her because he could kill her tomorrow, freeze her, then dump her two months from now."

"Exactly," said Bomb.

It was a ticking clock. But they'd no idea for how long it might tick. They could have weeks; they could have days; they could have hours. They'd never know. That made it crucial to find the Butcher as quickly as possible. So where did you start searching for someone who abducted children and then sexually abused them before dismembering them?

She tipped fish food into Fish's bowl and watched him suck up the bits as they drifted down past him.

She said, "I'll need a list of all known sex offenders in the tristate area."

"Already on it."

"And a list of anyone who's been suspected of child sex offenses in the last… five years."

"That's going to be trickier."

"How tricky?"

"That's the problem – I don't even know if such a file actually exists, let alone where to find it. I'm guessing I'll have to hack various databases and compile my own."

"Pity." That was time they couldn't afford to waste. But then, if someone was innocent, where was the justice in adding them to a list of *potential* child molesters? If you studied everyone's life, unveiled all their darkest secrets, wouldn't everyone on the planet be listed as a *potential* perpetrator of some crime? Just because they were on the list didn't mean they were ever going to commit that crime. Going from such a list could send her on such a wild goose chase that it cost Josie her life. But what other option did they have?

Tess said, "You got a time frame for a file?"

"Like I said, I got squat on this, so I can't even guess."

"But you can get it?"

He laughed.

She hadn't found a server yet Bomb couldn't access, a firewall he couldn't breach – given enough time. In fact, she wasn't even sure there was one. Every system had a weakness. That was why governments and corporations continually spent millions developing more and more impenetrable software with more and more complex encryption ciphers. Luckily for Tess, for every door, there was a key. And Bomb was an expert locksmith.

She said, "I've got some ideas, but none of them are going to bring quick answers, so that list is a Level Four, Bomb. Okay?"

"Four. Got it. Uh-oh, give me a sec."

"Sure." Bent over to watch her Japanese fighting fish feeding, Tess frowned as a bang came from the other end of the phone.

A moment later, Bomb said, "Sorry about that. Had to shut the door. Byte has just used her litter and, I tell you, you won't believe something so cute can produce something so vile. Man, the stench – it's like the Devil's overdosed on chili."

"At least she used the litter this time."

"Oh, don't remind me. I had to junk a keyboard on Tuesday."

"Your keyboard? Oh, hell." Poor Byte. Bomb didn't even allow dust to touch his precious gear. "I hope Jules managed to scrub it clean." But even as she said it, Tess cringed, picturing Jules as yet another entry on the long list of Bomb's ex-housekeepers.

"Maybe she could have, but she's here to look after the house, not Byte. And, anyway, like Byte was supposed to know."

Wow. Consideration for both a housekeeper and a pet? Unbelievable. Tess had been pleased when Bomb had canceled Animal Control coming to take away Byte, but this was a major breakthrough. And it was about time. Bomb had been alone too long. Way too long.

After the incident with his sister, Bomb had shut himself away from everything and everyone. Apart from a few online cronies, his only contact with the outside world had been his phone conversations with Tess, seeing her as a kindred spirit – someone else with a mission to change the world, someone else with a remarkable expertise, someone else with no life.

His work with her just gave him even more reason to lock himself away. Tess had had to battle to persuade him to have a housekeeper, someone to take on part of the crucial role his sister had played as caregiver. But an employee was just that – someone you paid to be in your company. Tess had struggled for a way to break Bomb out of his self-imposed exile. Every day she fought to give strangers better lives. With all the work Bomb did to help her achieve that, he deserved one himself.

What better to show him pure joy than a playful ball of black fluff? She hoped Byte would prove to him there was more to life – sharing, caring, wonder, awe... Maybe enough to tempt him to finally leave his house again for more than just medical appointments and food runs.

She was sure he suspected that it was she who'd left the abandoned kitten in a cat carrier packed with food and litter on his doorstep, but he'd never said anything, so she wouldn't either. It would be like defrocking Santa and finding your dad standing there in nothing but tighty whities – the magic would vanish.

By providing not just company, but physical contact – something everyone needed in one form or another – Byte was a tiny step forward. A minuscule step, but still a step.

Tess said, "So, this file – let me know the moment you've uploaded it."

"Will do."

At that point, there was nothing else to say regarding their new job, but Tess didn't sign off. In fact, she didn't do anything and didn't say anything. She knew what she wanted to say, what she needed to say, what was eating away at her like a tumor, but she'd said it so many times already over the past two weeks. She'd hoped she wouldn't have to ask again. But… Talk about a pregnant pause.

Finally, Bomb said. "Listen, you're going to have to let this slide for now, so you can focus on this job."

She heaved a sigh. "I know." She pictured the guy in the silver car – the killer who'd wrecked her life.

"Like I said, we'll get him. It's just gonna take time. Because there aren't any traffic cams where you saw him, I'm having to back-trace every single silver car that might have gone through that junction from the cams on all the neighboring streets."

"Yeah, I know. You told me that. I just thought we'd have something by now."

Bomb snorted a laugh. "Tess, I don't think you're getting the size of the problem here. For example, I picked up a silver Ford Taurus on East 122ndStreet but couldn't get a shot of the driver, any passengers, or the license plate until it turned onto Lexington. There I got the plate and driver, but it wasn't until it hit the corner of 119th and Second Avenue that I finally found a camera that got a side angle and showed there was no backseat passenger."

"Ah." Tess winced. She'd known he was doing his best, but just hadn't appreciated that even Bomb's 'best' had its limitations. "Okay, I get you now."

"You sure? Because as far as I can figure, we're looking at seventy-two silver cars that *could* have hit that intersection around the time you were there. That's seventy-two separate routes to track across the city, hacking cameras until I can get clean shots. And it's doing that in between all our other jobs."

"Okay. Thanks, Bomb."

"Hey, anything, anytime. You know that, Tess."

Anything anytime, yes, she knew he'd do that for her. But his tone implied something else. As if he wasn't doing it to find the guy, but merely to appease her.

She said, "I'm sure it was him, you know."

"I know."

"You know I know it was him, or you know I think it was him?"

"Does it matter?"

"Of course it matters. Bomb, I need you with me on this."

"And I am."

"Really? You don't think I might have imagined seeing him?"

She heard him sigh.

"Tess, you were working a job concerning an old man getting shot in his convenience store and, that very same day, despite seventeen years of failure leading up to that day, you just happened to see the guy who killed

427

your own grandpa in his store? Would it be unreasonable to think that was a little coincidental?"

"So you don't believe me? You think I imagined it?"

"Now, I didn't say that."

"You might as well have."

"So I'm not allowed to question this? I just have to take everything as gospel?"

"Look, you can't—" She huffed. And shut her mouth instead of blurting out something she'd later wish she could take back.

Numerous times over the years, she had sworn she'd spotted her grandpa's killer – a face in a crowded mall, a passenger passing by on a bus, a customer in line at a café. On each of those occasions, she'd only glimpsed the man as he moved away, or only caught him from the corner of her eye, or he'd been so draped in shadows she wasn't sure what she'd seen. And on every single occasion, when she'd scrambled around to get a better look, she'd immediately known she'd been wrong and that it wasn't him.

This time…

This time there'd been no glimpse, no snatched look from the corner of her eye, no shadows to make her mind play tricks.

No, this time she'd stared him fully in the face. Up close. In daylight.

This time, she wasn't wrong. This time, it was him!

But Bomb was right – after the false leads of the past, who wouldn't harbor reservations over what she'd seen?

"Bomb, I'm sorry. Just do what you can."

"Just because I question something doesn't mean I'm not with you on it."

"I know. Thanks. For everything."

"Hey, I mean it – anything, anytime. Good hunting, Tess."

Bomb was right to question her. If he didn't, he wouldn't be doing his job. Still, she needed him to trust her on this. That guy in the car *was* the guy she'd hunted for seventeen years. There was no doubt. No question. And when she found him again, she'd kill him.

Bomb was right about something else, too – she had to put the killer from the silver car to the back of her mind so she could focus on this job. As with the mugger at the ATM, if she lost focus, she could be surprised and someone could gain an advantage over her. Next time, she might not be as lucky as she had been with the mugger and a momentary lapse in concentration could get her cut, or killed.

But more than that, there was a little girl in dire need of rescue. And something in the back of Tess's mind clawed at her, begging for attention. Was there a key to this job that she was missing?

Chapter 08

TESS BOOTED UP Bomb's suite of software on her tablet, opened the mapping module and input the data they had on the six confirmed Butcher abductions. A map of Manhattan materialized, with six red dots scattered around the lower part of the island. She input Josie Ecker's probable abduction location and another red dot appeared in the same area.

So, Downtown it was. An area famous for the architectural magnificence of One World Trade Center, the money-manipulating marvel that was Wall Street, and the cultural melting pots of Chinatown and Greenwich Village, Downtown was now to become famous for quite another reason – as the hunting ground of the Bronx Butcher.

Tess input more data for the first victim, Elise Mortensen. A yellow zigzag line appeared on the map, showing her probable route home from the friend's home she'd been visiting before she'd been snatched. Other information appeared, including a blue dot showing her school and green dots highlighting the nearest playgrounds and age-appropriate entertainment venues.

Tess added data for all the abductees and then gazed at the brightly colored map covered in zigzags and dots.

She sighed. "Yeah, right." Aside from some very minor interaction, none of the data overlapped enough to reveal any sort of pattern. "Like it was going to be so easy."

If it had been, the NYPD would have solved the case and caught the guy already.

Swiping her hand over her touch screen, she activated a number of options and filters. The application overlaid the public transit system and the more major thoroughfares, including the direction of traffic flow. Tess studied how the abduction areas linked to various parts of the island to judge which routes the Butcher might have taken.

There were still no obvious connections or patterns.

Tess hit the Search button on Bomb's software. She watched the yin and yang symbol rotate while the application analyzed databases he'd enabled it to access over the Internet. After a few seconds, it cross-referenced the data it had gathered online with the data Bomb had supplied.

Again, she sighed. The software confirmed the victims were not connected through their extended family, parents' employment, education, healthcare, and all manner of other possible areas. A number of fields had come up blank, which she'd pass to Bomb to explore, but, so far, she had squat.

Other than the fact the Butcher liked slim girls with long hair and blue eyes, they had nothing at all to go on. Not that his taste – their sole clue – was any help. If Tess walked out onto any street in the city and threw candy into the air, she'd lose count of the number of hands reaching for it belonging to slim girls with long hair and blue eyes. Manhattan was positively heaving with potential victims.

Fantastic.

She paced across to her refrigerator, her feet slapping on the bare wooden floorboards. Having poured herself a smoothie of kale, pineapple and spinach that she'd prepared earlier and left to chill in a jug, she stood and looked out at the gray slab of air hanging over the city.

"What am I missing, Fish?"

She glanced over at him. His red fins gliding like angel's wings, he mouthed something, but she was sure it wasn't the solution. She smiled. A crime-solving fish – it was a wonder Hollywood hadn't done that yet.

Maybe she and Bomb were coming at the problem from the wrong angle. Maybe instead of looking at the victims for clues, they should concentrate on the killer, not least his motivation: why would a man abduct a string of kids, sexually abuse them, then hack each one of them up with an axe?

Searching for answers to handling the problems in her life, Tess had studied Eastern wisdom during her time in China. While she hadn't found what she'd been searching for, she had found truth in many of the ancient teachings. Sadly, in the West, such teachings were generally only used by pretentious dicks who loved spouting vacuous platitudes. However, that didn't mean the original wisdom was flawed, only the person using it.

Sun Tsu, the author of *The Art of War*, the definitive work on military strategy, had supposedly said, 'To know your enemy, you must become your enemy.' Whether Sun Tsu had said it or not didn't matter. What did matter was the truth in the words: if you didn't understand your enemy – know their needs, weaknesses, goals – how could you hope to defeat them?

Tess fired up her onion routing software to enable her to surf the Internet with total anonymity. And today of all days, she needed that anonymity.

People thought the Web was a happy place because it gave them so many happy things – music, movies, holidays, friends. The odd troll was a pain, but with the wealth of wonders the Web bestowed upon everyone, the Internet was a twenty-first-century miracle.

Luckily for them, ordinary people didn't have to go where she was going to go, didn't have to see what she was going to see. The Web could be a shiny wonder crammed with glittering toys for young and old… or it could be the deepest, blackest hole in which hid man's greatest atrocities.

People thought the dark side of the Web involved embarrassing photos, or being slandered by someone they trusted, or, worst of the worst, identity theft. That was the dark side of the Web? How innocent people were.

Tess entered the Deep Web. The darkest part of the Internet where even the search engines didn't want to go. Would she find what she was looking for?

Chapter 09

EVERYONE HAD SEXUALLY perverse fantasies. Everyone. Problems occurred when people tried to make those fantasies a reality. The more perverse the fantasy, the bigger the problem. And, man, did some people have problems – she knew because she'd encountered a lot of them. Sadly, not through pleasure, but as a means to completing various jobs.

Still, her having suffered endless degradation, humiliation, and self-disgust wasn't all bad – as was often the case, life had a strange way of working out.

Using her writing talent, she'd penned six series of erotica short story ebooks which she now sold through various online retailers. It was surprising what people would pay for – she usually cleared a few hundred dollars per month. Not that she saw any of it with three rent payments every month to cover all her safe houses as well as all her other expenses. Still, it did keep the IRS happy, her appearing to be a hardworking, tax-paying, law-abiding citizen.

Double-checking her TOR software was making her anonymous, Tess ventured further into the Deep Web. People thought of the Internet as a limitless playground and information source – it was, but the sites the majority of the population visited only accounted for around three percent of the Internet, a minuscule amount. The real Internet, where the other ninety-seven percent of the information lay, was invisible to most people because everyday search engines didn't index it.

However, if you wanted to blow the whistle on government corruption, the Deep Web provided the tools to anonymously reach out to journalists. If you were in college and couldn't be bothered trekking all the way over to your dealer's place for weed, the Deep Web could arrange for it to be mailed straight to you. If you were in a disastrous relationship and needed to escape, the Deep Web could put you in touch with nice people who'd bump off your partner for as little as twenty thousand bucks.

Ordinary people thought 'their' Internet had everything. It didn't. But the Deep Web did.

Tess ran searches using TorSearch and Evil Wiki, glanced over the results, and then dove into the sleazy underworld of the Deep Web – its forums, its media sites, its peer-to-peer sharing. Despite the twisted perverts she'd met in the past, she was not prepared for the perversity of the people she found and the dreams they wanted to fulfill…

Considering its size, what's the best way to give a horse head?

How can I create barbs on my dick like those on a tiger's?

Looking for grooming buddies in NY-NJ-CT area. Got pro video gear.

The Deep Web, the online place most people didn't even know existed, wasn't just deep, it was dark. Very, very dark.

Tess followed their one lead: the victims were preteen girls.

Wading into a world of men helping each other to use children in the most vile of ways, she searched for a hint that the Butcher had visited this part of the Web and, believing he was safe, had left some form of trail.

After nearly two hours of fruitless searching, Tess shuddered. She tossed her tablet aside. She felt soiled. As if something had vomited all over her and she couldn't find any water to wash off the stinking filth.

Tess was more sexually liberated than ninety percent of the population, yet there were lines that should never be crossed. Bestiality, sex organ modification, pedophilia... Hell, just how many thousands and thousands of sickos were there out there? How many did she pass on the sidewalk without batting an eye because they looked just as normal as everyone else?

The Butcher wasn't just sick. By doing what he did, he was spreading the sickness: he was feeding perverted people's dreams, encouraging others to expand their own twisted repertoires, showing people that anything was possible. The weak, the twisted, the just plain evil would listen. Listen well.

She had to stop him. Had to stop him now. But how?

Despite all the physical evidence they had, the police were missing something. Something vital. They had enough to nail the guy if he'd ever been printed or had his DNA sampled, but unfortunately, he hadn't. But who was to say the Butcher was working alone?

An accomplice might never have been processed by the police to have any records on any database. That meant known offenders was a legitimate starting point. At least until something more solid developed. She was sure it was. But that would be exactly what the police would have done, yet they'd come up empty-handed. She had to see what the authorities couldn't. Or what they'd seen, but had dismissed as irrelevant.

Her gut told her there was something about the Butcher that was just wrong, but she couldn't put her finger on what that was.

At the most basic level, most people were inherently logical. Infuriatingly so, at times. It was how psychologists predicted behavior – a specific stimulus prompted a specific response. Some responses to stimuli were so conditioned, behavior could be predicted with an almost mathematical certainty.

However, the mindless violence aside, something about this killer just didn't add up. Logically, what he did simply didn't tally with his supposed reasons for doing it. When she looked at this job, she couldn't help but see 2+2=5. Something was very, very wrong. But what?

It was no good. She had too many unanswerable questions when what was needed was clarity.

Tess grabbed her coat and her little black backpack, which she'd already packed with the usual essentials, and left.

The chill air giving people's cheeks a red glow, Tess zipped her jacket up to the neck. In the same way a driver maneuvers their vehicle without consciously thinking about every tiny operation, she strolled through the streets taking virtually no notice of her path, her fellow pedestrians, or the traffic. She couldn't help it. She knew she should remain alert at all times, but questions about this job wrenched at her too hard. There was something very odd about the Butcher. Very odd.

Not just that he was a cruel, twisted killer. No. Something else. Something that just didn't sit right. She'd been doing this job for long enough to know to trust her gut and her gut was saying there was more to this if she could just dig through the superficial outer layers to the truth.

Before she knew it, she was standing beside the lake in the park and beneath her favorite willow tree. She unslung her backpack, placed a small mat at the base of the trunk as protection from the damp and cold, and then sat. She looped the strap of her pack through her arm for security and then breathed in the view.

Mallard ducks glided by on the lightly rippling water, water black under the slab of unforgiving sky. With dark plumage and speckles of white on its breast, a large waterfowl floated by too. She hadn't seen that bird before. Was it now nesting here, or had it simply dropped in while on its winter migration?

In these serene surroundings, within seconds, she felt her heart rate dropping, her tense muscles relaxing, her mind starting to glide on thoughts with the elegance of the ducks on the water. It was like arriving home after a long and torturous day at work.

Tess closed her eyes. And her mind flew.

It was said Sir Isaac Newton discovered gravity while sitting under a tree. Urban myth went further by claiming he'd discovered it when an apple fell on his head. Tess didn't believe the urban myth. Neither did she believe Newton formulated his theory on gravity purely because he saw an apple drop from a tree.

Inspiration was seldom the child of random events. If it were, the whole world would be making remarkable scientific breakthroughs all the time. No, inspiration came from a state of mind: a state in which you were receptive to the unusual; a state in which you allowed your thoughts to run rampant, unhindered, and unrestrained; a state in which you allowed yourself to endlessly ask the same question – what if…?

She had to achieve that state. And achieve it as quickly as she could so she could end that monster.

As great clouds drifted across the sky, great thoughts drifted through her mind.

Finally, she opened her eyes.

She drew a long, slow breath, rejuvenated by the tranquility, beauty, and clarity of her special place. Tess had her answer: if she couldn't trace the pedophiles in the digital world, she'd trace them in the physical one.

She knew just where to start.

Chapter 10

TESS SMILED AT the plump woman with the straggly hair struggling to keep one of her sons from climbing over her couch like an animal. The stuffing bursting from a hole in the armrest suggested his climbing was no isolated occurrence. Tess also noted the hole in the left knee of the woman's jeans – it was not a hole because it was the fashion. No, Mrs. Rebecca Alcott was not one of life's winners. But was she a big enough loser to grab Tess's offer?

Rebecca shrugged, "I'm sorry, but I don't think I can, Ms. Gambini."

"I can go up to a hundred and twenty-five bucks a day." Tess leaned closer and lowered her voice. "And if you don't tell the tax man, neither will I."

Sucking through her teeth, Rebecca grimaced. "I don't know."

The woman looked to one of her other children.

Tess followed her gaze. On the TV, an animated movie about penguins was playing, its DVD box tossed nearby. Lying on the floor in front of the TV, a skinny little girl with long sandy hair dragged a wax crayon across paper. With all of the disproportion, but none of the talent, a drawing of a girl standing with a penguin looked like a Picasso painted on a particularly bad day.

Tess patted the coffee table. On top of a selection of dog-eared gossip rags, she'd placed her passport, a credit card, and her business card. Each proved who she was: Deanna Gambini, senior investigator for Baker & Tanner Investigations.

Tess said, "You've seen my ID, so you know I am who I say I am. Plus, you can speak to my boss, or one of the NYPD detectives I've worked with in the past." Rebecca could speak to Bomb or one of the two detectives who actually did know Tess as Deanna.

Rebecca looked at the ID. She heaved a breath and rubbed her chin.

Tess glanced at all the photos of Theresa May Alcott on the mantel and across the wall of the living room: Theresa May singing in a school choir, Theresa May in a Halloween costume, Theresa May skipping in the street. But it wasn't Theresa May now lying on the floor watching penguins. Theresa May was lying somewhere very different.

The photo of Theresa May most New Yorkers would recognize was nowhere to be seen – the photo of her that had been published in the *New York Times*, her the Butcher's third victim. A pretty eight-year-old girl with a mischievous smile – it was by far the best photo of the bunch, but it obviously brought back too many memories to display, it having been plastered all over the media for weeks.

Rebecca dithered still, so Tess went in for the kill.

"Mrs. Alcott, it can't be easy bringing up four kids on your own, so here's what I'm going to do. Either you can accompany little Mary Jo and me – all expenses paid – or I'll go up to two hundred bucks per day. And I'll give you a week in advance. No refunds whether I take her for the whole week or just today."

Tess needed a kid, and she had money. Rebecca Alcott had four kids, and barely a dime. It was a perfect match. From the condition of the apartment, Tess could probably *rent* one of the Alcotts for a couple of hundred bucks for a week, let alone for a day, but these kids didn't deserve to suffer because they'd been born to poor parents, so she'd upped her offer.

Of course, there was no guarantee every single penny wouldn't be blown on smokes, booze, and lottery tickets – it didn't look like the Alcott household had a five-year financial plan to which they stuck with religious fervor. However, from the photos and the way Rebecca spoke, there was a chance the money might go to family days out, ballet lessons and Xbox games, or maybe just a good meal and heating every day throughout the coming winter.

Rebecca's voice lightened. "A full week in advance and no refunds?"

"Fourteen hundred dollars." Tess patted her jacket's inside breast pocket. "If you want it, it's all

yours. Right now. If not, don't worry, it's no trouble –
I'll just move on to the next name on my list who I've
an appointment with in…" Tess glanced at her watch,
"…forty-five minutes."

Tess looked up and smiled. She had no list, she
had no appointment, but she had pitching skills.

Rebecca said, "And all you're going do is walk
her in the park and stuff?"

"That's all."

"So she'll be safe?"

"Oh heavens, yes. See, to complete my
investigations, I just need a legitimate reason to be in
areas where kids are about. Believe me, if I had a kid of
my own, I wouldn't think twice about having her do
this. Mary Jo will have a ball. Trust me."

"Fourteen hundred bucks?"

"In your hand, right this second."

"And all I have to do is sign that document?"
Rebecca pointed to the paper on her table.

"Just to say you've received the money, so my
boss doesn't think I'm screwing him over – you know
bosses. And to say you'll keep everything we discuss
confidential."

"And you really think you can find the bastard
who took my Theresa May?"

"I never like to say I can guarantee anything,
but… you darn watch me."

Rebecca snatched the pen and scrawled her
signature on the bottom of the confidentiality
agreement. Then she held out her hand.

Tess smiled and counted out fourteen hundred dollars into Rebecca's palm. Rebecca leaned right over, her gaze glued to the mounting money. The document meant little legally, but psychologically it meant Rebecca was less likely to talk about this meeting than if she'd signed nothing – every little bit of anonymity reduced the risk of Tess hitting trouble.

Rebecca couldn't stifle her joy. She ran the bills through her hands and then, even though she'd watched Tess count every single bill out, she counted again.

Tess studied Rebecca. When this woman was a little girl and had dreamed of the future, was this squalor and struggle the picture she'd seen in her mind?

How people dreamed. And how easily they abandoned those dreams and accepted mere existence in place of happiness.

Why?

Few people had the courage or determination to live life to the fullest, to follow their true passions, instead choosing to merely drift from one fad to the next, from one dream to the next, from one moment of satisfaction to the next, forever looking for, but never finding, that one thing they all craved: fulfillment. But if you didn't know what something looked like, how could you ever find it?

But why was she judging only Rebecca? Despite all Tess's courage and determination, had her life turned out as she'd dreamed it would? Maybe she and Rebecca weren't that different after all.

Or maybe neither of them had found fulfillment because it didn't exist. Maybe a life of struggle, mundanity, and disappointment, punctuated only by the odd brief moment of joy, really was all there was to life.

Having confirmed the fourteen hundred dollars to herself, Rebecca smiled, squashed the money into a fat wad and stuffed it into her hip pocket.

She looked at Mary Jo lying on the floor, still coloring her picture. The little girl spoke one of the lines from the movie in time with the character.

"She just loves this movie," said Rebecca.

"Yeah?"

"Oh, yeah. She'll play it over and over. It used to drive me nuts but she never tires of it."

Pulling Mary Jo up off the floor, Rebecca said, "Hey, sweet pea, you're going to the park with your Auntie Deanna. Aren't you the lucky one!"

Lucky?

Well...

It wasn't like Tess was going to tie her to a stake and leave her out in the open, but bait was bait.

Chapter 11

HOLDING MARY JO'S hand, Tess meandered through Columbus Park. Elderly Chinese people chatted in Mandarin while lounging on benches, and on the open-air upper floor of the building at the far end, a handful of people performed Tai Chi.

For a couple of minutes, Tess and Mary Jo watched two old men sitting at a concrete table playing Xiangqi, an ancient Chinese version of chess. Mary Jo didn't exactly watch the game so much as watch the old man on the left with bags under his eyes the size of Tess's Lapsang Soushong teabags. He reminded Tess of Joe Corrigan, the detective she knew from the Fifty-Sixth Precinct. What was it about aging that so many people ended up with so much extra skin?

The old man moved one of his pieces, a cannon, over the river, the narrow break in the middle of the playing area, and onto his opponent's side to threaten one of his elephants. Just as he had after each of his other turns, the old man then dipped into a white paper bag of candy. This time, however, he smiled at Mary Jo and held out the bag to her.

Mary Jo pulled back to Tess's side and clutched the cuddly penguin that Tess had bought her to win her over. But Tess could understand Mary Jo's trepidation: the little girl's sister having disappeared, everyone must have drilled into her that strangers weren't to be trusted.

Tess said, "It's okay."

Mary Jo shuffled closer to the man, dipped into the bag, and took an oval lemon candy.

Tess hunkered down and whispered into the little girl's ear.

Mary Jo looked at the old man and repeated what she'd been told to say. "*Shear shear*."

"Ahhh!" The old man beamed. He applauded Mary Jo. "*Bu keqi*." He offered her another candy.

The little girl giggled and took one.

At the other side of the concrete table, stood a fat guy wearing a T-shirt with big red letters that proclaimed *'I ♥ NYC'*. He took a photograph with a DSLR camera of the old men playing their odd version of chess. He looked like just another tourist. Except, while he was nonchalantly gazing around, Tess could have sworn he left his finger on the shutter release button as he slowly brought his camera up from focusing on the game to focusing on her.

She frowned. Had he really just snapped her photo? So what was he – some pervert who jerked off to pictures of strangers he saw in the street?

As he turned back to the game, he caught her eye. He didn't react in the least. Instead, he continued to gaze around the park like a perfectly innocent tourist.

If he'd photographed Mary Jo, Tess would have had to investigate, but she was in the middle of hunting down a serial killer, with a kid in tow, and she wasn't even sure if he'd actually snapped a shot of her or not. This was no time to become distracted by minor incidents, no matter how irksome they were.

However, before telling Mary Jo it was time to leave, Tess took a good look at the guy. Apart from his girth, his one identifying feature was a crescent shaped scar next to his left eye. She made a mental note of that then scrutinized him again.

He appeared oblivious to her.

Maybe he was innocent. Maybe not. But if that camera pointed anywhere near her again today, the guy would need a new T-shirt: *'I bled in NYC'*.

Pushing the incident to the back of her mind, Tess whispered to Mary Jo, again.

Mary Jo frowned at her, so Tess said it once more.

Waving goodbye to the old man, Mary Jo made a fair stab at repeating what Tess had told her to say. "*Zie chen.*"

The old man laughed and rolled back on his stool. With a thick accent, he said, "Very good Chinese." He took Mary Jo's hand and placed his bag of candy in it.

The little girl gasped, eyes wide with delight.

450

Tess appreciated the old man's gesture, so she made one of her own – she gently bowed her head to him. He did likewise.

Mary Jo had butchered the Mandarin, despite Tess having given her the easiest phonetics she could, but what could she expect from a six-year-old who'd probably never even left the city, let alone the country?

As they wandered for the gate, Mary Jo repeatedly twisted around to wave at the old man. *"Zie chen! ... Zie chen!"*

Smiling, the old man waved back. *"Zai jian."*

Hand in hand, Tess and Mary Jo headed for the street.

Tess had forgotten how comfortable she felt amongst the Chinese. Meandering around here, she could almost imagine being back in the little park near her old apartment building in Shanghai.

Yes, if it wasn't for Su Lin's presence, she'd visit Chinatown regularly. Okay, Su Lin was only one Chinese person amid the hundred thousand plus that resided in Chinatown, so their paths might never cross, but Tess couldn't risk getting drawn into that circle. Not again. She'd barely escaped the last time.

A shiver ran down Tess's spine at the thought of walking straight into Su Lin this very moment.

Oh God, what if she did?

Now?

Su Lin had to be someplace, so why not here?

Right here, right now. It was as good a place as any.

Tess walked a little faster. Anxiety clawed at her and her breathing quickened as she anxiously studied the faces in the immediate vicinity.

Chapter 12

AMBLING ALONG WORTH Street, Tess checked out the occupants of a silver Chrysler as it cruised by. Not *him*. Big surprise.

Even though it hadn't really taken them out of their way, visiting Columbus Park had been a mistake – all of the Butcher's victims had been Caucasian. Maybe if she wasn't constantly distracted by every goddamn silver car on the road, she'd have realized her misjudgment before trekking all the way here. She had to focus. And that meant forgetting Su goddamn Lin as well. Hell, what was she doing to herself? She had to get a grip. Especially with a kid in tow.

City Hall Park had already been a bust too. Mary Jo would start flagging soon, so Tess had to do something to keep the little girl's interest and, thereby, her compliance. Besides, Tess was thinking on too big a scale with parks thus far. She needed something where kids could just be kids.

She crouched down to Mary Jo and checked that her coat was fastened up to the neck properly. "Well, squirt, how about we go and find some slides to play on, huh? Would you like that?"

Mary Jo grinned. "Yeah."

This was Tess's kind of kid – barely said a word, happy to do virtually anything asked of her, never caused any fuss. Yes, if she were guaranteed to get one this well behaved, she might even consider having one herself. *Might*. One day. In the future. The far distant future.

Tess already knew Playground One was closed for renovation but that didn't matter as there was another park just a short stroll away.

As Tess and Mary Jo crossed the wide intersection at the end of Worth Street and onto Oliver Street, angry voices and honking car horns grew louder and louder. A mob surged straight at them, chanting, brandishing placards, and waving to motorists, who honked their horns in support.

Oliver Street being narrow, with the buildings close to the road because of the width of the sidewalk, the mass of protestors was like an impenetrable wall of anger surging right for Tess and Mary Jo.

The little girl gripped Tess's hand in both of hers, quietly whimpering, obviously spooked by the vehemence of the mob.

Tess stroked the little girl's head. "It's okay, Mary Jo. There's nothing to worry about."

Marching from Alfred E. Smith Playground, the site from where the Butcher had snatched his first victim, the mob was protesting at the abject lack of

454

progress the authorities had made with the case. The city's parents were scared. Many were keeping their kids locked indoors when not in school. And understandably so. Tens of thousands of terrified parents had slim, blue-eyed preteen daughters – potential targets they imagined the Butcher couldn't wait to abuse.

Tess guided Mary Jo onto the steps of the Baptist church and up next to one of the two massive stone columns, hoping its solidity would help the frightened little girl feel protected.

Only feet away, the protestors marched past on their way to City Hall.

Mary Jo still whimpered.

Tess crouched down to be on her level so she wouldn't feel so alone, so afraid, and hugged the little girl to her, cradling her face into her chest and trying to cover her ears without upsetting her.

The mob stomped by, chanting in unison, "Protect our kids. Arrest the pedophiles. Protect our kids. Arrest the pedophiles…"

Tess could understand their fear, their outrage, their disillusionment. The parents were so desperate, the idea of slamming all the city's known pedophiles behind bars appeared a logical solution. But they were wasting their time. If you were going to fight a battle, you had to pick one you could win or you'd lost before you'd even struck the first blow. Arrest the pedophiles? Like City Hall would ever do that?

Although…

Because of federal law demanding it of them, convicted child abusers had to make their presence known when they moved into a neighborhood. This meant people knew exactly which of their neighbors harbored dark secrets. If the Butcher wasn't caught soon, who was to say vigilantes wouldn't try to protect their loved ones by lashing out at every suspect around? Hell, there could be public castrations on street corners for miles around.

Maybe it wouldn't be long before the city's pedophiles themselves were begging to be safe behind bars.

The mob disappearing along Worth Street, their chanting became quieter and quieter by the second. So much so that Mary Jo dared to peek out at the world once more.

Tess said, "It's okay, Squirt. See? They've all gone."

Mary Jo peered around to check.

"Okay?"

Mary Jo nodded.

"So, shall we go find those swings and slides and have lots of fun?"

She nodded again. And cracked a tiny smile.

A leisurely stroll took them to Alfred E. Smith Playground. As soon as she saw it, Mary Jo's eyes lit up and she tugged at Tess's hand like a dog with its favorite toy. No pretty flowerbeds you could look at but not touch, no old men playing weird games, no meandering paths to trudge along at a sedate pace. No, on one big rectangular slab of asphalt, kids played on slides, on swings, on jungle gyms.

At the gateway in the black wrought-iron railings, Tess let go of Mary Jo. The girl immediately tore away towards the slides.

Tess shouted, "Be careful, squirt. And stay where I can see you." Not that that would be much of a problem in such a compact area.

Tess dawdled after Mary Jo.

She noticed three figures near the playground's restrooms, not playing on the slides or swings – they were way too old for that. Their presence was wrong. Why would guys, maybe eighteen years old, choose to hang out in such a small space so close to kids?

Sitting on a bench, two young moms smiled at her, one of them heavily pregnant. That was invitation enough.

Tess ambled over. She said, "Nice little playground you've got here."

The pregnant one said, "It's great, isn't it? You new to the area?"

"No, no. My niece is visiting so we're having a day out and as soon as she saw the slides it was all *'Auntie Deanna, Auntie Deanna, they've got slides. Please, please, please, please, please!'*"

"Awww, bless her," said the one with black spiky hair, a little boy sitting in her lap, his face buried in her shoulder. She nodded to him. "This one fell off one of the platforms and hurt his knee. But he's been very brave about it." She nuzzled him. "Haven't you, eh, Tobes?"

He peeked out, obviously curious to see who the new arrivals were.

Sweeping her bleached hair off her face, the pregnant one said, "Maybe Toby would like to show" – she looked at Tess – "Deanna, was it?"

Tess nodded. "Deanna, yeah."

"What a lovely name."

Tess smiled. "Oh, thank you."

The pregnant one said, "Maybe Toby would like to show Deanna's niece how high he can go on the swings." She pointed to a little boy in blue, beating the ground with a stick. "And take Thomas too."

Tess smiled at Toby. "Oh, Mary Jo would like that. She's not very good on the swings so she'd love an expert to give her some tips."

His mom said, "There you go, Tobes, you can show us all how it's done, huh?"

The freckled boy smiled. "But don't push me. I want to do it by myself."

She held her hands up. "Okay. Okay. You're a big boy now, so you go show Mommy what you can do by yourself."

Off he scooted.

"Please." Toby's mother gestured to Tess and then to the space next to her on the bench.

"Thanks."

"I'm Stace." She gestured to the pregnant woman. "Lucy."

458

Tess nodded. "Nice to meet you." She pointed at Stace's son. "He seems like a great kid."

"Thank you. But they all are at this age, aren't they? I tell you, it's the happiest time of my life."

"Enjoy." Lucy snickered and patted Stace's knee. "Because once he hits double digits that'll change real fast."

The women laughed.

Tess forced a smile. It was important that she ingratiated herself here. But idle chat? She'd rather go toe-to-toe with a knife-wielding psycho any day of the week than laugh at clichés and feign interest in other people's kids.

"So," said Lucy, "any of your own?"

"Not yet." Tess rolled her eyes. "Still waiting for the right guy, you know."

Lucy snickered again. "Hell, I've been married twelve years and I'm still waiting for him."

They laughed again. This time, Tess's laughter was genuine because she found the comment funny. They seemed like decent people. Maybe this was the place she'd been hoping to find. Especially as the women had taken the bait. Now, could she land a good catch?

Perverts couldn't sit in a schoolyard ogling kids, but there was no law to stop them from sitting in a park to read a book… and look up every so often at whoever else was there.

Parks were the ideal place for locating fresh targets – spot a kid in a park, tail them, snatch them wherever was convenient. Easy. So easy. In fact, it was thought the Butcher had snatched Theresa May, Mary Jo's sister, as she left a playground similar to this one. Tess would give anyone hundred-to-one odds-on that this was the way she'd find the leads she needed.

Tess called to Mary Jo. "Mary Jo, honey, stay where I can see you." There was absolutely nothing to worry about at that moment, but Tess needed an 'in'.

Lucy said, "Oh, don't worry on that score. She's good and safe here."

Tess shrugged. "Well, you can never be too sure these days, can you? Not with whack jobs like the Butcher around."

"Yeah," said Stace, "you have to be on your toes because it only takes a second, doesn't it?"

Lucy nodded. "True. But lightning never strikes twice."

Actually, lightning had been known to. Likewise, many a criminal had been caught because they foolishly returned to the scene of their crime. But Tess didn't correct them. That wasn't the way to gain trust.

Again, she glanced at the three figures near the bathrooms as a teenage boy waltzed over, shook hands with the taller of the three, then waltzed away again. That was smooth – to the untrained eye – but she knew exactly what was going on. Unfortunately, she didn't have time to deal with that now.

Tess said, "So it *is* safe here? You don't get weirdos hanging around anymore?"

Stace turned to Lucy. "There was that one a couple of months back."

"Oh, yeah. The fat guy with the beard."

"Yeah, he never had a kid with him but he kept hanging around, what, four times in the space of three weeks?"

Lucy said, "Five – he was here the day you saw your chiropractor."

"Oh, really?" Stace seemed genuinely surprised. "Yeah, there was something just not right about him. I don't know what, but, you know how some people instantly give you the creeps?"

"Oh, God, yeah," said Tess.

"That was this guy. Big time."

This was just the information Tess needed. "So, what did he look like?"

"Oh, don't worry, he won't be around here again," said Lucy.

Tess pushed them. "Yeah, but if he does and you're not here, I need to know for Mary Jo's sake."

"He was, like" – Stace looked to her friend – "what, six foot?"

Lucy nodded. "Yeah, around that. With glasses and a gut bigger than mine." She smoothed her hands over her baby bulge.

Stace mimed feeling some imaginary mound on her chin. "And with this big black beard. All matted. Like, ewww." She cringed.

Tess nodded. "Six foot; big gut; glasses; gross beard. Got it." She smiled, "Yeah, I can see why he'd give anyone the creeps."

Lucy said, "Oh, you won't miss him – he's a real looker."

They all laughed.

Excellent, using her 'bait'had paid off and provided her first lead – a description of a potential pedophile, maybe even the Butcher himself. She'd cross-reference that with the list of names Bomb was researching.

Now that she had the details, it was time to move on to the next playground to see if anyone there could corroborate Lucy and Stace's suspicions, or if she could find a description of another potential pervert to investigate. Sadly, she feared Bomb's list would be substantial, so at least this way, she could narrow it down to *possibly active* pedophiles instead of having to investigate every single one he'd found. No way would she have time for that – God only knew how many days Josie Ecker had left.

Something caught her eye. She didn't want it to, but she couldn't help herself. A teenager on a skateboard glided up to the three guys near the bathrooms, shook hands, and then glided away again. It looked innocent enough, but looks were so deceptive. That was why fighting the war on drugs was fighting a losing battle – the 'enemy' tactics were so entrenched in deception that, most of the time, those buying and selling the drugs were invisible.

She stared at the three young men. The exchange of money for drugs in a simple handshake had been flawless – an untrained person would likely never realize a drug deal had taken place at all.

Tess huffed. She really didn't want to get involved, but…

She turned to the two women. "Would you mind keeping an eye on Mary Jo for a moment, please?"

"Of course, no problem," said Stace.

"Thank you." Tess stood.

Stace turned to Lucy and began discussing what sounded like some god-awful reality TV show.

Tess had no time for such inanities – a televisual happy pill to help the masses forget how purposeless their own lives were by focusing on the purposeless lives of others.

No, she had no time for that – she had her own reality show about to start.

Who would she vote off?

Chapter 13

TESS SAUNTERED OVER to the bathrooms. At the thought of an impending confrontation, her adrenaline kicked in. She felt it infusing her body with power, coursing through her muscles to energize them. Great. Except, she knew the side effects could be deadly. Literally, for some people. The fight-or-flight response caused tunnel vision, auditory impairment, and diminished rational thought. She couldn't allow fear to control her – if she wanted to walk out of this park, she had to control it.

She breathed in for four seconds, held the breath for four, and then exhaled for four. She repeated the process as she walked. Gradually, her slow breathing slowed her heart rate and calmed her mind.

As she neared the three figures lurking by the bathrooms, one of them, a pudgy guy in a blue coat, nudged the taller buck-toothed one and nodded at her.

All three of them staring straight at her, the taller one whispered something and they all laughed. She knew that look – lust.

Tess didn't mind men ogling her – it gave her power over them because they always overestimated their potential and underestimated hers. To seal the deal, she swung her hips for them. Yeah, she loved being ogled.

She looked directly at the taller one and nodded to the corner of the small one-story building housing the bathrooms. The three guys looked at each other, puzzled, but then followed her around the corner, no doubt more out of curiosity than anything else.

Out of sight of everyone else in the playground, Tess faced them. "I know what you're doing."

"So?" A skinny guy with a red top looked unbelievably bored.

"So, do it someplace else."

The tall one turned and pushed his pudgy friend to go back to their spot.

Tess said, "I've got photos on my phone. Do you want me to call the cops?"

They froze. Then turned to face her again.

One by one, she stared them in the eye. "You can't deal here. Not with kids around."

The one in the red top loomed closer. He held out his hand. "Phone."

Standing at an angle to them, Tess stood her ground, but held her hands up submissively, palms out. "Hey, I don't want any trouble."

Red Top said, "You should've thought of that before flapping your big mouth. Phone!"

The tall guy joined him, puffing himself up to be as threatening as possible. "Didn't you hear the man? Give us your fucking phone, bitch."

Tess kept her fence up. From their attitude, they obviously weren't skilled fighters or they'd have seen that while her hands looked to be held up submissively, they were actually already in the perfect position to strike or protect herself – a 'fence' someone had to get over to attack her.

She said, "Do you think it's right to deal when there are little kids everywhere?"

Red Top huffed and glared at her from the corner of his eye. "Phone. Now. Or do you think it's right for little kids to see a grown woman bleed?"

There were just three simple rules to successfully taking on a small gang of untrained thugs.

Rule One was to appear weak, so they thought the fight was already over, when in reality it hadn't even started.

"Okay!" Tess said. "Please! Let me get it." She moved her hands to unsling her backpack. "I don't want any trouble."

Red Top smirked. He winked at his tall friend, already celebrating his victory.

As in many sports, games of chance, or magic performances, Rule Two involved making people watch the wrong thing, thereby giving you the opportunity to move before anyone could realize what had happened.

To give her the moment she needed to put one of them down immediately, she distracted Red Top by throwing her backpack in his face. The other two obligingly turned their heads to follow the bag with their gaze.

Of all the rules, Tess liked number three the most. In fact, it was usually the third she liked best whenever she devised a set of rules.

Maybe three was her lucky number.

Maybe it was the way the word 'three' rolled off the tongue.

Or maybe, just maybe, it was because most Rule Threes involved her beating the living crap out of whoever was standing in front of her.

She rammed a kick into the tall guy's gut. He crumpled backwards, mouth agape as he wheezed.

Having tossed the bag aside, Red Top fired a haymaker at her.

Instead of moving away from the danger, she moved towards it. She stepped closer to him, her left arm bent up at the side of her head for protection. Not only did that mean the punch swung behind her, but it put her in the ideal position to launch her own attack.

She smashed her right elbow up into his face.

Crashed her left elbow sideways into his head.

Whipped around and slammed her right elbow back over her shoulder and down onto him.

Red Top reeled back. Head wobbling like a drunk's. Blood streaming down his face.

Gaping mouthed, the third of the trio, Pudgy, had obviously frozen with the shock of seeing his two friends so brutally attacked. He snapped out of it. Kicked at her.

She sidestepped.

Caught his leg. Held him.

Thundered her shin into his groin.

Palm heeled him in the face. Twisted and swung him around and into the tall guy.

They fell to the asphalt a mass of twisted limbs.

Bleeding, Red Top leapt at her. Swinging punches wildly.

She covered up.

A boxer covered by holding both his forearms up in front of him. That was a weak defense on the street – it left both sides of your head open. A direct strike to the temple or neck could not just knock a person out, but if hard enough, could actually kill them.

Tess tucked her chin into her chest, held the back of her head with her left hand, so her bent arm protected the left side of her head, and wrapped her right arm around her jaw, elbow angled up. She could see out, but no one could hit anything but the top of her head – and anyone trying to hit her would likely break their hands on her elbows.

Red Top fired in another punch.

Untrained fighters didn't pick targets. Their minds warped by adrenaline and fear, they worked on pure instinct. Instinct didn't say, 'Hey, look, her guard is too high. You could get a nice jab in under her ribs.' No, instinct screamed, 'Go for the head! Go for the head! The head! Head! Head!'

Tess ducked and wove as Red Top's fists flailed at her.

His wild haymaker crashed into her elbow. The delicate bones of his hand smashed into one of the hardest parts of her body.

He squealed and recoiled in pain.

Tess struck.

She grabbed his head.

Pulled.

Kneed him in the body. Once, twice, three times.

Holding his head and twisting around, she threw him over her hip.

He splattered into the ground.

Instinctively, she pulled her hand back to crash a palm heel into his face.

A voice cracked the air behind her. "What … the … fuck!"

Fists up, she spun to defend herself, ready to punish whoever stood in her way.

With her hands on her hips, Lucy stared at her. "Are you fucking crazy?"

Tess lowered her arms. "What?"

"What the fuck have you done this for?"

"For the kids. You do know these losers are dealing drugs?"

Lucy said, "You think we're stupid? Of course we fucking know. But who the fuck do you think got rid of the pervert with the beard?"

Tess felt herself frowning. "What? What are you talking about?"

"So, they sell a bit of weed, but when they found out about that weirdo, who do you think beat the holy crap out of him so he wouldn't ever come back here?"

"But…" Her mind in a whirl, Tess struggled for words. "Do you really want your kids to see them day in and day out, like it's normal, like it's acceptable?"

She pointed at Tess. "I think you better fuck off before I call the cops."

Tess pointed at the whimpering lumps on the ground. "They're drug dealers."

"All I see is some crazy bitch who pounded on a bunch of harmless kids." Lucy folded her arms. "So, what's it going to be?"

Chapter 14

MOMMY SCREAMED, "MICHAEL!"

Sitting in the middle of the floor in Christie's pink bedroom, Mommy sobbed. Tears streamed down her sunken cheeks. Saliva drooled from her gaping mouth. It felt like someone had sliced her open, pulled out her innards, and was twisting them around and around into knots.

"Michael!"

Where was he? Why was he never there when she most needed him?

The sinews on her neck straining, she bent forward as she screamed again, "Michael!"

Footsteps pounded on the stairs.

"Michael!"

Panting, he dashed in.

Blubbering, Mommy pointed to the little girl sitting on the side of the bed in her white summer dress. Silent. Still. Well behaved.

"What is it, Helen? What's wrong?"

She struggled to get the words out, her sobbing breaking them up. "Chr—Christie." Her hand trembling, she pointed at the little girl. "Chris—Christie. There's something—something wrong with Christie."

Michael scooted over to the bed. He looked down at the girl. Crouched in front of her. Stared into her face. Then he looked back at Mommy. Looked back at Mommy with that half-baked expression he knew she hated. Why did he do that? And why was he doing it now? She needed him.

Michael said, "What am I looking at? What's wrong with her, honey?"

"What's wrong with her? What's..." She flung her arms up. "Can't you—can't you see?"

He shrugged. "I, er... Oh, do you mean... er..."

Mommy's breathing shuddered as she sobbed. "She—she won't talk to me." She snorted in a breath, her nose blocked. "She won't talk to me, Michael."

Michael looked at the little girl, who merely gazed into space. He shook his head. "Helen, it's not..." He huffed. "It's, er..."

Mommy reached out to him. "Fix her, Michael. Please. Please, Michael. Make it all perfect again. Please."

He crumpled to the floor in front of Mommy. "Oh, Helen." He put his arms around her. "Don't you remember? She's on pills so she'll behave, so she'll be the little girl you deserve."

"She's a doll, Michael. A goddamn doll! I need a baby. How can I be a wonderful mommy with… with that?" She stabbed a finger at the little girl.

He stroked Mommy's hair. "Oh, honey, we've tried that so many times and it doesn't work. At least this way, you can have Christie back with us."

"Christie talked to me. She told me everything. Everything. I want that again, Michael. I *need* that again."

He sighed. "But what if she turns out like all the others? What if all she does is scream for her mommy?"

Mommy pulled away from his embrace. "I'm her mommy!" She slapped him on the arm. "I'm her mommy. You hear? No one else. Me, Michael. Me! Now make her talk to me."

"Honey, I don't know if—"

She put her finger to his lips. "It will work. This time I know it will. I have a good feeling about this one." She wiped her palms over her cheeks to brush the tears away. "Promise me. Promise me you'll give me my Christie again."

"I…"

"Promise me!"

"I'd like to promise, Helen, but—"

She screwed her face up again as fresh tears welled, the empty ache inside her twisting around and around like a knife. "Michael, you know what we have to do if this one doesn't work. I can't keep getting my hopes up, can't keep getting Christie back, and then losing her all over again." She whimpered. "I just can't."

He hugged her and stroked her hair. "It's late, Helen. You need rest. Let's get you to bed and come at this fresh in the morning."

"But—"

"Shhh... I promise, honey, one way or the other, I promise you'll have Christie again."

Chapter 15

EXITING A CONVENIENCE store, Tess pulled the ring on a can of soda and handed it to Mary Jo, who was already munching on a candy bar. The crisp autumn sun had given the little girl a real rosy glow. Sadly, the weather had done quite the reverse for her bare hands.

Seeing Mary Jo's fingers turning a pale shade of blue, Tess had bought her some fur-lined mittens. Unfortunately, instead of keeping her hands warm with them, every time Tess looked away, Mary Jo turned them inside out to brush the fur against her cheeks.

Chocolate and a soda would mean her hands were too busy to play with fur and would warm up.

Needing to keep her energy levels up, Tess peeled a banana for herself and dug in. Fruit would've been a better option for Mary Jo too, but produce didn't endear an adult to a child the way chocolate did. Whoever engineered chocolate-flavored kale would become a billionaire overnight.

"Where are we going next, Auntie Deanna?" asked Mary Jo.

They'd already covered two small playgrounds that morning, but received only sketchy information of little value.

"I know where there's a lovely little park with some wonderful swings and slides, and some cute little ducks you can feed and—"

"And pandas?"

"Oh, I'm sorry, Squirt. We can't go to the zoo today because…" Oh, hell, what excuse was it she'd used yesterday? She couldn't use the same one – Mary Jo was too quick for that, as she'd found to her cost. "We can't because it's Animal Holiday Day."

The little girl frowned up at her.

"You've never heard of Animal Holiday Day?"

Mary Jo shook her head.

"After working every day to make children happy, the animals like to have a day of treats just for them – they like to read books, eat ice cream, play video games."

Mary Jo gasped. "We can go and read the penguins a story! Can we, please? Can we?"

Tess stared down into the big blue eyes pleading up at her. She'd killed more people than the FBI's ten Most Wanted combined, so why did she feel so bad denying this little girl something so trivial? "I, er…"

"Sammie Taylor says the animals in the zoo are even bigger than the ones on her TV. And her TV is *so* big. It's like…" Mary Jo stretched her arms out as far as she could reach. "Are animals that big? Really? Are they?"

"Well, some animals are very, very big, yes, but others are very, very small."

"So are the very, very big ones mean to the very, very small ones?"

"No, they're all nice to each other because they all live in different areas."

"Like vegetables?"

Tess frowned. "Like vegetables? Why like vegetables?"

"Well, in the supermarket" – Mary Jo pointed to her left – "apples are here and" – she thought for a moment and then pointed in front of her – "green things here" – she pointed to her right – "and oranges are here. But I don't like oranges. They have yucky white stuff."

Tess smiled. "No, that white stuff is awful, isn't it?"

"It's urgh!" Mary Jo made a disgusted face and stuck out her tongue.

Tess liked oranges, but a little white lie would help them bond more, which would be useful in persuading the little girl to do what Tess needed instead of what she wanted herself.

Nodding, Tess said, "So, yes, the zoo is like vegetables." What had happened to that polite little girl that barely said a word?

"So, can we go? Pleeeeeease?"

Tess crouched down to her. "I tell you what, squirt – and this is a promise, so you know I mean it –

if we don't go to the zoo today, or tomorrow, we'll go twice next week. Okay?"

Grinning, Mary Jo jumped up and down.

Hand in hand, they meandered down the sidewalk, Mary Jo skipping along and singing some made-up song about going to the zoo.

Tess didn't like deceiving the little girl, but she didn't have any choice. Besides, deception was such a gigantic part of her life, she didn't think she could ever be outright truthful with anyone.

On occasion, she even lied to Bomb.

As for Josh? Hell, it was scary just how much crap she'd fed him. But deceiving people was her life. Without it, everything would fall apart. It was the only thing that made it possible for her to do the good she did and wipe the scum off the streets.

Tess stopped dead.

Nibbling her candy bar, Mary Jo looked up at her. "Auntie Deanna?"

"Just a moment, Mary Jo."

Could that be the answer? Could that be the key to solving the whole Butcher job and saving Josie Ecker?

Her phone rang – Bomb. She answered it.

"Yo, Tess, I finally uploaded your list of names. Sorry it's taken so long but it's been a hell of a job."

"Bomb, sorry, but I have to go. I'll get back to you ASAP."

"No problem. Ciao."

She hung up. She couldn't let a conversation ruin her train of thought.

While Mary Jo munched on the last bit of her candy bar and gazed at the people browsing at a newsstand, Tess took a long slow breath and cleared her mind.

Her life was a complete lie to everybody. Absolutely everybody.

Why?

So she could get away with doing the things she did.

What if the Butcher's life was a lie, too? What if he only committed those monstrous acts to fool everybody so he could do what he really wanted to do? What if pedophilia was an elaborate decoy? That would explain why no one could find him – because they were looking for an imaginary person. You couldn't find a lie. No, you had to find the person who told it.

Surprising herself, she gasped.

Those 'monstrous acts' – did he even commit them? If the whole pedophile persona was a stunt to hide his true motivation, were the rapes fake, too? What if the thought of sex with a child repulsed him just as much as it did an ordinary person?

She realized she was standing and staring into space with her mouth wide open. She shut it and tried to look normal.

She'd known something was completely off about this job, about this killer. Was that it? Was all they knew about the Butcher a complete lie?

That would explain everything. Well, everything except why he snatched the girls to start with. This idea could lead to a gigantic wild goose chase, or it could be a major breakthrough in solving the case. But how could she determine which it was likely to be?

She smiled.

She knew just who to see and what question to ask.

Chapter 16

"TESS!" THE SCRAWNY man in the blue medical scrubs grinned and held his arms wide as he scurried towards her.

She smiled. "I hope you've washed after being elbow deep in there." She pointed to the cadaver on his stainless steel table, a Y-shaped incision in the chest and the black skin peeled back.

Yep, it was good she hadn't risked bringing Mary Jo along. One glimpse of that and the little girl wouldn't have made it through the night without waking up screaming for months. But since dropping her back at home, things had seemed kind of quiet.

Strange. Tess had never wanted kids – never felt that maternal gnaw that most women did – yet, the last few days had been... Fun? Instructive? Heartwarming? Challenging? She wasn't sure how to describe it, but at least she'd gleaned some insight into why so many people needed kids to make their lives complete. So would she be flushing her contraceptive pills the moment she got home? Oh, yeah. And then she'd be emailing the guy with the barbed tiger penis to see when he was available to impregnate her.

With a beaming smile, the scrawny man threw his arms around Tess. She hugged him back.

"Hey, it's been too long," said Doctor Myron Bickle, ME, patting her on the back.

She shrugged. "It's been… what… a couple of months?"

Breaking away, he said, "It was…" His left arm across his body, he rested his right elbow on it so he could stroke his chin while gazing into space. After a moment, he pointed at her. "Vincent D'Angelo. You wanted to know if the lividity might suggest he'd been moved not once but twice."

"Man, you always amaze me with that memory of yours."

"That's as may be, but Vincent D'Angelo was eighteen months ago come December."

"It's been that long?"

"Uh-huh. Uh-huh."

"Wow. Who'd have thought it?" She punched him on the arm. "So, how'd it go with you and that nurse from Saint Catherine's, huh? You dog, you."

"Oh, yeah – Melissa." He smiled, puffing himself up to his full height to look her square in the eye. "Yeah, that went really well. Yeah. Er… For a while, but, er, you know, not every relationship's going to work out, is it?"

There was nothing like building up a guy's ego to get him to do what you wanted. Sometimes it was so easy it was almost embarrassing. "What did you do? Nail one of your lab techs and she found out?"

He laughed. "Something like that. So, how about you? Seeing anyone?"

"God, no!" An image of Josh flashed into her mind.

His smile broadened. "Great. So still loving the single life?"

"Hey, can I help it if I've got needs one man can't fill?" Josh flashed into her mind again. And a pang of guilt twisted in her stomach. That was odd. That had never happened before. Not over him, nor any of the other guys she'd laid. And that was some list, so a new sensation was most surprising.

Myron laughed. "Same old Tess."

His gaze drifted to her boobs. And lingered. When it finally drifted back up, she gave him the most wanton smile she could.

He leaned back, resting one hand on his second coroner's slab, the empty one. His posture opened up his chest and thrust his groin forward. Very manly.

He smirked. "So, what can I do for you today?"

For the third time, Josh flashed into her mind. Oh, this was like God was playing some sick joke on her. What the hell was wrong with her? Had she married the guy? No! She was fucking him. That was all. *Fucking him*. There was no commitment; no involvement; no sharing. Fucking. That was what there was. Fucking and nothing but fucking.

Then why the hell wouldn't he get out of her head!?

She willed it to go.

But his image wouldn't disappear.

She wasn't having this. She was not having a man interfere in her life. Not having a man influence what she could and couldn't do. Not having a man upset the balance of her world and threaten her work. Oh, no. If she couldn't will him out of her head she'd drive him out. The bastard! And she knew just how to do it.

Chapter 17

"**COME ON, BIG** boy," said Tess. "Fuck me hard. Come on."

The polished metal like ice on her bare skin, she gasped as she lay back on the stainless steel coroner's slab.

Between her thighs, Myron panted as his spindly hips thrust him into her.

She glanced over at Mr. Josiah Worthington on the next slab, his innards laid bare to the world. He didn't look much older than she was. What dreams had he had? What goals had driven his life? What greatness had he envisioned? And what poor choices had brought him to this place five decades too soon?

It was amazing how many dreams people had over their lifetime. And even more amazing how few of them they realized.

Why?

Because people always thought they had far more time than they actually did. Always thought there was no harm in leaving things till tomorrow, or next week, or next year. The result? Most people ended up on a cold steel slab having achieved only a tiny fraction of what they could have done, what they'd longed to do.

All because they got that one simple thing so wrong.

Would it have been any different for Josiah if someone had told him the exact date on which he'd be sliced open on this cold slab?

Maybe, maybe not.

It wasn't only procrastination that held people back, but fear.

Fear of failure, fear of success, fear of rejection. People didn't like change almost as much as they didn't like the disapproval of their friends and family. Between procrastination, peer pressure, and change, people were pretty much screwed. It was no wonder so few people held to their dream and dedicated their life to seeing it realized.

She looked at Myron. Sweaty, panting Myron.

So was this the childhood fantasy she'd longed to be realized?

Hell, she pushed Bomb to get a life, yet look at the piece of crap she was living.

Christ, no. This wasn't her dream. This wasn't what she'd wanted. Josh or no Josh, this wasn't living.

She wriggled further up the stainless steel slab, pulling away from Myron. But he gripped her thighs and pulled her to him again.

Like hell was he doing that. She needed information, so she didn't want to upset Myron, but this wasn't going to happen. Not now.

Again, she glanced over at Josiah. Looking for strength in his failure.

But she didn't see Josiah Washington.

On the cold steel slab, her tiny body slashed open from top to bottom, bloody innards bared, lay Josie Ecker.

Josie Ecker would have dreams.

Josie Ecker would have seventy years to see them realized.

Josie Ecker would have a chance for greatness.

If she lived.

Tess looked up at Myron. Red-faced, sweaty Myron.

When Tess was a young girl, she'd needed someone to rescue her from the brutal life she'd been pushed into. But no one had come. And now she was here doing this. Josie Ecker deserved better. She deserved the chance for a proper life. Could Tess deny Josie that chance?

She wrapped her legs around Myron's bare butt and pulled him deeper into her. "Fuck me, big boy. Come on. Fuck me now."

He mauled her boobs. That was always a good sign things were coming to a climax.

She said, "Go on, baby. Go on."

He panted harder. Thrust faster.

"Give it to me now!"

He slammed into her and cried out. He bit his own arm to stifle the noise.

Tess heaved a great sigh of relief. "Oh, man, that was good."

"Yeah?" Holding the condom, he pulled out of her.

"God, yeah. You really hit the spot that time."

Myron grinned. He wiped his dick on his blue cotton cap then tossed the cap into the bin of scrubs waiting to be laundered.

Fastening his trousers, he stood at the main door, watching her dress. As she fastened her own trousers, he unlocked the door.

He ambled back. "So, while I'd like to believe it was, you didn't come here today just because you had an itch only I could scratch."

"The Butcher."

He held up his hands. "Whoa, I can't get into specifics on such a high-profile case. You know that."

"Listen, I'm not expecting the complete file, just an odd tidbit or two."

"Tess, please, I said No. Now, don't push me on this one."

"Myron? Come on, man."

He strode over to the main door and held it open revealing the hall beyond.

He said, "I'm sorry, Tess, but as much as I love your visits, that's too big an ask."

"Seriously? You're kicking me out?"

He refused to make eye contact. Instead, he stared into space and yanked the door even wider open.

"Myron, it's me." She smiled at him. "Come on."

He didn't even look at her.

"Please," he gestured to the hallway. "If you don't mind, I've a great deal of work to get through."

Fantastic. She was damn sure he held the key. But if dropping her panties for him didn't work, how the hell could she get the info she needed out of him?

Chapter 18

TESS STORMED FOR the doorway. "Fine. If you're getting so much snatch you don't appreciate my visits, I'll find someone else next time I have an 'itch'."

Playing hardball was risky, but she'd bet he hadn't even been alone in a room with an eligible woman since her last visit, let alone banged one. But no matter how risky it was, it was the only play she had.

Myron's jaw set as she marched past, but he still didn't look at her.

Hell, he wasn't going to stop her. Damnit.

She skulked down the hallway, its striplights making the cream ceramic tiles on the walls gleam as if slicked with water, giving the area a sickly, unnatural feel. Walking as slowly as she thought she could while still appearing to be storming out, she headed for the exit at the far end. And it got closer and closer.

Tess's shoulders slumped. Goddamnit, he wasn't going to break – he was really going to let her walk out. That meant she'd blown it. Probably her only chance.

Oh Christ, what the devil was she going to do now to find the Butcher?

Weary from the disappointment, she limply reached for the steel handle of the exit.

"Wait!" Myron called from down the hallway.

Tess blew out a breath with relief. Oh, thank God.

Slowly, she turned.

"This is off the record?" He knew she did freelance journalism and appreciated the *favor-for-a-favor* way of the world.

She dawdled toward him as if she really didn't care whether he was going to give up what he knew or not. "Hey, we've got a good thing going here. Would I screw you over and ruin it?"

"So long as that's abundantly clear."

"Off the record. Got it. Until you give me the go-ahead..." She zipped her lips shut.

He beckoned with a wave of his hand for her to join him in the room again.

Tess scampered back.

"Thanks, Myron." She leaned in and kissed him on the cheek.

He pulled back from her, then whipped around and peered down the hallway, as if anxious someone might have seen the kiss. The hallway still deserted, he shoved the door to.

Staring straight into her eyes, he said, "This is all off the record. I can't stress this enough. Okay?"

"Okay."

"And some specifics are completely off the table."

"Okay."

"Well, okay then." Another wave of his hand invited her to ask her questions. "So hit me."

She dove straight in, fearing he'd change his mind at any second and yank open the door again.

"Am I right in thinking the victims were kept in cold storage after being dismembered?"

He stared at her. Obviously deciding whether to answer or if that was one of the specifics he wanted to avoid. It didn't matter, his hesitation meant she was correct – the victims had been frozen.

She said, "Okay, so the rapes. Is it possible the rapes were committed postmortem?"

Again, he simply stared at her.

"Myron, you've got to give me something, man."

He snorted a deep breath in and then blew it out. "Okay, what I think you want to ask is this – hypothetically, can I tell if a child has been sexually abused pre- or postmortem? In which case, the answer would have to be: generally, yes."

"Generally?"

He held up a finger. "However, if a body has been frozen and then suffered extensive decomposition and insect activity, that could prove problematic."

"How about telling if the sexual abuse was caused by a man performing intercourse, or by penetration with a foreign object?"

He squinted at her. "Who have you been talking to?"

"What?" His question threw her for a moment. "No one. Why?"

He frowned. Obviously in deep thought, his gaze drifted through empty space.

What had she stumbled upon that he had to think about so intensely? Could it be the breakthrough she'd idly dreamed it could be?

Myron rubbed his forehead.

"Myron? What is it?"

"Tut, tut, tut." He gazed down at the floor rubbing his mouth.

Finally, he looked up and pointed at her. "You haven't paid anyone for information?"

"What information? I'm asking questions because I don't have any information."

He marched over to the door, peeked outside, and then locked it again.

This was going to be good. But what was it?

"Myron, what is it?"

He drew a deep breath and raked his fingers back through his hair.

He said, "So far, we've only found four of the six torsos."

"Yes, I know. So does the media. That's not a secret."

"Three were very badly decomposed, but the fourth…" He took another deep breath as if still debating whether to reveal anything or not.

Tess waited. She didn't want to push too hard – yet – in case she spooked him and he clammed up completely.

Finally, he said, "The fourth showed clear signs of sexual abuse, except, for a girl of that age, the damage to the labia and vaginal entrance and the amount of internal bruising were incongruous with penile penetration. Especially for a live subject."

"So if the Butcher didn't have intercourse with her, what did he do?"

He looked at her from the corner of his eye. He snickered. "You're not looking for information, are you? You're looking for confirmation – you already know."

Tess had thought the Butcher might have abused the girls postmortem to throw the police off the scent, to make them believe it was all about sex when there was something else he wanted, but now? Now, her suspicions ran far deeper.

Umpteen times, Myron had stated that he wouldn't give specifics, but if she stated information as opposed to asking questions, his non-denial would be answer enough.

But she wouldn't get a second chance at this. Could she think on her feet quickly enough to get all the information she needed?

She said, "That fourth girl – the Butcher faked the signs of sexual intercourse with her."

No answer.

"You didn't find semen in any orifice of any of the girls."

No answer.

"You're starting to think these abductions are not sexually oriented at all."

Again, no answer.

So if the Butcher wasn't a pedophile snatching girls for sex, why was he taking them? A myriad of questions whirled around her head.

Why would a grown man kidnap a prepubescent girl?

What could he get out of such a relationship?

And why would he take a girl, but then fake having had sex with her instead of simply having it?

She was making a glaring assumption there. Just like the police and every single person who'd followed this case with horror and outrage.

One question clawed its way to the front of her mind – why would a grown man kidnap an eight-year-old girl?

A grown man?

That was one glaring assumption if ever there was one. What if the Butcher wasn't male?

Or what if he had a female accomplice? Children generally trusted female strangers more than men – it wasn't just that they were less threatening, but because of the maternal aspect too.

Whichever was the case, it changed the game completely. Talk about throwing a proverbial spanner in the works – she'd taken her investigation in totally the wrong direction, so no wonder she was hitting dead end after dead end.

But that ended now.

She'd come here for answers. And she'd found them. All the answers she could ever have hoped for. Unfortunately, she'd also found a question. A huge question – why would a woman, or a couple, become serial kidnappers who eventually murdered their victims?

Chapter 19

TESS SLID ALONG the brown vinyl into the booth in the middle of Grossman's Diner.

With a Marilyn Monroe beauty spot, but with the similarity ending there, a dumpy waitress stood before her. "Do you want to hear today's specials?"

"Does Pete Cornish still work here, please?"

"You want to talk to him?"

"No, thanks, but I'll take two pieces of apple pie and an orange juice."

The waitress toddled away. At best, Cornish was a mediocre cook, hence his position at Grossman's and not the Four Seasons, but his apple pie…!

She stared out of the window. As dusk slowly enveloped the city, a silver Ford drove by. And a silver Toyota. And a silver Mercedes. And another silver Ford. She scrutinized each one. Was disappointed each time.

She turned away. Of all the colors of car her grandpa's killer could've been in, why did it have to be the most popular one on the road?

Gazing down at the matte black table, she started to dissect her conversation with Myron.

Josh flashed into her mind.

She couldn't help but think she'd done something wrong, yet all she'd done was her job: she'd needed information, so she'd used a commodity in her possession to trade for it. Where was the problem?

She picked up the ketchup bottle and turned it around and around in her hand.

The problem was that if Josh knew what she'd done, he'd be upset.

So?

That was his problem. Why should she be concerned with it? Since when did it matter what other people thought of her?

Her job was vital. Through her work, she made a valuable contribution to society and made the city a safer place for everyone. It wasn't like she was married and had screwed some guy just for money, or out of lust.

Hell, being a detective, Josh did pretty much the same job she did.

Yeah, except he got a nice fat paycheck, medical insurance, and regular hours with time off.

What did she get? She didn't even get a simple thank-you, let alone payment. No one cared if she starved because she couldn't afford food, if she froze because she couldn't afford rent. She did what she did to survive.

She slammed the ketchup down. Jesus, missing people, caring about their feelings and what they thought of her – what the hell kind of pussy was she turning into!

A child's life was at stake.

Why was she getting hung up on other people instead of assimilating the new information she'd uncovered?

Her gut had always told her there was more to the Butcher than a brutal killer. Firstly, he didn't just go for young, pretty girls, no, he chose girls with a particular eye color, body shape, and hair length. He was very selective.

Secondly, considering the length of time he kept the girls alive, there was very little vaginal tearing or bruising.

Finally, despite him leaving behind ample DNA evidence, meaning he didn't care about the police finding it, there was no semen present in or on any of the bodies.

Sex was not his primary motivation. Indeed, it very probably was not any motivation at all.

Why would he fake being a pedophile? What could he be doing that was so horrendous that appearing to be a pedophile was so much better? When he—

The waitress clattered a glass of orange juice and two pieces of pie on one large plate onto the table. "Enjoy your meal."

Her train of thought completely lost, Tess said, "Sorry, can I get the pie to go, please?"

"Sure." The waitress picked the plate back up.

Tess downed half the juice.

If it wasn't the number of silver cars cruising by the window, it was relationship issues; if it wasn't relationship issues, it was the activity of the employees and her fellow diners. Tess needed somewhere with as few distractions as possible.

If the Butcher's past victims were anything to go by, Josie Ecker should have a good few days left yet. Unless the little girl had done something particularly bad to piss him off. For all Tess knew, the Butcher could be standing over Josie with his axe right that second.

Tess needed to find Josie. Needed to find her fast. But who had her? And why?

That was the secret to solving the riddle – why? If Tess could fathom *why* someone had her, she was positive she could uncover the *who* of the puzzle.

Why? Talk about a mystery.

If only Josie could keep the Butcher happy for a little longer.

Tess had wanted to save Josie because no child should suffer such a gruesome fate.

But now?

Now, things had changed. Now there was a different reason.

It wasn't because of the new information and the mystery of what nightmare the Butcher subjected his victims to.

It wasn't because she'd befriended Mary Jo and seen that a child could actually be a person Tess could care about.

It wasn't because the Butcher was a serial killer who didn't just kill his victims but destroyed entire families.

No, it wasn't any of those.

One day, one day long ago, a small girl had suffered pain, suffered abuse, suffered a life no child should even have known existed, let alone experienced. The problem was that 'one day' had repeated over and over and over. For years.

Every day, the little girl had prayed it would be the last such day. Prayed someone would come, prayed someone would see her suffering, prayed someone would rescue her.

And every day she'd been disappointed. No one came. No one cared. No one saved her.

Tess didn't want to save Josie; Tess *needed* to save Josie.

Through saving Josie, Tess might save a small part of that other little girl.

Through saving Josie, Tess might save herself.

But to do that, she had to find Josie.

In a city of eight million people, how did you find one terrified little girl, hidden away in the dark from prying eyes?

If only Tess knew how much time they had. If only she knew where to start looking. If only she knew Josie was safe at that very moment.

But she couldn't know.

All she could do was imagine the horrors the little girl was facing.

Alone.

In the dark.

Praying for help, but receiving only torment.

If she was still alive, what horrors might she be facing that very second while Tess sat safe and warm, casually enjoying a glass of OJ?

Chapter 20

IN THE PINK bedroom, standing beside the three shelves crammed with cuddly stuffed animals and immaculately dressed dolls, Mommy shouted, "And you won't be wanting this either, will you?"

She yanked the head off the hand-painted porcelain doll she'd bought at an antiques store in Chelsea and flung it to the floor. It landed on top of a panda with stuffing bursting from its abdomen, a teddy bear with no arms, and a doll that looked like its head had been caved in by the heel of a woman's shoe.

With the baby monitor in his hand, Michael dashed in, panting for breath. "Helen, what the devil's gotten into you?"

She scowled at him. "Don't you dare use that fucking tone with me, Michael."

He shrank back. He looked at the pile of toys on the floor, then back to her. "What is it? What's gone wrong?"

"That's gone wrong." She jabbed her finger at the little girl curled up on her bed in the corner of the wall.

Michael said, "Christie? What's she done?"

"What's she done?" Sneering, Mommy looked at the girl. "*What's she done!*"

Mommy threw a smiling furry dolphin at the child. It hit Christie on the arm, but harmlessly bounced off.

The little girl shrieked an earsplitting cry.

Michael winced.

When the little girl ran out of breath and stopped, he moved over. "Christie, everything's fine, sweetheart. There's no need for that."

He reached out and gently laid his hand on her shoulder.

She shrieked another piercing scream.

He pulled back.

Mommy said, "See. See! Every time. Every single time I go near her, that's what I get. I give her a life that other children can only dream about and this is how she repays me. It's not fair. It's not goddamn fair."

She flung her arm across the top shelf and all the toys tumbled to the floor.

Michael put his head in his hands. "This is what I was worried about." He heaved a breath and then shook his head. "I was frightened this would happen when you said you wanted me to reduce her medication."

Mommy scowled at him again. "Oh, so it's my fault, is it? My fault for giving her *everything* and just *hoping* for the tiniest bit of appreciation in return?"

He looked up at her with a strange resignation in his eyes.

"You fix this, Michael. You fix it now."

He heaved another deep breath.

"Christie," he said, "I need you to be good, sweetheart. Okay?"

He moved his hand toward the child. He could see her watching from the corner of her eye, through her hair hanging down over her face.

The moment he got within twelve inches of her, the screaming started.

He pulled his hand back and looked at Mommy.

Mommy said, "If you can't fix this, you know what has to be done."

He hung his head.

"Michael. ... Michael..." She would not be ignored. She shouted. "Michael!"

The little girl flinched and clawed the walls to squeeze further into the corner.

He looked up. "I'll try, Helen. But... it might take time. So just bear with us. Okay?"

She leaned down to him, so close her spittle hit his face when she spoke. "How can anyone be a wonderful fucking mommy if they haven't got a fucking baby?"

She stormed away.

At the door, she spun. She stabbed a finger at him.

"Fix it. Tomorrow." She scowled. "Or you know what to do."

Chapter 21

LYING IN HER bed, gazing at her white ceiling, Tess heaved a great sigh. She picked up her phone from beside her and held it up to look at the time: 11:27 a.m. She heaved another sigh.

She'd been lying like this since her 6:30 alarm. And she'd lain like that for hours the previous night. And for what? A whole lot of nada.

Aside from her special spot beside the lake in the park, lying in bed was one of the best places she'd found for brainstorming – it was like a poor man's deprivation tank. Today, it simply hadn't worked – inspiration had not come a-knocking.

She'd considered getting up and going through the files Bomb had sent on known and suspected pedophiles, but yesterday's revelations at the morgue suggested that would be fruitless. So what should she do?

And therein lay the problem – she had absolutely no idea.

She'd already sent Bomb on one wild goose chase, which could already have cost Josie Ecker her life. She had to get the new plan of action right. Had to get it right now. Had to unveil what was really going on so she and Bomb could put all their efforts into finding and saving Josie.

Deception was the key. Why would the Butcher want the authorities to believe he was a pedophile? Why would he fake having sex with children? What could possibly be in it for him?

As if that wasn't riddle enough, why did he keep the girls? Why keep them for weeks, some even months, and then kill them? Hack them to pieces and toss them away like so many bits of trash? And that was exactly how he thought of them – as trash. You couldn't hack up something you cared for and toss it in the East River, in a dumpster, in a cage for animals to feed on. So why would he do that? Why would he snatch a child, care for it for a few weeks, then discard it?

Could it be—

Tess's phone rang. She knew it wasn't Bomb from the ringtone. No, it could only be one person because only one person had that number, an Internet number being routed through Bomb's custom-built Web telephone exchange. And it wasn't the number for Tess Williams.

She answered. "Deanna Gambini."

Rebecca Alcott said, "I'm sorry to bother you, Ms. Gambini, but Mary Jo just won't stop talking about all the fun you two had and she's desperate to say hello. Do you mind?"

Tess snickered. How strange. A kid wanting to talk to her? But she hated kids! Or at least hated the common concept of them – as a must-have life accessory. "Er… no, of course not. Put her on."

"Auntie Deanna!"

Tess had to hold the phone from her ear, Mary Jo was so excited her voice was deafening. She said, "Hey, squirt."

"Auntie Deanna, I've drawn a picture of you for your refrigerator. Can you come see?"

"Ohhh, that's so great. Thank you, Mary Jo. But I'm sorry, I can't come right now. But I'll come by and look just as soon as I can. Okay?"

All the excitement drained from Mary Jo's voice. "Okay."

"Hey, I tell you what – you draw a picture of you standing next to each animal you want to see in the zoo and then when we go next week, we'll put them on the cage so they'll always remember you. How about that?"

Mary Jo's voice all but exploded with joy once more. "Me and penguins?"

"Of course you and penguins."

"And elephants?"

"You bet."

"And lions?"

"You and every animal you've ever seen on TV. That okay?"

"I have to start."

Clattering noises came down the phone.

Tess heard Rebecca's voice in the distance. "Mary Jo? Mary Jo?"

The voice came louder, clearer. "Ms. Gambini, Mary Jo's just run off. Is everything okay?"

"Yes, don't worry. Everything's just fine. I guess Mary Jo just got a little overexcited, is all."

Rebecca said, "Excited? 'Excited' isn't the word for it. She's barely stopped talking about all the fun you guys had and how you're going to the zoo next week. Thanks ever so much, Ms. Gambini."

"It's my pleasure, Mrs. Alcott. See you soon." She hung up.

Tess stared into space for a moment. Then smiled.

It was highly doubtful she'd have time to traipse around a zoo just for the fun of it, especially with a child she barely knew, but it was kind of nice to know she'd managed to connect with the little girl. Maybe there was hope for her to live some sort of ordinary life yet.

The smile faded.

A frown formed.

What had she been thinking of before the call?

Something had clicked into place in her mind.

Kind of. She was sure it had.

But what?

Something she could follow.

Something that might lead to the Butcher.

But what in God's name was it?

"Oh, hell."

Tess laid back on the bed. Stared at the ceiling. Tried to lie in exactly the same position she was in before the call. Coaxed her mind into the same state it was in when the possible breakthrough had happened.

What the devil was it?

What had she been thinking about?

What images had she pictured?

What phrases had she used to express her thoughts?

What idea had sparked…

Trash.

Bits of trash.

Yes. That was it.

Trash.

The Butcher had tossed away his victims like so many bits of trash. You only tossed out something you didn't care about. But you took it in in the first place because you *did* care about it. Why would he care about kids that weren't his own?

She gasped. That was it! That was the missing piece of the puzzle she'd been hunting for. The piece that unlocked everything.

Chapter 22

TESS GRABBED HER phone.

The answer was so obvious. Why the hell hadn't she seen it sooner?

The Butcher cared about kids that weren't his own because that's what he was trying to make them – *his own*. He wasn't abducting kids for sex; he was abducting kids to build a family.

She placed a call. "Hey."

"Yo, Tess. How you doing with the files I uploaded?"

"Bomb, I don't think that's the answer. I think we've been looking for the wrong kind of suspect."

"What do you mean?"

"According to the ME, the crimes might not be sexually related."

"Might? We're going to risk a kid's life on *'might'*?"

"This is the key, Bomb. I know it. The Butcher isn't grabbing kids for kicks, he's trying to rebuild a family."

"Rebuild a family? I don't follow."

"I think we're looking for someone, or maybe a couple, who's lost a daughter and is trying to replace her."

"So, if he's looking for a new daughter, why rape, then butcher the kids he takes?"

"To throw everyone off what he's really doing. Everyone thinks he's a pedophile, yet the ME has no conclusive evidence of any rapes."

"It still doesn't explain why he kills them."

"Because they don't work out. To him, it's like getting a new pair of shoes – if they hurt your feet, you junk them and look for another pair."

Bomb remained silent for a moment, probably while he mulled over the idea. Hardly surprising, it was a big idea to get your head around.

Finally, he said, "So now we don't even know if we're looking for one person or even a whole family."

"No, but now we know what kind of people we're looking for and there'll be far fewer that fit the profile. I want a Level Five on every family that's suffered the bereavement of a girl, six to ten years old, blue eyes, long hair, slim build, in the two years leading up to the first victim being taken."

"Got it. Anything else?"

"Just those names. ASAP."

"Will do. Ciao, Tess."

If she was right, she'd have to move fast, so she couldn't rely on public transport. Immediately after she'd hung up, she phoned her local car rental and booked a compact, something that would blend in on any street and which didn't have satellite navigation – the last thing she wanted was an onboard computer able to place her at the crime scene.

Putting her phone down, she smirked. If all went well, later today, the Butcher would discover there'd be no cozy psychiatric cell for him with three squares per day. Hell, he wasn't the only one who could hack people up and make them disappear.

Chapter 23

SITTING ON THE bed, Michael smoothed his pudgy hands back over his bald head and groaned. He shook his head. Three scratches streaked across his cheek where he'd been raked by a small hand.

He looked back at the little girl curled up in the corner on her pink bed.

He said, "Please, Christie, you've got to take the pills. If you don't I'll have to hurt you again, and make you swallow them. Is that what you want?"

No response.

"Christie?" Michael touched her arm.

She shrugged him off.

"Come on now, Christie, be a good girl." He reached out with the pills.

She screamed and lashed out, hitting his hand. The pills flew from his grasp and across the room.

He hung his head again. Sighed. For a few moments, he sat on the edge of the bed simply staring at the floor.

Finally, he drew a deep breath and went onto his hands and knees, searching for the pills.

Turning towards the door, he stopped. He slowly raised his gaze. Mommy stood in the doorway, her countenance as dark as the dried blood on the axe in her hands.

Michael sank back to kneel on the floor. He raised his hands defensively. "Please, honey, please. I just need a little more time." He pointed at the girl. "Christie's already doing much better. See? See how quiet she is? Just give me a little more time. Please."

Chapter 24

TESS DREW THE drapes and flicked on her living room light. She'd been so engrossed in studying the case, she hadn't realized it was now pitch black outside. Trundling back, she gazed down at a huge, collage-like map of Downtown created by printing out individual sections on letter-size sheets of paper. She sat on her brown rug in the middle of the floor and stared at the map. She hoped that seeing every tiny nook and cranny of the area might spark some vital insight.

The map also displayed all the victim information she'd input earlier. When Bomb provided the new list to her of families who'd tragically lost a young daughter, Tess hoped the combined pattern would help them narrow down the number of families to investigate.

She gazed at all the colored dots and zigzagging lines representing places and routes. Why did the Butcher limit his hunting grounds to such a relatively small area? There were eight million people in the city, so why didn't he strike further afield? Surely he knew that by limiting his hunting area, the authorities had a better chance of finding him. What was so special about Downtown that he never went anywhere else? There had to be a connection of some sort, but what?

She scoured the map. "There's something I'm not seeing, Fish. What the hell is it?"

And then she saw it. Or, to be more accurate, didn't see it. Didn't see it because she hadn't printed it.

She inhaled sharply. "Holy crap!"

She snatched her tablet. Resized the map of New York City on the screen to see more.

There!

That was it.

She'd bet any amount of money on it. Why hadn't she seen it earlier?

Why? Because she hadn't been looking for it. But now, it was so obvious.

She jabbed her finger at a point on the map on her tablet. "That's it, Fish. He's there. He's goddamn there!"

She grabbed her phone. Called Bomb. He answered after only two rings.

"Tess, I'm still on with it. There's a lot of data to collate for what you're asking."

"Forget that. Listen, concentrate on Brooklyn. Only families in Brooklyn."

"Brooklyn? Why Brooklyn?"

"Because animals don't shit where they eat."

"You've lost me," said Bomb.

"Check his exit routes from where he snatched the girls – all easy access to Brooklyn via the Manhattan Bridge, Brooklyn Battery Tunnel, or Brooklyn Bridge."

"Yeah, but we can't base our entire strategy on an easy escape route."

"I'm not. Think real estate – how big a house can you get in Brooklyn for the price of an apartment in Manhattan? And what do you get with houses that you don't get with apartments?"

"Er… Ohhh, basements and attics."

Tess said, "Where better to stash a kid away from nosy neighbors?"

"Hey, I don't want to jinx it, but I think I might have something. I'm uploading a file now."

"What you got?"

"I'll tell you in just a sec…"

She waited. But Bomb said nothing.

"Bomb?"

"I'm just looking for the right bit."

Again, she hung on. Hell, it was like waiting for the dentist to stop drilling to fill a cavity – it just went on and on and on, as if time had stopped flowing.

"Bomb!?"

"Er… I've got it somewhere…"

"Bomb, you're killing me here!"

"Ah, found it. Michael and Helen Thorsen. 275 Lower Jessop Way, Brooklyn. Lost their seven-year-old daughter, Christie, eleven months before the first victim was snatched."

"Sounds interesting."

Tess surfed to Bomb's darknet and downloaded the file while Bomb continued to fill in the details.

He said, "That's only half of if. Wait till you see a photo of the kid. And get this – they'd been trying for a child for sixteen years before finally succeeding thanks to IVF. But it put them in hock up to their eyeballs. Two weeks after Christie's death, the mom was admitted to *Bartholomew's Psychiatric Unit*. She spent three months locked in there."

"Jesus," said Tess. "She had a total meltdown after losing her kid?"

"Not surprising, considering what they'd had to go through to have one."

Tess opened the photograph of Christie Thorsen on her tablet. Blue eyes, slim build, long dark hair – a ringer for Josie Ecker and all the Butcher's other victims.

She said, "It's them, Bomb. I know it is. It's them."

Tess had him. She had the Butcher. And she had Josie Ecker. If only she could get there in time.

Most of her jobs involved punishing the guilty for their sins. Ninety-nine percent of the time, she administered retribution on behalf of the dead. Despite the tens of kills she'd made, barely anyone even knew she existed, let alone that the innocent had been avenged. She didn't want glory, she didn't want accolades or wealth, but, very occasionally, she ached to know that what she'd done had actually helped the victim's loved ones. That what she'd done mattered. Not just to her, but to those suffering. However, most times, the victim's family didn't even know their loved one had been avenged. They were left with the agony of believing their loss had gone unpunished. That no one cared enough to do anything. And to protect herself, Tess could never have it any other way.

This time would be different. This time, the victim might still be alive. This time, Tess wasn't merely seeking vengeance and craving justice. No, this time, she was on a rescue mission – she was going to save Josie Ecker.

Chapter 25

SLOWING TO LOOK through her car window, Tess saw 275 Lower Jessop Way lying in darkness, as were most of the other houses on the street – little gloom-laden boxes all in a neat row. She peered up the strip of lawn along the side of the house and noted she could see straight into the backyard. No fence on the property meant there probably wasn't a dog she'd have to contend with. Good.

But what *would* she have to contend with?

Everyone had a dream. Something their heart ached for. Even she did. But the problems began when a dream metamorphosed into an obsession. Tess's dream was a dream. She knew that and treated it as such – she controlled it; it didn't control her. But for some people, dreams stopped being merely dreams – largely unattainable desires – and become drugs that fueled their psyche. Just as a junkie could lie, steal, even kill for a fix, so could someone obsessed with their dream.

The Butcher had a dream that had become an obsession. He'd killed to see it realized. That was how far he'd go. So what was she walking into? Who was she walking into? The public files on Helen and Michael Thorsen portrayed them as decent, law-fearing people. What else had the available information got completely wrong?

Bomb had hacked the Department of Buildings and discovered 275 had both a basement and an attic. But which would be the better option to secrete a kidnapped child?

Tess parked a couple of blocks down the street and slunk back, pulling on the last of her combat armor – her titanium-alloy-reinforced leather gloves. She already had her body armor vest under her jacket, and her titanium forearm and shin guards, but she couldn't help wondering how effective they'd be against an axe-wielding psycho. A small caliber handgun, a small blade, a baseball bat – her armor could easily handle those. But an axe? That was a whole other level of deadly force.

Despite it not yet being midnight, she passed no other pedestrians. A few cars drove by, but there was no reason for their occupants to take any notice of her – she was just an ordinary woman meandering along an ordinary street.

As she stalked closer to the house, she continually breathed in for four seconds, held it for four, then exhaled for four. Steadying her body was not hard; instead she focused all her effort on steadying her mind. A steady mind could overcome impossible odds.

Facing the unknown was frightening. Even for those vastly experienced in guerrilla warfare, espionage, or crime. In fact, that rush was a big reason some people ventured into such arenas.

Tess didn't crave that rush; her only craving was for making a difference. If that put her life at risk, so be it. Her life wasn't really worth that much in the grand scheme of things anyway. She'd never cure cancer, never solve the energy crisis, never create a literary masterpiece, so she'd be no great loss.

Not fearing death, and thus not fearing what she had to lose, gave her a clarity most people could never know in life-threatening circumstances. When a person was lost to panic, they were lost, period – their capacity for rational thought diminished to such a point, their death invariably resulted from their own stupid decisions, not the direness of the situation into which they'd been plunged. By having no such overpowering fear and by controlling her reactions to what little fear she did feel, Tess could not only survive most situations, but turn them to her advantage by relying on the panic of others.

With no one in front of her, and double-checking there was no one behind her, she slipped up the driveway of 275 and into its backyard.

At the back door, Tess conducted her final check – she ran a hand down the outer edges of both forearms to ensure the three-quarters-of-an-inch titanium alloy strips lay velcroed in the optimum position for blocking blows. Satisfied, she similarly checked both shin guards.

Stronger than steel, her ergonomically contoured titanium guards could spread the impact load of a baseball bat, so a blow didn't break her bones. But an axe? That was one weapon against which she wouldn't like to put the effectiveness of her guards to the test.

Being in hock, the Thorsens didn't have an alarm system. Nor the most modern security features securing the house.

The back door's lock was of a common pin tumbler design. As usual, Tess first tried a simple rake technique to pick it, but the pin sets failed to pop into place properly, leaving the door firmly locked. So much for the down-and-dirty method.

A pin tumbler lock was usually operated by between four and seven pin sets, which were small metal pins that slid up and down inside cylinders within the lock – all up and the lock opened, but if even only one stayed down the lock remained tightly shut. The secret to lock-picking was in discovering how many pin sets a lock contained and then judging the very specific order in which each one could be teased out of the way.

Replacing her rake, she selected a J-shaped pick tool to use with her tension wrench. She probed with the pick tool. There were five pin sets. While gently levering the lock around with the wrench, she delicately manipulated each pin in turn and, one by one, eased all five driver pins above the shear line and into the open position. In less than twenty seconds, she had the door unlocked.

But she didn't go in.

Chapter 26

TESS WAS ABOUT to encounter the Butcher, a man who'd hacked up at least six children with an axe. Feeling an adrenaline rush starting to surge and her emotions starting to take a hold of her, both of which would cloud her ability to think rationally, she waited a moment and drew a couple of long slow breaths. Then, like a shadow disappearing in the dead of night, she vanished into the darkened house.

Once in and with the door shut again, Tess lit her tiny penlight. She shone the beam down, where it revealed parquet flooring. She didn't need a big flashlight because she only needed to see where she was walking, not illuminate entire rooms. Her feeble light was ideal, being less likely to disturb the house's occupants or arouse suspicion if seen through the windows from the street.

The kitchen was just a kitchen. But then, what had she expected? Body parts hanging from the ceiling, dripping with blood?

A shopping list clung to the refrigerator under a magnet shaped like a puppy; two mugs idled in the sink, probably from a bedtime drink; with a circle in thick black ink, a calendar of wilderness scenes suggested the twenty-sixth of the month was of some importance.

Yes. Just a kitchen.

It could belong to anyone.

Tess heaved a breath. But it had to be the Butcher's kitchen. Had to be. Everything pointed to that. *Everything*. If she was wrong, she had no leads to go on. And Josie would be as good as dead.

No. This was the place. She was sure of it.

The first priority was to discover if Josie was still alive and, if so, put her in the car, where she'd be safe. The second priority was to deal with the Butcher. Ideally, she'd have liked to have dealt with him first, but without knowing if he was working alone or not, she couldn't risk engaging him while his accomplice could be free to hack up Josie.

Tess couldn't help but picture Mary Jo trapped in this house. No matter their motivation, how could anyone do something so monstrous to someone so innocent, so defenseless? She needed to find Josie. She needed to find Josie alive.

As she'd entered on ground level, the basement was the obvious first choice to search. Tess crept along, lightly testing each footstep so creaking floorboards wouldn't give her presence away.

Michael and Helen were supposed to be a loving couple, so they might be upstairs asleep together in bed, just as a loving couple should be. Tess could creep up and barricade them in, or kill them in their sleep. But if the available information on the couple was so wrong, in so many ways, her priority had to be Josie's immediate safety.

After a few steps, she panned her penlight's beam around the walls to check for a door which would hopefully lead to the basement. In the half-light, she thought she could make out the outline of a door around fifteen feet away. She made for it.

Nearing, she saw it was indeed a door. Positioned in the side of the staircase, it could only go down – she'd found the basement.

Tess's heart hammered as she reached for the handle. What would she find? And would anything find her? For all she knew, she could be walking into the Butcher's secret lair, where he'd be standing proudly polishing his axe.

She turned the door knob.

In the dead of night, it screeched as its rusty innards scraped against each other.

Tess froze.

Winced.

Held her breath.

Strained to hear voices, footsteps, screams…

Nothing.

Turning the knob as slowly as she could, she eased it around. The door opened silently.

Tess stepped into the Butcher's darkened lair.

And closed the door behind her.

Yes, she'd found the basement, but what would she find in it? A terrified little girl, desperate to be reunited with her mother, or hacked-up limbs and a bloody torso a mother should never have to see?

Chapter 27

AS TESS STEPPED down onto the first step, the hairs bristled on the back of her neck.

Before her, a wooden staircase descended, gradually disappearing, swallowed by utter blackness.

What would she find waiting at the bottom?

She took another step down.

But the step creaked.

Tess froze, wincing. The hairs bristled even more.

As gently as she could, she lowered her full weight onto the step.

On one side, holding cans of paint, cleaning products, and the odd tool, a wooden framework supported shelving which followed the stairs into the gloom. Nothing suggested a child was hidden somewhere.

Tess prayed she'd made the right call.

But she had.

She was certain.

She shivered at the thought of the gore she might be about to discover.

Of all the gruesome killers she'd known, none had been so brutal, none so evil, as this one.

A voice in her head told her to stop, to turn back, to run and avoid the horrors that waited below.

Fighting to ignore that voice, she took another step. And another. Walking as gingerly as possible to avoid the creaking wood waking the sleeping monster.

She panned her light into the depths of the black pit before her. The beam too faint to illuminate anything, she couldn't help but picture the endless bloody horrors that might be lurking – severed limbs, swinging axes dripping with blood, gutted torsos…

Tess struggled to breathe slowly to control her fear, to hold back the panic she knew was bubbling just below the surface of her calm mind. But even the most battle-scarred warrior is still but a frail person.

Her mouth unbelievably dry, she licked her lips. Her palms felt sweaty. And her heart hammered ever harder.

Creeping down into the bowels of the house, she scanned the blackness ahead for the faintest sign of hope, of life, of… anything.

Finally, Tess reached a solid floor. Through the gloom, her penlight panned the basement – some work areas, some tools, some dark shapes, endless shadows, and…

Tess's stomach tightened.

She stared into the far corner.

Into the blackest of shadows.

Oh, God.

She realized she'd held her breath, so she exhaled gently to be able to breathe deeply again.

Drenched in darkness, barely visible with her light, lay a long, light-colored chest. A freezer.

Tess didn't want to look in the freezer. She didn't want to look and see Josie's eyes staring up at her, eyes as cold as the ice crystals in them. She didn't want to. But she had to.

She padded into the shadows.

With each step, her stomach scrunched tighter, her heart hammered harder.

Please, don't let it be Josie.

Please, please, don't let it be Josie.

Her hand reached out for the freezer lid. Slowly. She didn't want to touch it. Didn't want to lift it.

Her fingertips caressed the lid.

It was hard. Brutally cold. Lifeless.

The voice in her head screamed at her – *Don't lift it. For God's sake don't look inside!*

She eased it up.

The movement creating a pressure wave, a cloud of deathly cold air wafted out and drenched Tess.

Inside lay the darkness of a coffin.

She paused. Drew a slow breath. Then shone her light inside.

Chapter 28

TESS SCREWED HER eyes shut and turned away. "Oh, God, no."

She drew another deep breath, struggling to slow her heart rate, to keep her emotions in check as the grotesque image burned into her memory forever.

Oh, the poor child. What kind of a nightmare had she lived through only to end up here?

Tess didn't want to turn back and look inside, didn't want to see what lurked within, but she had to be sure of what she'd only managed to glimpse before the horror of it had forced her gaze away.

Opening her eyes, she looked inside again.

A leg.

An arm.

A foot.

All frosted white.

All wrapped in plastic sheeting.

And below the severed parts.

Peeking out from between the gaps.

A face.

Iced-over eyes stared lifelessly into space.

A little girl's mouth gaped, as if about to ask a question.

Poor, poor Josie Ecker. The world might be filled with horrors and darkness, but there were also moments of unbelievable brightness – love, hope, laughter, dreams, achievement. Every child deserved a life in the light, yet so many were dragged into the shadows. Poor Josie.

Tess closed the freezer. For a moment, she slumped against it. She'd desperately needed to save Josie. Ached to save her. She'd wanted it so much she'd envisioned it happening. Now… Now, she felt totally drained, felt stupid for believing she could make a difference, felt so incredibly empty.

And then she felt something else.

Then she felt fury.

She pushed herself off the freezer. The Butcher was going to drown in a pool of his own blood. She'd stand over him and watch his last bubbling gasp for air with joy in her heart.

Feeling the rage flowing through her body, Tess turned for the stairs. Muscles bristling with energy for the fight, senses alert to the tiniest of sounds or smallest of movements, she mounted the first step to climb back up to the kitchen. But as she gingerly lifted her foot to climb to the second step, she stopped, leaving her foot dangling in the air.

She glanced back at the freezer.

A lifeless ice-riddled face glimpsed through the gaps between severed limbs could be Josie. Or it could be a victim yet to be identified. What if Josie was still alive and down here? Tess could never live with herself if she left now, only for the police to discover Josie's body later and for forensics to reveal that, tonight, she'd probably still been alive. No, Tess needed to know. The Butcher was asleep. He'd still be asleep in a few minutes. Right this second, she needed to know, one hundred percent, that Josie was dead.

Tess turned back for the basement. She had to go further. Had to know the truth.

Heading into the shadows to explore, she used her four-second breathing technique to still her emotions, to control her fear, to keep her alive. But the sickness churning in her stomach made her all too aware of her own frailty.

Her inner voice screamed at her. Screamed to turn, to scramble back up the steps and out of the back door as quickly as humanly possibly.

She ached to follow her instincts. Ached so much it hurt.

But one thought pushed her on into the blackness – Josie Ecker might still be alive down here and Tess could never cope with knowing she'd abandoned a nine-year-old girl to face such evil all alone.

Tess had to know. Had to know if Josie was still alive.

She shuffled forward.

A wall loomed out of the darkness. A wall where there shouldn't have been a wall. A room within a room. Was this where he hid his victims?

Tess reached out and felt it… soft, cloth-like, spongy. She ran her hand over it. How odd. What the hell kind of room could it be?

And then it clicked.

Years ago, when trying to fund her lifestyle, she'd undertaken some session work playing her cello for any band, composer, or orchestra that needed such services. On one occasion, she'd played in a homebuilt studio above a garage and the walls had felt like this, being made of carpeting over panels of thick industrial foam – cheap DIY soundproofing.

This was it.

This was the Butcher's secret lair.

This was where Josie could be. The Butcher must have built the soundproofing on the outside because he didn't want to destroy any decoration inside the room.

Tess crept on.

A door reared up before her.

Tess approached.

Oh, God, what was she going to find? Blood and guts, or hope and dreams?

She reached for the handle.

Again, metal scraped on metal as she turned it. Tess winced, but she had to open the door. Had to know what was beyond it. She turned it as gently as she could.

But with the handle fully down, the door stuck. Tess pushed. It was sticking on the frame somewhere. She didn't want to push harder for fear of the noise it would make. But she did.

A light thud. And the door opened.

Tess hesitated.

In her mind, she saw Mary Jo.

Saw Mary Jo bloody, dead, in pieces.

Tess shut her eyes and twisted her head away, as if she could turn from the nightmare image in her mind.

She drew a slow breath and crept inside.

Shining her light around, she could see it was a room decorated for a young girl. But was the girl still inside?

She crept further in.

A squeaky, unnatural voice said, "Mamma."

Tess jumped. "Jesus!" Her heart rate rocketed in an instant.

No one leapt out of the shadows to attack.

She eased out a breath slowly to calm herself and then shone her light at her feet. Broken dolls and cuddly animals lay scattered across the floor, dismembered just like the Butcher's victims.

Dear Lord, did he torment his victims by showing them what he was going to do to them?

At the far side of the room, a bed lay under a mess of bedcovers. It looked empty. But was someone lying in it, balled into a protected mound?

Was this Josie?

Please let it be Josie. Please!

Silently, Tess stalked over to the bed.

She reached out a hand. Closer and closer to the heap of bedcovers.

She snagged the pink sheet. Again, she took a deep breath. What would she find when she whipped it away? Bloody gore or a whimpering child?

Wincing and holding her breath, Tess braced herself, then ripped the cover off the bed.

Nothing.

"Oh, God no." Tess was too late. It was Josie in the freezer. Poor, poor Josie.

And millions of people still believed there was a God. Bring them here. Let them get down on their knees and praise Him after seeing this hellhole, after seeing what He'd allowed happen to an innocent child.

An empty hollow in the pit of her stomach clawed at her.

It hurt. Hurt so much.

Hurt like an accident unexpectedly snatching a loved one from you.

She'd needed to save Josie.

Desperately.

Just once, she'd needed to be there to save the victim instead of only avenge them. Just once. After all she'd done for so many victims, was saving just one person, just one child too much to ask for?

Shoulders slumped, Tess turned back and trudged across to the doorway. But with each step that empty hollow faded as she was consumed by blazing fury. A fury only one thing could satisfy.

Easing the door open, Tess pictured the Butcher, pictured him bloody, pictured him broken, dying, pictured him—

Something stopped her dead.

She gasped.

What was that?

Chapter 29

TESS SPUN BACK to the room. Had that really been a tiny noise behind her?

She was certain she'd heard something. Certain. But… Maybe it was merely the darkness and her emotions causing her imagination to run wild in this Godforsaken place.

Again, she scoured the room.

Empty. Just like before. So what could have made that noise?

Her ears strained for the slightest sound. She wasn't even sure what she'd heard to know what she was listening for.

The silence mocked her.

But still she listened.

She frowned into the darkness. Straining. Hoping. Searching.

Nothing.

Nothing but blackness.

Nothing but silence.

Nothing.

Her shoulders slumped again. She turned for the door. But something made her freeze.

There! That noise again.

She felt her eyes widen as hope bloomed in her heart.

The same noise – a tiny ruffling sound as if cloth was rubbing on cloth. Like... Like a wool robe against a carpeted floor?

Tess peered at the deep, dark shadows below the bed. Could there still be a chance? Could she still save Josie?

Tess crept back over to the bed. Crouching, she held her breath. It could be a mouse. A rat. Even just a large cockroach. She mustn't get her hopes up. Mustn't.

But she couldn't help herself.

Please let it be Josie. Please let it be Josie. Please!

Slowly, she leaned down to peer into the darkest depths under the bed.

Something lashed out.

Tess recoiled. Her fist automatically raising to pummel the attacker. But nothing leapt out.

Regaining her composure, Tess whispered, "Josie?"

A hand lashed out at her.

A tiny hand.

A little girl's hand.

Not wanting to spook the girl, Tess didn't shine her flashlight directly at her. Instead, she held it in front of her, at arm's length, and pointed it back at herself, so the little girl could see her.

"Josie? Don't be frightened. I'm here to help." Tess angled the light so it illuminated both of them.

Curled up facing the wall, the girl said nothing. She shuffled closer to the wall, clawing her arms around her and pulling her legs up to squeeze into an even smaller ball.

"It's okay," whispered Tess. "I've come to take you to your mommy."

The little girl turned a fraction and looked at her from the corner of her eye.

Tess shone the light full on her own face so there'd be no scary shadows. She smiled. "It's okay. I'm here to help you, Josie." She reached out. "Let me take you to your mommy."

"My real mommy?"

Oh, what this poor kid must have endured. "Yes, your real mommy. She's waiting for you. She misses you."

It was obviously too much for the child and she burst into tears. "Mommy!"

Tess reached over and pulled her to her. "Shush, shush, shush, honey. You have to be quiet so the bad people don't hear us."

The kid blubbered. "Mommy!"

Tess picked her up. Hugged her. Stroked the back of her head. "Shush, honey, shush. Everything is going to be okay now. I've got you."

The kid buried her face in Tess's shoulder and wrapped her arms and legs around her to cling to her. Tiny fingers clawed at Tess's back as if the little girl was frightened this was all just a dream that could vanish any moment if she didn't hold on tightly enough.

Tess felt tears welling in her own eyes. To think she'd almost left and abandoned Josie. She clung to the little girl, the little girl she'd saved.

To regain her calmness of mind, calmness needed to ensure they both walked out of this hellish place alive, Tess breathed slow and deeply. Gradually, her overwhelming emotions – fury, relief, horror – subsided.

Tess whispered, "I'm taking you to Mommy now, Josie." She shone her light into the open doorway. "Look, the door's open."

Her cell door finally open and nothing blocking her from leaving appeared to ease the little girl's hurt and she stopped crying so hard.

"That's it," said Tess. "That's it. Let's all be as quiet as we can so we can get out of this nasty place and find Mommy."

Tess stroked Josie's head and slowly the crying subsided. "There's a good girl."

Holding the light on them both, Tess eased Josie's head up so she could see her face. "Yes, what a brave little girl."

But this had been the easy part – the hard part would be getting out in one piece.

"Now, listen, Josie, because this is really important. You have to be very, very quiet. Okay? We're going to go home now, to see your mommy, but you can't make any noise. Understand?"

Josie nodded.

"Here's what I want you to do." Tess eased her face back into her shoulder. "You have to hold on as tight as you can and keep your face against me like this. And no matter what you hear – no matter what – you can't look. Okay? Just keep your face here."

If something spooked the girl and she screamed, the Butcher could come hunting them with his axe. If he caught them by surprise, there was no way Tess could fight to defend them both while holding Josie. But she couldn't risk putting her down either. Couldn't risk the little girl stumbling and clattering something to the floor while screaming in shock or pain. Tess had to carry her so they could escape in total silence. It was their only hope.

She held the girl's face into her shoulder. "That's it. Just stay there and we'll go to your mommy. Okay?"

Josie nodded.

Tess turned for the door. Now she just had to get the little girl out. With everything going so well so far, maybe this was going to be far easier than she'd feared.

Chapter 30

TESS SHONE THE light into the doorway to the main part of the basement.

Still empty.

Thank, God. She heaved a relieved sigh. This was incredible. Things couldn't be going better.

She'd worried the girl's crying might have drifted up through the floor and alerted the monsters upstairs, but so far, she couldn't have dreamed of an easier rescue.

Shining the tiny beam before them, Tess retraced her steps, moving quicker this time, because she knew what to expect. They crossed the basement and reached the foot of the stairs which led up into blackness.

Tess whispered. "Remember, Josie, don't look and hold on tight. And stay very, very quiet. We're nearly there. Okay?"

Josie nodded.

Tess lightly stepped onto the first step, worried the extra weight she was carrying would make it creak and give away their escape. It didn't.

Neither did the next.

Nor the one after that.

Though Tess's heart burst with ever more hope and her mind filled with ever greater confidence as they mounted the wooden staircase in silence, Tess knew she couldn't be complacent. Though her subconscious screamed at her to run, her rational mind forced her to be carcful, to take her time, to remain just a silent shadow flitting invisibly through the night.

Finally, the top step reared out of the gloom.

Tess cringed, realizing she'd forgotten which step it was that had creaked loudly on the way down.

Was it the second or third from the top?

Still, they were almost out, so it barely mattered.

Gingerly, she made her way toward the door at the top.

The second step down grumbled as she put their weight on it, but the darkness now holding fewer fears, it was nowhere near as loud as her imagination had led her to believe. It was way too quiet for anyone outside the basement to ever have heard.

Tess squeezed Josie to her. She barely whispered, "Almost there. Shhh."

At the top, she reached out for the door handle, praying it would turn silently this time if she turned it slowly enough.

She winced.

Turned.

Slowly.

Slowly.

Slowly…
She felt the latch give.
Carefully, she eased the door open.

Chapter 31

STANDING AT THE other side of the door, Helen Thorsen screamed at Tess and Josie. She held a baby monitor in one hand. A raised axe in the other.

Tess flinched. Gripped Josie harder.

And despite what Tess had said, Josie looked.

Engulfed by panic, the little girl shrieked and fought to climb over Tess's shoulder, to break loose, to run from the monster before her.

Tess fought to hold on to her, to keep them both safe.

But Helen moved in to crash the axe down.

Tess knew exactly how to defend against an unwieldy attack from a middle-aged housewife, so she readied herself.

But Josie had grabbed a shelf behind Tess and now yanked on it to try to break free.

Helen screamed and swung the axe.

Unable to close in and disarm her, Tess threw her arm up. She just managed to deflect the blow off the titanium guard down the outside of her forearm.

The blade embedded in the drywall.

Struggling to hold Josie while absorbing the force of the blow, Tess lost her footing.

She fell.

She and Josie tumbled down the stairs, arms and legs flailing in the air.

They crashed to the hard floor at the bottom.

Screaming, Helen ran down the steps.

Tess rolled away from Josie and tried to push up, but cried out. Excruciating pain shot through her torso when she tried to move her right arm. She must have dislocated her shoulder in the fall. She crumpled to the floor.

The basement now dimly lit, someone having flicked on a light, Tess pushed up with her left arm and looked back.

Helen reared over her with the axe.

Tess rolled aside.

The axe hit the floor.

The woman swung her weapon again.

And again Tess rolled out from beneath the deadly blade.

As Helen heaved the axe back for a third strike, Tess kicked Helen's feet out from under her. The woman crashed to the floor.

Tess rolled and rolled across the floor to give herself some space.

She caught a glimpse of Michael Thorsen sitting halfway down the stairs, head hung. He said, "It's over, Helen. It's over."

Tess pushed up onto her knees. She clutched her shoulder as pain again shot through her body.

Helen clambered to her feet. Picked up her axe. Raced at Tess.

Grabbing the top of a workbench, Tess pulled herself up.

The woman heaved the axe back over her shoulder to slice Tess in two.

Tess lunged.

With her good arm, she blocked the axe handle in mid-swing. Wrapping her arm over both of Helen's, Tess trapped them against her ribs.

She headbutted the woman.

Kneed her in the crotch.

Helen dropped the axe. Staggered backward.

Tess hammered a kick into her gut.

The woman doubled over, clutching her stomach and gasping for air.

Tess smashed a knee into her jaw.

Helen crashed over backwards. Slammed into the floor. Blood poured from her face.

Spinning around, Tess swept up the axe.

Heaved it over her shoulder.

Slashed it down into the woman's midriff.

Helen screeched. Her arms and legs shuddered wildly as if she'd been electrified.

From the steps, Michael shouted, "Helen!"

He flew down the steps.

The axe squelched as Tess heaved it out of the woman. She stepped back for a better angle to attack the man, but tripped over Josie's leg.

Tess crashed to the floor, losing her grip on the axe.

By the time the man reached the bottom, the woman lay unmoving in a huge pool of blood. He gazed down at his dead wife, then down at Tess. "You evil little fuck!"

He grabbed a wood chisel from his workbench.

Squealing in pain from her shoulder, Tess scrambled up.

Michael rushed Tess, slashing the razor-edged chisel backwards and forwards.

With two good arms, even for her, it was hard to defend against a wildly swinging blade, but with only one arm…

She backed away.

Slashing wildly, he lunged at her.

In an instant, Tess crouched low and shot forward under the deadly blade. She slammed her good shoulder into the man's right thigh.

He crashed to the floor on top of his wife.

Tess immediately pushed back up to her feet, adrenaline combating her pain.

Turning onto all fours, the man tried to clamber up. But Tess leapt into the air and, with her full body weight, hammered her elbow down between his shoulder blades.

He collapsed onto his wife, face first into her blood-soaked gut.

Lying on top of him, Tess hooked his right arm between her legs and trapped it; his left she locked with her good hand and heaved it back against the joints.

Pushing down with all her weight, she forced his face into the bloody guts.

He struggled.

His breathing gargled.

His legs kicked.

But Tess rolled her weight further onto his head.

She squeezed his right arm between her legs.

Heaved back on his left to rip the joints apart.

Rolled forward.

Smothered his head with her body.

He kicked.

Bucked.

Made muffled, gargling wails.

Finally…

Silence. Stillness.

Tess waited a moment longer to ensure she'd done the job right, then rolled off.

She gasped and clutched her shoulder.

For a few moments, she lay on the floor gasping for air.

Her breath calming, she pushed up, grimacing with the effort.

"Josie." She staggered towards the little girl curled in a loose ball on the floor, but stopped, panting for breath.

Tess glanced around at the carnage. There'd be no easy way to disguise what had happened here to hide whatever DNA evidence she and Josie would leave behind. Once she had the little girl safely in the car, it might be best take the severed body parts to dump in the East River and then to torch this place.

Yes, that was a good plan. There'd still be a police investigation, but one nowhere near as exhaustive as if the authorities realized it was the Butcher they'd finally found. The less of an investigation there was the less chance the authorities had of discovering Tess's involvement.

Yes, that was a decent exit strategy. Before torching the house, and her shoulder permitting, she might even carry the man and woman upstairs and lay them in bed to confuse investigators even further.

Clutching her shoulder, Tess trudged over to the little girl.

"Josie, it's okay, honey. It's safe now. Come on, we're going to see your mommy."

But the little girl didn't look up.

"Josie? ... Josie?"

Tess crouched beside her and gently held her shoulder. "Josie, you're safe, honey. They can't hurt you anymore."

Still the little girl didn't look up or make a sound.

"Josie?"

Oh, God. Tess felt the girl's neck for a pulse.

Tess screwed her eyes shut. "No. Please. No."

She'd come here to save the little girl, but instead, falling down the stairs onto her, she crushed her. Instead of being Josie's savior, Tess was the one who'd killed her.

Tess sank to the floor. And sobbed.

Chapter 32

"LOOK, MOMMY, PENGUINS. Mommy, penguins!" Mary Jo pointed at a big black-and-white penguin lumbering over the rocks in its enclosure and then to another darting through the water in their pool.

"Penguins, Mommy. Real penguins!" She held her arms wide. "And they're this big!"

Tess had honored her commitment to the Alcott family by finding Mary Jo's sister's killer and now she'd honored her commitment to little Mary Jo herself by showing her live penguins. Now, this relationship had to end. It could never lead anywhere and sustaining Deanna Gambini's identity could be dangerous. And not just for Tess. With the work she did, anyone close to her could be a target of some psycho out for revenge.

Tess's mantra kept her alive. It meant survival. It was simplicity itself.

No feelings.

Ever.

For anyone.

It couldn't be simpler.

"Okay. Got it," shouted Tess, stopping the video recording on her phone. She waved the little girl over. "Shall I send it now, or do you want to see it first?"

Mary Jo scampered over. "See it first."

Tess crouched down and played the video.

With a beaming smile, Mary Jo watched it. When it ended, she flung her arms around Tess. "I love you, Auntie Deanna."

Tess hugged her back, but she had no idea what to say. So she said the only thing she could think of that seemed appropriate. "I love you too, squirt." And it felt good.

Hugging Mary Jo, Tess couldn't help but think of Josie Ecker and how no one would ever hug her again. Tess had needed to save Josie, but instead, she'd been the one who'd killed her. Could the authorities have tracked down the Butcher quickly enough to save Josie before he hacked her into little bits? Maybe. Maybe not. But Tess had needed to save her. Needed to.

Tess dealt with so much death that, just once, she'd wanted to see a light at the end of the dark and dismal path along which she trudged. Just once, she'd wanted to know, beyond a doubt, she'd changed the world for the better. Not by taking a life, but by giving one.

Could the police have saved Josie? She'd never know. But the knowledge she'd killed the little girl would haunt her forever.

Tess squeezed Mary Jo. She felt a warm glow emanating from her chest. It felt good to be close to another human being. Someone normal. Innocent. Someone for whom each day wasn't filled with death and vengeance, but sunshine and birdsong, and laughter.

So what about her mantra? Why the hell couldn't she follow the single most important rule in her life?

To protect the Gagliano family from crime boss Arnold Ryker, Tess was already maintaining one false identity she should have shredded. To keep another of her alter egos alive was pushing things way too far. Even just retaining Deanna's telephone number went against so many of her security protocols.

Tess sighed.

Would keeping just one extra phone number be that bad? Really?

She sighed again.

Doubts were weakness. And weakness killed more surely than any knife or gun. If she could no longer be one hundred percent certain she was doing good, no longer commit one hundred percent to her work, no longer be objective about the people she encountered, maybe it was time to get out. Retire before being 'retired'.

But where would she go? What would she do?

As long as it was a long, long way from here, did it matter?

She smiled. She didn't really know why, but she suddenly felt lighter; the world seemed brighter. She felt… free.

She pulled back from Mary Jo. "So, squirt, what about those elephants?"

"Yeah!"

Tess's phone rang.

Standing up, she answered the call. "Hey, Bomb."

"Tess… I think I've found him."

"Yeah? Who have you found?"

"The guy from the silver car. The guy who killed your grandpa."

The End

Continue the pulse-pounding *Angel of Darkness* adventure. Check out what other readers are saying about the next book.

"Another cracking instalment of the series. It just gets better and better."
P. Flanders

"This was a roller coaster of a read… I Could Not Put it Down"
Hillel Kaminsky

"Wow! An explosive installment… A great read with real insight and wisdom from a strong and very likeable protagonist."
Julie Elizabeth Powell (Top 1000 Reviewer)

Continue the adventure with *Nightmare's Rage* (book 07). Use a link below to get that book, or grab the 3-book edition which includes *Nightmare's Rage*, *Shanghai Fury,* and *Black Dawn.*

3-Book Edition
http://stevenleebooks.com/24tp

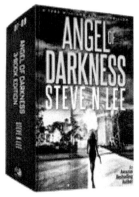

Nightmare's Rage
http://stevenleebooks.com/tz0q

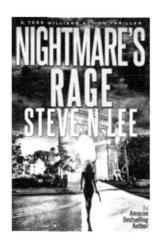

Nightmare's Rage

Angel of Darkness Book 07

Nightmare's Rage extract

SWEAT BEADING ON his brow, Mikey smiled down at Ray with all the sincerity of a priest sermonizing on the Ten Commandments while dreaming of being balls-deep in his blond-haired choirboy.

Lying on his back on the black vinyl exercise bench, Ray blew out a breath with a loud shushing sound as he heaved a weighted barbell off his chest for the eighteenth time.

"That's the God's honest, Ray," said Mikey, standing at the foot of the bench. "I swear as God's my witness." He kept that smile on his face, a smile as greasy as his wavy black hair.

A single droplet of perspiration trickled back over Ray's shaven head as he strained up his nineteenth lift. Despite its hypocrisy, he had nothing against religion. Except when others used it to lie to his face.

Mikey shrugged his weedy shoulders. "Look, I'm as pissed as you are about things."

The buildup of lactic acid causing his arm muscles to tremble, Ray set his jaw. He heaved one last time. But the bar stopped going up before he'd locked his elbows. If it fell back down with so much weight on it, it would break his ribs, or his neck. But he'd have this lift. It would not beat him. No way.

He strained harder.

To his left, Andre moved to grab the bar, but immediately pulled back under the glare Ray shot him.

Ray grimaced. Tapping into those final reserves which always saw him achieve his goals, he pushed with all his will. He would not let this meaningless piece of shit beat him.

The blood pounding through his veins, he felt his face screw up and start to redden with the pressure.

He heaved.

Let out a great straining breath of air.

And, with trembling arms, powered the bar aloft, locking out his elbows.

On either side of him, Ted and Andre grabbed the ends of the barbell and lifted it back onto its stand. Either guy looked big enough to have lifted it one-handed.

Ray dabbed his face with a white cotton towel, being careful to dab and not to rub to avoid dragging and stretching the skin, which would cause wrinkles. He wasn't vain, but it was pointless being handsome if you didn't take care of yourself.

He sat up. When it was he who'd done all of the work, why was it Mikey doing most of the sweating? Without a word, he offered Mikey the towel.

A look of confusion flickered across Mikey's face, then he said, "I tell you, once I find out who's been skimming off the top, believe me, are they gonna pay."

Mikey just wouldn't let that smile drop. Yet, all the while, down by his thigh, he flipped his cell phone over and over in his hand. It was strange he was so nervous when God was vouching for him.

Standing, Ray turned to the wall-length mirror along the back of the gym. He clenched his hands in front of his body and tensed his muscles. Though he'd have to measure them later, he was sure his biceps had developed further, while the definition of his triceps was becoming far more pronounced. He smiled. One hundred and eighty-three pounds of chiseled muscle. Hell, if he was gay, man, would he hit that!

His gaze shot across the length of the mirror. Other than he, his two men, and Mikey, the place was deserted and the steel shutters were closed over the windows to the street.

"See," said Mikey, "the problem is you just can't trust nobody these days. Nobody."

"Anybody," said Ray, without looking at the guy.

"Excuse me?" Mikey craned his head, as if being a couple of inches closer would raise his IQ.

Ray said, "You can't trust anybody."

Mikey nodded. "That's what I'm saying. Nobody. It's like there just ain't nobody you can trust to get the job done without them wanting to sneak a cut."

Ray heaved a breath and rubbed his brow. Some days, it seemed he was surrounded by imbeciles. He finally turned to face Mikey.

"Here's what we're going to do, Mikey. One: you're going to give me the names of all your contacts so I can get to the bottom of his. Two—"

"Hey, you don't wanna be bothered with—"

Ray wagged a finger at him. "Ah, ah, ah, ah, ah..."

His hands up submissively, Mikey said, "Sorry, Ray."

Ray continued. "And two: you're going to tell me what really happened."

Mikey's eyes widened and he gasped as if in surprise.

"What?" He held his arms wide. "Ray, I'm the injured party here – I'm gonna have to make good for whoever's been ripping us both off."

Ray picked up a five-pound barbell weight. He tossed it in his hands.

He looked at Mikey. "Do you know why I use free weights instead of fancy machines like that?" He pointed to the bench press machine with its elaborate steel cable pulley system, stacked adjustable weights, and V-shaped lifting bar.

Mikey's mouth dropped open but no words came out as he gazed blankly back.

Holding the weight in just his left hand, Ray slung his right arm around Mikey's shoulders. "It's very simple. See, it's all about character."

"This" – Ray pointed to the machine – "is a machine for pussies who want to think they're real men, but don't want to have to put in real effort. It's easy, it's cool, and most of all, it's risk-free because you've got all kinds of safety features built in, so any time you want to quit, you can just let the bar drop and either go grab a Frappuccino, or beat one out over the boy band poster you've tacked above your bed."

Ray pointed back at the free weights bench he'd been using. "That, however..." He smiled reassuringly. "That develops character. Oh, it won't necessarily give you bigger muscles than the machine, and it's nowhere near as cool looking, but what it gives you is worth a million times more – it gives you 'will'. See, people think it's muscle mass that makes you strong, but they couldn't be more wrong – it's your mind." He pointed to his barbell. "You quit on that and drop it, you ain't going for coffee, you're going in a casket."

He smiled again at Mikey. "You see what I'm saying?"

"I, er..."

"You've gotta take risks, Mikey. Risks." He patted him on the shoulder as friends did. "It's the risk–reward ratio – if there's little risk in doing something, you can bet there's little reward in doing it too. You've got to push yourself to be the best you can be. Otherwise, what's it all for? You might as well take a nine-to-five in a goddamn candy store, am I right?"

Mikey nodded halfheartedly. "I can see—"

"Risk–reward ratio, Mikey. That's what it's all about. So, I find myself asking, 'When the risks are so great, who's got the most to gain by screwing me over?' And do you know whose name I keep coming up with?"

Mikey threw his hands up submissively again. "Hey, as God's my witness, I'm telling you, Ray, it—"

"Mikey, Mikey, Mikey, you're missing the important point. Of course, I'm upset at being ripped off, but I can respect the person who took that risk. That shows real strength. You follow me?"

His annoying smile replaced by a studious expression, Mikey nodded.

Ray continued, "And credit where credit's due – whoever came up with that method of skimming shows real flair. I mean, the brains to come up with such a new angle... whoa! So, I'm thinking – what other masterpieces has this guy got going and how can I get in on the action?"

He clamped his hand down on Mikey's shoulder. "Now, which is it, Mikey, are you just the dumb schmuck who got caught shafting his boss, or are you my new moneymaking dynamo?"

Mikey hung his head. "The skimming... I, er..." He huffed, lifted his head and gazed away into space. "I—I got the idea from a movie. I'm sorry, Ray. It won't happen again. God's honest."

Mikey's voice became more upbeat. "But I got a great idea for cutting coke to make an extra five percent, easy. Maybe more."

"Five percent?" said Ray.

"Minimum. My guy's looking into it already."

Ray nodded. An extra five percent profit would be great. But like everything else in life, profit came at a cost. Some he could bear, others...

Mikey smiled. "I'll call him as soon as we're finished here. Believe me, I'll pull out all the stops on this one. Just for you, Ray."

Ray smiled back at him. "See how the truth helps us move forward with everyone happy?" He held out his right hand to shake.

Mikey shook Ray's hand vigorously. "Ray, I'm real sorry about the skimming. But I'm gonna make it up to you with the coke. You just watch if I don't."

"Thanks, Mikey. I appreciate that. You don't know what honesty means to me."

Ray smashed the five-pound weight into the side of Mikey's head.

Mikey crashed onto the floor.

Ray stabbed a finger at him. "I trusted you, Mikey. I trusted you. And you repay me by stealing from me?"

As if in slow motion, blood gushing from his head, Mikey slung a wavering hand onto the black vinyl seat of the bench press machine.

Ray leaned down to him. "The God's honest truth? Just how stupid do you think I am?"

More as an automatic survival response than a conscious decision, Mikey tried to get up. His whole body shook with the effort. He heaved himself onto his knees and then sprawled across the black seat, gasping from the exertion.

Ray smirked. "Risk–reward, Mikey. Risk–reward. You took the risk, now here's your reward."

Ray snatched the metal spindle which users inserted into the machine's stack of weights to select what they'd like to press. He grabbed Mikey's head, slammed it down on the bench, then punched the spindle through his temple.

For a moment, Mikey flailed his arms like a drunk trying to swim. Then he lay still.

Ray turned to Andre. "Get me Mikey's coke guy." He stormed toward the door at the back of the gym marked 'Private'. He didn't turn around but merely slung his arm back towards the body. "And get rid of that pile of shit."

Truth be told, he'd liked Mikey. Well, liked him in the sense he hadn't disliked him, which wasn't the case with most people. Yeah, he'd kind of miss the guy. But he couldn't have someone so close showing such disrespect.

Hell no.

If he'd let Mikey get away with that and word got out, everyone would turn on him. And not just his competitors, but his own men, who would figure he'd gone soft so now was their chance to make it big. Now that was the God's honest truth. And he should know – that strategy had worked for him.

But strolling for the door, Ray couldn't help but smile. It had been so long since his last time, he'd forgotten the thrill he got out of ending someone. Yeah, maybe it was time he got a little more involved on the streets again. Security cameras at every turn, GPS tracking on phones, and forensics goons who could put you in Sing Sing because of a single eyelash they found at a crime scene, man, had it taken all the joy out of his business.

Okay, he lived a great life, but there was nothing like getting real blood on your hands. There was an honesty to it. An integrity. A sense of achievement. You didn't get that sitting behind a desk delegating jobs.

Maybe there was some sort of technology that could confuse cameras so your image didn't show up, or a cream you could smooth on to sabotage DNA traces. He'd have one of the guys research that.

In fact, if there wasn't anything like that available, he'd find someone who could make it happen – he'd make a killing selling gear like that. Hell, he was a goddamn genius. There could be more money in that than drugs – everyone needed to evade the law: dealers, thieves, traffickers, smugglers, enforcers, counterfeiters... Hell, the marketing possibilities were endless. Jesus, he'd clean up!

He yanked open the door. Ahead lay a narrow corridor and a private staircase up to his penthouse apartment.

Now, which girlfriend was he going to call? Tonight's events had given him such a buzz, if there was a tournament for it, he could fuck for America.

Chapter 02

Ambling past apartment 3F in the meticulously clean pastel green hallway, Tess stopped and removed her glasses. She massaged her eyes and then blinked a few times. She looked at the door beside her and then away to the far end of the hallway, allowing her eyes to focus and refocus to regain their natural balance. She hadn't wanted plain glass for the lenses because, close up, savvy people could tell such glasses were fake, but these lenses were straining her eyes.

Replacing her glasses, she continued on.

Butterflies started in her stomach.

Her target, Thomas Conroy, had served time for aggravated assault. He'd been free for six years now, with no subsequent offenses recorded or investigated, but that didn't mean he'd been clean, only that he'd been careful.

As the apartment numbers climbed toward the one she wanted, she could feel the fear rising in the back of her mind. She saw images of her bloody and mangled body; glimpsed feelings of pain and darkness and anguish. Generally, fear killed more people than any knife, gun, or psychopath. Unrestrained, fear became panic and panic made a bad situation deadly.

Of course, the easiest option in a bad situation was to run. Run and never look back. Run until the danger was far, far behind you. Unfortunately, escape was often not a viable option. When it wasn't, you had to be sure fear was working for you by energizing your body, making it resilient to pain, sharpening your reflexes, but never allowing it to escalate into panic. Panic invariably meant someone was taking a trip to the morgue.

Calmness, on the other hand, could make a deadly situation manageable. By embracing the insight fear gave you in alerting you to a dangerous situation, while controlling how much of a grip on you that fear got, you could not just survive a life-threatening encounter, but even turn it to your advantage. Having faced all the killers she had, that was one of the main reasons she was still breathing.

To rein in her fight-or-flight response, Tess controlled her breathing to calm her heart rate and mind. She breathed in for four seconds, held it for four, exhaled for four, and then repeated as she walked.

At the door to apartment 3F, she snuck a look in her compact. Her shoulder-length brown hair scraped back tight, she wondered if she'd gone too far aiming at prim and unattractive. But she wasn't entering Miss America; she was trying to pass for everyone's most hated kind of pencil pusher. She rapped on the door.

A moment later, a man in a taupe robe answered. In mid-yawn, he said, "Yeah?"

Instantly, there was no more fear. No, now another emotion consumed Tess. Just as primal. Just as unpredictable. Just as deadly. Now, there was rage.

In her mind, Tess pictured herself leaping at Conroy, pinning him against the wall by his throat and ramming a thumb into his eye so he'd give her what she needed. She could all but feel his squidgy eyeball in her fingers. He knew the man she was hunting. Knew him so very well. Knew what he did, what suffering he caused, and what nightmares he forced others to endure. Knew, but did nothing.

Her blood pounded through her veins, coursing adrenaline through her body and making her muscles cry out with excess energy. Her entire being screamed at her to strike, to feel his blood warm and wet on her hands. But just like fear, rage could force the most intelligent of people to make the dumbest of mistakes.

She clenched her fists. Held in the pain. Held in the suffering. Held in the heartache and broken dreams. After waiting the best part of two decades, she was so goddamn close. So close. She'd never been this close before. Never. She couldn't blow it now. Not after all she'd pushed herself to do to reach this point. No, she had to stick to the plan.

"Well?" he said, staring at her as if he half-expected her to ask if he'd heard the Word.

His robe closed sloppily, hanging partly open, she glanced at his waxed chest.

Pussy.

She liked men who were men, not preening prima donnas who needed more mirror time than a beauty queen at a pageant.

God, how she ached to hear him shriek as she literally tore him limb from limb.

It would be so easy. So right.

Guilt by association was a damn good reason.

So what was she waiting for?

***

Continue the adventure with *Nightmare's Rage* (book 07). Use a link below to get that book, or grab the 3-book edition which includes *Nightmare's Rage*, *Shanghai Fury*, and *Black Dawn*.

3-Book Edition
http://stevenleebooks.com/24tp

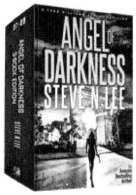

Nightmare's Rage
http://stevenleebooks.com/tz0q

Free Library of Books

Thank you for reading *Predator Mine*. To show my appreciation of my readers, I wrote a second series of books exclusively for them – each Angel of Darkness book has its own *Black File*, so there's a free library for you to collect and enjoy.

A FREE Library Waiting for You!

Exclusive? You bet! You can't get the *Black Files* anywhere except through the links in the *Angel of Darkness* books.

**Start Your FREE Library with *Black Files 04-06*.
http://stevenleebooks.com/tfbm**

Make Your Opinion Count

Do you know that less than 1% of readers leave reviews?

It is unbelievably difficult for an emerging writer to reach a wider audience, so will you help me by sharing how much you enjoyed this book in a short review, please? I'll be ever so grateful.

Don't follow the 99% – stand out from the crowd with just a few clicks!

Thank you,

Steve

Copy the link to post your review of *Predator Mine*:

http://stevenleebooks.com/34ty

Copy the link to post your review of *Angel of Darkness Box Set 02*:

http://stevenleebooks.com/6gbu

Free Goodies – VIP Area

See More, Do More, Get More!

Do you want to get more than the average reader gets? Every few weeks I send my VIP readers some combination of:

- news about my books
- giveaways from me or my writer friends
- opportunities to help choose book titles and covers
- anecdotes about the writing life, or just life itself
- special deals and freebies
- sneak behind-the-scenes peeks at what's in the works.

Get Exclusive VIP Access with this Link.

http://stevenleebooks.com/wcfl

Angel of Darkness Series

Book 01 – Kill Switch

This Amazon #1 Best Seller explodes with pulse-pounding action and heart-stopping thrills, as Tess Williams rampages across Eastern Europe in pursuit of a gang of sadistic kidnappers.

Book 02 – Angel of Darkness

Set in Manhattan, Tess hunts a merciless killer on a mission from God in a story bursting with high-octane action and nail-biting suspense.

Book 03 – Blood Justice

Blood Justice erupts with the intrigue and red-hot action surrounding a murder. Thrust into the deadly world of crime lords and guns-for-hire, only Tess can unveil the killer in this gripping action-fest.

Book 04 – Midnight Burn

An unstoppable killing-machine, Tess demands justice for crimes, whatever the cost. But even 'unstoppable' machines have weaknesses. Discover Tess's as she hunts a young woman's fiendish killer.

Book 05 – Mourning Scars

Crammed with edge-of-your-seat action and vengeance, this adventure slams Tess into the heart of a gang shooting and reveals the nightmare that drove her to become a justice-hungry killer.

Book 06 – Predator Mine

Bursting with nerve-shredding intrigue, this page-turner plunges Tess into the darkest of crimes. And dark crimes deserve dark justice. Discover just how dark a hero can be when Tess hunts a child killer.

Book 07 – Nightmare's Rage

If someone killed somebody you loved, how far would you go to get justice? How dark would be too dark? How violent too violent? Vengeance-driven Tess is about to find out in an electrifying action extravaganza.

Book 08 – Shanghai Fury

Tess Williams is a killer. Cold. Brutal. Unstoppable. In a white-knuckle tale of murder, mayhem, and betrayal, discover how her story begins, how an innocent victim becomes a merciless killing-machine.

Book 09 – Black Dawn

Everything ends. Including a life of pain, hardship, and violence. Tess has sacrificed endlessly to protect the innocent by hunting those that prey upon them. Now, it's time to build a new life for herself. But a news report changes everything.

Book 10 – Die Forever

A brutal gang is terrorizing NYC. Tess's hunt takes her to one of the deadliest places on the planet, for one of her deadliest battles. How will she get out alive?

About Steve N. Lee

Steve lives in Yorkshire, in the north of England, with his partner Ania and two cats who adopted them.

Picture rugged, untamed moorland with Cathy running into Heathcliff's arms – that's Yorkshire! Well, without the running. (Picture jet-black bundles of fur – that's their cats.)

He's studied a number of martial arts, is a certified SCUBA diver, and speaks 10 languages enough to get by. And he loves bacon sandwiches smothered in brown sauce.

Use the link below to learn more – some of it true, some of it almost true, and some of it, well, who really knows? Why not decide for yourself?

http://stevenleebooks.com/a5w5

Printed in Great Britain
by Amazon

22038819R00330